THE SLAVE-OWNER'S DILEMMA

or

The Ghosts Of Mulberry Hall

By

Simon Holder

Copyright © Simon Holder 2024
This book is sold subject to the condition that it shall not, by way of trade or otherwise, be lent, resold, hired out, or otherwise circulated without the publisher's prior consent in any form of binding or cover other than that in which it is published and without a similar condition including this condition being imposed on the subsequent publisher.
The moral right of Simon Holder has been asserted.
ISBN: 9798301117442

This is a work of fiction. Names, characters, businesses, organisations, places, events and incidents either are the product of the author's imagination or are used fictitiously. Any resemblance to actual persons, living or dead, events, or locales is entirely coincidental.

To my darling wife Xiaomei, who supported me immensely during the research and writing of this novel.

Also to those brave and noble 19th-century people who made Britain the first country to abolish slavery.

By the same author:

The Revolution of the Species

A topical, terrifying and plausible environmental thriller

For the Love of a Life

An unusual international love story

It's All In The Script!

A dastardly, humorous thriller involving a present-day TV soap opera set in the 18th century

A Cultured Pearl

... and other tales of Love, Longing, Mystique & Hope

All available on Amazon/Kindle

CONTENTS

PROLOGUE 1

BOOK I

CHAPTER 1 *Mulberry Hall is created* 6
CHAPTER 2 *Tobias* 16
CHAPTER 3 *An Awkward Situation* 22
CHAPTER 4 *Alice* 29
CHAPTER 5 *Confusion* 33
CHAPTER 6 *The Plot Thickens…* 39
CHAPTER 7 *An Unexpected Situation* 43
CHAPTER 8 *The Plan & Its Consequences* 49
CHAPTER 9 *Complications Arise* 59
CHAPTER 10 *Further Complications Arise* 64
CHAPTER 11 *Pride and Prejudice* 70
CHAPTER 12 *A Fear Is Endured & Another Is Resolved* 76
CHAPTER 13 *A Tricky Situation Develops* 82
CHAPTER 14 *Lucinda Concocts A Proposal* 87
CHAPTER 15 *An Arrangement Is Made* 94
CHAPTER 16 *Two Babies and a Mutual Surprise* 97
CHAPTER 17 *An Awkward Development* 100
CHAPTER 18 *An Engagement Banquet, A Complication & A Concern* 105
CHAPTER 19 *A Wedding, An Awkward Situation & A Discovery* 110
CHAPTER 20 *An Embarrassment, A Confrontation & A Surprise* 116
CHAPTER 21 *An Altercation & An Agreement* 126
CHAPTER 22 *A Meeting, A Rumour & A Conspiracy* 133
CHAPTER 23 *The Plot Thickens* 136

CHAPTER 24 *Secrets, A Body & A Prospective Tree* 147
CHAPTER 25 *Suspicions, A Twist… & A Proposition* 150
CHAPTER 26 *A Shady Deal, A Meeting… & A Delicate Situation* 157
CHAPTER 27 *A Sticky Situation & An Acquiescence* 162
CHAPTER 28 *A Lull, A Panic, A Birth… & A Dastardly Plan* 171
CHAPTER 29 *The Act's Early Legacy* 175

BOOK II: 1822

CHAPTER 30 *The Children Become Adults…* 177
CHAPTER 31 *An Unexpected Meeting* 181
CHAPTER 32 *Anticipation… & A Surprise Revelation* 187
CHAPTER 33 *An Admission, A Plan & A Dark Deed Uncovered* 192
CHAPTER 34 *A Devious Postulation, A Singer & A Decision* 198
CHAPTER 35 *An Engagement, A Singing Teacher & A Removal* 205
CHAPTER 36 *An Unexpected Truth & A Plan For Revenge* 210
CHAPTER 37 *A Hidden Threat, A Realisation & An Advancement* 220
CHAPTER 38 *A Proposal, An Escape, A Performance & An Emigration* 224
CHAPTER 39 *A Trip To Bakewell, A Meeting & An Admonishment* 233
CHAPTER 40 *Approaching Nuptials, A Further Offer & An Escapade* 239

CHAPTER 41 *A Confirmation, A New Experience & A Realisation* 247
CHAPTER 42 *Things Come Dramatically To A Head*..253
CHAPTER 43 *The Marriage & An Unexpected Guest*..261
CHAPTER 44 *A Decision, An Explanation & Defiance*...272

BOOK III: 1832

CHAPTER 45 *Finances, Rankling Revenge, A Plot & Acts Of Parliament*..284
CHAPTER 46 *Stark Realisations & A Momentous Decision* 292
CHAPTER 47 *A Plan Is Proposed & A Brawl Avoided*...304
CHAPTER 48 *Decisions Made, A Thwarted Plan, A Flight & A Murder*..311
CHAPTER 49 *An Arrival, A Confrontation & A Protraction*...322
CHAPTER 50 *A Despicable Deed*..........................333
CHAPTER 51 *A Discovery, A Resolution & A Departure* 338
CHAPTER 52 *A Tricky Confrontation, A Revelation & Conjecture* 345
CHAPTER 53 *A Journey, A Meeting, A Plan & A Warning* 354
CHAPTER 54 *A Plan Thwarted, Suspicions Arise & Evidence Is Found*..365
CHAPTER 55 *The Net Closes In* 374
CHAPTER 56 *A Change Of Heart, A Confrontation & A Conclusion*..385

CHAPTER 57 *A Change Of Plan & A Resolution* 395
CHAPTER 58 *A Marriage & A Change Of Heart...* 397
CHAPTER 59 *A Letter From Italy & A Welcome Setback* 400
CHAPTER 60 *A Reunion, A Relief & A Debt Repaid* 403

EPILOGUE 411
ABOUT THE AUTHOR 416

PROLOGUE

Jamaica, 1774

The young boy, inquisitive as ever, looked out over the ripening sugar-canes swaying in the light breeze, an imprecise blur of yellow and green as they danced in the evening sunlight. It was his fourth birthday and he had, on that day, acquired the excitement of coming adulthood, as if lace curtains had been drawn from a window, revealing a vista full of beauty and promise. Yet at the same moment, a disappointment had also begun to gnaw at this perception, as if perusing such a beautiful landscape had suddenly revealed the most ugly of buildings, despoiling its balance and harmony; the unwelcome annoyance tugged at his feelings, affecting this most considerate of children, the sense of unease tainting his innate belief of English fair play, which he instinctively knew he had inherited from his mother. He turned to look at her: she was very ill and reposing on a bed which had been placed on the veranda of their white-boarded colonial home. Even at that tender age, he knew she was not long for this world, despite the attentions of her personal maid, Akusia, who, with her lilting Jamaican accent, was mopping her brow and administering a concoction of sweetened mango juice which she occasionally poured from an iced jug into a tiny glass for easy consumption. Akusia was sweet – he loved her almost as much as his mother. Yet she was different – as were all the people who worked on this huge estate and on that seminal day it had occurred to him that everyone who worked was black, and everyone who did not was white, which confused him. His father, Grayson Grimley, ran the plantation with a strong hand, yet although he was firm, he was fair, and the boy, Walton, had been appalled when once accompanying him to another sugar plantation and seen their workers with the scars of lashings on their backs and tattered, indecent clothing about their bodies: some were in irons of varying degrees of restriction, too. His father's workers were much better looked after, he had noted, and when he had spoken to his mother afterwards about what he had seen, she went very quiet and gave a forlorn, passionate sigh, as if regretting that her sheltered son had witnessed the known barbarities inflicted upon the people at other plantations. She then explained that, whereas his father treated these slaves far better than any other owner – it had been the first time he heard that word and needed to ask what it meant, causing his mother even more consternation and not a few tears – they were referred to as workers here on this estate to imbue them with some dignity. His father gave them medical attention, too, for which he was ridiculed by the other owners: the prevailing orthodoxy if a slave was too ill to work was to shoot him and buy another – doctors cost more than a slave. This revelation changed the young boy's life: he knew that – as the only child – he would eventually inherit the estate and determined that when he did so he would treat his slaves as well as his father, if not better; and with the sweet, caring Akusia as a role model, he would indulge them with compassion as human beings, not property.

At that time, however, the economic side of his nascent benevolence was unknown to him and would, in time, test his morality and compassion to the full…

England, 1806

The Napoleonic Wars had been raging since May 1803 and would continue until November 1815… but after Lord Nelson's victory at Trafalgar on 21st October, 1805, a sense of relief and nervous national optimism had become apparent. On the death of his father, Walton had inherited his title, yet with no place to call home in England – his father had used the sale of the family house many years before to buy the Jamaican plantation - it was then that the newly ennobled Sir Walton Grimley had decided to return to the mother country. As the French threat remained he had bought some land in the north on which to build his house, where any invasion would be less destructive: it would be the south which would bear the brunt in that event. To add weight to that decision, a parliamentary seat – as well as a beautiful tract of land amounting to some two thousand acres - had become available near Bakewell, Derbyshire, in November, 1805: this was just far enough away from the Duke of Devonshire's seat, Chatsworth, to not appear as a competitor for, despite his significant wealth, he by no means had that particular family's depth of finance. To tide him over while his new mansion was being built he bought a small house in the centre of Bakewell which was just big enough for him, a butler and a maid to live in: his housekeeper would for now live nearby.

He then went about making himself known around the town and further afield as a man of wealth and influence, who would soon have a stately pile to demonstrate his importance.

Due to his pivotal moment as a young boy when his sentiments against slavery became as strong as they were, he decided to stand for election in the hustings of 1806. He stood as a Whig and secured the seat with a decent majority, despite being virtually unknown in the area; yet his inherited title had stood him in good stead and, along with a spirited campaign for the betterment of the workforce – and some carefully targeted bribes, as was common at the time - he had secured the seat, his cheery, no-nonsense disposition inspiring the local population. His hustings, however, had concentrated only on domestic matters but it was his conscience regarding slavery that had guided his intentions: that, however, was rarely mentioned for now - he was canny enough to know that the deprivations of his local electorate would trump any interest in the morality of the slave-trade and whilst many ordinary people around the country had slaves as investments which paid them annual interest, the number in this mainly poor, rural area was small.

The parliament was a coalition of Fox and Grenville supporters on the Whig side and Addington supporters for the Tories; termed the Ministry of all the Talents, it was led by William Grenville as Prime minister and although it only lasted a few months – Parliament being dissolved by King George III in 1807 - Sir Walton Grimley soon became known as a man of purpose and respect. With a new administration led by the Duke of Portland, Sir Walton's first act was to be a champion of the Royal Naval Squadron, which chased other countries' slave ships from the seas and helped repatriate many people; and where slaves had little clue from where they had been taken from, Freetown – a colony which British philanthropists had set up in Sierra Leone for freed slaves in 1787, (his year of conscience, as he would later call it) the town eventually became a thriving, homogenous and ethnically diverse city, a glimpse into a future which was not at that time commonplace.

Yet despite these auspicious beginnings, slavery would not be finally abolished until 1838 and his personal life would soon be a reflection of its contradictions.

So it was into this melee of fractious politics that Sir Walton Grimley found himself as his house began to take shape…

BOOK ONE

CHAPTER 1

Mulberry Hall is created

The deep red brick carcase of the building stood in stark contrast against the darkening sky; with the roof not yet built, the setting sun's warm rays cast long shards of fulgent light through the tall, slender openings where the windows would one day go, the 'golden rule' of the dimensions a parody of the coloured beams of light as they fell onto the scratchy, rubble-strewn grass below; these oblong patterns were either illuminating or avoiding the piles of joists, ropes, picks, shovels, buckets, sacks of mortar, bricks, blocks and pulleys littering the ground in disarray. This chequered chaos of light and dark contrasted with the stacks of locally quarried stones completing the scene, their diminution in size from their Carboniferous provenance almost pleading for no further desecration of the timeless, wild beauty of the Derbyshire Peak looming large in the distance, where its height still attracted a gilded crown.

The master builder, Josiah Prentice, picked his way

through the chaos and carefully placed his tools into the capacious leather bag which lay open on the back of his cart; his nag, Bessie, was silently enjoying the rich grass beyond the rubble under a newly-planted but thriving mulberry tree but as soon as he called her she came to him, which she always obediently did. The day was over and the other workmen had been dismissed until Monday, for Sunday was the Sabbath, when both this man and his beast could look forward to some sleep – the former after a few pints in his favourite Bakewell tavern, the latter with some oats steeped in cider, a tradition which had started by accident when Josiah accidentally dropped a flagon of the liquid and the broken container's contents saturated the grains; but Bessie had loved it and henceforth it became a weekly treat for his beloved steed.

Josiah was a genial, slightly nervous young man of twenty-three with a wiry, muscular frame, the tufts of manhood on his face not yet as developed around the mouth as his chin, which grew sporadically and unsurely, giving him an unfinished look - just like the house he was building. He had been apprenticed to his father, also a master builder, at the age of sixteen, who had been fortunate enough a couple of years ago to meet the purchaser of this land and subsequently contracted him to build this stately home; yet soon after starting the project, he had died after falling off some scaffolding. The owner, Sir Walton Grimley, had been impressed by the son's knowledge and ability and had requested that he continued the build, which Josiah was grateful to do, despite it daily reminding him of his father's demise…

He hitched Bessie to the cart and looked back at the week's work; the top layer of bricks had been completed and the first of the parapet's stones in contrasting limestone had been laid across them; the gaping window spaces would soon not be looked through from the outside but the interior, where the striking view – enhanced by the beautiful tree which would give the hall its name – stood as a softening distraction to the otherwise chaotic and austere panorama.

'Mulberry Hall', he mused in his mind, as he mounted the cart and gently muttered, "Home, Bessie"; Bessie moved off as a sudden chill complemented the gathering gloom, adding a menacing aura to the building's outline, as if a blot on this brave but often challenging landscape; "But it will soon be beautiful," he consoled himself, as his project receded into the background.

Josiah knew Sir Walton Grimley to be a good man who had inherited his father's Jamaican plantation, title and money on his death, which had been caused by deep despair not long after his wife, Sir Walton's mother, had died. Josiah had voted for Sir Walton, too, as had his father, both knowing he had decided to build something of beauty in the 'mother' country, not wishing to live in Jamaica – where he felt ashamed of looking out every day onto the toiling, displaced workers of his vast sugar plantation, mostly supplied by brutally obliging tribal chiefs in west Africa who wanted rid of their local ethnic enemies. Yet Sir Walton had made it clear to them both that, by treating his slaves more fairly, his father had also looked upon this situation as a relative favour to them as much as a good business transaction for him and although he had known deep down that the premise of slavery was wrong, consoled himself by giving his subjects good conditions, plenty of food, pleasant accommodation, less work and fewer, if any, beatings than many unenlightened owners he knew were guilty of.

Now just turned thirty, Sir Walton had developed into someone who was physically somewhere between stocky and slim with good, if slightly short, legs, sandy-coloured straight hair and a face which displayed his moral dilemma to any who knew it; yet those were very few as he had kept to himself his fourth birthday decision to double down on his father's relative goodness. His only flaw, if there was one, appeared to be that despite knowing what he wanted to achieve in life he never quite knew where to start from. Except in this particular instance: for what he had not told anyone was that he had impishly decided to bring one of his more dutiful workers back to Bakewell when his house was finished to show not only that he appreciated loyalty and diversity of cultures but also because he knew it would cause a local stir; people of colour were quite usual in London by this time but up here in Derbyshire acceptances such as these took somewhat longer.

The man Sir Walton had mentally earmarked to become his manservant in this new home was a particularly handsome slave on his Jamaican plantation; currently his estate foreman, Tobias had also been appointed to this more personal position when Walton was in residence in Jamaica because he had demonstrated a calm and astute ability. Tobias would, therefore, eventually be despatched to England when Mulberry Hall was finished; he was an honest, intelligent man whom Sir Walton felt should have a better chance in life. The man was also unmarried, so would not at this time bring a wife and family; perhaps that might happen later when the house was up and running - and if he could find a suitable girl to match the man's qualities.

Sir Walton, too, was still unmarried and had made it clear that he had little intention of becoming so - he liked the freedom from fawning which the marriage market entailed, desperate suitors parading their daughters only for his fortune and any dowry; the local taverns supplied him with all the pleasures he needed and that was that.

Until he met Alice. This meeting would change everything... but whether for better or worse only time would tell.

*

It was November by the time Mulberry Hall was almost complete; the roof was on, the plastering finished and only some detailing needed to be done in the main rooms – mostly cornicing, niches and gold leaf in various places; the late summer and autumn had been kind and the workmen had managed to complete the building a few weeks earlier than anticipated. Now, rather than labourers, carpenters, bricklayers and stonemasons, it was mostly artisans who flooded the rooms – carpeters, painters, gilders, wood-carvers and so on – who lent a more esteemed tone to the building. Sir Walton had announced his imminent arrival from the less conspicuous temporary house he owned in Bakewell and wanted to move in; he had also acquired the services of a well-known landscape gardener with the appropriate name of Samuel Hedges and was keen for him to start the laying out of the lawns, lakes and terraces before the harsh northern season cloaked everything in frost and snow. Then, with the basics established, the internal continuation of the project could continue through the winter, after which the external works would re-start with increasing speed as spring's key unlocked the land.

THE SLAVE-OWNER'S DILEMMA

The entrance hall, Great Parlour, dining-room and withdrawing-room had been mostly finalised and Sir Walton had arrived at the house to oversee the placing of many bespoke artefacts and gewgaws collected on foreign travels, as was the fashion of the time. Lumbering cartloads of furniture, paintings and statues were being delivered, the gentle but long incline from the half-finished gate to the entrance causing even the strongest horses to sweat despite the rapidly decreasing temperature; Sir Walton, situated mostly in the parlour, stomped about in his leather riding-boots ordering this and that to be placed here and there, then changing his mind and ordering repositioning, causing a backlog of arriving treasures to mount in the entrance hall, which itself needed organising. Josiah was in a state of turmoil as these were obstructing access to the upper rooms where other workmen were trying to complete their tasks and had no need of these extra hazards.

Just to add to the confusion, Mrs. Burrows, Sir Walton's housekeeper in his Bakewell home, had arrived to see if she would accept his offer to live in the new hall which would dissociate her and her husband Giles, the butler, from their trusted suppliers and tradespeople in Bakewell, built up over a number of years when in service at a previous home. Discomfited, hesitant and somewhat nervous, the added responsibilities of such a much larger house nine miles from the town was not something she had really wanted to do; yet Sir Walton, being an obstinate but kind-hearted man, had offered she and her husband wages well above the norm: whilst this was to be welcomed, they were both aware they would now have nowhere to spend it.

Giles had decided to stay in town while he could and leave the decision to his wife, who, now standing in the middle of the chaos that was the entrance hall, suddenly heard the stentorian voice of Sir Walton addressing her.

"Ah, Mrs. Burrows, 'pon my soul – welcome to Mulberry Hall."

'Mulberry Hall?' she thought to herself, *'What a stupid name – I see no mulberry here.'* (Why she had not seen such a resplendent tree was due to winter approaching and it had been surrounded by high boarding to protect it from the elements as much as by any carelessness from so many workmen.)

"Good morning once again, Sir; slightly in need of some order here, it would seem," as she intimated the chaos around her.

"Indeed," he concurred, "but what a splendid place this is going to be, don't you think?"

"Yes, Sir," she answered, still not a little overcome by its size and hardly daring to think how many rooms for staff there must be upstairs to cater for all the needs of such a huge place - which she would be duty-bound to oversee. "And not a little, daunting, Sir," she demurred, more as a point of view than a criticism – she would not dare risk any form of that to her master.

"Come, come, Mrs. Burrows – this is progress!" he almost shouted in his exuberance and, suddenly seeing his building manager, called out, "Ah, Mr. Prentice – when are the upstairs rooms going to be furnished with all this?" referring to the piles of boxes and artefacts surrounding them all.

"When you've told me where to put them, Sir," Prentice replied, slightly waspishly.

"Ah – well, talk to Mrs. Burrows here, my housekeeper: she'll give you an idea where to put them for now – we can always change them later," and he disappeared back into the Great Parlour. Mrs. Burrows and Josiah Prentice looked at each other and – despite both being overcome by the enormity of their respective tasks – found themselves gently laughing at the circumstances they found themselves in.

An hour or two later, Mrs. Burrows and Mr. Prentice had toured every last inch of the house, and whilst the former was somewhat tired by the experience, she recognised that it was a beautiful construction and appeared to be very well built, a point she made to Mr. Prentice.

He, buoyed by the compliment – which was seldom given to a man of his lowly position – was effusive in his thanks and instantly took further to Mrs. Burrows who was, he had come to realise, an attractive, tall, slim woman with an ample bust decreasing into a pointed waist; despite having exceeded her bloom some years previously, her handsome being was topped by lustrous, long auburn hair collected into a resplendent summit. They found themselves laughing freely about a number of trivial yet relevant points to their respective positions and a bond began to emerge. It transpired he had noticed her slightly corpulent, balding husband in the town due to his butler's dress but had never met him formally… and could not help thinking that the attractive and well-preserved Mrs. Burrows was rather too good for him; he thus found himself musing that most housekeepers he had known were usually buxom and comely due to being in the constant proximity of food - something that the vast majority of the population were not privy to. However, when he later met the prospective cook, a Miss Shaw, he was instantly aware that, despite her leaner years, she was somewhat the opposite in stature – and conformed more to the usual than Mrs. Burrows did.

*

Despite her reservations, Mrs. Burrows had decided to accept the position as Sir Walton Grimley's housekeeper, a choice that her husband Giles seemed keen for her to do – despite himself confirming he wished to stay in town and find another job; they would be able to see each other on her monthly four days off, which she had negotiated with Sir Walton, along with an even more outrageous demand for much higher wages, both of which she thought Sir Walton would rebuff but unexpectedly agreed to. Giles, having worked as Sir Walton's butler for almost two years and others for over ten previously, had put aside enough money over time (helped by ongoing pilfering from the butler's financial allowance for wines and victuals) to have bought the tiny house in Bakewell's nether regions from which his wife left for Sir Walton's house every morning where Giles resided, joining her husband there; this tiny abode would now suit them both on the rare occasions they would meet... and unbeknown to his wife would allow him a certain licentiousness with one of the barmaids from his favourite town tavern.

This declination of such a good position by Elspeth Burrows' husband had been met with a certain disdain by Sir Walton, who disliked any change of trusted staff intensely and had become not a little testy as a consequence. Yet by now, the house was otherwise settling into its daily routines and whilst the expansion of staff numbers had been a major headache for Mrs. Burrows and the cook, who together had interviewed and taken on several footmen, parlour-maids, laundry-maids and a seamstress, the butler was a position that Sir Walton wished to appoint himself. Finding no-one that he liked, despite several applicants, his thoughts turned to his initial decision of importing one from Jamaica whom he could both teach and put into a position of reliance and internment. Tobias, he increasingly felt, would be the perfect candidate for the job and even more suited to being his butler than manservant; his calm authority would be much needed for the running of Mulberry Hall - an asset somewhat lacking in Giles Burrows. Tobias would also never be able to present the dilemma of leaving as Sir Walton owned him. His mind made up – and due to travel to Jamaica from Liverpool within a fortnight for a couple of months – he would bring back the man on his return. He would also enjoy the local reaction to probably the only black butler in the north of England and again rather warmed to the idea of its novelty.

Yet, as so often with perfect plans, fate would present other interpretations…

CHAPTER 2

Tobias

Sir Walton looked out over the valley below in the dazzling sunlight, the sea of tall, ripe green sugar canes occasionally being dotted with the dark skins of the slaves – no, his workers – toiling there, then disappearing again as they backbreakingly bent over, cut the stalks and then stood up again. A shudder came over him despite the heat and he imagined, with the fervour of a recurring nightmare, how he himself would feel being in that terrible position. Tired, overworked, resentful, few rights and no chance of escape except mortality. Whilst he had instructed his slave-masters to be kind and respectful of their charges and would only allow beatings for theft, murder or attack, this had only happened once with a hot-headed young man who had tried to kill one of his slave-masters; so once again he felt proud of his compassion by treating them as humans rather than chattels, feeding and housing them well and providing decent clothing. Despite that one unfortunate instance, his plan had worked well: his slaves had never, to his knowledge, been treated badly and they obviously respected his latitude. Indeed, his comparable geniality had been confirmed to him by his faithful foreman, Tobias, who knew only too well of stories from other plantations where physical abuse was liberally meted out daily as a matter of course. This added to Sir Walton's frequent thoughts of slavery being morally wrong and he had talked several times to trusted friends in the Lords about its abolition; indeed, he had even supported the <u>Committee for the Abolition of the Slave Trade</u>, formed in 1787 by a number of Evangelical <u>Protestants</u> and Quakers when at Cambridge University and, also, as a young man about town in London. The rub was that, if he stopped using slaves when everyone else continued to do so, what would happen to his fortune – and the dignity of having his new testament to wealth, Mulberry Hall? Nevertheless, he knew he wanted to abolish the practice if he could and it was made known to his slaves that, having been wrested from their homelands due to unprincipled tribal chiefs and greedy traders, if they were mistreated by his slave-masters they would be given the opportunity to be allowed home – if they knew where that actually was. Fortunately, only that one miscreant had been dismissed and, not knowing where his homeland was, now rotted in Kingston jail. No others had wished to rebel and he often mused whether – under his more benign management – many on his plantation actually had a better and safer life than they had experienced in Africa where famine, animal or tribal attacks and disease were commonplace. Yet he also frequently wondered what future generations would think of slavery and whether its abolition would cause upset and rancour with such huge displacements of people finding themselves with no true roots in alien countries and little prospect of improving themselves – especially without any basic education or sense of local tradition. Thus he had decided, with increasing daily resolution, to do more to have this practice abolished – but only once his fortune was secure and Mulberry Hall finished. Although this was a conflicting decision, he justified it as an altruistic standpoint because, by using his inherited wealth, he would not allow his own workers to fall into total poverty. And even taking Tobias back to England would be a small but important start...

When asked, Tobias had seemed keen to accompany his master back to the mother country, only being worried about the crossing – although, this time, not in chains with hundreds of others but in his own cabin – and the prospect of the wet and often freezing English weather. Nonetheless, he felt that it would be better to be in England where he would force himself to be the best archetypal Englishman he could manage and be respected for who he was rather than his skin colour denoting him as a social inferior.

The day of departure arrived and Tobias was given a hearty send-off by the other slaves; he had been a good friend to them and a conduit of any grievances through being Sir Walton's foreman. One young girl was weeping openly and he wondered if there had been any intimacy between them as Tobias was weeping too, fleetingly embracing her and darting a kiss to her lips – which made Walton even more troubled by what he was doing - taking Tobias away from the only people he knew well and had an affinity with. A few yards down the track, overcome by compassion for the relationship he might be destroying, he ordered the driver to stop the cart and asked Tobias directly if he would rather stay in Jamaica after all to be with this young girl. But Tobias was resolute: "No, Master," he said with tears in his eyes, "I want to be an Englishman. And one day, perhaps I can come back and marry her."

"Well, Tobias; would you like her to come with us? She could be very useful in the house... and she seems a pleasant girl."

Tobias' eyes brimmed with tears but said it would be better for him to return in years to come and marry her then, when he would have enough money to buy her freedom. If he didn't leave, he would be a slave forever and thanks to Sir Walton, this was his life's opportunity.

With that, Sir Walton nodded to the driver and the cart rolled on. They had a ship to catch, after all…

*

With their close proximity on the long voyage, Sir Walton found Tobias to be even more intelligent and canny than he had supposed; he was articulate, witty and had a sense of humour which made him wonder how it had been acquired. The answer was that Walton - having granted Akusia access to his small library – had used that privilege to teach Tobias to read, whereupon he had consumed most of the books there. On learning this, Walton told him that his library in Mulberry Hall would soon be twenty times bigger than that one and Tobias could help himself to all the books he wanted as long as it did not interfere with his duties. Tobias was almost overcome with thanks and Sir Walton noted once again some tears in his eyes - whether of gratitude or anticipation of the chance of a better, fuller life, he was unsure: but what he was sure of was that he had made a good choice and this handsome, muscular and emotional man was someone he could trust as his butler – and much better than the resentful, bone-headed hopefuls he had interviewed at Mulberry Hall for the job… He was also aware that Tobias would be much cheaper than Mrs. Burrows' husband, Giles, who had declined the job anyway; Walton had been happy to keep Mrs. Burrows as he liked and respected her, but she had forced a high wage and time off from him so the approaching prospect of the unflappable Tobias in a butler's attire – and at a much reduced price - made him even happier.

*

After a frighteningly cold, rough crossing occasioned by gales and mountainous seas, their little ship finally arrived in Liverpool. From Jamaica, Sir Walton had written to Mrs. Burrows to alert her to their imminent arrival but when they docked and there was no-one there to meet them it became obvious that they had arrived before the letter. Going into one of his testy moods – not helped by the dockers' disdainful looks at his fellow traveller of unusual colour dressed in such relative finery – he managed to find a lodging for a couple of days while he sent for his coach and horses to collect them. Staying at a hostelry, his humour was not pacified by the stares of the young maids working there who made little secret of their attraction to his handsome travelling companion...

Eventually the coach arrived and after resting the horses for a night, they embarked at dawn to get as far as possible before another two or three nights en route; one never knew how long these journeys would take and navigating the Peak District on unmade roads frequented by highwaymen and instantly changeable weather was daunting enough on its own. For added security, he therefore hired a craggy local man with a pair of flintlock pistols whom, Walton hoped, would be able to fend off any unwanted attentions.

They eventually arrived back at Mulberry Hall without any major incident, apart from the carriage becoming stuck in a hole near the top of High Wheeldon which took all their energy – and the help of a local farmer's Percheron horse - to dislodge.

On hearing the sound of the carriage approaching, Mrs. Burrows flew around the house mustering the staff to welcome their master, some of whom had little idea of what Sir Walton Grimley looked like, having been taken on in his absence. Yet Sir Walton had omitted to tell her that there would be someone accompanying him so as they all bowed or curtseyed whilst Sir Walton descended from his carriage, Mrs. Burrows, on rising but not expecting another passenger and seeing Tobias for the first time, was almost unable to get up again as she set eyes on this beautiful man from across the seas – many seas – and found her legs weak and in an unexpected and embarrassing swoon.

CHAPTER 3

An Awkward Situation

Mrs. Burrows had never experienced a swoon before and its occurrence shocked her morality as much as her composure; she was not so much a deeply religious woman as one who gave it passive acceptance. Yet the total convulsiveness of the moment devastated her whole being and compass; his smooth skin appeared to have been burnished by polishing oil and his shapely legs were the best she had ever seen – muscular without being bulky, their outline highlighted by his new white breeches; even the fact that these were mud-spattered due to the incident at High Wheeldon only gave them a sense of reality rather than of a dream. As he stepped down from the carriage, she could also tell he was courteous and mild-mannered and when Sir Walton introduced her and Tobias bowed slightly, taking her hand gently for a moment, a thrill of desire went through her nether regions which she had never before experienced. Somewhat flushed and befuddled, she fluttered about introducing the other servants to Tobias as Sir Walton climbed the palatial steps requesting tea, food and sherry – in no particular order but as soon as possible.

After some tea in the Great Parlour, where Sir Walton

described to Tobias once again what he expected of him (having done it several times on the long voyage) it was down to Mrs. Burrows to take Tobias down to the servants' hall where the less opulent surroundings at last made him feel less of a trophy and more of a human being. Mrs. Burrows then had a dilemma: normally, one of the footmen or maids would have shown him to his quarters behind the butler's pantry but she could not bear to let him out of her sight until every curve, ripple and atom of his personage had been assessed; so she told the head footman, Percy, to fetch Tobias' small stock of belongings from the entrance hall, scattered the other servants to their duties around the house like a mother hen and then took Tobias there herself, closing the door behind them.

It was no wonder that the young maids were all of a flutter, too, and giggling behind cupped hands at the obvious discombobulation of their normally unflappable housekeeper.

*

After a week, the initial disturbance to the female staff had settled down into a wistful longing, any chance of plotting an excuse to be with Tobias for even a fleeting moment being jealously taken. Tobias, being unused to this restricted yet obvious attention – and due to his upbringing as nothing but a slave – was bemused and confused by this. Yet he had already, at an early age, experienced the joys of passion with his sweetheart Alice in Jamaica, whom he had loved very much, as she had him; but both being very young at the time they had left their passions untold. So the attentions of the 'master class' in England – however lowly in the hierarchy of the time – confused and frightened him: he did not wish to show any favour either to the more sensible Mrs. Burrows or the flirtatious young maids as he knew this would sow division and almost certainly lead to his return to Jamaica. So he steered a polite course between them all and was careful not to excite any expectations in any of them.

However, as the weeks progressed, he did find himself becoming increasingly attracted to Mrs. Burrows. She was not exactly a beauty but was slender and had a lovely smile on the rare occasions she allowed one; her blue eyes, gleaming like sapphires, sparkled when something humorous momentarily took her by surprise and her whole persona seemed to glow with the moment; her teeth – normally covered by a prim, purposeful expression - then appeared too. Yet on occasion Tobias was aware that her enforced distancing due to duty and social mores appeared to be tearing her apart, as if battling inner conflicts between desire and propriety, and Tobias, despite his lack of experience in his new country, picked up these discords, making him feel both sorry and excited at the ardours he was sure she was hiding. However, this feeling of fragility and torment had the effect of attracting him to her even more. To boot, she was quite educated as well – at least compared to Tobias – and in her less guarded moments suggested books from Sir Walton's expanding library that she felt might help him better understand his new country and impart to him knowledge he had previously been unaware of. To cap it all, she had a beautiful natural aroma which – due to the privations of ablutionary opportunity - only became stronger between bath days.

This quietly insistent feeling of affinity with Mrs. Burrows did not disappear even when the more outward intimations of the parlour-maids were offered. No, he was learning the English ways and God had given him a heaven-sent opportunity which he was not going to jeopardise.

He had met her husband, Giles, on a handful of occasions and concluded he was a worthless man puffed up by his own feelings of superiority. Yet passing her door one night and hearing the sounds of a guarded intimacy on one of his clandestine visits when Sir Walton was away, Tobias' first stirrings of jealousy had become apparent. From then on, he confidently felt that he was at least the equal of Giles but still did not have the self-belief or confidence to display it.

Yet time – of which there was plenty at Mulberry Hall - would soon produce a determining result.

One day in early autumn, a chill wind sprang up and the temperature in the draughty building plummeted accordingly. With Sir Walton once again in Jamaica, a slight latitude had become apparent in the household and Mrs. Burrows ordered a number of large pans of water to be boiled on the kitchen range so everyone could warm themselves with a tepid bath if they so chose – which they all did. So, turns were taken to look after the boiling, distribution, filling and emptying of the servants' bath, which was brought in from the coach-house and positioned in Tobias' butler's room for its proximity to the kitchen and because it had a fire – and a lockable door.

The various maids went in first and shared the first tranches of water, which allowed the next batch to boil to a greater heat; then the footmen went in, one by one, bath by bath, and then a few other servants who had been availed of the same treat by the suddenly overtly generous instruction of Mrs. Burrows. She then disappeared to fulfil various duties around the house while the servants severally washed and warmed themselves. Tobias had positioned himself in the library to do some stocktaking, ordering and accounts so that the return of Sir Walton in a week or so's time would not be inconvenienced by any deprivations.

Two hours later – and assuming in that time that all would have had their baths before returning to their duties – he descended the back stairs to the servants' hall and, off-handedly, thought to replace his papers into his strongbox. The place seemed quiet and empty, the servants all having presumably had their baths and now continuing their obligations around the building. He tried the door and, finding it unlocked, progressed into his office. There, he heard an audible stilted cry and realised he had stumbled into his pantry where a naked Mrs. Burrows was standing in the bath, washing herself down.

Tobias immediately covered his eyes and hastily apologised but the glimpse of her unclothed body glistening in the candlelight and her firm, bedewed breasts projecting proudly through her long, wet hair which caressed them as it reached almost to her pudenda, was one of the most beautiful things he had ever seen in his relatively short and restricted life. He turned around in embarrassment and was about to exit to safety when he heard Mrs. Burrows' soft but suddenly commanding voice calling him back. Tobias stopped but did not dare look again, terrified that his intrusion would mean the end of his career and he would be saddled with shame for the rest of his life. Yet the softness of her voice, applied to the image in his mind of this beautiful woman behind him, had caused a thrill in his loins he had only ever once manifested with Alice so he felt further compelled not to look again.

"Tobias – come back."

"But, Mrs. B-"

"Tobias. Come back in and close the door."

"But…"

"And then lock it behind you."

With his eyes looking at his black, silver-buckled shoes, he did as he was told and then stood there, looking in her direction but with his eyes firmly closed.

"Tobias – open your eyes."

"But, Mrs. Burrows…"

"Just do as I ask you, please…" The voice was more insistent this time. He hesitated, though; for although technically they were of the same superior rank in the hierarchy of servants, in this case - being of slave stock and there only due to Sir Walton's magnanimity – he felt inferior and duty-bound to do as she said. He took a deep breath, sighed and opened his eyes; the image which had burned into his mind was almost the same, yet even more beautiful now as she had stepped out of the bath, so revealing a very pretty set of ankles. He suddenly noticed how her feet, too, were beautifully formed, untrammelled by the everyday obligations which had affected her hands.

She stood there as a smile of sublime conquest crossed her face and she beckoned him to her. "Undress yourself too, my dear Tobias," she whispered as he got so close he could smell the lavender oil she had applied to her bath, which aroused Tobias further despite desperately trying not to be affected. He did as he was told and when he was naked too got back into the bath, instructing him to do the same. They sat at opposite ends of the tiny receptacle as she guided him into her very own; "It's just as beautiful as I had imagined," she said sweetly, as the water ebbed and flowed with their movements; suddenly, both climaxed at the same time, both trying decorously not to make the noise their bodies were desperate to express.

They lay there for several minutes. Then, the sound of a scullery-maid dropping a pan in the kitchen reminded them of their predicament and the moment was gone. Quickly, they silently got out of the bath, dried down and dressed again. Then, while Mrs. Burrows hid behind the door, Tobias opened it and told the scullery-maid, Fleur, to do a chore at the other end of the house; when she had gone, Tobias came back and, opening the door to his pantry, intimated Mrs. Burrows could now leave.

"That will not be the only time," she stated silently but resolutely as she passed him, deposited a kiss on the cheek and then added, "This is just the beginning of something special." Then she disappeared into the furthermost areas of the vacuous building to calm her troubled but very satisfied body down...

CHAPTER 4

Alice

At that same moment in Jamaica, Sir Walton was on his horse inspecting the vast magnitude of his estate when he spied the young girl whom he had briefly encountered with Tobias when they had left for England almost a year before. He pulled up his steed and guided it over to the girl, beckoning her closer as he did so.

Alice had recently acquired her eighteenth birthday and the bloom of young womanhood had suddenly gilded her; she had almost overnight, it seemed, passed from being a child to a slim, beautiful young woman and Sir Walton was suddenly overwhelmed by her presence. She, shy and fearful at what her master might ask of her, stood a little back but he gestured her closer.

"I met you some months ago when I took Tobias back to England, didn't I?" he asked. The girl nodded.

"Alice, isn't it?" he enquired. The girl nodded again.

"And you were a friend of Tobias, weren't you?" She again nodded. Then, with feeling, added, "Yes, Master; he was a very close friend of mine."

"Yes, he mentioned you once or twice on our voyage."

Sir Walton looked at her; such a pretty young thing, he

thought. Yet he would never touch one of his slaves, however attractive, despite this being commonplace amongst the other slave-owners. But no, and he nearly drove on – then a thought crossed his mind.

"Would you like to see him again?" he enquired. The girl hesitated, then nodded animatedly. "It would mean you'd have to come back to England with me…" he cautioned. She looked surprised but hopeful, then said, "Yes Master – I would like that very much." He pondered for a moment; if he could make both of his slaves happy together, he would like to do that. It would be good for both of them. "Jolly fine, then," he said. "I think Tobias was sad to leave you so… get yourself ready to leave in a few days. Come to my house this evening and Akusia will kit you out for the journey. The other things we can arrange back in England."

"Thank you very much, Master," she said with an excitement in her voice. "I would like that very much."

"Capital. Don't forget to tell your parents."

"I don't have any parents, Master; they died on the crossing from wherever I was taken from."

"Ah… well, sorry about that… Er, well, tell your friends and come around tonight, as I say."

Then he rode off, leaving a bewildered but happy young woman to contemplate her good fortune. And he was doing it so she could be with Tobias! Her feelings about her slave owner were now of an even better disposition, she admitted to herself. Yet the future suddenly daunted her: would Tobias want her? Well, she wanted him… but that was now beyond contemplation – the die had been cast and she was going to England to become an Englishwoman, however lowly… and her heart was overjoyed…

*

It was the day before Sir Walton's likely return to Mulberry Hall and the house's normally oppressive silence was punctuated by the sounds of sweeping, polishing, wiping and carpet-beating; since the episode in the bath just over a fortnight before, Mrs. Burrows' humour had improved immeasurably and her grip on the household's necessities had correspondingly lapsed, so now it was incumbent upon her to sharpen up before the master returned and might feel that standards had slipped. Not only would that be bad for her references regarding any future employment but it would mean being separated from Tobias, who had consumed her soul entirely: it was not only the physical wonderment of his being but the tenderness and urge to learn that she found so consuming. They would both read a book then discuss its contents, philosophy, style and points the author was making... and so the beginnings of a stimulating cerebral relationship had begun alongside the now very physical one.

For Tobias, this extraordinary meeting of minds and bodies had transformed him into a more confident young man and the humour with which Mrs. Burrows teased him was returned with wit and perspicacity, much to their mutual pleasure. The other servants had noticed a lightness of being between the two and, although the couple tried very hard to keep any glances or sentiments away from them, it was not long before tongues started wagging and rumour became the talk of the house – especially with the parlour-maids who were generally indignant and jealous of such a possible development between the young Tobias and the older Mrs. Burrows...

Into this unusual melee of gossip and intrigue, the young stable-hand posted at the top of the hill to alert them to their master's carriage when it was sighted a mile or so away, suddenly rode at a gallop through the gate with the news that Sir Walton was approaching. The usual panic ensued as Mrs. Burrows and the rest tidied themselves and put away any hint of domestic apparatus, then lined up outside as the coach arrived.

The carriage duly swirled into the crescent in front of the house and, as it pulled up and its owner descended, they all bowed and curtseyed as they were expected to do. They were somewhat bemused, however, when Sir Walton – rather than striding up the steps for liquid refreshment as was his wont – turned back to beckon someone else out of the carriage. Looks were exchanged – had Sir Walton found a companion? A bride, even? All eyes narrowed onto the door as a slight, pretty dark-skinned girl dressed in white lace and satin shoes tiptoed down the carriage steps, her gloved hand being held by Sir Walton. The surprise was palpable; was their master about to marry someone from Jamaica? Exchanged looks and muted gasps were prevalent as the couple turned to face the entourage; Mrs. Burrows was surprised – nay, shocked - by this vision and suddenly felt anxious for her conquest of Tobias: had the master brought this waif-like girl back as a partner for her new paramour?

As for Tobias, his blood ran cold as he realised what the master had done – and all for him... he had brought back his sweetheart. He knew immediately then that life was going to become very complicated indeed.

CHAPTER 5

Confusion

With the suddenness of the situation, Tobias had no chance to ascertain Sir Walton's calculations and could do no more than greet Alice in the distant way that was the norm - as if she were a stranger. Her eyes beamed as she shook his hand, but she had been instructed by Sir Walton on the long journey not to betray any allusion to any previous closeness as it 'was not done' in England in these circumstances. More pertinently, as the long voyage had progressed, his interest in the girl had become something more than altruism: he had found himself becoming obsessed by her. Yet his moral rectitude dictated that he could brook no dalliance with Alice and upon seeing Tobias found himself severely envious of his new butler's past liaison with this sweet girl. Mrs. Burrows – having known Sir Walton longer than anyone else in the house – suspected her master had done this for Tobias' benefit but was understandably discomfited by this new situation.

Alice was overwhelmed by the grandeur, size and opulence of the house but Sir Walton had swept her up the steps and into the main hall before any serious eye contact could be exchanged between her and Tobias. He sat her down in the Great Parlour as her excitement and disbelief at her luck made her wonder if this was all a dream and that she would soon wake up and find herself still nothing but a poor, vulnerable slave girl on a sugar plantation in Jamaica.

Sir Walton rang for Tobias, who reluctantly answered but was told to serve tea and cakes for the young girl; she desperately wanted to talk to – no, embrace – her past lover but Tobias' face remained implacable save for a brief instant when Sir Walton momentarily turned away and he gave an expression which implied he could do nothing about this and could not speak to her now. She seemed to understand and turned back to her benefactor as Tobias left.

A few minutes later, Amity, one of the maids, brought in tea, sugar, milk and cakes on a silver tray, their matching receptacles each displaying Sir Walton's crest. She cast a puzzled look at Alice, then silently left, the door closing behind her. At that seminal moment, Alice realised that if this was going to be her life at Mulberry Hall it would be both stifling and frustrating – especially if Tobias was to be kept away from her... and she wondered whether she had done the right thing agreeing to come to this remote place in such a damp if beautiful country.

As for Sir Walton, Alice's presence had aroused many demons in his soul: he had honestly brought her over to be a companion – a wife, even – for Tobias but the naïve charm and unexpected intelligence of the girl, who seemed amazingly prescient despite being illiterate and with very little education, had made him envious of her having too much exposure to his butler. Thus he had not given her a room in the servants' quarters at the top of the house – not for now, anyway – until he had sorted his inclinations and their corresponding complications. Instead, he installed

Alice in one of the most beautiful rooms in the house, which overlooked the reason for the house's name. The view was stunning, and in the far distance, between a cleft in the Derbyshire peaks, the spire of Bakewell church could just be seen when the mist did not occlude it. Yet he had to admit to himself that this charitable gesture was borne of the realisation he wanted Alice for himself and his morality was at odds with his desires; so he only hoped that his infatuation would soon pass and then life could continue as normal.

Yet it was inevitable that, at some point, the opportunity for a rendezvous between Tobias and Alice would become possible and this happened on the third day after her arrival.

At breakfast that morning, Sir Walton announced that he would be riding into Bakewell to do some business there and told Alice that she should avail herself of the books in his library – she could look at the pictures, if nothing else - just at the moment Tobias entered the room with some letters. Hearing this information, Tobias returned a minute later with a tiny note for Alice secreted under a serviette, having seen that she had soiled the one previously laid out for her. He intimated to the napkin as he did so, then left; Sir Walton eventually departed the room, explaining to Alice that he would take her into Bakewell another day when the weather was more clement.

As soon as he had left the now empty room, Alice pounced on the serviette and looked at the note. Knowing that Alice was illiterate, Tobias had drawn a picture of some books and a clock drawn to show the time of 11 o'clock. She was aware of how to tell the time and saw that this was in a half-hour's time. She rose and left the room, going back to her quarters to ensure she looked her best for the assignation and her heart beat rapidly as she climbed the stairs, her voluminous dress an unwelcome impediment to her destination. In her haste, however, to see her past lover, she forgot to take the note with her and, a few moments later, Amity returned to clear up and saw the missive. Being jealous of Tobias for not having chosen her as his paramour, she took the note to Mrs. Burrows with the story that she had found this and wondered whether it was for her; then, triumphantly laughing to herself, left the room and told some other maids what she had done, much to their pleasure and Mrs. Burrows' discomfort.

Actually, Mrs. Burrows was more than discomforted – she was furious; it was bad enough that Tobias wanted to see Alice at last – of course he did; it was that she knew Amity to be a scurrilous girl and knew exactly why she had shown it to her. Yet there was nothing she could do.

Alice entered the library just before 11. It was the first time she had been there and found herself overwhelmed by its size and the number of books it already contained; she knew there would eventually be more as half the bookshelves were empty, as if waiting to be fed with the literary tastes of the time. A few seconds later, she heard a door open at the far end and saw that it was a concealed entrance hidden behind what appeared to be a full bookcase but was, actually, fake, the supposed books only being the spines of some unfortunate savaged tomes.

Alice ran down the library to Tobias and kissed him earnestly on his lips and, although he returned the emotion, he was stiff and distant in its application. Feeling the slight rebuff, she took a few paces back and looked at Tobias, her pleading, moistening eyes implying, 'Why?'

"Dearest Alice," he whispered; "It is indeed wonderful to have you here but the Master gave me no idea of his intention when he left, so seeing you was a huge surprise – no, shock – to me…" He tailed off, not knowing how to continue.

"Shock?" she reiterated. "But Tobias - we were lovers." There was a pause, then, "Weren't we?"

He nodded his head but looked even more troubled. "Alice, when we were in Jamaica together I had no idea that what has happened to me would be so. At that time, I knew we would be together one day – but through the master's goodwill, he brought me here. Perhaps, after some years, I might have come back for you but… things have changed and we cannot have a relationship here."

"But Sir Walton told me he was bringing me back here for you," she almost shouted, "so you had a companion and perhaps we could be married and have children here."

"Yes, my dear Alice, I know all that. But… well, things have changed. Don't tell anyone else but I'm in a relationship now."

"Where? In the town? Are there some other people like us there?"

He shook his head. "Not that I know of, my dearest Alice, no…"

"So… who, then?"

"I cannot say… It's a difficult secret. And if I betray her, then I might be sent back to Jamaica – or at least cast out of here. And I cannot risk that."

Alice was devastated. "So what am I going to do here, then?" she exclaimed. "I'm without purpose in this place now. I will have to return to Jamaica! How can you do this to me?"

"Make the most of your time here," he advised. "Learn to read, the English ways... how to play cards... learn the piano... I don't know. But I cannot be with you." With that, his eyes full of tears, he disappeared back down the stairs. Alice was heartbroken and just stood there, sobbing and then sinking to the floor as she banged the precious Persian carpets with her tiny fists.

At the other end of the library, behind a huge draughtproof screen, stood Mrs. Burrows; whilst she had heard everything and felt sad for the girl, she was not going to give Tobias up for her, and her lover had unwittingly confirmed that fact.

Alice went up to her room and cried her eyes out. Mrs. Burrows descended the stairs and acted as if nothing had happened. But inwardly, she was happy. Very happy indeed.

CHAPTER 6

The Plot Thickens...

Tobias returned to his pantry and locked the door. He put his hands over his face, allowing the tears to seep through his hands. He felt a terrible sense of betrayal to his previous love who, as ever, was innocent of anything bar a deep affection for him. Yet circumstances had intervened and he still found himself thinking of Mrs. Burrows – or Elspeth, as she had instructed him to call her during their intimate moments. Yet he wondered what he could do to assuage his guilt regarding Alice, only after much contemplation realising there was nothing. The poor girl was adrift on a sea of emotion, loss and despair due to being in the wrong place at the wrong time when he had left Jamaica. Momentarily, he wished that Sir Walton had not stopped to question whether he would like Alice to come to England with him for it had made his life complicated and hers... well, impossible. Trust him, he thought, to have been the slave of the only compassionate slave owner on the island, who actually cared for his charges to a far greater degree than the majority. Yet this charity had now brought only sadness and recrimination.

Upstairs, Alice cried ceaselessly and rued the moment she had found herself in Sir Walton's view as he rode past and then approached her with his offer of coming to England if she wanted – and then hated herself further for accepting it. Yet her innocent love for Tobias had run deep and she could have had no intimation that this situation would occur. So she sat up, dried her eyes and thought hard about what she could do – for she had to do something. Taking her life came to mind, as it often had when in Jamaica with the prospect of being a chattel for her whole life of hard work and subjugation... then a resolution came to her. Did she wish to return to Jamaica with Sir Walton the next time he returned? No, certainly not. She had an opportunity here to become someone, something... God had blessed her with a golden chance and she must grasp it. She had youth on her side and – if the comments were to be believed – not a little beauty. She sat bolt upright and became calm and calculating as a way out of this setback began to clarify. In the next moment, the young girl had shed her childhood innocence and become a calculating adult as, slowly, a plan began to emerge.

*

Sir Walton had arrived in Bakewell and, feeling slightly bewildered due to reasons he could not fathom, left his horse at the livery stable for some rest and nourishment and repaired to his favourite tavern to flush out his woes with a surfeit of ale. There were some pretty girls upstairs whom he had used on occasion to his great pleasure but today something stopped him from acquiring their services, despite their discreet waves and smiles of encouragement as he arrived. He was vexed but could not put his finger on why and, whilst he recognised that fact, he still could not divine it.

Suddenly seeing his ex-butler Giles descending the

stairs on the arm of a pretty young thing whom he had not seen before, he surmised in an instant that his former employee had quite obviously been unfaithful to his wife, his housekeeper, Mrs. Burrows: and that was why he had wished to stay in Bakewell, he mused… no 'entertainment' at Mulberry Hall. As Giles quickly left, the young woman passed by him and he noticed that she had an olive-coloured skin, which he instinctively found disturbingly attractive. Obviously a descendant of a shipwrecked sailor after the dispersal of the Spanish Armada, he concluded. And then it dawned on him: the reason for his unease was that she reminded him of Alice. He had to admit to himself that whilst his initial thoughts were true altruism for the new butler he had wrenched from Jamaica, the thought of this beautiful young girl being around had also been a factor… Not to use for himself, but to have as a pretty trinket with which to help entertain his bibulous and licentious friends. In short, she might have been good for encouraging business… And then the stark admission dawned that he found Alice attractive… *very* attractive - desperately so, in fact. A thrill went through his loins as he accepted the fact and, like a fog lifting, his clarity of thought returned and his spirits rose accordingly: this was why he had subconsciously not wanted to put Alice in with the servants, he concluded, as doing so would make her seem inferior and he would not be able to put her on the pedestal he wished for her. The next few ales slipped pleasantly by as his machinations – helped by the liquor – crowded his mind. He had invited Alice over for Tobias and that was the main reason. Or was it? He found himself wrestling with his conscience as to whether this poor, beautiful young woman was here for him or Tobias and concluded it was both. Then, having realised that point, he admitted that it was more to do with him. He had never wished to marry so that he could be legally available for all the flotsam and jetsam of society that crossed his path and if, if, he made Alice part of that equation then he would have to give her a title for credibility... But then he would have to marry her! No! He could not do that, no, no, no... But still Alice's sweet smile and dazzling white teeth, contrasting with her silky black face, were playing havoc with his reason and he resolved to force she and Tobias to marry, which he knew they wanted to do anyway; then she could be put in with the other servants and that would absolve him of any lustful inclinations for the dear, sweet, beautiful girl.

Or so he hoped.

CHAPTER 7

An Unexpected Situation

The weather, which had been dull and soggy, had matched Alice's tearful mood perfectly; yet as the basics of her plan had taken shape, her personal clouds lifted in concert with those outside. So she decided to assess the situation head on and go for a walk around the grounds to clear her complexion, mind and also to refine her plans.

On her amble, she determined to ask Sir Walton if he could teach her to read, which would avail her of his presence every so often; this would also have the effect of annoying Tobias and whoever it was who had compromised him, stolen his heart or blackmailed him. In addition, this would encourage a naïve-looking liaison between herself and Sir Walton, despite the full knowledge that he would not allow this to happen, for English society would never accept her openly – only where it could be covered up, denied and brushed aside, as was the rule in Jamaica. But never here in prim and proper England! Then she could distribute rumours around the gentry she would meet and he would have to pay her off; then – once she found who was compromising Tobias - she could either elope with him and they would be free go together somewhere else, or she could leave him completely and use her windfall to buy a property and create her own business.

As the breeze disturbed her clothing – a beautiful ice-blue dress that Sir Walton had bought to accompany the white one she had worn on arrival at Mulberry Hall - this new-found confidence made her wonder why he was being so good to her; she was aware that Sir Walton was a kind man who genuinely liked and admired Tobias but why, then, was he in the servants' quarters while she had a room to herself in the main house? With a chill brought about by a change in the wind's direction, she complemented its effect with the sudden idea that Sir Walton was loath to let her go because he found her attractive. Her! Not a duchess or baroness but *her* – little slave-girl Alice! She had even been given his surname as her true parents' names had been lost - she was Alice Grimley! Redemption? Possibly... Lust? Perhaps... With that, her plan became clearer: she was in a position to use him, despite this not being in her nature as, being a slave, she had never before had any opportunity. Then she argued that he had used her companions in Jamaica, whether he was fundamentally kind or not. Surprisingly, she felt little remorse about this conclusion of thoughts that might ensnare the man who had freed her - but who had also compromised the man she loved – and whom she thought had loved her, too. Yet her enslaved situation and recent circumstances had made her see that the world was what you made of it and sometimes it was necessary to use one's wiles, looks and abilities to create opportunities. After all, that was what slavery had taught her – take what you can, when you can; consequently, she felt an existential urge – with no disgrace attached – to grasp the one possibility which had presented itself.

She walked back to the house in high spirits… only to be met by Tobias as she entered the main hall.

*

Mrs. Burrows, too, had not emerged unscathed from her entanglement with Tobias. That she had compromised him was obvious, and she had done it purposefully, leaving the door unlocked in the hope he would eventually enter. In fact, she had stood in the bath waiting for his 'surprise' appearance for so long that the water had been in danger of becoming cold: another few minutes standing there and even their ardour would not have been enough to warm it. And now she felt guilty; not for what she had done but for the circumstances which had now unfolded: the unexpected arrival of Alice who had been nominally betrothed to Tobias but could not have entered the house at a worse moment. A week or two before and none of this would have happened. Still, she was glad it had for she had never felt so fulfilled – so much so that her numbskull husband had immediately become a distant memory. She was happy he had declined the position at Mulberry Hall and that Tobias had replaced him – in both her affections and her bed. Yet they had to be careful: Tobias' sexual prowess was magnificent, as was every sinew and muscle of his beautiful body. She was powerless to reject him any time he wanted her, which had been frequent and exhilarating. He had become slightly hesitant since the arrival of Alice and she knew why but it had not impacted his abilities; yet she was frightened at what would almost definitely ensue if this escapade persisted but was unable to defy it. And that was the truth. She had subsequently dreamed nightmares of being cast out as a fallen woman and Tobias, too, would be incriminated in her wake and probably sent back to Jamaica. And what would she do with any child? She knew a lady in the town who was proficient with knitting-needles but that was bloody and dangerous; perhaps she could pass it off as the child of Alice and Tobias as a lustful tryst of redemption – despite obviously mixed-race babies not being at all usual in the wilds of Derbyshire: that would kill off all speculation of any child's parentage – any baby she had by Tobias would be thus and not black, which would squash that lie. And that was also presuming she could somehow pass off any pregnancy without detection. She found herself almost cursing the arrival of Tobias who had engendered these feelings within her. Then, despite her despair at the circumstances she found herself in, realised she could never curse him because she was deeply, irrevocably, in love with him.

*

Tobias and Alice were in the library, whence he had guided her when she unexpectedly met him in the hall; his pretence for taking her there – if one were needed – was that he wanted to teach her how to read and was keen to give her the first lesson. Yet she had been guarded, curt and offhand with him, as if the huge disappointment of her rejection had deeply hurt her – as, indeed, it had. She had a growing sense that it was more than disappointment but betrayal - and this sentiment piqued her new-found resolution, tinted with a hint of revenge. What he did not know – nor she revealed – was her resolute plan to improve her wealth and standing in society with the one thing she could use: her youth and beauty.

She acceded to the short initial lesson but only because it was an excuse to be with him for a while, however uncomfortable. She also knew that any help was necessary in her quest to learn to read, this being her gateway to knowledge and success: she needed all the help she could get. She was alone and vulnerable, and knew it.

After about a half hour, Tobias shut the book and sighed. "I'm so sorry, dearest Alice," he said remorsefully, the weight of his situation and weakness by temptation from Mrs. Burrows a burden on his soul. "There was nothing I could do about it. If only you'd come even a few days earlier," he wept, "none of this would have happened." Alice stayed silent, enjoying the power she suddenly realised she had over him and men in general, letting him burble on without any comment. After a while, he looked at her and pathetically asked, "Will you ever forgive me, Alice?"

She looked down and then stated in a hard tone, "I don't know, Tobias. We'll have to wait and see. I think it's up to you." '*Actually*', she thought, '*it's not. It's up to me – and I'm going to succeed*'. Her ultimatum to Tobias needing no further embellishment, no other comment was made and eventually Tobias stood up and slunk away down the back stairs to the servants' hall.

She was glad, and about to make her way up to her palatial room when she heard Sir Walton's horse arriving: it was now or never. She left the library and made for the Great Parlour, where Sir Walton always repaired after a ride. It was essential to put her plan into action as soon as she could…

*

As Sir Walton returned, the same chill wind which had inspired Alice had induced much the same effect on him as he rode home, clearing his mind and ridding him of the effects of his alcoholic excesses.

He strode into the entrance hall and immediately saw the lovely Alice leaving the library. "Ah, me dear Alice," he boomed. "I want to talk to you." He waved and beckoned her into the Great Parlour. He was going to divulge his plan.

What he did not know was that she had one, too.

CHAPTER 8

The Plan & Its Consequences

Tobias returned to the servants' hall and found himself in the company of Miss Shaw, the cook, and a subdued Mrs. Burrows who was sewing but instantly concluded that he must have just been speaking to Alice, such was his sad demeanour. Miss Shaw was her usual chatty self, babbling away like a brook in full flood, contrasting with the quietness of the other two. Tobias raised his head and directed a request to Mrs. Burrows: "Mrs. Burrows, could I have a word with you in my pantry, please?"

"Of course, Mr. Tobias." (She called him this as Tobias had admitted to never having been given a surname other than Grimley, being his master's property, dropping the salutation only in intimate moments). He was waiting for her and closed his pantry door behind her, slumping onto his chair and inviting her to do the same on the one across his desk. A silence pervaded the room for a moment as neither knew what to say next. Eventually, he uncupped his hands covering his face and just said, "Dear Elspeth... I feel I have betrayed both of you."

Mrs. Burrows looked at him and felt sorry for the predicament she had forced upon Tobias but was adamant she would not change her resolve to have him for herself for as long as she could until scandal – a baby too, perhaps – forced them into a different situation, whatever that might be. Eventually, she stated solemnly, "Well, Tobias... I am not letting you go. We're slaves of circumstance, I'm afraid."

"As is Alice," he said quietly. "Literally."

"But you didn't know she was coming here, did you?" Hearing no reply, she asked more menacingly, "Or... *did* you?" He shook his head. "No, I did not – not at all. The master suggested her coming with us as we left Jamaica together all those months ago but I said 'No' as I thought she would be a distraction to my doing well here."

"She's certainly that now, though, isn't she?" Mrs. Burrows opined waspishly. Tobias noticed an unexpected bitterness in Elspeth's riposte; the situation was obviously affecting her as deeply as it was him. "Well, I have told her that I cannot change what's happened, and what is must continue to be," he said dejectedly. Mrs. Burrows' spirits lifted a little. Softening somewhat but trying to help the predicament for herself as well as for Alice, whom as a woman knew had been compromised in a ghastly situation, she suggested a solution. "Perhaps I can ask around and see if there's another house she can work in relatively close by – or even in Bakewell. She's a sweet, pretty thing," she added generously, "and it's not her fault."

"Or mine," Tobias corrected. It was Elspeth's turn to be chided.

*

Upstairs in the Great Parlour, Sir Walton and Alice were facing each other, perhaps rather closer than would have been expected in polite society. He had sat at the end of a large settee which faced an identical one opposite; there was a low gilded table between them and a luxurious armchair at the end, facing down between the two. Sir Walton had expected the shy girl to sit opposite him but she had instantly and purposefully availed herself of the armchair, right next to him. This had both surprised but pleased him, especially as her proximity allowed him to enjoy the faint whiff of scent which she had found provided in her room.

Awkwardly, he tried to begin his explanation of why he wished to see her. "Er, Miss Alice… as you know, I wanted Tobias to have someone whom he knew well to be his companion here. However, er, since we spent some time together on the voyage, I found, er…"

"I think I know what you're trying to say already, good Sir," she said ostentatiously, leavened with a wry smile and a cheeky expression, her perfect teeth displayed as an adjunct to fulfilling her plan and augmenting it at the other end of her body by exposing a pretty, stockinged ankle. (She knew she had perfect teeth – everyone told her that at some point or another). Sir Walton found himself slightly flustered by what he had hoped was a step in the right direction for his advance but quickly found she seemed to have arrived ahead of him. Yet Alice's apparent calm was a chimera: under her stiff dress and corset her young heart was beating frantically. Knowing that if she was too forward or grasping that she could wreck her plan and end up on the streets destitute, unwanted and avoided due to her colour, she mentally chided herself for perhaps being too open and going too far; even during the short time she had been at Mulberry Hall she had realised that propriety trumped all and any pretensions could be easily misinterpreted – or even interpreted absolutely correctly to her detriment, she cautioned herself.

Regaining his composure, Sir Walton started again. "As I say, my reasoning was for you to have a friend here, one of your own kind, so to speak…"

"Tobias and I were not married, Sir. We were close friends."

"Ah, yes… of course… close friends…" Then, after moment: "How close?"

"Sir! A young girl such as me in my humble position does not disclose intimacies of any kind to someone I only met so little time ago!"

He was suddenly impressed by the social norms she had so quickly picked up and realised once again that she was as intelligent as she was beautiful; accordingly, his respect for her deepened. As did his lust. "Quite so, my dear – how forward of me. I apologise."

She laughed – a skittish, young, naïve laugh full of gaiety and abandon. He realised he was becoming mesmerised by her. Not for the first time…

Feeling a little put in his place, he tried another tack: "Miss Alice, I am a wealthy man, thanks in great part to the toils of your people… and I would like to both help you and do something for them to repay some of that hard work." He knew that wasn't strictly true – he wanted to impress her and help himself. He did not think she would understand that subtle statement: but she did. So she answered, "Dear Sir, you are a good man and I would like to help you, too. You have been very kind to me and Tobias and we both appreciate it, so thank you." She did not mean this in its entirety either but was learning fast how to play the game of seduction. This was now all for her, not Tobias. So she asked, with an askance elfin look that promised everything

THE SLAVE-OWNER'S DILEMMA

but confirmed nothing: "Sir, what is it you wish me to do for you? For there is something you want, is there not?"

Sir Walton was flabbergasted. She was playing with him… and he was enjoying it! The wonderful girl – no, lady, with all this ability! How on earth did she acquire this wit, living on a slave estate in Jamaica? Was there more to her than met the eye? Did she have a secret? He decided he did not care; here she was in front of him, almost certainly understanding his guile but not admonishing him for it! How fortunate was that? And all her words caressed by her sweet soft Jamaican accent, which added mystique to every syllable!

He broke out of his reverie and smiled, saying, "Miss Alice, I think you understand me. And I you, methinks. So I shall be very open with you and stop beating about the bush."

"I am pleased, Sir; I dislike subterfuge so do, please, be open with me. Then we can continue this discussion without prevarication until its conclusion."

"Ah… well… er, well… Indeed." He blew out a sigh, composed himself, and then spoke. "I first saw you as Tobias and I left for England, when I perceived you as a little girl with no future - but knew Tobias would love you if he had the chance. So I suggested to him that you came with us, even if then I was unsure it was a good idea. He declined but I knew he was sad to leave you. I didn't think anything more of you until I saw you again, what, twelve or thirteen weeks ago? In that time, you had changed from a girl to a beautiful young woman. I had no designs on you then" - that word 'then' hung in the air for a moment, which Alice was astute enough to comprehend – "and so I thought you would be welcome here – a pretty face and a companion for Tobias, as I said. But over the course of the trip from the plantation to Kingston, the voyage to Liverpool and the coach journey here, I realised you had something exceptional – a wit, common sense and beauty which I began to find quite compelling -"

"Thank you for your compliments, Sir, but -"

He waved her interruption aside and continued: "That was why I bought you those two exquisite dresses in Liverpool, to see if your beauty would be as vibrantly and exquisitely suited to our class – *my* class - as I had wondered. I was almost hoping it would not, and I could let you have Tobias and that would be that." He was becoming redder and a sweat was forming both on his forehead and under his lip so Alice – who, it has to be said, was warming quickly to the man due to his flattery, honesty and bumbling bravado – was tiring of waiting and just wished him to say what she knew he wanted to. In that moment, she decided she was in such an advanced position of control that she would ask the question for him.

"Dear Sir Walton. Do you wish to have me as your wife?"

The question completely astounded him. Floundering, he started muttering inconsequentially: then there was a pause, where she just looked at him with a playful smile on her sweet lips as this elevated, educated knight blubbered like a child. Chaos had enveloped him, driven by desire, appreciation, surprise, reputation, class, race, what people would say and more. Then a calm descended upon him and he just said, breathlessly, "Oh, you sweet thing; no, not your wife but... well..."

"Your mistress? Lover?" she asked playfully. Before he could answer, she continued, "Well, if I cannot be your wife, Sir, then I must have certain assurances. After all, a poor young girl like me – utterly homeless without your goodwill - has need of some recompense or I will not fit into your high society and be nothing. And without that standing, then you would not like me anyway, would you, Sir?" By throwing the onus back onto him, she had hoped to goad him into a position where he would have to offer her something substantial or she could not accept.

Stunned, his thoughts were like a raging inferno. Yes, he wanted her – desperately – but whilst he did not wish the moment to disappear he had to think clearly, which this delightful girl was making impossible. As he tried to clear his head of his tortured emotions, Alice felt sorry for him; if her plan succeeded, he would be vilified by his peers, society and prejudice. He had told her on the voyage that he was, intrinsically, against slavery and there were people in Parliament whom he knew well whose instincts were – like his - to abolish it. Yet he had confided that this would take time… She had admired him for his stance and relative humanity – after all, it had been his father's estate which Sir Walton had inherited when he died, not his. He had lived almost permanently in Jamaica but had wanted to live in England and, when his father deceased he used the lush earnings to buy this land in Derbyshire. She watched as the machinations in his head replayed themselves on his turbulent face. A nice face, in fact, she thought. He was quite handsome, actually, and had a good head of curly, sandy hair; his nose was mildly bulbous but its unusual shape was rather attractive, like a mole on an otherwise beautiful woman – a deformity which emphasised all the other copious attractions. Indeed, she had seen many such by observing the pictures which hung about the Hall. Her eyes descended lower and she took in his slightly stocky but well-proportioned figure. The beginnings of a paunch were there but that was due to the good life she was now hoping she might share with him, however secretly. He had good legs, too, she could see. Not a bad catch, whatever the other problems that may arise…

All these thoughts, fears and summaries were only a few seconds long but seemed to both of them like an eternity. Then abruptly, Sir Walton stood up and exhaled a huge sigh; he looked at her in a slightly strange way then leaned over and took her tiny gloved hand; Alice was nervous – had her openness been too much, her guile too obvious?

"How about a thousand pounds a year, a small house where you can live nearby, a servant or two – although not Tobias, of course… a dress allowance, a carriage… but any philanderings will incur my gossiping to all and sundry to your great disgrace." His proposition both startled and surprised her. Was he really offering to be this open, this generous and – most importantly – this dismissive of what society expected? Did he realise the opprobrium he would encounter if – and, inevitably, when – the arrangement became known? She put this to him.

"Damn the lot of 'em!" he countered. "I will have to keep you 'aside', so to speak, for a while at least. But I am confident that your wit, beauty and… and… sparkle – yes, that's the word, sparkle - will soon make the ladies jealous and the men so envious they will all wish to know you."

"But wouldn't you wish to marry someone of your own class or race, Sir? Surely, despite your generous offer, I would still just be a trinket for you, your little dark secret?"

He laughed. "Dark secret – ha-ha, I like that! But no, I have no intention of keeping you secret. We will introduce you gradually and people will just have to get used to it. I don't care – I have found a woman I hope to grow to love even more than I think I do now!"

"But what would happen if you *did* want to marry someone more suitable, then, Sir?"

"We would have to come to an arrangement. But if I have you now, Alice, that will be like signing the agreement."

"We will have to keep it completely secret," she noted, precipitously becoming aware of what her machinations had wrought.

"Of course – at first," he replied. "Then, we shall see."

The unexpected enormity of the offer crowded over her: she had not expected such largesse, both financially and emotionally, and felt compelled to make sure he understood what he had done. "But, Sir, I understand that you cannot be seen by your peers as I am of lowly birth and, of course, the other thing." He nodded, speechless; this illiterate girl had read him like a book and although he was completely willing to accede to her terms, he foresaw many problems. But he did not care. How could he let her go? She was astonishing.

"All I want at this moment, dear Alice, is you."

'At this moment', momentarily caused doubts but she was aware he seemed earnest so, with a rush of blood to the head, she responded, "I want a signed contract, though, Sir, before anything happens. You can do that now, if you wish…" this last being said in hope rather than expectation.

Yet he took her point and went straight to his writing desk. Taking out a piece of headed notepaper, he wrote an agreement detailing his proposal and signed it. Then he read it to her and asked, if she agreed to the terms laid down, and to make her mark on the document, which she swiftly did by actually signing her name.

"Who taught you to do that?" he enquired. "I thought you couldn't read."

"I am learning, Sir, and writing my name was my first ability."

"Tobias?" She nodded, slightly concerned this might wreck her plan.

Yet Sir Walton was not now going to be put off and said breezily, "Well... well done, Tobias!" and, brushing the hint of association aside, he embraced her and gave her a kiss on the lips; she was pleasantly surprised by their sweetness, although no such surprise troubled him – hers were as sweet as ripe cherries, as he had expected. Then he opened the door slightly to ensure that no servants were present and told her to go to her room and prepare herself for him.

She did so but on the way up the stairs she felt the presence of Tobias and wondered whether she should make sure the contract was what she had agreed to; not being able to read very well yet, this was the most dangerous part of her escapade – at least for now. But she could not ask Tobias – it was too cruel: this was not a situation created by him but unwittingly by the man who had a kind heart and had wanted to help them both... so she rushed to her room and hid the paper in the lining of her dress – the latter which she then removed for her master's imminent pleasure.

The contract was duly 'signed' carnally not long after...

CHAPTER 9

Complications Arise

It was now early summer and Lucinda Noncey had just turned eighteen. Her father, Lancelot, was keen to marry off his pretty daughter, his income having been savaged by an investment in canals which was taking far too long to apprise him of any financial returns. Thus, the arrival of his only child at the age where she could be 'put about', as he termed it, had come in the nick of time. He needed a dowry and, although he was not aristocracy but a member of the supposedly inferior 'mercantile class', he had made his money in iron implements and building materials for commerce and trade during Britain's burgeoning industrial revolution; in short, he had done well, despite the current trough in remuneration, and aspired to be of the same class as his aristocratic betters. Indeed, the snobbish upper-class slur of being 'middle class traders' was now wearing thin as it was this emerging strata of society who now had the money. Except Lancelot. Not yet, anyway, and he was hoping he could elevate his social standing – and bank balance – by marrying Lucinda off to a wealthy baron or knight of the realm. The trouble was that his social circle included few such people… yet one of them was Sir Walton Grimley. He had never met the man but had already sold some building materials and many implements to his master builder, Josiah Prentice, for the construction and maintenance of the former's new mansion, Mulberry Hall.

Although the land nearest the front of Sir Walton's house had been laid out, the parklands beyond – especially the excavation of a large lake – were still a work in progress and, hearing about this, Lancelot had contacted Sir Walton in the hope of supplying further goods and implements to help him construct it. He had subsequently succeeded in being invited to the house for the possible provision of further supplies of shovels, forks, picks, hoes, saws, pipes, diverters and other newly-designed and more pertinent accoutrements for the wealthy man's continuing project. Including, perhaps, his delightful daughter…

Sir Walton had written back to agree to a meeting and called in Josiah Prentice, who, by now having totally completed the main house, was now fully responsible for the practical part of the parklands' construction under the authority of the landscape designer, Samuel Hedges.

The day duly arrived and Lancelot was travelling on his cart, which contained a number of new product examples, sketches - and his sweetly-smiling daughter. They had taken two leisurely days to get from Wirksworth, staying at an inn in Bakewell. Whilst this meant passing Sir Walton's estate and then going back, Lancelot had done so for two reasons: first, it gave him a chance to meet people in the town who would be likely to know Sir Walton Grimley, so giving himself some foreknowledge of whom he would be dealing with and, second, he had wished to eschew the uncomfortable, flimsy and open cart which had transported them thus far and – at great extra cost – had hired a covered, more robust and expensive-looking one for the final stage of the journey: this self-made man knew that a good initial impression was everything.

As they arrived, they noticed a small but extravagantly-modelled house off the main drive being constructed and wondered why it was necessary when such a vast mansion was only two hundred yards away. He also wondered why he had not been engaged to supply the materials, which annoyed him.

When the coach was spied, a footman was despatched to the lake excavation area to bring Prentice and Hedges up to the house for the meeting. On descending from the carriage, Lancelot and Lucinda were both surprised to be greeted by Tobias, never having set eyes on a person of colour before; as for Sir Walton, he was just as surprised to find himself in the unexpected presence of an attractive young lady.

Sir Walton was pleased with the discovery of the new and improved implements available which would help his estate's beautification further, and also of young Lucinda, whose bright eyes and chirrupping personality helped the sale along immensely. Lancelot's spirits duly rose – not just for the magnitude of the ensuing order but by Sir Walton's apparent attraction to Lucinda. Yet while this was true – Sir Walton was always partial to a pretty young face – his clandestine love for Alice was still firm and developing well; he had even hired a governess to teach her how to read better – and to keep her away from Tobias. Her ability to learn had astonished him: soon, he suspected, the governess would be unnecessary, much to the woman's probable discomfiture.

As for Tobias, he was racked with despair. The iron grip Mrs. Burrows had on him was intense and she had made it quite clear that if he left her she would accuse him of rape and assault; it would be her word against his and who would a judge and court side with if that came to pass? He would be imprisoned or sent back to Jamaica – perhaps both – and even if Sir Walton believed him, the difficulty he would have defending him would be detrimental to his societal standing. Not that he didn't like Mrs. Burrows – he deeply did, and their lovemaking was fulfilling and exciting. Yet being under her thumb made his feeling at being freed from slavery returned to much the same state as before.

Alice, however, was very happy; every day, she would leave or return to her room – or Sir Walton's bed - via a specially-constructed secret corridor that linked their rooms; during the day, she would spend time observing the construction of the house he was building for her. Once completed, this would lower tensions in the main hall and she would be able to live a freer life; it would not be long before Sir Walton would start introducing her to his acquaintances and then she would be able to do the social rounds just like any aristocratic lady. Such was her influence on Sir Walton that she knew he would fight her corner whatever prejudices were thrown at him – or her. But for now, she just had to lie relatively low while all the pieces fell into place...

Lancelot and Lucinda left a few hours later, with a hefty deposit for many new tools and materials having been agreed – much influenced by the man's vivacious and fun daughter. Sir Walton watched her climb into the carriage from the Great Parlour window and noted that, as she did so, she looked appreciatively back at his new monument to wealth and plenty, as if sizing it up in her mind with an eye to becoming its lady. He enjoyed her prettiness, wit and vivacity and thought back to Alice's observation about what would happen if he suddenly did wish to marry an Englishwoman and his answer, "We would have to come to an arrangement." Yet he still adored Alice – more so every day, in fact; but it might make things easier if he had a wife like Lucinda… but he would never give up Alice, whatever happened. She had stolen his heart and he knew it. Yet he knew also that Lucinda's sudden appearance could cause some disruption.

CHAPTER 10

Further Complications Arise

Lucinda left Mulberry Hall with some regret at not having impressed herself upon Sir Walton as much as she had hoped regarding her father's other business plan – her marriage to him. He, whilst ecstatic with glee at the huge order for implements that the man had bestowed with the help of Lucinda's charm and beauty, wondered, like Lucinda, whether that supplementary adjunct to his scheme had landed firmly enough for Sir Walton to ask for Lucinda's hand. She confessed to herself that she quite enjoyed helping her father with the sales of his wares and had met some very pleasant young traders as a result; yet none were as aristocratic or influential as Sir Walton. Or as rich.

"He's a good catch," Lancelot murmured as they passed out through the tall, iconic gates; "You did yer best, me gal, ye did yer best. At least we have a healthy order book now – so it's a nice new pair of shoes for you as a thank you..."

Lucinda tore her eyes away from the receding mansion. She loved her father – Papa, she called him - and wanted to help all she could: since dear Mama had died three years previously – whom they had both adored deeply – her affection and respect for him were magnified as he strove, in his grief, to keep going with the business in the face of severe financial difficulties and depression. The thought of a life at Mulberry Hall with Sir Walton had immediately struck her as a good outcome for her father and not such a bad one for her, either: Sir Walton was quite good-looking, not too fat yet, very rich and had a wittily sarcastic sense of humour; what with the other hardships bearing down on her father, Sir Walton's rumbustious behaviour and almost certain irrepressible wenching – she'd noticed the glint in his eye as he looked at her - were insignificant bumps in the road by comparison with his benefits.

"Papa?" she said.

"Yes, my dear?"

"I have a plan." The coach hit a large stone, causing them to lurch forward a moment.

"A plan, my dear?" he asked as composure was restored. "What sort of plan?"

"When it's the next time to return here – with the new implements – you're going to be ill."

He looked concerned. "Ill? I feel as fit as a fiddle – I'm not going to be ill."

"Yes, you are. It'll add pathos."

"Pathos?"

"Yes. If I return alone with the new tools he'll be sad for me that you're ill and I will have to address him directly. And that might be useful. To both of us."

A flicker of comprehension crossed his face. "Ah… So you liked him, then…"

"Well… certainly 'enough'," she stated resolutely.

*

"Are you all right, Mrs. Burrows?" asked Tobias as he entered. She was sitting at the servants' table, her shoulders half across it with her drooped head in her hands, almost sighing rather than breathing.

She sat up as robustly as she could and looked at him as the parlour-maids busied themselves around the kitchen and said quietly, "Ah, Mr. Tobias. May I have a word with you, please?"

"What's the matter, Elspeth?" he enquired as the door to his pantry closed behind them. She sat heavily in an armchair and started crying quietly.

"Elspeth, my dear... tell me... what is it?" he said as he knelt down to be closer to her tearful face.

"'It'", she answered bitterly, "is a baby."

There was a moment's pause: they had both dreaded this possibility. Eventually, he ventured warily with, "You're pregnant?"

She nodded. "Now we're finished," she said. "If I can't get rid of it then I'll have to leave. The master won't have it and I'll have to either go back to my husband – heaven forbid – or leave the area and bring it up on my own somewhere. And if anyone sees the baby, they'll know it's yours, too," she added with a slight vindictiveness, "and then you'll have to leave, too. It's all your fault, Tobias."

"My fault?" he riposted, both surprised and not a little hurt: "I think it was you who chased me, Elspeth. I admit I was agreeable to the situation but... well, you can hardly blame me."

"She threw her arms around his neck and gave him a wet kiss, the tears cascading down her cheeks onto her dress and Tobias' starched collar. "Forgive me," she said. "It's just I couldn't resist you... you were the most beautiful thing I had ever seen in my life. But now I've ruined yours. You should be with Alice – why didn't you agree for her to come with you when you had the chance and then this would never have happened?"

"It still might have done," he responded softly. "I found you attractive, too, you know. And you've taught me so many things…"

"Probably all the wrong ones," she said with a forced smile.

They laughed together – laughs of despair when there is nothing else left to do.

"Thanks to my skirts I can hide it for a few more weeks but… Oh, I'm finished." And she cried again.

After a minute or two, she stopped, sighed deeply, and stood up. "I'll go into Bakewell on my day off and find the lady with the knitting-needles. She might sort me out."

"It's my child, too," he responded softly. "I don't want you to risk that. I'll have a talk with Sir W - "

"No, you won't!" she almost shouted. "He'd fire us both on the spot! Oh, you lovely, innocent person… this… us… it's not 'done' here. And my husband will kill me anyway if he finds out. Much as I try to forget the fact, I am still married to that nulling cove!" Tobias felt helpless. She was right, though; and Alice could not now resolve the situation – especially seeming to have come out of it well as they both knew, Sir Walton having taken a rather expensive shine to her: she could do no wrong. And they both had their suspicions as to why he was building a small house so near to the main one …

"I have things to do," she said, suddenly standing up purposefully, the movement causing her to clutch her stomach as a pang of pain assailed it. Then, pathetically, she added, "It'll all work out somehow." But they both knew she didn't mean it.

Tobias stood up too and said, "I'll come up with a plan."

She gave him a quick kiss on the lips, wiped away the tears on her apron and swept out.

*

Alice was learning to ride with the young groom, Archibald. Like almost everything she did, she had taken to it with alacrity and had 'a good seat'. Yet she wished she could ride in a proper saddle, not this silly side one, which prohibited her from going faster; it was all so safe, so *sedentary*...

Yet she conceded that the position was just as well, as she had noticed that some strange, unusual feelings in her womb area were becoming more pronounced; she was also sure her stomach was larger than before, and a strange sickness had affected her recently, usually around daybreak. Whilst she was competent at anything she tried, though, her youthful innocence and joy at the unexpected state of luxury and privilege she found herself in somehow occluded her realising that she was with child.

To any other observer, this would have been obvious: her sexual relations with Sir Walton had been ecstatic, liberating and frequent; indeed, there was already a furrow running down the new carpet in the secret corridor between her room and his. However, her youthful fecundity and relative innocence in these matters must have been apparent to him in that she would at some time be in the condition she unknowingly now found herself: but such was his desire for this beautiful young girl that her fruitful condition was ignored, obscured by a miasma of lust; after all, he was rich and could pay for any eventuality. The remoteness of Mulberry Hall ensured a high degree of privacy, too, so any resulting effects of his libido could easily be hidden from the surrounding population and his servants; and if they were indiscreet enough to leak the results of any supposedly inappropriate behaviour, then he could pay them enough to keep quiet or even dismiss them without payment or references.

For him, life was good. For Alice, she had at first unwittingly, then innocently, but finally calculatingly, ensnared him; so at this moment, life, she believed, was good for her, too.

CHAPTER 11

Pride and Prejudice

Elspeth Burrows had taken advantage of one of her monthly days off to visit the lady with the knitting-needles – another month's delay would certainly make her predicament even more dangerous: the horse and cart she had travelled on amplified every tilt, hole and stone it passed over and the movement had considerably worsened her constant discomfort. She left the horse at a livery stable at the far end of the town and walked the remaining quarter mile, quickly passing the end of the street where her own house with Giles lay and pulled a shawl over her head lest her ghastly, oafish husband might see her.

The Bakewell back street she eventually arrived at was dirty, ramshackle and reeked of desperation; she wondered again whether she should proceed down it. Ragged, barefoot children were everywhere, as were a few of their destitute parents who had somehow avoided the workhouse. The leaden skies and wet ground from a torrent of earlier rain completed the picture of desuetude, a compilation of poverty, despair and helplessness. She stepped a few yards into the street when suddenly the enormity of what she was doing made her stop, as if an invisible, ghostly hand had arrested her. But if she had the child, she thought, it would be a half-caste and probably tormented for the rest of his or her life; on the other hand, the procedure was dangerous, painful, tricky and not certain to remove the foetus she had inside her. She had not told Tobias of her plan but realised she was risking her life now for both of them; yet with this child growing inside her she would soon be on the streets with no work or money and Tobias – for whom she had so completely fallen – would be cast out too. Yet she did not blame him: it was she who had fallen for this beautiful, intelligent and compassionate man and had compromised him, for which she felt guilt but no regret. He was everything she had ever dreamed of, despite never having known this until she had first set her eyes upon him. And it was his child, too; would he be angry if she went ahead with her plan? Probably, but she was hopeful he would understand…

A little unwashed boy, an urchin with ripped clothes and lice visibly crawling in his hair, approached her and, having observed Elspeth's clean, respectable attire, held out his hand for a farthing or two. Her child would end up the same as this, she shuddered, as would she if she did not go ahead. She discreetly put a finger to her lips to denote secrecy – she could not afford to give them all a farthing – and slipped him a coin. The boy said nothing but ran off around the corner where there was a bakery; at least one poor mite would eat today, she thought benignly…. Then she turned purposefully back to face the wretched street and decided to proceed.

*

Alice was being very sick. She had, by now, realised her condition and was terrified; would Sir Walton throw her out now, his lust satisfied and her situation untenable for the social mores that would engulf him? Would she never live in the house he was constructing for her and withdraw the annual stipend he had promised? There had been a written, signed agreement, of course, and now that she could read this seemed to be watertight. Yet she had heard some of the prattling parlour-maids talking about 'having one in the basket' and had soon realised its meaning; perhaps she could confide in one of them what to do? Yet that was risky; they were all jealous of her and did not like the fact she could order them around – which she never did: but that was not the point. She could confide in Mrs. Burrows, she thought, but there was a frost between them and she was fairly sure that this was due to something going on between her and Tobias: perhaps that was what his words, "There was nothing I could do about it. If only you'd come a few days earlier," was all about... Sir Walton would be back from one of his London jaunts in a few days, would find her with child and callously send her away. She burst into tears.

*

Lucinda had made a visit to the Hall with some new plans and an implement her father had designed which could easily bore a round hole through soil, into which piping of the same circumference could be inserted; this, she was going to tell Sir Walton, could more conveniently cut a swathe through roots and stones, so reducing digging and covering time and helping water drainage into the lake where it needed to be. Yet she had been thwarted by the fact that Sir Walton was away and angrily realised she would have to plan her visits more carefully for when she knew he would definitely be there. More annoyingly, she had used up their best implement, which had been much liked – and kept - by Josiah Prentice, so now her father would have to invent some other device to justify her next solitary visit to Mulberry Hall!

On her way back down the drive in her covered cart which had hidden the new implement from view, she had noticed that the smaller house near the Hall had advanced by quite some degree since she was last there and, seeing nobody about, her curiosity was pricked and she turned towards it up the track which would, one day, be conveniently metalled.

The sun was setting – hence no builders – and so she entered. The house was dark inside as the roof had been completed and the gloom was difficult to get used to; but she could just make out the main shape and size of the rooms, and gingerly went up the majestic but rubble-strewn stairs to a room above, where the last slivers of sunlight illuminated the darkness better. It was then that she heard shuffling noises and a young girl crying from the floor above.

She suddenly felt she should leave and began quietly retracing her steps downstairs, inadvertently kicking a lump of brick - which fell over the edge of the unbalustraded staircase and crashed into the entrance hall below. The crying upstairs stopped and then a voice came out from the darkness above her: it was not hostile but restrained, with a slight accent she could not instantly place: "Who's there?"

Lucinda had to reply, and responded into the gloom, "Sorry... I'm Lucinda Noncey, daughter of Lancelot Noncey who's supplying implements for the building of this house and the lake. I was curious about this building, being so close to the main hall and why it's needed. The other looks big enough to me." This last was said with a slight laugh to offset any hostility from the unseen being. There was a pause. Then the voice replied, "Sir Walton is building it for me." Again, the accent confused Lucinda: where was this person from?

Then she heard a tinderbox open and after a few moments a candle stutteringly gave birth to a modicum of light; within its halo of brightness stood one of the most unusually beautiful young girls she had ever encountered – augmented by her not being of the colour she had expected. Not knowing what to do, she curtseyed and apologised for being in her house and said she would leave immediately. However, the young girl carefully descended the stairs, peering at her. Lucinda could see the tears on her cheeks and noticed she was wearing mostly a bedcover – presumably so her clothes would not get soiled – and was barefoot. "How did you get here?" Lucinda asked clumsily, not really sure how to address this young girl whom she supposed was a secret; for if Sir Walton was building it for her, then he must know this beautiful young girl well.

"I came from Jamaica," the girl answered. "I was a slave… but now… well, in some ways, I still am."

Lucinda felt some compassion for the girl but suddenly the whole situation fell into place. She knew Sir Walton was a slave owner and was unmarried; so he must have brought this girl over as a concubine and was building this house to hide her away in secret. Well, that was certainly not 'done' around these parts and instantly she saw a way of ingratiating herself into Sir Walton's company - and this pleasant little house. Or even the whole estate. She summarily felt she had more to offer than this girl and her flirtatious rapport with Sir Walton had been apparent: so yes, she could entrap him and become the lady of the estate. And if Sir Walton wanted to keep his little secret, that would be fine by her as long as she had everything else. But she would ensure everyone would know about it if he did not comply.

She smiled sweetly, triumphantly, and made her apologies and excuses as quickly as politeness would allow as she left. Alice watched her go and started crying again. She had instinctively liked Lucinda and wanted a friend. Once again, she felt alone and frightened…

CHAPTER 12

A Fear Is Endured &

Another Is Resolved

Elspeth started to bleed profusely as the needles were inserted into her womb - the pain was insufferable; she had a wedge of wood between her teeth and the large tot of rough rum she had consumed was of little help to soften it. She tried to cry out but the haggard and filthy woman instantly covered her mouth with some foul-smelling cloths – if she was caught she would either be in prison or the work-house, or branded as a witch. Suddenly, Elspeth could bear it no more and threw up her hands: even a lifetime of poverty was not worth this and she suddenly felt very afraid. Yet in her mind she knew this clumsy old woman might already have caused the foetus to abort; and if she was even luckier, the harridan might have already rendered her barren and she could then continue being pleasured by Tobias with no consequences – what bliss that would be!

The woman stopped: "But I think I've got the little bleeder," she said contemptuously, "So no point in stopping now."

'Little bleeder'? That was her child! How dare this hell-hag talk like that about this tiny person the love of her life had created in her! Common sense must prevail: Elspeth shook her head violently: "No, stop!" she said as much as she could with the wood between her teeth: "I can't bear it any more."

The woman looked at her: "You'll not get yer money back, me dear," she said threateningly through the only two blackened and rotting fangs she retained. Elspeth nodded vigorously. She had to hope that her plan would come true: the pain was throbbing, inexorable and intense, as if her whole abdomen was in a fiery ferment. Anything would be better than this, anything…

The woman withdrew the bloodied needles and wiped them on an already blood-stained cloth – much of which was not hers, Elspeth surmised. Oh, what had she done? Soon she would be thrown out of Mulberry Hall, Tobias would be no more and she would probably contract some terrible disease which would kill her. Well, perhaps that would be a better solution… and retribution, too.

The woman gave Elspeth another tot of rum and helped her off the table which was just large enough to also contain a few eating implements, she now noticed; it was about the only piece of furniture in the room and was obviously the scene of multiple uses. She was feeling dizzy and nauseous now and the room spun about her, although whether she was at the centre or the edge of the vortex was unclear. She had taken the precaution of bringing some clean cloths with her from the Hall and stumbled towards her bag to achieve them… but her legs gave way and she fainted, banging her head on the wall as she fell.

*

Sir Walton had just arrived home from London and was keen for some relations with his little heart-throb. He ordered Tobias to give him a flagon of burgundy and a hearty snack to be presented: after such gut-foundering exertions as the four-day ride on his horse, he needed sustenance to see him through his intended more joyous ridings on Alice. He then told Tobias to call the girl to him as soon as he could find her.

Ten minutes later, a light knock on the Great Parlour door was followed by Tobias announcing the presence of Alice and he then discreetly left.

As the door closed, she curtseyed to Sir Walton and then they both ran across the room towards each other and embraced. Instantly, however, he had noticed she had been crying and also looked a little plumper than he remembered from before his three weeks away.

"You look sad, my little poppet," he said after they had kissed passionately on the lips. "Is something wrong?"

There was a pause as Alice receded a pace or two then looked at him with an almost frightened expression. Then, she said unsurely, "You do love me as much as you say you do, don't you, Walton...?"

He peered at her. "Well, of course I do," he said, feeling slightly deflated as if there was some doubt in her mind.

"It's just that... oh, I hope you won't find me unattractive now..."

"No!" he exclaimed. "Whatever it is, I will love you forever."

"Ah... I hope you will mean that still when I tell you..."

"Tell me what? You haven't fallen for someone else have you? Tobias, for example?"

"No, Sir – he's -" No she mustn't say anything about her suspicions regarding Tobias and Mrs. Burrows. That would be unseemly.

"Well?" he enquired, with an edge of annoyance in his voice.

She had to tell him and, taking a deep breath, blurted out quietly, "Sir, I am with child – *your* child."

There was a moment which lasted a second but seemed like an hour as she contemplated his reaction. What would he think? Had she been sloppy with the cap he had often asked her to wear, which wrecked their lust but gave some protection against… well, this? Then his face was wreathed in smiles and he advanced towards her, throwing his arms around her, kissing her cheek as tears of joy cascaded down his cheeks. "Capital! Wonderful! I'm so pleased!" Then his expression changed a little and he became more subdued. "We'll have to keep it a secret, though, my dear little Alice – at least for now. But to be honest, I'm delighted: in fact, I was beginning to wonder *when* you might fall pregnant and, now it's happened, I'm the happiest man in the world! My seed works!" He hopped and danced about the room with pleasure, which surprised Alice, finding his reaction slightly childish as well as unexpected. "So you won't throw me out, then, Sir?"

"Throw you out? Never!" Then his face darkened slightly as he added, "Of course, all the things we mentioned before will have to be observed… But I'll get more builders into the place so I can hide you away in comfort in your new house sooner."

The words 'hide you away' caused some concern in Alice's young breast but soon his obviously truthful exuberance swamped her and she, too, was dancing around the room with him. Suddenly, though, he stopped and said, "Dear Alice, you have made me feel happier than ever before and I am so happy to be the father of your child – whatever the colour or sex! But no more dancing now – we must think of the child – *our* child!"

Then they embraced again and he finished off the flagon of burgundy. Alice was so relieved that she flopped into the chair on which she had first planned her entrapment of him and wept with pleasure, too.

*

Mrs. Burrows stayed the night in Bakewell, away from her husband's home, in a cheap inn, trying to get over her faintness and loss of blood. The weather was bad, a dull mist and specks of drizzle blowing in the chilly air; this, at least, had given her the excuse to keep the shawl over her head as she had made the slow, painful walk from the abortionist. The shawl was also of use in that she spied her husband with a pretty young barmaid not so discreetly paraded on his arm as they left an inn; he was drunk. 'He'll soon be in trouble,' she had thought as she pulled the garment further across her face, hiding down an alleyway until they had passed. As she watched him disappear, she contemplated how her savings – achieved through years of frugality - had come in useful and, although the risk of being recognised in any lodging was a danger, she was glad to find that the inn she had chosen to stay at was fortunately being run by a new couple from York who did not know her. She had told Tobias, too, that she would not be back for a night – possibly two – as she had things to talk to her husband about. A lie, of course… despite the dangerous position it put them in. Tobias would have been fundamentally against her getting rid of the baby as it was against his Christian principles - drummed into him by a missionary on the plantation - and he had given her a wry look as she departed the Hall; well, at least he would be pleased about that, she thought. As long as it survived, which she doubted, as the pain was still intense. That would absolve her guilt as well as all their problems for now, she hoped: she could tell Tobias that miscarriage was a natural happening and quite normal.

Whether he would believe her or not was another matter. And sex with him – that beautiful, uplifting, life-defining act which made all other worries disappear – would have to go on hold until she was better.

That was the worst prospect of all.

CHAPTER 13

A Tricky Situation Develops

As Lucinda Noncey made her return to the burgeoning mill town of Wirksworth, she reflected on how lucky she and her father were to be resident there; its growing prominence as a town of cotton-mills had occasioned the creation of many new machines, tools and implements which her poor hard-working father had slowly managed to capitalise on. He had started on farm implements but as the Industrial Revolution had arrived – and by working all hours - he had mastered and then created many of the new industry's needs; consequently, many newly-thriving industrialists had started patronising him and his livelihood had increased immeasurably in quality. Yet he was in poor health and his ingenuity was now in such demand that she was worried he might suddenly be overcome with promises of new innovations and expire. Her mother had died of poverty, perhaps her father now would do so due to his success; it was only in the last three or four years that his fortunes had changed – but more to her own benefit than his. It was this that had given seed to her plot of finding a wealthy man to marry so she could use his money, not only to help her father's business expand but also relieve him of his crippling workload: she was not by nature a grasping child but loved her father so much that she wanted to do anything to save him. Thus her plan had developed over the long journey back to her home. The chance meeting with this unexpected black girl had given her plans a fillip: the girl might be beautiful – she could not deny that – but she was fairly sure that if Sir Walton's obvious dalliance with her was discovered, then society would disdain him; she could help with that – do him a favour, in fact! So if she, Lucinda, could ingratiate herself with Sir Walton – she knew he liked her as there had been a spark in his eye when they met – and then marry him, she would keep him on the right side of acceptability! Whilst angered that he had not been there so she could impress herself upon him more earnestly, the chance meeting with the girl had given her a motivational boost. Her kind thoughts for her father sat in direct contrast to the fate of the poor girl but she brushed those thoughts aside and awkwardly made herself believe, therefore, that she would do this more for altruism than avarice.

It would have extensive consequences.

*

Mrs. Burrows stayed in the inn for three days, sending a message to Tobias that she had been unavoidably caught up with 'business' in Bakewell and could he please inform the master, if he had returned? He could say that she had caught a bad cold and did not want to pass it on to the household; any shortcomings would be rectified by extra hours to catch up. Having paid a young lad to deliver the message, however – and the extra night at the inn with its attendant livery charges – her savings were now much reduced so she declined to eat that day to save money...

much to the disbenefit of her strength and recovery.

The next day was brighter, however, and she decided she felt well enough to make the ride back to Mulberry Hall. Her womb was marginally less painful than the day before but the movement of the horse and cart jarred with every bump and hole as before: she was certain she was bleeding again and by the time she arrived she was in such pain - and so weak - that she felt as if she would fall off the cart rather than descend from it gracefully. So she was glad to see the stable lad running to get Tobias as her horse and vehicle were heard from a hundred yards away.

Tobias ran down the passageway from the servants' hall to the back door and rushed out into the yard, just in time to discreetly catch Elspeth as she slid to the ground. One of the scullery-maids had come out with him and, together, they half escorted, half-carried her to her room at the top of the house - on the way being observed by a surprised Alice who had just bathed after an excessive bout of licentiousness with Sir Walton.

*

A few minutes before, Sir Walton, on hearing the sound of the horse and cart and subsequent commotion, had gone from his bedroom into the dressing-room at the side of the house which overlooked the yard and witnessed Mrs. Burrows collapsing and being carried into the servants' hall. He had not seen Mrs. Burrows for a few days but that was nothing unusual; wondering where she had been and why she was in such a state, he rang for a footman but was more pleased to see Tobias.

"Ah, Tobias," he said as his butler entered. "What's wrong with Mrs. Burrows?"

The question took Tobias by surprise: he had not

realised they had been observed. "Well, Sir," he began, but having only just realised himself why she was indeed in that forlorn state, was stuck for an answer. Sir Walton looked at him.

"Well, Tobias?"

"I think she may be with child, Sir," he said, suspecting the truth was a better response than a lie.

"Hmm. Strange. I didn't think she'd seen her husband for months. How on Earth could she…?"

"I don't know, Sir. That's none of my business."

"I should hope not, Tobias." Then there was a pause and he smiled a little: "Mind you, a damned good-looking woman. Perhaps she's got some secret lover, eh? Couldn't blame her… Never liked her husband much, I have to say. She'd be much happier with someone like you, Tobias," he said innocently. Then, with a gleam in his eye, he added, "And I daresay you wouldn't mind either, eh, Tobias?" He laughed: Tobias had never seen him like this before. Alice must be doing him a lot of good, he thought. But then panic struck him: was Sir Walton implying that he knew about him and Mrs. Burrows? Had one of the jealous parlour-maids said something?

"Thank you, Sir," was all he could think of saying.

"Right. Well… tell Mrs. Burrows to take it easy for a few days while she wonders what to do about it. Don't want any more screaming babies around the place, do we?"

"Any *more*, Sir?"

"Ah… well… they make a lot of noise, don't they? I like peace… Anyway, thanks for the explanation, Tobias. Give Mrs. Burrows some chicken broth – laced with a lot of gin – and a couple of eggs; that'll get her on her feet again in no time. That's all, Tobias…"

"Yes, Sir." Tobias left and closed the door. His heart was pounding. Why had he told him of her pregnancy? How stupid! Now they'd both be thrown out; Elspeth's condition should have been hidden, never discussed or admitted. But what did he mean by not wanting any *more* babies?

Then the penny dropped and he felt as sick as his dear Elspeth did.

CHAPTER 14

Lucinda Concocts A Proposal

A few days later, Lucinda, alongside burnishing her plan to ambush Sir Walton into marrying her, found herself helping her father design an implement she had thought of; any new tool or device seemed to be eagerly accepted by Sir Walton and she had desperately wanted to invent a new one in order to justify another journey to Mulberry Hall. Since her return home, she had found the anticipated goal of a sweet-smelling blackmail of Sir Walton too much for her to control and could not keep herself from thinking about it. Such was her creativity, however, she had designed a prototype device for her father – which was simple enough but would complement his earth-boring device; an iron T-shaped junction-pipe which would not only fit with the ones he had designed before but, its corresponding pipes being of a slightly different, larger and mildly egg-shaped dimension to others on the market, the flow would not only scour the bottom to allow a stronger torrent but also ensure that the buyer – in this case, Sir Walton – would have to stick with these products above anyone else's. It could be promoted as a vast improvement to the previous pipes they had sold him and would also fit snugly into the hole made by their previously-introduced boring-machine.

In their small foundry, they designed and cast the samples in three days; they were happy with the result and soon Lucinda found herself in her father's cart – again alone, as planned - with the new products, heading for Mulberry Hall.

Tobias had told Mrs. Burrows of Sir Walton's reaction to his blundering betrayal of her condition and their first argument ensued; in fact, it became so heated at one point that she thought she might abort the child there and then. Consequently – and with the first bad blood between them - they both resigned themselves to being eventually dismissed.

*

Alice's house was not far from completion and the same would eventually be true of her pregnancy; yet it had not been easy for her, especially as she was alone for long periods when she was not 'required' by Sir Walton, so as the weather improved and spring approached, she spent more time walking around the estate. She had made such rapid progress in learning how to read that the governess had been dispensed with far earlier than expected and now that the mulberry tree was again coming into full foliage she enjoyed taking a book or two from the library and reading them under it. The only problem was that despite being supplied with ever more voluminous dresses to cover up her condition, even this artifice was beginning to look awkward.

As for Mrs. Burrows, the same problem, the worry of her situation and subsequent employment was such that it caused her to ask Tobias to request of Sir Walton some time off under the precept of seeing her father, who was now poorly. Her hope that the baby had been destroyed and would have miscarried had not happened and – whilst she now worried that it would be deformed by the intrusion of the knitting-needles - had eventually been forced to ask Tobias to put the question to Sir Walton, rather than risk asking him herself.

Sir Walton was in his dressing-room when Tobias found him and, having posited the question, to Tobias' relief readily agreed; but as Tobias parted with the permission, Sir Walton enquired, "So if she wasn't pregnant, then, what was the matter with her?"

For a moment, Tobias was stumped, then stutteringly came up with, "No, Sir – I believe she was not. Obviously, Sir, we do not discuss such personal things but I think it was food-poisoning, Sir – not from here, of course, but when she went to see her husband last."

"He probably tried to poison her himself," was the gruff response. "Doesn't know when he's well off, the silly scroof. Saw him in the town the other day with some little floozy… must be mad," and went off muttering. Tobias quickly withdrew. As he descended the back stairs, he heard the hooves and clattering of a horse and cart arriving in the yard and immediately followed a footman out to meet this unexpected arrival. Sir Walton, too, heard the noise and went to his dressing-room window to observe what he instantly realised was a new cart, emblazoned with Lancelot Noncey's name and profession; it was obviously his own extensive patronage of the man that had allowed him to afford such advertising and this annoyed him slightly as the man must be charging him too much; however, when Lucinda descended from the vehicle – without her father - his temperament changed somewhat; he subsequently searched out some more respectable clothing without waiting for his valet…

Alice, who had been taking advantage of some weak sunshine, was reading under the mulberry tree and had seen Lucinda's arrival as well. As the cart turned through the arch by the side of the house into the yard, she recognised the young woman from the nocturnal meeting in her house and suspected that Sir Walton would find her attractive: so she removed herself from under the tree and went to the yard to see what this lady's visit proposed. Her disquiet was amplified by the fact that she heard Tobias asking Lucinda to wait while he fetched the master – but who then immediately bounded out of the door to meet her. Alice turned away – but was sure she had been glimpsed by the new arrival, who shot her a deprecating look.

A few minutes later in the Great Parlour, Lucinda was chattily showing Sir Walton some brochures explaining the new products her father had just invented – with her help, of course! Visibly impressed and increasingly interested in both her wares and her captivating personality, Sir Walton listened as Lucinda breathlessly extolled the virtues of these implements and improvements – and how they would increase water flow, divert it into two different directions, fit the hole bored by her father's previous invention, and also – the best part – despite being of an improved shape would also fit the products previously purchased. She also had the very same samples in her cart, of course...

Josiah Prentice and Samuel Hedges were summoned and the little party went down to the lake excavations, the men each carrying a sample or two of Lucinda's wares; in doing so, they passed Alice who had discreetly returned to beneath the tree but was surprised that none of them acknowledged her presence, presumably due to the twittering tones of Lucinda, she surmised and – to the men's ears – complementing the beautiful sounds of nature. Alice was suddenly afraid…

The meeting by the lake concluded, Sir Walton noted that Alice had left her position under the tree and had therefore been bold enough to ask if Miss Noncey would care to join him for a spot of lunch after her long travels, to which she readily agreed. Tobias was told to get Miss Shaw, the cook, to provide a small but nutritious lunch for the lady whilst they discussed costs and terms in the Great Parlour.

For Alice, this caused increased anguish: Sir Walton had promised her that he would love her forever… yet the caveat that perhaps he might need to find someone 'more suitable' as a front for his acceptance in society had been blandly said; and here was a pretty young girl who would be just that – even if she was from the supposedly despised trading classes: yet she was also of the same race. Alice again wondered whether she would, after all, be cast aside…

*

Day by day, Mrs. Burrows had begun to feel better since her return and the pains and cramps in her nether regions had receded: yet the child was getting bigger within her and with it her fear that it would be deformed. She had taken the two weeks off 'to see her poorly father' which Sir Walton had allowed – he had even given her five pounds for the journey and any medicines she might need to supply her father with; this kindness made her even more distraught, though, as she was sure he would not countenance accepting her baby by Tobias and reprimanded herself for the weakness that her lust had landed them both in - a conflicted situation which even Sir Walton's benevolence would surely never accept. As such, she felt even worse as she was betraying him. When she had left, she had mostly done so in the hope that the child would be lost or stillborn during that time or on the journey but this solution had not materialised: she could now feel it kicking ever more strongly. On top of that, as she had confided to Tobias on her return, she did not actually have a father – he had died many years ago. And so her mendacity accrued concern in tandem with her guilt.

When she had returned, she too noticed that Alice was plumper round the girth than before and her complexion was ever more radiant – so she wondered with a chill whether the father of the obvious pregnancy was Tobias; Sir Walton obviously adored the girl but he would never have had any sexual relations with her, she thought; so on top of all her other concerns she became ever more anxious that it must have been Tobias who had impregnated Alice since her arrival at Mulberry Hall. And this was after she, Elspeth, had ensnared Tobias for herself. Tobias, mostly oblivious to these conflicting concerns, could only see that Elspeth Burrows was beginning to look stressed, drawn and haggard and, worse, was increasingly wary of her sudden mood changes and shortness of temper.

One day, with the servants all about the house doing their chores, Elspeth found herself in a dreary mood in the butler's pantry with Tobias; quite suddenly, she gave vent to her unease and accused him of having an affair with Alice under her very nose. Tobias was astonished and hurt: he managed to control the anger which subsequently rose within him and – having checked that the door was firmly closed - availed her of the truth: that Alice was pregnant by the master and he, Tobias, had nothing to do with it. Yes, he had made love with Alice once when in Jamaica but that was almost three years ago now so he could not, would not, touch her again for fear of angering Sir Walton who had given him – and Alice – so much. He was concerned for Alice, of course: he worried that Sir Walton would throw her out – baby and all – if someone 'more suitable' were to be found. Indeed, the pretty, chirpy, engaging young Lucinda Noncey was again upstairs with him at that very moment, selling her wares - and herself, no doubt - in no uncertain fashion.

He was right: as he had suspected, Sir Walton and Lucinda were discussing a very sensitive contract – but nothing to do with tools or implements.

CHAPTER 15

An Arrangement Is Made

That evening, Sir Walton and Alice were taking dinner as usual together in the dining-room; he was subdued as if burdened with a weighty contradiction which, inevitably, cast a pall over the thoughts of Alice, too. Again, she could hear in her head him saying 'someone more suitable' which, in her haste to ensnare him and protect her future, she had agreed to; yet they had got on so well and their love-making was so ecstatic, that she had thought he really would love her forever, despite the complications of the time. She had learned that most men of position had mistresses – even up to and including the King – but somehow she thought that this would be different and that one day, as situations such as hers became more common, the sentiment regarding her race and colour would disappear. Yet she had come to love Walton: he had been good to her and she was soon to move into the house he had built expressly for her with many of the benefits and promises he had made already fulfilled; she had the princely sum of one thousand pounds in her own bank account in Bakewell, too, a bespoke carriage coming next week from York and her own horse to ride or pull it as she needed when her condition allowed. And yet... the closeness he had shown to this Lucinda Noncey disturbed her and she increasingly felt it inevitable that she would be superseded by this woman for all the wrong reasons.

Sir Walton was, however, wrestling with the same dilemma: he did truly love Alice and was keen for her to have his child, whom he would look after and cherish as much as he would its mother; Alice would always be his favourite and – he felt – would keep her attractiveness far longer than Lucinda would, who was only so due to her youth: Alice was naturally beautiful and would remain so whatever her age, he just knew. Lucinda would soon become plump and matronly after a few children and her cheery sense of humour would probably go the same way, too, he feared: in short, the girl would become unattractive, boorish and curt. Yet his position and the mores of the times could not be compromised too much: so as long as he could keep Alice, either secretly or in plain sight – and Lucinda would not rock the boat - all would be well.

His instinctive rapport with Alice meant he knew what was troubling her and eventually, after a long silence which seemed louder than the ticking and chiming of several clocks around the house, he sighed and told Alice the situation: as he spoke, he could see the tears welling in her eyes: she truly loved him, he could see, and this made him love her even more... so he rose from the table and walked around it to embrace her; their lips caressed each other's and that same mutual sweet taste passed between them; then Alice was crying and so was he, both professing their everlasting love. Yet with his caveat that this was how it had to be, he explained that Lucinda, too, would have to accept the situation if she wanted to be Lady

Grimley, help her father and be fêted in society. That was the deal, the contract... as for the pending child, this would forever be his and Alice's – and there would almost certainly be more in the future.

After this, they went up to his room and made love as best they could and before he fell asleep he murmured the words, "Alice, darling, I will love you forever."

"Me too," she sleepily replied.

"All will be well," he summarised before a heavy slumber enveloped him. He was the happiest man in the world, he thought as he did so...

Alice wanted to think the same but lay awake, foreseeing discord. She would not be wrong in that supposition.

CHAPTER 16

Two Babies and a Mutual Surprise

A s lives progress, it is common for expectations to be challenged, moderated, changed or even dismissed when circumstance reveals the absolute, undeniable truth. Such was the situation when, three weeks before Christmas, Mrs. Burrows' waters broke and she went into labour. Four days later, chance would have it that Alice went through the same; unlike Mrs. Burrows, however, she was resident in her own new house, away from the main Hall and in a place where Sir Walton could clandestinely attend to her, spending hush money on the best doctors to deliver the child without any expectation of his secret being subsequently betrayed. A nursemaid was also employed for help and company. As for Mrs. Burrows, she had to be whisked upstairs to her tiny room in secret: the word was that she had suddenly been consumed by a terrible inexplicable seizure yet all but the naïvest of maids knew the truth: Tobias immediately instructed silence from the staff and to discreetly cover for the inevitable gaps in service caused by Mrs. Burrows' predicament - concealment was paramount: any servant breaching, speculating or revealing what they all secretly knew would be summarily dismissed. When the truth inevitably came out, knowing of Alice's situation with the master, he would explain his own concealment - but wagered that as they each had a similar secret to keep, they were unexpectedly complicit: surely some understanding would therefore be forthcoming? This admission would only come out *in extremis*, of course and it would be a risky moment but it would have to be taken one day. Perhaps he and Elspeth would be dismissed but, deep down, Tobias was confident that the master would ultimately be supportive. Sir Walton would also, Tobias hoped, not wish to lose his housekeeper. Or himself.

The only potential surprise for both Elspeth Burrows and Sir Walton Grimley was what each had omitted to expect: that both children would almost certainly be born black. The prevailing hierarchical supposition was that a mixed-race child's colour would obviously be Caucasian: it would only be much later that research by Gregor Mendel into the laws of genetic dominance would show that the dominant colour would, in most cases, be the darker hue. But Elspeth had started worrying about this possibility, too – her lust would be permanently on show and she would be branded, she feared, forever; as for the more worldly Sir Walton, he would revel in the surprise, at least privately, as he could boast of his modern attitudes and poke two fingers up to the establishment; it would also boost his credentials in his parliamentary support for the abolition of slavery – whatever that meant for his finances.

*

Mrs. Burrows' child was a boy – healthy and fortuitously unimpaired despite his foetal attack by knitting-needles; furthermore, his hue was somewhere between his parents'... Alice's child was female and as dark as she was. Both were agreed to be – as those who were in the exalted position of being able to compare both, such as Tobias - extremely beautiful.

Into this pot of intrigue and secrecy stepped the almost innocent Lucinda Noncey. 'Almost' as she had achieved her objective but would inevitably be marked by its tensions; although she had been told firmly by Sir Walton of his love for Alice and that she would forever be with him as his 'dark secret' – he had always liked that phrase – if Lucinda did not like it she would have to find someone else; but as wealthy titled landowners were thin on the ground, she had reluctantly acceded to his wishes and promised to abide by his directions. The arrangement would benefit her father – if not herself so much – and she would just have to accept it. She would be Lady Grimley, after all; who knows, she might even be able to get rid of this irksome Alice along the way. Whatever happened, it would be she, Lady Lucinda Grimley, who would be the one attending society concerts, operas, banquets and the high life, fêted and received as an equal and chased by licentious young dukes, earls or whatever while Alice was closeted away in the draughty northern countryside as a trinket; and if Sir Walton could do what he had done, why not could she? A house in London would be a start…

CHAPTER 17

An Awkward Development

Sir Walton stirred in the middle of the night, woken by the sound of a baby crying. In his mind, he was confused: his child was with Alice in the house he had built for her and unless the night was very still or the breeze was casting itself in his direction he doubted he would have heard it. He listened again: there it was... The crying was definitely in this house and yet seemed to be somewhat stifled, as if someone was trying to quieten it. Then it stopped and he went back to sleep.

In the morning, however, when Alice joined him at breakfast in the main house, he discreetly asked if their daughter – whom they had named Sophie – had been crying in the night. Her answer was negative – Sophie had been asleep all night with little more than an occasional burp or sigh, a wonderfully tranquil child.

"So where did the crying come from, then?" he enquired gruffly. "It sounded as if it came from upstairs."

Alice, being privy to Tobias' and Elspeth's situation and the need for diplomacy, tactfully responded, "My dear Walton, it was probably a bird squawking or, perhaps, a fox? Or a peacock?"

"No peacocks here," he said: "I won't have any of those

THE SLAVE-OWNER'S DILEMMA

on my estate – too damn noisy."

She dared not say any more; she did not want to compromise Tobias – or even Mrs. Burrows.

"Are any of the servants with child?" he suddenly darted at her.

"No, Sir – I am sure not." This at least was true: Mrs. Burrows had already delivered her infant.

"Hmm."

She tried to change the subject. "When is Miss Noncey coming to live with us? Well, with you," she added, slightly tartly. She was not looking forward to this woman's presence, dominating and interfering with her life and being the receiver of any fawning and acclamation rather than her. But Sir Walton was not to be sidetracked and rang for Tobias.

"Tobias," he said as his butler arrived; "Is there a mewling child in the house?"

Tobias flushed, fortunately unseen by his master due to his complexion: "I think not, Sir. I have not heard one myself." Actually, it was he trying to stifle the baby's cries.

"Am I the only one to have heard it?"

"I believe you must have been, Sir."

"Send in Mrs. Burrows, would you? I need to discuss some housekeeping with her. Haven't seen her for ages."

"She's been a little poorly – the after-effects of the food-poisoning, Sir."

"Still? That was weeks ago. I want to see her for myself."

"Of course, Sir." And he left.

Alice did not wish to be in the room with Sir Walton when he was like this: Mrs. Burrows would feel compromised if she was there, too, because although the housekeeper knew about her – of course she did - Alice was unsure whether Mrs. Burrows knew that she, Alice, was aware of Mrs. Burrows' predicament and did not want to put her in an awkward spot. So she made an excuse to check on Sophie and left for her own house.

A few minutes later, there was a knock on the door and Mrs. Burrows was summoned in. Sir Walton took one look at her and was shocked; since he had last seen her some days ago she had lost weight and had taken on a gaunt, bloodless appearance, like an old parchment bedecked with writing which had been erased. Her skin was not taut as it had been and her face bore an expression of melancholy, despair and fear.

"Mrs. Burrows," he gasped, "you look dreadful. Are you all right?"

"I'm fine now, Sir," she replied weakly, a slight wheeze in her voice. "I had a dose of food-poisoning, Sir."

"Yes – so I heard. Not Miss Shaw's fault, I hope?"

"No, Sir; it happened whilst I was away seeing my father."

"But surely you're over it by now?"

"I'm bearing up, Sir. Thank you. It's been a difficult time over the past few weeks and it has knocked me back a bit. I am improving slowly, though Sir."

He stared at her; something was not right with the once-irrepressible, positive Mrs. Burrows. "I heard a child cry last night," he stated blandly, avoiding her eyes, yet noticing that she stiffened.

"At what time was that, Sir?" she enquired dismissively.

Ah... about two o'clock, I think..."

There was a pause. "Possibly a cat, Sir? There are no babies here… except Miss Alice's, Sir. Was it hers you heard, possibly?"

He was gazing at her; despite being thinner, he surmised her breasts were bigger than before and a tiny stain of liquid was apparent under one of them. He felt she was covering something up; "Is it a child of yours, Mrs. Burrows?"

A flash of terror crossed her eyes; then quite nonchalantly, purposefully and with a slightly aggrieved tone in her voice, she replied, "I wish that were so, Sir, but since my husband left the premises for… for another woman… I have had no chance of any child, especially living out here in the wilds of the country, Sir."

He suddenly felt sorry for her and quietly dismissed her, wishing her well and offering the services of his doctor if she needed him, which she thanked him for and then disappeared. He thought for a moment or two; he realised that the chances for a child in her position were minimal and was glad as he did not want to lose her; he was a kind man and if she was in trouble he wanted to help her; he still didn't believe her, though. Yet the obvious truth had not yet dawned upon him.

*

Mrs. Burrows rushed into the servants' hall past all the staff having their breakfast and straight into the butler's pantry where Tobias was nervously waiting for her, closing the door behind her. She fell into his arms, quietly sobbing. "He knows, he knows," she whispered through the deluge… "He asked me if I had a child…"

Suddenly tense, Tobias pushed her to arms' length and asked, "What did you say?"

"Nothing, dear Tobias… I just said perhaps it was Miss

Alice's but he didn't take that. And my breasts are weeping, too – I'm sure he noticed..." He took her back in his arms.

"Perhaps we should tell him after all," Tobias opined.

It was her turn to push Tobias to arms' length: "No! I have lied to him now! I can't go back on that! He'd fire me for lying... if not for the other thing, too..."

She went back into his arms then asked, "Where's Edward?"

"Don't worry – Alice's nursemaid, Florence, is looking after our son; gave him a drop of gin to keep him quiet and I gave her a shilling to do the same. I just wish Sir Walton would go away again for a few weeks until Edward has learned to sleep through the night..."

"Not much chance of that with the master's engagement party coming up," Elspeth noted. Tobias nodded. "Well, for now... our child will just have to be unreal... like a ghost."

"A ghost?"

"For now, yes; the ghost of Mulberry Hall."

CHAPTER 18

An Engagement Banquet,
A Complication & A Concern

Lucinda was preparing to leave home together with her father to go to Mulberry Hall. She had told him of her prospective engagement to Sir Walton without disclosing the conditions of the arrangement - that would have been the end of it; what father would want his daughter wedded to a man with a live-in mistress – especially of a different race – notwithstanding the benefits of this particular liaison? She was also concerned that he was becoming frailer by the month, despite his joy at Lucinda having snaffled one of the most eligible squires in the country and so did not wish to avail him of any fact that might unduly stress him. So now they were going to stay at Mulberry Hall for two nights for a banquet and ball - and so that Walton could officially ask Lancelot Noncey for his daughter's hand in marriage.

The day arrived and they set off in the old cart which had previously delivered implements - and then the young Lucinda Noncey - to her prospective husband. The new one, sporting their business name and credentials, had unfortunately broken a wheel and there was not the time to repair it; so as not to look too impecunious – despite the anticipated dowry which would solve all Lancelot Noncey's financial ills – they would travel once more to Bakewell in the old one and there hire a more resplendent carriage: they could not afford to look like relative paupers now. Alongside some minor new implements - and as large an order of the new 'scouring pipes' that the cart could accommodate without it breaking or killing the horse - were their belongings for the festivities. The weather was fortuitously bright for early March and a stiff breeze helped them on their way, the sun cheekily popping out from time to time as if to remind them of its benign, warming and heartening best wishes...

Back at Mulberry Hall, the mood was less propitious; since Elspeth Burrows' audience with Sir Walton, Tobias had decided to take his son at night to a small folly on the estate which had just been finished and would eventually overlook the lake; being new, it was reasonably dry and had not been colonised by insects, mammals or reptiles. It was essentially a small room with niches that would eventually accommodate statues; it had a good, solid door so was a good place to hide the baby at night, nestling in rugs and blankets within Tobias' strong arms. The worst part was not the cold but the dangerous trek across the pasture from the Hall to the folly which at night was a dangerous place, being criss-crossed by ditches, holes, machinery, tools and pipeworks. A torch was out of the question – he had to rely on his instincts; then, as the sun rose, he could at least see again but his shoes became wet with dew and festooned with mud, seeds and bracken, tearing his silk stockings which then had to be hastily repaired by his lover, Elspeth.

THE SLAVE-OWNER'S DILEMMA

There was the added concern that if Sir Walton rang for him in the night he would not be there to respond: how he would explain away that potential situation was not something he had yet found an answer to...

*

The day before the banquet, the Nonceys had arrived at Mulberry Hall somewhat earlier than expected and a footman had shown them to their rooms in the absence of Tobias, who was nowhere to be found. He had had a bad night with his son, who would not stop crying – there was obviously something wrong with the child which his infancy could not articulate - and at the moment of the Nonceys' arrival Tobias had been returning to the Hall but forced to hide behind a hedge; only when the guests had gone inside could he cross the greensward between the hedge and the house by a side entrance, his child bundled up in a blanket, its head covered. However, with Sir Walton having been summoned, on passing a window at the top of the stairs, he had seen a furtive Tobias crossing the greensward with what looked like a bale of bedding, holding the top preciously as if trying to protect something valuable. Bemused, he descended the stairs and, a few minutes later the Nonceys were being presented to him in the grand reception hall. They then proceeded into the Great Parlour.

The moment came when the pleasantries were exhausted and so the point of the meeting was addressed: Sir Walton cleared his throat and took a large draught of sherry for fortification and then launched into his request for Lucinda's hand in marriage.

"So, my dear Mr. Noncey, sir; to the main point of the meeting..." He spied a look of terror in Noncey's eyes as if he was about to ask a question of his implements and might have gone off his pretty daughter - but the relief on his face as the permission was requested soon cleared his expression of any anguish. He could now take life more easily with the dowry of two thousand pounds and a never-ending contract for tools and devices which would see him right for the rest of his life. His face, now glowing like a beacon, was animated by the question but also burnished by the two schooners of claret he had already imbibed. "Dear Sir Walton; I would be truly grateful – er, delighted – if you would marry my sweet, lovely Lucinda. Thank you, Sir – I am trustful that you will not be disappointed by your choice."

Whilst Sir Walton's answer was not quite in the effusive spirit Lancelot Noncey had expected, he smiled and rang for Tobias to bring in some champagne and delicacies. A few moments later, Tobias entered – but Sir Walton was perturbed by the fact that his stockings and shoes were marked with mud. He shot him a look as he said, "Thank you, Tobias... some champagne and light victuals for our guests at this auspicious moment" as he intimated Tobias' shoes with his eyes.

"Forgive me, Sir; I was caught out in the damp a little earlier but had to respond as quickly as I could to your call before I had the chance to address my clothing. I apologise, Sir; it will not happen again. I will retrieve the champagne and victuals, Sir," and he left.

"A charming fellow," said Lancelot helpfully. "Are these people good servants?"

"Excellent. They are hard-working, courteous and do whatever you ask of them."

Lucinda felt that this last stated virtue was particularly pertinent as she imagined her intended husband having licentious couplings with the young girl Alice in her own house: she, Lucinda, was the face of propriety but Alice was the true object of his desire... and she suddenly felt slightly sick.

*

The engagement banquet, attended by the worthy locals of the area - and less nearby earls, dukes, duchesses, knights and ladies for show, pomposity and ballast to fill the huge ballroom - had gone well; indeed, much hilarity, gluttony, imbibing, music and dancing had been experienced at Mulberry Hall. Yet the one person who was not invited was Alice, an omission not lost on Lucinda...

After this event, but before they left two days later, Lancelot and Lucinda had been jovially introduced to Alice by a sheepish Sir Walton, who had referred her to Lancelot as 'my special servant for anything the others are either not good at or as someone to read to me until my dear wife Lucinda is betrothed to me...' which unnerved Lucinda further; yet her father suspected nothing and went off in a satisfied manner. Lucinda, however, was beginning to wonder what she had involved herself in and now had the whole journey back to Wirksworth to think about it.

CHAPTER 19

A Wedding, An Awkward Situation & A Discovery

It was now April and spring's burgeoning of nature matched the spirits of those who occupied the Hall, now augmented by a large number of extra staff to prepare for the wedding which was planned for the start of May. The lake had now been fully excavated and the bottom lined with clay, various walls had been built to enhance its beauty, create a promenade and make it more permanent, a jetty and a boathouse built and plans for a large marquee to be assembled on the newly-levelled lawn in front of the house put forward. The mulberry tree would be included inside it at the end, under which the upper table would be placed, with ten large round tables around the space serving ten people at each. It was the busiest this piece of land had ever encountered since its creation thousands of millennia before…

Mrs. Burrows was still somewhat frailer-looking than she had once been but had finally thrown off the remnants of her poor condition and although retaining a slight haggardness had put on a modicum of weight and was becoming a noticeably attractive woman again. Their son,

Edward, had fortunately outgrown his early pains and was now as quiet as Alice's daughter, Sophie; while Alice had the luxury of a nursemaid to look after her child when she was not required by Sir Walton, Mrs. Burrows had been obliged to hide Edward behind a clothes screen in her attic bedroom on a tiny bed made of woollen bales. Yet as he grew bigger and wanted to play, they had to find a solution to their predicament as he would soon start crawling and crying due to his confinement: so he could not stay there much longer.

Mercifully, when the wedding day arrived, the sun shone and although there was a slightly bitter breeze the lower temperature could not douse the feeling of happy expectation in the air. By this time, Sir Walton had forced Alice and Lucinda to meet more often and had privately told them to be 'friends' – and no dissent from either would be accepted. Alice, being a pragmatic, friendly and kind girl – and still aware of her good luck – had accepted the arrangement but was wary of her rival, whom she knew had ensnared Sir Walton more as a useful bank balance for social climbing than as a husband. Lucinda, meanwhile, smiled and laughed prettily as if a subscriber to the instruction… but beneath the surface there lurked a jealous resentment which she was already planning to utilise for the betterment of herself and the plight of Alice. This sense of vengeance would have been sharpened further if she had been privy to the exquisite love-making between Sir Walton and Alice the night before her betrothal.

*

Lancelot and Lucinda entered St. Michael's, the old village church; the assembled guests – mostly the gentry in ostentatiously-concocted and colourful outfits – turned to see the couple walk down the aisle, a slightly forlorn-looking

Alice being bridesmaid, holding Lucinda's silk train in her small hands. To those who lived far away and had not been told of this young girl, the mood soured but, when Tobias too appeared with Mrs. Burrows and the usual servants, they turned away again, presuming that she must be Tobias' daughter or sister and, either way, a new slave. This was both a challenge and a joke for Sir Walton, who wished to remind people of his Jamaican business interests and also his acceptance of different races into his entourage. Yet although Lucinda was happy to have landed this paragon of the gentry, neither she nor Alice were happy with the conditions for very obvious conflicting reasons.

The ceremony over, the crowd made their way back to Mulberry Hall where the banqueting, drinking and jollity continued unabated for many hours. Tobias, Miss Shaw and Mrs. Burrows were eventually allowed to join the throng after their main duties had been performed, as were the Mulberry Hall servants, the temporary and auxiliary staff then expected to run the evening to its conclusion; for this they were very grateful, all observing that Sir Walton was indeed a very good master.

Yet the wedding night with Sir Walton's new wife did not go as well.

While Lucinda had a sweet face and an engaging personality, he had obviously never seen her naked before and this was, to put it mildly, a disappointment. She was attractive enough down to the waist but thereafter her thick legs and ankles, voluminous buttocks – previously always covered by crinolines and yards of material – were not to his taste. All he could think of was Alice and what he had done to her; he chastised himself for not just marrying her, whether to the annoyance, disbelief and disdain of his

THE SLAVE-OWNER'S DILEMMA

friends and wider society or not, but there it was: he had done it and would have to live with it. And the arrival of an heir would sort things out, he mused. Yes – that was the point of all this; so of course it would...

After managing as best he could, he stayed awake as Lucinda fell into a deep sleep. At around two o'clock in the morning, a nightshirted man with a flaming torch crossed from the stable yard to what he would now call Alice Lodge - and a sleepy but tearful young black girl was woken by a rather drunken, sad and contrite man who embraced and kissed her passionately ... which inevitably led to much more besides.

Through all this, the little Sophie slept soundly in a cradle at the end of her mother's bed, oblivious to the upheavals of her parents' liaison – and even less so what these would eventually inflict upon her.

Sir Walton returned to Lucinda's bed in the early hours after Alice had fallen asleep; he had looked at his daughter as he left and kissed the child, which smelled of sweetness and mown hay, pausing for almost a minute to breathe in this essence before reluctantly returning quietly to his marriage bed.

On arrival, Lucinda woke and threw her arms around Sir Walton, kissing him profusely; whilst he reciprocated, his guilt and recent intimacies with Alice – whom he now realised even more forcefully was truly the love of his life - precluded any further liaison for him. As for Lucinda, the enjoyment and release which the first act of losing her virginity had revealed left her wanting more - so was disappointed when her new husband rather curtly declined.

*

After bathing and getting ready for the wedding

breakfast, the newly-married couple awkwardly descended the stairs as the servants and invited guests clapped them into the dining-room. Yet it was obvious not all was well and when young Alice entered the room a little later – to be over-welcomed and cornered by a chinless young foppish duke – her pleading eyes for escape towards her aristocratic lover were picked up by a subdued Lucinda.

The new bride was once more aware that her husband's heart undoubtedly lay with Alice, not her; she had hoped that the first night with him would extinguish all his attraction to the girl and whilst her first ever enjoyment of sex had been a wonderful revelation, she knew she would now have to try harder to wean her new husband off her rival. Whether it was by stealth, deceit, looking prettier or being more useful or concupiscent, she was unsure; but if none of those worked, she would have to be more devious, unscrupulous and demanding… That was, in fact, her true nature, she coldly admitted to herself – not the sweet, beguiling, fun, witty and engaging young woman she had always projected herself to be or had displayed to Sir Walton. So, in that cold, calculating moment, she concluded she definitely had to be rid of Alice… and as soon as possible.

As the guests started to drift away, she asked her husband if she could meet the servants more personally: as she was now Lady Grimley of Mulberry Hall, she ought to get to know them better and what their duties were. Sir Walton was happy with the request – why not? So he pointed out the servants' stairs and instructed his wife to go down and meet them. Eager to find out what had happened to Alice, he turned away after Lucinda had rounded the corner, with the intention of removing the foppish limpetlike duke from his beloved paramour.

Lucinda arrived in the kitchen to find that the servants were not there; she rightly assumed that they must all be away about the house and grounds attending to guests and their daily duties, so she decided to look around. She took in the huge table where they created meals and ate, the enormous open fire with its slow-turning spit, the pots, ranges, dishes, kitchen implements, knives, bonesaws, hatchets and more, then found herself at the start of a short corridor at the end of which was a room marked 'Butler's Pantry – Private'. She knocked on it but there was no answer. Opening the door, it was obvious the room was empty... except for some slight movement behind a screen at the far end, and a quiet gurgling. Intrigued, she approached the screen and looked around its edge.

There in front of her was a beautiful baby with a smiling face, robed in warm but coarse bedclothes. Instantly, she imagined that this darkish child must be Alice's, being looked after by the servants so that the secret – although known by all – could yet be kept away from prying gentry eyes.

A feeling of hard resolve gripped her again: a plan was emerging. She swiftly left the sprawling set of basement rooms and emerged into the fresh spring air.

CHAPTER 20

An Embarrassment, A Confrontation & A Surprise

Sir Walton found his *inamorata* awkwardly walking around the grounds with the chinless duke, who had not allowed her to escape him, despite Sir Walton's earlier efforts. On noticing Sir Walton, her eyes immediately transmitted a renewed, panicked expression for help and soon the wet young man had been discharged on the pretence that Walton had some urgent private news to impart to his young charge. Grumpily, the duke drifted away and was soon to be seen with another object of his lubricity showing far more interest.

"My dearest," Walton breathed to Alice; "forgive me – I have done a terrible thing."

"And what is that, my dear Sir?" she asked sweetly, but with a tinge of concern.

"I have married the wrong woman: I should have stood by my beliefs and married *you*!"

For an instant, Alice was taken aback; "But you explained all this to me, my dear Walton; you couldn't do it as I am not... appropriate. But we have the most wonderful situation, do we not? We are happy, I can bring up Sophie and you can do all your business with your real wife who can give you an heir who will be acceptable to those you have dealings with. I have understood and am mostly happy with that. Compared to what my life might have been, I'm in heaven – despite the complications," which was added with a keen edge as she saw Lucinda in the distance bearing towards them.

"Yes, yes... I know... It was me that constructed this artifice! But, oh, my dear Alice, you are so forgiving, so... wonderful, that – "

She put her finger to her lips and quietly said, "Don't kiss me, my dearest... a dark cloud is heading this way and I fear it might bring a storm upon us if we discuss this further," and she smiled sweetly, knowing he would understand. They always just did, he suddenly realised...

He winked at her, mouthed a kiss and turned resolutely away as if he had just reprimanded her, and was soon in the company of Lucinda, arm in arm, and chatting pleasantries and obsequiences to all and sundry, a rictus smile implanted upon his face.

Eventually, between these politenesses, Lucinda observed, "You appeared to be in a very earnest conversation with that Alice girl..." which was laced with a mild sarcasm; "So what were you talking about, dear husband," this last word which she emphasised slightly. "Oh, this and that..." he countered evasively.

Then she stopped and faced him, after ensuring there was no-one else near enough to hear what she said next. "Dear husband, I have just discovered something which I suspect you do not know about. Or, if you do, I believe you have not told me."

"And what is that?"

"As you know, I went into the servants' hall ... but I found no-one there, as they are all around here doing their duties... so I have not yet had a chance to meet them sufficiently."

"Ah, well – there'll be other times..."

"Hmm. But did you know that Alice has a child?"

Sir Walton's blood froze. "What do you mean?" he stuttered.

She could see he was on guard, angry, even; but his apoplectic look did not give anything away... yet.

"I think Alice has had 'relations' with your butler, Tobias."

"Impossible!" he blurted. "The man is a saint."

"Even saints have weaknesses, dearest."

There was a moment as he collected himself. Then: "So what makes you so sure?"

"I have found a dark-skinned baby in the butler's pantry."

"A dark-skinned baby?"

She nodded.

"But I'd have known about it... It can't be."

"Well... I can show you if you wish..." He was becoming annoyed by her gloating supposition now... "So where did you find this... child?" he enquired.

"As I said – in the butler's pantry."

"Well, it's more likely to be Tobias's, then."

"But every child needs a mother," she sniggered.

Sir Walton was stumped; yes, he knew Alice had a child – his child; but why was it in the butler's pantry? No, it wasn't – he had seen his daughter that morning and the nursemaid was there in Alice Lodge looking after her. So had Tobias made love with his sweetheart while he was away in Jamaica? No – impossible: he had only gone for two months and Alice was not pregnant when he returned – nor would there have been time to give birth and hide it. But Tobias… "Did you ascertain the sex of the infant?" he suddenly asked her.

"I would wager it was a boy, my dear."

Suddenly, he felt a load lift from his mind: well, it couldn't be his then – Sophie was most definitely a girl! His countenance lightened, which was quickly noticed by Lucinda, who said in her chirruppy way, "You look relieved, Sir!"

"Ye-es… but I still think I should look into it."

"Indeed… so how long has Tobias been here?"

"Oh… about two, two and a half years…"

"And Alice?"

"Ah, er… well… not so long; about eighteen months, I think."

"So it's possible, then…"

"What?"

"That it's Alice's child."

"No! As I say – it's impossible. I would have known." '*She's playing with me now*,' he thought; fortunately, he felt he was on solid ground.

"Then it must be Tobias's."

"Hmm…" He had to conclude that she must be right. Then the sounds of a baby crying in the night came to him. And why was Mrs. Burrows so frequently unavailable and always tired – and had been so haggard and lifeless for such a long while? And the wet stain over one of her breasts… The fact that the child was Tobias's was overwhelming; but was the mother truly Mrs. Burrows? Surely not... But he had to tread carefully; this woman – this wife he had married – was out to cause chaos at his expense: or, at least, to blackmail him. And she did not yet know about Sophie... That would cause another explosion. He suddenly felt weak and compromised: he did not like that. Or, he realised, his new wife! God help him – what had he done?

*

By late afternoon, the guests had all disappeared and a relative feeling of calm spread across the estate; but not in Sir Walton's mind. He sent for Tobias and sat on one of the chairs in the marquee to wait for him, a large decanter of sherry in front of him, accompanied by two glasses. This was something which had to be addressed man to man and a surfeit of libation would certainly help him - if not the usually restrained Tobias.

Tobias soon joined him and asked of his master's pleasure.

"Sit down, Tobias," he said firmly.

Noticing a frost in his command, he said, "As you wish, Sir," and did so.

"Have a drink, Tobias – I think you might need it."

Concerned at his master's unusually frank demeanour, he slowly, anxiously sat down and accepted Sir Walton's proffered drink.

Sir Walton looked around to ensure no-one was within earshot and leaned close to him and said quietly: "I shall be blunt, Tobias. Word has reached me that you are father to a child here."

Tobias looked shocked and went to protest but Walton held up his hand and leaned even closer to him: "No need

THE SLAVE-OWNER'S DILEMMA

to say anything yet that you may regret saying," he said resolutely but kindly: "I am not reprimanding you – yet, anyway – and I only want the truth; but if you lie and I find out that this is so, I will have to dismiss you. So just tell me the truth… now, please."

Tobias was as drained as his dark skin could reveal: he contemplated his fine buckled shoes, the frilled cuffs and expensive sleeves of his butler's uniform with a fear that all he had achieved would suddenly be taken from him. Yet there was nothing he could do: if he lied, as the master said, and then found out, it would definitely be the end of his time here – and Mrs. Burrows' – who would probably be even more disgraced being a married woman. Albeit an unhappy one. He took a deep sigh then, with tears welling in his eyes, he looked at his master and said, "It is true, Sir."

There was a pause. Then, "I see. One thing I think I know but have to ask is… the child is not Alice's, is it?"

"No, Sir! She is *your* charge. I would never - "

He put his hand up again stop him. "As I would have thought. So, then… who *is* the mother, pray? One of the parlour-maids?"

"No, Sir!"

"Well? Who is it, then?"

There was a pause as he wrestled with the betrayal of his dear companion: "It's Mrs. Burrows, Sir."

The silence which ensued made the noises of the estate around them become more audible, only the subdued shouts of the servants clearing up the invasion breaching the otherwise tranquil surroundings.

"I see," he eventually said. Instantly, Tobias rose and said, with a lump in his throat, "I will leave immediately,

Sir, if - "

"Sit down," said Sir Walton decisively, then paused to think. Then he continued: "I do not blame you necessarily, Tobias – just give me the facts." Tobias sat. "But before you give them to me, be absolutely honest – that's all I ask. Then I will make my decision." A plan was already forming in his mind; he just needed to understand the reasons...

Tobias told him the truth: his meeting with Mrs. Burrows, her deep yearning for him – and, eventually, the admission of his for her... the complication and despair of Alice's unexpected arrival and the fact that by that time it was too late to start a relationship with her for the obvious reasons – as well as the obvious situation which became apparent between his master and Alice.

There was a long pause; Tobias' heart was pounding and he felt faint...

"How old is the child, Tobias?"

"About six months, Sir." *'About the same age as Alice's,'* Walton thought...

"And what is its name?"

"Edward, Sir."

"A boy... Does Mrs. Burrows' husband Giles know about all this?"

"I believe not, Sir."

"Good – let's keep it like that."

"I believe he has a lady or two in the town, Sir."

"Yes – he does: I've seen him with one of them." Another pause. "Are you a godly man, Tobias?"

"I try to be, Sir."

"Yes, I'm sure you are – that's another reason I asked

you to join me here... So do you think Mrs. Burrows would divorce him?"

"I think she hates him, Sir – so the answer would probably be 'Yes'. If she ever could..."

"And you would marry Mrs. Burrows?"

"I would have to, Sir."

"A damn fine-looking woman..."

"Yes, Sir – she certainly is, Sir. And very passionate, Sir."

They both looked at each other, a wry smile on each of their faces growing as the male bond grew suddenly stronger between them – and an understanding between races and genders despite different circumstances. "I think we are much the same, Tobias..."

"In some ways, perhaps, Sir."

"I, too, have a secret, Tobias."

"Sir?"

"I have fallen deeply in love with Alice."

"I think I knew that, Sir."

"Indeed. But now I'm saddled with the woman who has caused all this marriage frippery," and he waved his hand around at the general chaos around them. "But it was a necessary evil to conform with the times we live in."

There was another long pause, each reflecting the situation they found themselves in.

"I like you, Tobias."

"And I like you too, Sir – you have been most kind to me."

Sir Walton sighed and, with a sense of resolve, looked him in the eye and said: "And there is another part to my secret: Alice has a child by me. A daughter – Sophie. There – I have told you everything, so now we are mutually tied."

The astonishment was written all over Tobias' face. He knew, of course – but it was better that he kept that one secret to himself. So he just said, "Congratulations, Sir."

"And to you, Tobias." A long pause ensued, Sir Walton cogitating and Tobias wondering what would happen next. Then he looked Tobias in the eye and said, "Tobias, I have a plan."

"And what is that plan, Sir?"

"You will tell Mrs. Burrows I know about your boy and that I am sympathetic. Do the other servants know about your child?" Tobias shrugged his shoulders and sighed, "Probably, Sir. I have forbidden discourse on any such speculation but… well, it must be very obvious, Sir…"

"Then, in deepest secret – and on pain of dismissal – they must keep that secret; I suspect that one or two suspect of my own situation, too, and they must realise the same restrictions… In the meantime, you will move your child to Alice Lodge, where Alice's nursemaid, Florence, will look after your child along with mine…" He tailed off, looking into the distance as he did so. Then, abruptly, he looked at Tobias and enquired, "Does Alice know of your child with Mrs. Burrows?"

"Indeed, she does, Sir."

"Ha! I wondered why she was so evasive when I was speculating about Mrs. Burrows' condition!… the little prigstar! Just wait till I see her," he added jovially under his breath. Then he became more serious once more: "I will somehow evolve a divorce between Mrs. Burrows and her husband and pay him off handsomely: if he squeaks, it's the gallows for him. Our children will grow up together and I will employ a governess when the time comes. They will be confined for the most part to Alice Lodge and Mrs.

Burrows can have a room there, too - bigger than the one she has in the Hall - and be close to her child. You will have to stay in the butler's pantry as now because I need you at the centre of things…"

A finality of purpose seemed to be apparent between them so Sir Walton stood up and held out his hand. Tobias did the same, and an even firmer bond of respect and understanding was palpable. "And that, I think, concludes our very important and honest meeting, Tobias. You will, of course, tell Mrs. Burrows of my decision. I hope she will be grateful for the news."

"Indeed, Sir; I'm sure she will… and relieved, too, Sir, as am I, of course – thank you very much, Sir." There was a lull, but something burned in Tobias' conscience, so he asked, "Just one thing, though, Sir: it *will* be difficult to keep the children out of sight as they grow older…"

Sir Walton thought for a moment, then replied, "As far as this household is concerned, everyone will eventually know everything as circumstances become… necessary. But to the wider world, they will be unknown, as, sadly, my reputation demands it – especially with my standing in the Commons: if they knew I was having relations with a slave-girl it might sink my credibility. God knows why – but my enemies would find a way…" He tailed off, then looked back confidently at Tobias and said, "So our respective children will have to stay secret – at least for now."

"I see – like ghosts, Sir."

"Indeed – the ghosts of Mulberry Hall."

CHAPTER 21

An Altercation & An Agreement

The next day, Sir Walton rode into Bakewell. In his saddlebag he had a pouch with a large amount of cash and a hastily-written contract... As expected, he found Giles Burrows in one of the less salubrious taverns and wondered how the reprobate could afford his life of apparent wenching and libation. It had often crossed his mind he might have been guilty of embezzlement when working for him before, which made him further resent offering the man any more money but was a conditional part of his proposed plan; yet he wanted to do good for Mrs. Burrows. And, of course, Tobias: that man was the key – a decent, honest, hard-working and highly intelligent man, unlike the uncouth lout he was now walking towards.

"Mr. Burrows!" he called loudly, drawing the attention of the other topers; as a person of the local aristocracy, he wanted to be noticed in case Giles Burrows became violent or abusive. The man turned and looked at him: "Ah, good morning to you, Sir," he said as he unsteadily rose to his feet. "Do you wish me back at the hall, Sir?" this said with the hint of a sneer.

"Certainly not, sir," replied Sir Walton; "I want to do business with you."

THE SLAVE-OWNER'S DILEMMA

"Business? What sort of business?"

Sir Walton looked at the landlord and enquired of him: "Good sir – do you have a room I can do business with this damber in?" The landlord assented, being glad to get this drunken oaf out of the main tavern; although enjoying the money he brought through drinking and the use of his girls, there were times when his boorish behaviour became overpowering - so any respite was welcome. He showed the two men into a back room as Sir Walton requested a glass of claret, an inkwell and quill, and a pint of ale for Giles Burrows. The request fulfilled, the door closed behind them and Sir Walton noticed the man was somewhat edgy: a sign of guilt if ever there was one.

"I come with regard to your good wife, Mrs. Elspeth Burrows." The man looked at him, as if questioning that kindly adjective. "In short, she wants to divorce you." The man's faced remained implacable. After a pause, he smirked; then, his voice slightly slurred, said, "She can't divorce me – we're married,".

"Which is exactly why she wants to divorce you."

"I don't want to divorce her: she gives me money." Sir Walton believed this: he was a bullying type - thank God he now had Tobias as his butler.

"That may be so, but the poor woman cannot afford your habits and I wish to see that she is better accounted for."

"Then pay her more money."

"She is paid quite well enough."

"Then she'll have to give *me* more money." Again, that nasty sneer.

"That, sir, is what I propose." The man's face lit up, the ruddy, bulbous cheeks suddenly glowing with the anticipation of being burnished by more jollity.

"What's your proposal, Sir?"

"That I give you a one-off payment of one hundred pounds on the condition that I organise your divorce from Elspeth Burrows with the local vicar and that you comply unreservedly to the terms I have written here, to be witnessed by a member of the judiciary and signed by you. It will give you the right to live in your house as long as you wish or until you are deceased, whereupon it will revert to your wife. Or ex-wife, after this agreement."

"She'll kill me, then!", Giles retorted loudly, "so she can get it back!"

Quietly, Sir Walton responded, "I hardly think a woman of Elspeth Burrows' impeccable character would do any such thing. So I shall continue... After this agreement is signed and witnessed, you must never ever see, contact or spread rumour or bad intent about your ex-wife ever again, on pain of appearing at the assizes and being transported to the colonies for breach of contract." There was by now a look of disbelief and hatred on the man's face, so Sir Walton pointedly added an afterthought: "And, of course, if you kill *her* to gain the house, then it will be the gallows for you."

The man's eyes narrowed: "You want to marry her yourself," he said nastily, the sneer this time revealing some stained and blackened teeth. "In which case, *I* want more money."

"A hundred pounds and leave to stay in the house is more than enough for a rum cove such as you; with that you can settle your debts and set up a business. It's a good offer."

There was a pause, then he said, "Show me the money, then."

"Landlord!", Sir Walton shouted loudly; he was not going to run the risk of being murdered by this gross fellow and having his money stolen as well so wanted a witness. A moment later, the landlord knocked and entered: "More drink, Sir Walton?" he enquired hopefully.

"No – I want you as a witness to a planned transaction of money and the signing of a contract between this man and myself." Then with a glint in his eye, he added, "I'm sure this transaction will help your business greatly."

The landlord assented, the money was displayed and counted, but withheld until any contract was signed, much to the visible wrath of Giles Burrows. Sir Walton then requested the landlord ask a boy to send for the town's local churchman, as another witness' signature was needed. He doubted any god would look after this man's soul but, as they waited, he realised a lawyer would also be needed. "Justice Bateman is here in the tavern," the landlord responded; "Shall I ask him in?"

Sir Walton nodded and kept a wary eye on Burrows as he momentarily left the room: he had a pistol in his bag for security but hoped he would not need to grasp it as he was a poor shot, even at this range. But Burrows stayed seated, a louring and patronising leer fixed on his face. The landlord soon returned with the Justice so Sir Walton ordered another flagon of ale for Burrows, a bottle of claret for himself and the new arrival – and whatever else the landlord wanted.

Half an hour later, the man of God arrived, a thin, bespectacled, mousey man with a voice that matched and who shared the same form of teeth; after introducing himself as the Reverend Louwerse and entering into discussion as to his role, he assented and said he would do all he could to execute the contract and ensure that the man stayed within the confines of God's ordinance. '*Good luck with that,*' thought Sir Walton again, but gave the vicar five pounds for his parish. A divorce proceeding was arranged and the money was then left with the Justice until such time as the contract was settled, much to the protestations of Burrows who had imagined spending some of his good fortune immediately. The party then went their separate ways with the agreement that all would meet again at the same time and place two days later to finalise the arrangement.

Sir Walton returned to Mulberry Hall soon after to inform a rather relieved Mrs. Burrows of her new situation and the fact that her child would not be illegitimate any more if she wished to ever marry Tobias; also, that there would soon be no reason to fear her husband again.

Two days later, as agreed, the same people reassembled in the same room, with the addition of a frightened Elspeth Burrows: after she and Giles Burrows had signed the divorce contract in front of Sir Walton, the Reverend Louwerse and the Justice, Giles had grasped at the money as if it would suddenly be snatched away again and left the room – almost certainly to divest some of his fortune on his favourite harlot.

It was immediately obvious to Sir Walton that the lifting of the burdensome husband's influence – however distant - made for even better relations between the staff and Elspeth Burrows, who found they could better discuss issues now that she was in a lighter frame of mind; as Sir Walton had promised, she now had a room in Alice Lodge, where she would do a large number of her accounting and haberdashery duties while at the same time spending time with her infant child. Alice was also delighted, as it meant she was less of a clandestine shadow and more part of the general household; it gave her a companion for some of the time, too, when they would discuss the bringing up of their respective children. Yet Mrs. Burrows – or, more appropriately, her maiden name of Miss Yarley now that the divorce had been confirmed - was not allowed to share her room with Tobias until or unless they actually married: Sir Walton's generosity went a long way but, notwithstanding the original sin of fornication between them (which he was in no position to frown upon), he did not want to institutionalise their liaisons by allowing them to share habitation. He obviously knew they would conjoin from time to time when he was away in Bakewell, London or Jamaica, but openly rocking the boat with the clergy, his entourage or his society friends was a step too far.

After a few weeks, Sir Walton's marriage to Lucinda had steadied somewhat but he was careful not to let Alice know when they coupled for the purpose of an heir lest it upset her; he was less concerned about the situation the other way around, for Lucinda had been in on the deal beforehand and he felt she had been quite lucky to win him despite the awkwardness of the situation.

Lucinda also had her own business to do, not least keeping the expanding building works supplied with materials, innovations and new inventions which were still being supplied by her father, who had taken on a new lease of life now that his daughter's marriage had provided him with such a generous dowry.

Yet she still harboured resentment: she disliked the situation and dishonesty of being Sir Walton and Lady Grimley in principle when they were not so in bed; that delight lay with her adversary. Yet Lucinda found that she could not dislike Alice; she was so sweet and friendly that it was very difficult for her to despise the girl - which was actually what she earnestly really wanted to do.

CHAPTER 22

A Meeting, A Rumour & A Conspiracy

With the Hall and parklands having been completed in time for the wedding, life continued thereafter at Mulberry Hall in much the same way on a daily basis; most of the servants still had no idea that Alice had had a child and whilst they suspected Mrs. Burrows' secret, fewer and fewer had any idea what that was as time went on, servants departed and new ones joined - these sworn to silence regarding any matters to do with Mulberry Hall on pain of dismissal or even prosecution. Elspeth now went solely by the name of Miss Yarley and visitors to the Hall were never given knowledge of her child. What had been envisaged as a small withdrawing room at the rear of Alice Lodge soon became more of a playroom as the two children grew up together, their noise unheard in the main house unless the windows were open in summer, when they were sworn to playing in relative silence. So Sir Walton had a large walled garden built at the back, where they could not be seen by anyone from the house; thus eventually the fiction grew that both Miss Yarley and Alice were childless. Yet Lucinda knew all too well and, as her intended pregnancy refused to happen - despite their best intentions if not particular pleasure on Sir Walton's part -

she became ever more bitter and disillusioned with the situation she had agreed to. Tobias and Elspeth had decided not to marry, less due to the social mores of the time but rather because any wedding would draw attention to their situation; whilst Sir Walton had initially stipulated this condition, he had also come to agree that they might be ostracised or, worse, the townsfolk might turn against he himself for allowing it; so, to keep his reputation clear as a local member of Parliament, whenever there was need for them to visit the town for the market, business or pleasure, he strictly forbade any hint of intimacy between them.

Yet one day, in town, they had been observed having a little laugh together in an unguarded moment by a disgruntled seamstress called Jess, who had been dismissed from Mulberry Hall by Sir Walton a few weeks before after her over-zealous attentions for a stable-lad had been rebuffed; subsequently, she had not found work and been forced into prostitution, eventually being taken on in a tavern where she suffered the further misfortune of receiving Giles Burrows as a client. Inevitably, pillow talk surfaced and Giles - who had by now squandered his money and was in the mood to squeeze more out of Sir Walton's purse under the guise of blackmail – sensed a perfect opportunity. Having been gifted his little house through the divorce agreement, Giles soon found that Jess – with nowhere else to go – had taken advantage of the situation and moved in with him. Subsequently, their liaison became ever more focussed as a poisonous seed of revenge started to bloom between them, together reckoning that – despite Giles signing the divorce contract - he could argue he had been swindled, not knowing his previous wife was rumoured to have been having a relationship at that time with a black man, as Jess had soon told him.

In such a close rural and small town society, it was not long before the rumour took root - spread by Jess as she plied her trade - that the prior Mrs. Burrows, housekeeper at Mulberry Hall, was having 'relations' with this ex-slave; yet the upshot was not what Giles had expected for he soon started suffering taunts about his previous wife which angered him, putting him in an even worse disposition regarding his former life under Sir Walton than before. The added rumours that a child had been born - but to whom even Jess was not completely sure - only aggravated the situation. Yet the infant could not be Sir Walton's, they believed, as although his companion was a young ex-slave called Alice, for whom Alice Lodge seemed to have been built, surely a man of such propriety and influence would never have entered into a relationship with such a person.

In Giles' mind, then, this meant that any child could only be his ex-wife's and it was this that finally ignited a deeper and more dangerous revenge, fanned by the demonic Jess. She had also added further to the subterfuge by mentioning that she believed her previous mistress, Lady Lucinda, was desperately unhappy despite the money, position and privilege she had at Mulberry Hall – and had heard that there were many strange, unreported things going on there. It was even whispered that often strange noises at night and during the day had been heard emanating from Alice Lodge - wild children's laughter, bangs and bumps, screams and more besides, implying more than one child: with no allowed ingress except from a maid, Miss Yarley and a woman whose purpose was unknown, this prompted imagination to run riot further…

So it was not long before, between them, their plans for blackmail or revenge – perhaps both - had hardened…

CHAPTER 23

The Plot Thickens

Sir Walton had gone with Lucinda to London for a few days to visit the opera, give his wife an opportunity to do some shopping for the latest fashions and generally parade themselves about; Sir Walton also wanted to attend some debates in the Commons. Alice, of course, was used to his long absences and accepted it as part of her life, whereas Lucinda spent much of the time on the journey haranguing her legal husband, urging him to reject Alice as it was 'improper and unseemly' to have his mistress – a slave – living under the same roof as her. His answer, that 'Alice lives under a separate roof to us' did not improve Lucinda's temperament one jot and she prayed that something would happen to get this beautiful, sweet obstacle out of the way. Little did she know that, at much the same time, a supposed labourer had walked the nine miles from Bakewell to Mulberry Hall with the aim of gaining any employment, knowledge or scandal he could find... Giles Burrows. He knew the stakes were high but – still having a small amount of money left – had decided to buy some new clothes, grow a beard, clean himself up and go to Mulberry Hall under what amounted to a disguise; his pretence of looking for work to see what he could find

THE SLAVE-OWNER'S DILEMMA

was solely to use any gained intelligence to his financial advantage…

He walked up the long drive and, seeing the smaller Alice Lodge first, was intrigued. He had not been here since declining the offer to continue as Sir Walton's butler when Mulberry Hall was still being built: so, even though Jess had mentioned it, seeing this small but opulent building was unexpected. As he approached, he saw a small carriage-and-two leaving the premises and quickly darted behind a large topiary; as the carriage rumbled past, he thought he saw a pretty girl inside who flashed by in an instant; yet, had the light tricked his senses? He concentrated on the receding carriage, trying to remember that instant… and came to the conclusion that the person in the carriage appeared to be of a different hue to what he had expected. He knew the butler was a 'chimney-chops' as the rough Bakewell locals had nicknamed Tobias, but it took him only a moment to realise that it must be the master's young companion, Alice.

After the carriage had disappeared, he carefully resumed his journey to the house and, seeing the archway at the side which he surmised gave access to the stable yard, knew that this would also lead to the servants' halls where there would be someone whom he could talk to. As he approached the door, he affected a limp to improve his disguise in case he had the misfortune to meet with his ex-wife: all plans would be thwarted if she recognised him. The door opened and Tobias confronted him with a polite but curt, "How may I help you, sir?"

Tobias had been the talk of the town a year or two ago – but Giles had never met him – just observed him once in Bakewell. He reflected that this was the rapscallion whom

Jess's rumouring claimed had cuckolded his wife. An envious rage mounted in his chest but for now there was nothing he could do. He was struck by the man's bearing, his beautiful skin and deep voice but had inevitably taken against him, less due to his colour than because Tobias had taken the job he should, with hindsight, have accepted: without that decision, his thoughts asserted, his licentious "swiving with a surfeit of his cock-bawd's 'buttered buns'" would not have given him the severe dose of scalder from which he wondered he would ever recover... so an increased prospect of reprisal suddenly burned hotter within him.

"I am looking for a position, sir," Giles eventually replied, a tremor in his voice.

"What sort of position, sir?"

"Anything, sir; gardener, valet, footman..."

"There are none of those positions at the moment, sir. Although... there may be a space for some workmen on the estate... there are continuing building works, as you have probably noticed."

"That would suit me well, sir; how do I apply?"

"Go towards the lake and seek the master builder, Mr. Josiah Prentice. He might be able to help you."

"Thank you, sir; much obliged." There was a pause and then he forlornly looked at Tobias and enquired, "I don't suppose there's a tiny bit of food I could take, sir, is there? I've walked nine mile and I'm not a little peckish."

There was a pause as Tobias assessed him. His face was familiar from the town but he could not at that moment place it. So he replied, "Come into the servants' hall and I'll see if I can find you something."

"Thank you, kind sir..." and he followed Tobias in.

"What's your name?" Tobias asked as they walked down a long corridor.

He struggled for an instant – he hadn't thought of that. "Er, George, sir: George... Bargeman, sir." Tobias nodded; there was something not right about this man. Arriving in the kitchen, Giles spied Miss Shaw, the cook. Although he hadn't yet recognised any of the servants he had known during his time before in Bakewell, he was surprised to find her there. The woman did a double-take but then went back to her pastry-making.

Tobias gave the man some bread and soup; increasingly, Miss Shaw kept darting him looks and then, after a minute or two, called over a kitchen-maid, discreetly whispering in her ear; the girl glanced at Giles and then, wiping her hands on her apron, left the room. *'Gone to get Elspeth, I wager'*, he thought.

Then Tobias was bundling him out of the hall and out into the yard again, pointing down the gentle incline past where the mulberry tree stood and towards the half-full lake glinting further away.

"Thank you, kind sir," Giles said as he walked down the slope, "Much appreciated." He suddenly remembered that he had forgotten, in the surprise of entering the building he had spurned, to apply the limp he had affected and cursed himself. This was noticed not only by Tobias but also Elspeth – watching from an upper Alice Lodge window after a tip-off from the parlour-maid. Whatever his gait and whether he was now bearded or not, she knew it was him and instantly feared for Tobias; Giles had a violent temper and if – as she supposed – his money given him by Sir Walton had been exhausted, he would probably try something stupid, like blackmail. Or even murder.

*

Elspeth instructed the nursemaid to look after the children; with Alice on her way to a local meeting with the pastor who would advise any offspring of their godly duties when they were older, she could move fast. She knew that Giles would try to ingratiate himself into the Hall if he could, even though any employment would be blocked by Sir Walton. Further, he might even push to have his threat of sending Giles to Australia or the gallows expedited: the problem was that Sir Walton was not here now. So she had to waylay Giles in private if possible – she could not risk a public altercation - and tell him to return to Bakewell: there could be no chance of his returning here. In the distance, she could see him talking to Josiah Prentice who, now being the estate manager and a kind and pleasant man, would probably offer Giles work. Yet she did not believe Giles to be that clever – had he waited for Sir Walton to leave for two weeks? If so, how would he have known? A provider of victuals? A grudging or dismissed servant? The scurrilous seamstress Jess crossed her mind – she had left only a few months ago and might have suspected his planned expedition to London, being the Season... Yet it was common knowledge that work was sometimes available at the Hall... but asking for food of Tobias had snared him via the eyes of Miss Shaw, whom he had known when butler in Bakewell: typical. Stomach, drink and wanton women were always his priority above anything else... So the time to confront Giles was now. With a sudden sense of purpose, she left Alice Lodge and crossed the drive towards the lake; her pace quickening, the damp grass was making her shoes cold, wet and uncomfortable. Giles' back was to her as she saw him shaking hands with Josiah - as if sealing some sort of agreement: it was too late! All she then heard from Prentice were the distant words, "I will see you on Monday morning, then sir." She slipped behind the mulberry tree… she could not cancel the agreement as it would be considered as a gentleman's bond. Yet Sir Walton would be livid. She had to do something…

Giles passed within a few feet of her on the other side of the tree, a smug look on his face as if the first part of a devilish plan had been achieved. She saw him reach the drive, where he stopped to take in the main house, as if assessing its worth and how much he could blackmail Sir Walton for… And if her master's secrets got out about Alice's relationship with him, their baby Sophie and she and Tobias' child, Edward, then he would have a lot of ammunition to slander Sir Walton with… She could not let that happen – he had been too good to her; Giles had to be stopped by someone before he could destroy the whole estate… In an instant, she realised that this someone had to be her… she had to do something – and urgently.

Her thoughts returned to concentrating on Giles… she noticed that his gaze had shifted to Alice Lodge and – to her horror – noticed he was making straight for it. He must not go there – it was forbidden to all but her, Alice, a nursemaid and a couple of trusted servants… Alice was out – but her child Sophie was there and Edward, too; neither child must ever meet this dangerous and unpleasant man who could so easily have been Edward's father, she shivered… she must do something… but she could not involve Tobias: he was too kind – it was only his compassion, too, that had unwittingly taken Giles into the servants' hall. She had to do something… herself.

*

Alice had arrived at a small house near the village church; it had not been built as a rectory and was therefore smaller than usual, but it served well enough for the pastor and his wife, a hearty, buxom woman who was at least twice the size of her husband. They were studying the scriptures and Alice was learning about biblical episodes she had heard of in Jamaica but never fully learned about since her arrival in England.

It was soon time for tea and a large slice of cake and some jam scones later, the woman suddenly turned to Alice as if there was something on her mind.

"So who *is* your daughter by, then?"

Alice nearly choked on her scone. This was a question too far – and nothing to do with the scriptures. She did not even realise they knew she had a child at all; the fiction that she was nominally a companion to Lucinda and Sir Walton and priming herself for an eventual happy day in marriage to someone 'suitable' had obviously been breached and she worried about who else might know: this couple represented a lot of parishioners and it seemed unlikely they would have held back on their suspicions and gossip, the only currency the rural poor could exchange without cost...

Surprised at her dramatic reaction, the woman apologised but then nonetheless continued, as if charged with the zeal and righteousness of God: "It's all over Bakewell, love. The only thing people don't know is who the father is. And because you're... you know... not quite like us and any other person like you is, well, probably hundreds of miles away... we assumed it must be by the butler, Tobias."

Suddenly, the scriptures seemed less of a narrow path to God than a highway to restriction, guilt and prejudice. She made her excuses and left the house, outside which the coach-driver waited patiently; not expecting such a short visit, he had unhitched the horse so it could eat the luscious grass around the building but quickly re-harnessed it as Alice jumped in and slammed the door, holding back a mixture of anger and tears. The rector and his wife stood in the doorway, wondering what her abrupt departure meant but their deprecating looks suggested that they only thought the worst of her; as the carriage pulled away, she pulled down the blinds and wept copious tears.

*

Elspeth waited for Giles to get a couple of hundred yards in front and then ran through the main entrance into Mulberry Hall; she wished that Sir Walton were here but knew he would not be back until the morrow: he would have shot him on the spot as an intruder, she suspected... Come on, Elspeth, think... Then she remembered that, inside the Great Parlour, was a selection of weapons which had been in Sir Walton's family for generations: they were mainly muskets and pistols – but some fierce-looking swords in their scabbards were also displayed around the walls, souvenirs of battles long past. She furtively went in and chose a slightly shorter sword than most displayed there, then noticed a dagger underneath: she removed both and, carefully hiding them under her apron, left the Hall for the stable yard. Fortuitously for her, Giles was trying the main front door of Alice Lodge, which was always locked; this gave her a little more time to reach the side door, although by doing so she would inevitably reveal her presence long before reaching him. This door, too, would be locked but there was a coded rap which everyone privy to the secrets contained within the lodge knew. But as housekeeper, she had a key... Giles had continued trying to open the front door but, still failing, was now knocking on it; yet it remained shut – and his increased hammering only made his presence more menacing to those inside. She withdrew back behind the arch to think for a moment: the dangerous part was evading Giles' gaze as she approached: she had to risk it. She went out through the arch, stumbling as the sword caught in her clothing, her anger and intent blinding her for a moment as she swept across the expanse of grass between the two buildings as best she could. As she ran, she looked up and was relieved that she could not now see him – he must have gone around to the back and would now be skirting the walled garden, trying to find an unlatched gate... So she ran to the front door - which was slightly nearer than the side one - up the steps and took out her large ring of keys, which jangled in the clear air as she tried to find the right one. No, not that one... This one?... No... That was the problem, the front door key was seldom used so she was unsure which it was. As she fumbled, she heard a carriage coming up the main drive and saw that it was Alice's; she waved frantically at the coachman and after a few wild movements the carriage stopped and she saw Alice's tiny face enquiring as to why they had done so. Elspeth did not wish the carriage to reach the stable yard and fortunately she could then see Alice leaning through the window and telling the driver to instead take the carriage to the front of the lodge – she had understood Elspeth's wild gesticulations! The carriage then turned towards her as Elspeth found the right key and the door creaked open; then she was gesticulating for them both to hurry and soon Alice jumped out of the carriage, slammed the door shut and made her way up the steps as fast as her voluminous clothes would allow, Elspeth intimating silence and waving the carriage away; confused, the driver did so, the front door banged shut and Elspeth was re-locking it, coarsely, breathlessly whispering to Alice to go upstairs and hide herself and the children in a locked room, just as Giles turned the opposite corner where the side door was, only to see the carriage receding. Alice tried asking why but Elspeth just rasped, "Later," and Alice ascended the staircase. Elspeth ensured the front door was well locked as Giles banged on the side one; she ran to it and, in a voice she tried to disguise as not her own, she shouted, "This is locked – go to the front door!" and swept back to it. A few moments later, there was again banging on the front door: she took out the sword from under her apron and withdrew it from the scabbard, readying the unsheathed dagger in her other hand. Then, she took a deep breath and unlocked the door.

As it opened, Giles was unsurprised to see his ex-wife there, beckoning him inside; what he was surprised at was the fact that, as she closed the door, she revealed the sword from behind her back and plunged it into his stomach; he cried out and fell to the floor, whereupon she stabbed him with the dagger in the back, face, arms, legs – anywhere - in such a deranged way she only realised what she had done after one large pool of blood and several smaller ones started to spread across the marble floor. In just a few short seconds, the longstanding bane of her existence had been slain, each pool representing a year of hurt; yet her overwhelming relief only seemed to emphasise an eerie void, as if the journey from continuous unease to retribution had been extinguished too fast for estimation because it had all been so simple...

Elspeth looked back at the corpse: yes, Giles was lifeless: yet she felt more full of it than ever. Wisps of hair had dropped over her face in the frenzy, tickling her nose and cheeks: she swept them away with her hand and then saw herself in the large gilded mirror on the wall, her bloody hand having smeared two scars of red across her face. She looked terrible: yet despite being spattered with blood and her mouth flecked with foam, her demeanour was one of triumph, restitution and sweet revenge. She had killed her ghastly husband. She fell to her knees, suddenly exhausted... The Lodge was silent but for the ticking clock, resonating through the hallway like a slow march of destiny. Then, as the triumph of what she had perpetrated sank in, her ex-husband's blood doing the same into her skirts, she knew that if this was ever found out, she would hang. Instantly, getting rid of the body was the most important chore of her life.

Yet she could not trust telling anyone outside of Alice Lodge and hoped she could avoid any questions: but it was her doing.... so she had to clear up the mess on her own.

CHAPTER 24

Secrets, A Body & A Prospective Tree

It was a cold morning three days later and Josiah Prentice was wondering why the workman he had hired the last week had not turned up. Not that he really needed him… but he always wanted to help people and the man had seemed particularly needy. Well, he had been as charitable as he could be…

In the Lodge, the three days since the murder of her husband had been ghastly for Elspeth: she had immediately bolted both doors so no-one could enter whether they had a key or not and wrapped the body in an old blanket to soak up any blood that was still seeping out. Then she had gone to the kitchen and washed her face with water from a washstand; Alice had suddenly looked down from upstairs and let out a cry of horror at the bloody mess she witnessed and Elspeth had rushed up to imply silence and whispered, "It was Giles – he had come back to murder me and my child – yours too, probably – for he would not have known which was mine or not… so we must help each other." Alice had instantly understood the situation and run off to ascertain whether the nursemaid there had heard anything. She had then rejoined Elspeth with the news that the woman had fallen asleep with the children… Alice had then removed her nice dress and shoes as together they had dragged the body to the back of the house and out into the garden where encroaching darkness abetted the fact that the high wall precluded anyone seeing them from the Hall anyway. The body's passage had left a trail of smeared blood as it was dragged from the hallway; once in the garden, they had stacked it indelicately behind a burgeoning hedge - its burial would need some swarthier people, which would have to wait until later. They had then both set to with mops, buckets and rags to annihilate any trace of the deed within the building. Elspeth seemed motivated not just by guilt but also a contrasting righteous indignation - tempered by fear should the law ever catch up with her. Just before midnight, she returned to the Great Parlour and replaced the sword and dagger to their ceremonial places on the wall as she best remembered them...

Early the next morning, she went down to Josiah Prentice and requested the loan of two strong labourers who could come up to the lodge – now - with picks and shovels to dig a large hole in the walled garden for a tree she had ordered and might arrive any time...

Half an hour later two swarthy men had duly arrived; they were shown past what looked like a pile of dirty laundry airing in the garden to where she wished the hole to be dug and spent a nervous hour watching them create a deep hole. It had to be deep and round, she stipulated: any other shape would have aroused suspicions as to its true intent. When completed, she slipped the men five shillings apiece for their labours, asking each not to say what they had done as the tree was a surprise – for whom, she did not divulge. They looked doubtful – such a large payment surely meant the cover-up of a dastardly deed - but she reassured them with another shilling apiece and they returned to the lake.

A few nervous hours later, as dusk fell and the shutters were closed, the nursemaid was tasked with playing hide and seek with the children; then the two women somehow managed to drag the stiffening body from under the pile of laundry into the deep hole where it was deposited, in a foetal position, at the bottom. Then they lightly covered it with some earth and twigs, again topped off with the pile of laundry; this would be replaced by a tree when one could be appropriated…

It was not until past midnight that the deed, in all its manifestations, had been cleared up and Alice went to bed wondering what she had allowed herself to be an accomplice to. As for Elspeth, she dreamed of being sent to the gallows and hanging from it with her neck broken. Yet she was so relieved that her husband was no more that she was soon sleeping like the babies in the house, a slight, satisfied smile on her lips.

*

In the tavern, the landlord had become surprised by the total diminution of custom from his best client, Giles Burrows. In fact, he had not seen him at all for three days. He had heard him telling Jess that he was going to try and return to Mulberry Hall – which he knew was a dangerous thing to do as he had been privy to the signing of the clandestine deal's conditions – and so wondered whether Sir Walton had taken it upon himself to finish him off if he had discovered him.

What he did not know was that Sir Walton had not been there at that time… yet lack of knowledge in such instances frequently throws up irrational conclusions.

CHAPTER 25

Suspicions, A Twist... & A Proposition

Lady Lucinda did not go to Alice Lodge: it was her rival's domain and she would have felt uncomfortable there. As lady of the estate, she could visit if she wanted, of course, but Sir Walton had made it clear that this was an area that he would rather she did not go, especially as he did not want his wife to inadvertently – or purposefully - witness the amazing pleasures that Alice provided him with. These delights were still not evident with Lucinda, who – despite trying whenever occasionally possible to produce an heir for them both – resolutely did not become pregnant. Sophie and Edward were now each approaching three years old and had become inseparable yet it became obvious that they could not stay cooped up in Alice Lodge forever.

It was inevitable that young Alice would become pregnant again and, in late October, it became obvious that she was indeed once more in that condition. When the news reached Lucinda, she was angry, upset and emotional... and ever more envious of the pretty slave girl her husband was besotted by in her stead.

The tree over the body had started to grow by now and it seemed that the deadly deed had been banished from all history; Giles Burrows' disappearance had been much spoken about in Bakewell but, with no access to the estate or any clues to his whereabouts or last movements, people drew a blank and eventually he was forgotten.

Except by Jess.

In a strange way, she had become quite attached to Giles and, although she knew he was a wastrel, his disappearance meant that now she was living in his house alone; so she reasoned that - if she kept a low profile - she might be able to lay claim to it. With luck, after a while, people would get used to her presence and assume she had inherited or bought it. Subsequently, she took advantage of the opportunity and it was not long before she was expanding her clientele – and had taken in another two 'fallen women' to increase her wealth.

For her part, Elspeth had decided to stay away from the house as it harboured too many memories and any claim to it might lead to awkward questions regarding Giles which might ensnare her; so she pretended to forget it and hoped that no problems would surface.

But, of course, they did. One day a letter arrived at the Hall addressed to her; it was a weighty manuscript and her initial fears were correct when she opened it. By law, it said, she had joint ownership of the property bought by her husband some years before and, upon his disappearance and presumed death, after one year the property had to pass to her as there were no other possible beneficiaries. Except, possibly, a certain Jess Rigby. This shocked Elspeth: she had known the girl when at the Hall - she had been moody, lazy and predatorial, always trying to ensnare Jack who, as a loyal, upright and religious-minded stable-lad had had no interest in her and complained of her advances to both Elspeth and Sir

Walton. In fact, it was through Mrs. Burrows – as she had still been titled at that time - that the girl had eventually been sacked. So this was the harlot's revenge, she feared: the girl had obviously made a point of finding out weaknesses, secrets, rumours and scandal and was well aware that she might throw some unpleasant allegations Elspeth's way, so exposing the Hall's secrets to the detriment of her, Sir Walton, Tobias, Alice and their children.

The easiest option, then, was to cut any losses and sell it; yet she had always surmised that Giles had bought the house with money embezzled over the years from Sir Walton's food and drink allowance when he had been his butler in Bakewell - a fact which might well come up during the legal proceedings. Should they ask how such an apparently impecunious and spendthrift man had managed to afford such a pleasant, if tiny, property, she would be pushed to answer. So she filled in the forms as evasively as she could, stating that she would indeed like to sell the place and wish to invest the proceeds for when she was too old to work. Then she waited for a response.

*

It soon came – and its contents infuriated her.

To her horror, she found that Giles had used the house as collateral for a loan to subsidise his wayward spending but now that he was presumed dead the bank wanted their money back – or for her to preferably sell the property - which would only just cover his debt. However, at the time of his death, he had had been co-habiting with a certain Jess Rigby who had made a claim of fifty pounds against the amount: this threw Elspeth into a state of prolonged anger, which those at the house had never before seen in such a usually passive woman. Yet her sense of shame at the man she had married all those years ago in good – if unsure – faith only made her secret affection for Tobias deeper; for this, of course, she was grateful… and wished all the more to marry him and make her relationship with him legal – and the birth of their son, Edward. But then, to make matters worse, she then received a note from Jess Rigby, delivered anonymously during the night, stating that she knew all about Sir Walton's child with Alice and hers with Tobias; furthermore, she suspected that her lover had been 'done in' as she put it - and all truth and speculation would be revealed if she did not get her fifty pounds hush money. In addition, she had fallen pregnant and stated that it was obviously Giles' child, so an extra fifty pounds would help to bring it up.

Knowing the girl's flirtatious manner, Elspeth was fairly sure that any child's parentage could not be confirmed: it was just another ruse for more money. So after some discussion with Tobias, they came up with a plan: she would keep the house and pay the outstanding amount somehow. She replied to the lawyers proclaiming this decision – but carefully made no mention of Jess Rigby: it was not a moment to rock the boat – that could come later and she would arrange it herself. Furthermore, she did not wish to involve Alice or Sir Walton – not yet, anyway; the tempting idea of murdering Jess Rigby as well was not an option as it would be too obvious – the lawyers knew all about the girl anyway. She sensed, though, that Jess knew she was on shaky ground, too, hence the threatening letter… and it was this which had prompted the main part of their plan. It was a gamble and might mean the exhaustion of their savings… but the benefits would be worth it if their connivance bore fruit…

Knowing now where the girl was living, Elspeth had decided to face fact with presumption. But first, she had to prepare the ground...

The next morning, she concocted a meeting with Lady Lucinda on the pretext of ordering her some new finery for an upcoming ball at Lord and Lady Melwick's house some fifteen miles and three months distant. She got on well with Lucinda: they had both come from lowly birth and an uneasy female bond had been established between them. In Elspeth's mind, she had a hunch... and if it was what she surmised, then it was time to tease the possibility. So, in the course of the conversation, she asked Lucinda if there had been any hope regarding the conception of a child.

Lucinda looked forlorn at the question and tearfully confided that she felt Sir Walton would try to divorce her soon if she did not produce the heir which was now her only reason for being at Mulberry Hall. Heartened by this disclosure, Elspeth posed the question as to whether Lucinda had ever thought of adopting a baby under the pretence of it being her own; it was no secret that Lucinda seldom saw Sir Walton and sexual couplings were of a similar paucity, so the emotional gravity of two women who could talk to one another about such things she felt to be a strong card.

"What are you suggesting?" Lucinda darted at Elspeth.

"I mean, milady, that if I could perhaps find you a baby in a few months' time... you could start to pretend, you know, that it was yours. All you need to do is play increasingly tired and emotional from now on ... and we could gradually make it look as if you were about to, well... give birth."

A flicker of a smile crossed Lucinda's face. "Do you think I could get away with that?" she asked flatly.

"Well… why not? I can create an ever-expanding belly for you to wear under all your clothes… a little white-ish make-up to make you look peevish… frequent trips to the privy…"

Lucinda laughed; it was the first time in ages she had seen her do so, Elspeth noted. "But he would want to be there at the birth," she protested.

"I'm sure that – if he was not away in London or Jamaica on a ruse or something – which we could perhaps concoct… that he would return home a happy man -with an heir awaiting him."

There was a pause. Then: "What if it's a girl? He wants a son."

"That is something we shall have to pray for but… well, if it's a girl then we'll just have to try again."

"Which would keep me here another nine months longer."

"Exactly."

"Mrs. Burrows – you are a disgrace! But a wonderful one!" and clasped her to her chest. "I think it's my only hope… and I can never get him away from Alice so at least I'd be occupied – without any of the pain and discomfort of having a *real* child of my own!"

"As far as the world is concerned, milady, it would be your son, your flesh and your blood."

Lucinda suddenly went quiet, a look of burgeoning triumph on her face. "Mrs. Burrows, you are an amazing woman. Thank you. I hereby request you do all you can to make it happen."

"There is just one thing, milady…"

A dark cloud passed over her sunny face for an instant: "What's that?"

"I will need some remuneration – for the real mother, not me, of course…"

"Of course, of course… How much? Would fifty pounds be enough for the mother?"

"There is a lot to arrange… so, perhaps seventy-five pounds?"

"Why not? It's not my money… but if it keeps Sir Walton happy and me here, it's a drop in his ocean. So a hundred, if needs be!"

"I imagine that would be more than sufficient, milady," Elspeth agreed, betraying more than a hint of relief in her voice. "For now, though, just give me seventy-five pounds, if you can, and the rest when I have concluded a deal."

"Then, let's do it! At last – a bit of intrigue…" and she giggled profusely as she went to the end of the room, took out a small key from a chain around her neck and unlocked a small secret drawer in what looked like an ordinary marquetry chest. She took out a small coffer which Elspeth could just see despite Lucinda's back being turned towards her; she counted out the money, closed and locked the chest and returned, dropping the bills into Elspeth's hand. "Good luck," she said as she did so.

Elspeth curtsied and left, a happy woman in one sense and a worried one in another. Now she had to actually put the plan into action, which both scared and delighted her. For her, the best part was that, without Sir Walton knowing, she could repay him for all the good things he had done for her.

She just hoped that her hunch was correct.

CHAPTER 26

A Shady Deal, A Meeting...

& A Delicate Situation

The next day, Elspeth went into Bakewell with Tobias on the pretext of ordering various necessities for her and Tobias' work; it was market day and the town was busy, so the tavern would be full and she thus expected Jess would not only be there but busy, too... she waited outside for a while, hardly daring to enter the rowdy, bawdy atmosphere which was always even more rumbustious, cat-calling and loud on market days. Tobias had left her to busy himself with the market's offerings, knowing that his presence might attract too much attention and ruin Elspeth's plan.

She took a deep breath to summon courage... then entered the tavern.

It was gloomy and smoky, which contrasted violently with the bright day outside; the room was busy and various bar-girls and harlots – often one and the same, she haughtily reminded herself – were weaving in and out of the throng, pitchers, tankards of beer and wines adhering to the waving trays as they plied their way around the tables. Laughter and jollity thickened the tobacco-stained air further as she peered to pick out her quarry. Her eyes tilted to the top of the stairs where the upper floor saw most of the lucrative business; a slight red-headed girl was coming down the stairs in a flouncy fashion on the arm of a bucolic man who could have been her grandfather, his unsure steps due, she surmised, not only to a surfeit of grog but exhaustion at what he had just been pushing his tired old body to do.

Jess waved goodbye to him as he stumbled to the door, her face instantly losing its girlish grin as she turned away, the deed done, the potential money pocketed and a look of instant disdain on her face. Then she noticed Elspeth, the only female in the tavern with any hint of propriety, and her face fell. Elspeth glared at her and made towards her.

"What can I fetch for you, madam?" Jess asked frostily as Elspeth bore down on her; "A glass of sherry, perhaps?" suffused with a faint sneer which instantly reminded Elspeth of Giles.

"I need to talk to you urgently," Elspeth whispered, not without a hint of pressing malice. "I have a proposition for you." As she said this, her eyes dropped to the girl's waistline... yes, she was reasonably sure her hunch was correct.

"And what sort of proposition would that be?" Jess asked saucily, in the manner of coquettishly propositioning a male client.

"I believe you need money," she said, then added, "... now that your main source is no more."

The girl's face darkened. "Look, Mrs. Burrows," she said quietly but with a ferocity that startled her, "All I want is that house and the money. Me and Giles were happy, but now he's gone – and I think you had something to do with it." Elspeth kept cool, which was easy as the comment had chilled her to the bone.

"We don't need to do this through lawyers," she said stiffly lest anyone else heard; "I want to help you as much as me."

"I don't believe *that*," Jess riposted. "Apart from the money I want from you to keep me quiet, there's nothing I want from you. Or that I can do for you."

Elspeth thought quickly. "Not even the house itself – as well as the money?" she said even more quietly, as a loud guffaw and licentious laughter interrupted the conversation. Then, she added, "…and a way of getting a home for your unborn child?"

Jess shot her a filthy look. Then she leaned into Elspeth's face and hissed, "My child is *my* business!"

Elspeth took a deep breath, then leaned to her and whispered: "Indeed it is – but it's obvious you're in trouble, Jess; you have no leg to stand on regarding my ex-husband, or the house, and you know it; you obviously need to get this agreed quickly before your pregnancy shows because then you won't be able to work due to … well, you won't be in a position to do so, will you? Much as it pains me for what you did with my ex-husband, I want to help you in case the child is yours by him."

"Might be, might not," she stated carelessly.

The landlord was suddenly calling Jess over, demanding she stopped talking and got back to work. Jess lowered her voice and said, "I get some time off between clients in an hour or so… I'll meet you at my house."

"*Your* house?" Elspeth said pointedly; "For the moment, Jess, the house is still Giles's… which means – as his wife when it was purchased – I am first in line to keep it and will continue to be unless you help me. And – as I said – it will also help you. I'll meet you there shortly."

Jess gave her a final, vindictive look which threatened much but equally meant that she knew she needed the help Elspeth had offered.

"All right," she said, begrudgingly; "See you in half an hour. My next client won't take long – he never does." And she strutted off. Elspeth left as fast as she could and gulped in the fresh air outside which, although tainted with the dung of horses and the market nearby, smelled far sweeter than that of the tavern.

*

Elspeth sought out Tobias, who was in discussion with a local butcher, haggling over prices for the sale of a number of sheep, chickens and other livestock which looked on dispassionately, not realising their fate was being discussed. The men struck a bargain as Elspeth approached and the butcher tipped his hat to her as she arrived, saying, "Afternoon, Mrs. Burrows."

For a moment, being caught out by hearing her married name, which seemed so distant and loaded with fear, she replied, "Good afternoon, Mr. Hardy; trying to fleece my butler again, I see," as she laughed to sweep away the memory. The man laughed back and he and Tobias shook hands whereupon Tobias gave the man their agreed price. "Sold, then, Mr. Tobias; I'll go and get the receipt made up and you can pay me the rest when I deliver the animals to Mulberry Hall after butchering tomorrow." He disappeared into a nearby building and Elspeth recounted her discourse with the slippery Jess. Tobias frowned; "I hope you haven't told her too, much, Elspeth. Do you think she'll play?"

"I don't think she has a choice."

"Hmmm."

"Anyway, I'll find out soon. She wants me to meet her in what she calls 'her' house."

"The cheek of it," Tobias noted. Then: "Do you want me nearby in case she does something silly?"

"What can she do? She hasn't got a leg to stand on." She lowered her voice: "And even if I did lose the house and a lot of money, it still helps us and gets Lady Lucinda out of an awkward situation. Which further helps us, too."

Tobias nodded. "Let's hope so."

With that, Elspeth made for the house which, despite still being legally half hers, she had not been near for quite some time…

CHAPTER 27

A Sticky Situation & An Acquiescence

Elspeth waited behind the corner of a building almost opposite her previous home so that she could not be seen awaiting Jess; the less they were observed together, the better. Her house and the ones around it seemed more dilapidated than she remembered and the filth in the unmade road sent a shudder down her spine; had she really lived here with that ghastly man? She had not realised his unsuitability for her at the time they married, of course – it was Tobias who had latterly made her blindingly aware of that. So she had lived here, less than a half mile from Sir Walton's previous home which, although pleasant, had not been big enough to allow her to live in it – only Giles, a cook and a maid. Things were the other way around, now, she reflected; it was she who was living in relative splendour and comfort at Mulberry Hall with the man she loved, however circuitously... but she really *had* lived here, she mused, going to Sir Walton's house every day whilst Giles lived in comfort. What a hovel hers had become since she left. She shuddered again. Then she was aware of someone approaching... it was not Jess, though, but a young-ish man of obvious poverty whose inability to keep his probably one set of clothes clean cast a pall over his otherwise youthful appearance. She watched as he looked around furtively and then, seeing no-one, knocked on the front door. After no reply, she heard him say, "Jess? Are you there, Jess? It's me, Benjamin…" hearing no reply, he went back the way he came and disappeared. A thought suddenly struck Elspeth: was Jess using the house – her house – for further dissolute earnings – and on top of the work she was doing in the brothel above the tavern? Jess was a very needy girl, she surmised… or desperate… or just a slattern. Now she had even more evidence should she need it: and her spirits rose again.

*

Lady Lucinda was reading in the library when Sir Walton returned. He had been out hunting and she could tell by the way he stomped around that he had probably not managed to bag anything, which always put him in a bad mood. So for once she decided not to greet him in her usual wifely way – not that it was often reciprocated – and allow him to get over his annoyance with Alice. For that, she was at least grateful; whereas she only perpetuated his sour moods, Alice always erased them and he was pleasanter for the rest of the day than he would otherwise have been.

She had mulled over the plan that her housekeeper, Elspeth, had unexpectedly presented to her the day before, which had grown in importance within her so much so that already she was almost believing she was pregnant - with the idea, at least, if not the child itself! It would solve so many problems if the subterfuge succeeded. She was happier, too, as her father would be delighted at the news, however dishonest: he had been particularly stroppy the last time he had visited the Hall and found that she was still not with child, fearing for his business as if that was also part of the reproductive agreement.

The door opened and Alice came in; they both acknowledged each other, a mutual frost pervading the air between them, although Alice's was more due to Lucinda's opinion of her than the other way around; but why was Alice not with Walton, copulating away his bad mood, Lucinda wondered? Was he going off her? That would certainly not help her predicament, she recognised: if her husband suddenly wanted sex with his wife then her subterfuge would quickly be blown! It was something else she had to think about: she needed to contrive more excuses to keep him away from her when her fake pregnancy was announced.... Alice went to a cabinet and took out a book, explaining quickly that she and Walton wanted to share new knowledge together and gave a knowing smile which even Lucinda found disarming – it was so difficult to despise this girl as she wished to... They exchanged final pleasantries and Alice left with the book, which apparently concerned a discourse on the etiquette of different races, which Lucinda found strange; for her, books on useful practicalities like dress design, cooking, medicines and nature were more to her taste. Product design and subsequent new methods of manufacturing, too: yet it was hard to keep up with these developments as, in this fecund time of industrial revolution, by the time one book had been printed explaining new processes and products, superior innovations had already taken their place.

Then it struck her that Alice was reading books which were more cerebral than the ones she liked: Walton obviously adored Alice for her brain as well as her body and there was nothing she could do to change that. She realised once again that, quite apart from her inability to reproduce, he obviously found her boring. The frost subsequently returned.

*

Elspeth was suddenly aware of Jess' arrival and when the door was opened she quickly moved right in behind the girl so it could not be closed without her on the other side of it. Jess was somewhat surprised at her sudden presence, as much as Elspeth was by the untidiness of the room she found herself in. When she had lived there with Giles, it was a home – simple but clean: now it was a mess. It was not clean, either – perhaps the rooms upstairs were more welcoming for Jess' clients, but she doubted it; above all, an aroma of damp dirt, stale food and sex pervaded the fusty atmosphere.

Not wishing to stay any longer than necessary, she came straight to the point. "Jess, I know what you're trying to do and it won't work; I know you well enough from your time at Mulberry Hall – you're a grasping chancer and my stupid ex-husband was taken in by your deb– "

"Where is he?" she interjected aggressively.

"I have no idea – although rumour has it he has gone to America."

"I don't believe you."

"Well, it's none of my business any more. He went with you and spent a debauched life on what were supposed to be our savings – although I believe even they were acquired illegally."

There was a pause. Jess just looked at Elspeth in a cold, hard way and then said starkly: "Did you murder him?" Elspeth had not expected any interrogation and its vindictive bluntness caused her to be flustered by it, giving Jess further confidence to push her theory more harshly:

"You did, didn't you?" Again, that sneer.

"No, of course I didn't. That... that would destroy me completely. It would be a stupid thing to do. As I say, I believe he's fled to America to get away from his debts... his, his... problems... - and *you*, I daresay!"

"You 'dare say'," Jess responded mockingly. "Well, I think you did him in and I'm going to find his body. And when I do, you'll go to the gallows."

Elspeth had found herself completely thrown by this accusation; the belief in her ability to confront this wretched girl was being challenged and it was unnerving her greatly.

She managed to compose herself and just said starkly, "If you can find his body then you're better than I am – I lost him, body and soul, many years ago; you at least had the man I once loved in body. But if you do want to find him, then I suggest you go to America."

Jess just looked at her. Then, she sighed, glanced at the floor for inspiration and said, "So you want to buy my baby... Why? Can't you make one yourself?" Now she was taunting Elspeth and the sneer was again causing her anger to rise.

"No, it is not for me," she said crossly; "It's for a friend."

Another pause, then: "So tell me what you're offering."

"I will take your baby the moment it's born – whether it's male or female. I will give you seventy-five pounds - "

"A hundred."

"I'll see what I can do."

"A hundred or I won't accept – and your 'friend' can keep trying for the baby she wants so much. Probably the man's fault, anyway – usually is."

Elspeth was about to repudiate this but then swiftly realised that it would play into the girl's guile; she could hardly admit that the husband had a child already by someone else or it would reveal the baby's recipient. In fact, it was as if everything Jess said had a hidden meaning, implication, insult or potential trap. So she changed tack: "I was prepared to let you have this house, too," she said. "The way you have kept it, I don't want it any more. So it's seventy-five pounds or I walk away, you lose some easy money and a home and have a starving child off your back forever. It's your decision." Jess just looked at her, so she added, "But I want an agreement *now*."

Jess looked around the room, as if sizing it all up. Then she looked back at Elspeth, shrugged her shoulders and said feebly, "All right."

A surge of relief engulfed Elspeth; she would lose the house but that would solve many other nagging problems. It was also a complete break from her ex-husband. And she had already told Lucinda that it would cost a hundred pounds – money was of no consequence to her – so that she, Elspeth, could start saving again for the house she hoped one day to share with Tobias. It was not a fortune but it was still a very good start...

"When is the baby due?" she suddenly thought to ask.

Jess shrugged. "Dunno. 'Bout six months, I think."

Elspeth nodded, delved into her skirts and brought out a piece of paper, on which the agreement was written and put it in front of Jess. "Here's the agreement; do you have a quill and ink?" Jess looked around, a disdainful laugh playing on her lips. "You must be stupid," she said... "I can't read nor write – so what's the point of quill and ink?"

Another hurdle. Elspeth looked at the fireplace – there were some charred remains in the hearth. She rose and fetched one. "Do you have a mark?" Jess nodded. "That'll do."

"But I don't know what's written there."

"You'll just have to trust me."

That sneer again. "Trust *you*?"

"It's in your interests more than mine. I am losing more than you are gaining."

"Where's the money?"

"I have it about my person."

"Show me."

"Sign first."

The girl moved towards her, almost menacingly, as if she were about to assault her, then took a pace back, snatched the paper, went to a chair – there was no table – kneeled and used the hard seat to scratch her mark. To be fair, Elspeth thought, it was at least a florid and unique symbol. She inspected it, nodded, and before Jess could demand the money, took out a small leather pouch and gave it to her, jangling it to demonstrate its contents. Jess opened it and counted out the amount, nodded and went to sit disconsolately in the chair, her resolve deflated.

It was time for Elspeth to finalise the deal and leave: "Let me know when the baby's due and I will arrange everything," she said hurriedly, and departed. She closed the front door and was pleased to see Tobias a hundred yards away – she had not asked him to be adjacent but was pleased he was there… just in case; he would have gone in to see what Jess might have done to his lady if she had exited first. Elspeth waved at him to hide around the corner; the stakes were too high for Jess to see him as well, which might have made things even more difficult to explain…

The sun was setting as they travelled back to the Hall, a cold wind with a hint of snow lashing their trap as they crossed the valleys and fells; on arrival it was almost dark. Being somewhat windblown, Elspeth tidied herself up and then went quickly to the Great Parlour; she tapped on the door and Lady Lucinda's voice called her to enter. Seeing she was keen to hear any news, Elspeth regaled Lucinda with a slightly redacted explanation of what had happened, glad that Sir Walton was not there – and probably with Alice.

"And how much was the sum involved?" she asked after the narrative had been divulged.

"One hundred pounds, milady," she lied.

"But I only gave you seventy-five pounds."

"Indeed, milady; but having known the girl when she worked here I took an extra twenty-five pounds from my savings; I wanted to make sure I could get an agreement for you and I was right to, as it happened…"

"Hmm. A tidy sum for a wretched girl… I hope she doesn't make too much of it or people will start surmising…"

"Indeed, milady. But I think even she has enough intelligence to realise she will incriminate herself if she does. People will think she stole it from a client – or that's what we could put about; no-one would dare admit to having 'relations' with *that* girl for fear of being compromised."

"You're right – or let's hope so." Then she suddenly looked more urgently and said with a flicker of a smile, "So when is my baby due?"

"Within six months, milady."

"Six months?" Then, sotto voce, "I'd better start padding myself up!"

"It's all in hand, milady."

There was a lull, but Elspeth did not move. Then Lucinda

twigged; "Ah, you're waiting for your extra money – how silly of me," and she went over to the same marquetry cabinet as before and took out the requisite amount.

"Thank you, milady."

"I think it is for me to thank you, Mrs. Burrows."

There was another pause as Elspeth half-turned to go but then looked back at Lucinda. "Milady?"

"Yes?"

"Would you mind at all calling me Elspeth from now on, please?"

"Of course not. But why?"

"Being called Mrs. Burrows reminds me of my husband, milady; and we never got on. Well, not latterly, anyway. I believe he has gone to America."

"Ah. I see. Yes of course. *Elspeth*."

Elspeth left swiftly, her heart pounding, and closed the door behind her. Then she counted the money: to her astonishment she saw that Lady Lucinda had given her fifty pounds, not twenty-five. She felt grateful but guilty; another lie to be kept hidden.

CHAPTER 28

A Lull, A Panic, A Birth...

& A Dastardly Plan

Life continued at Mulberry Hall without much further adventure, except that Alice once more became pregnant; for Lucinda, this was a double-edged sword for, with Alice progressively unable to succumb to Sir Walton's lust, Lucinda had to concoct ever more reasons to repel him on the rare occasions he wanted her.

Elspeth had tidied up all the official hurdles and her house had been paid for, which now legally rested in the grasp of the conniving Jess. Whilst this was a good palliative to the ever more nervous Elspeth, at least that side of things had been settled – or at least that was what she hoped.

After a severe winter with deep snows, roaring fires and much eating and drinking to while away the frozen hours, spring suddenly announced itself, winter's white blanket disappeared and spirits rose in tune with the earlier daily arrival of the sun.

Sir Walton had been happier of late, the news of a legal heir giving him a boost to his demeanour, matched in opposite ways by Lady Lucinda and Elspeth who were the only ones – apart from Tobias, of course – to know of the subterfuge. Elspeth had been busy occasionally enlarging the padding that Lucinda wore about her girth, the only awkward moment being when Sir Walton imbibed a surfeit of claret at Christmas and had wanted to see and touch the pregnant belly of his legal wife. She had only just managed to thwart his advances by the help of Tobias opportunely offering him some crystallised ginger, after which he had fortunately fallen into a deep sleep.

All manner of ostentatiously-purchased baby paraphernalia had by now been obtained: the Hall was soon set for the approaching big day – only the terror that the plan might go horribly wrong playing on the minds of the three main protagonists. On their trips into Bakewell after the snow had melted, Elspeth and Tobias had kept close tabs on Jess' progress; on one visit, they encountered another worry in that the young boy Elspeth had witnessed – Benjamin, who was training to be a clerk – had debauched Jess more than occasionally and so was not unsure that he might be the child's father; yet he looked after Jess in her confinement, which was at least a blessing for the pregnancy – as well as Jess herself and Elspeth's plan.

Elspeth paid a local stable-lad in Bakewell to keep an eye on the house so that when the day of birth was imminent, the oft-present Benjamin could be whisked away on some pretext or another whilst the child was born; then the infant would be swiftly exported away from his true mother's presence as replacement for the incrementally growing padding around Lucinda's nether regions.

Nearly three weeks later, the breathless lad rode to the Hall and garbled the news to Elspeth, who quickly told Lucinda to confine herself whilst she and Tobias rode to

Bakewell to order some supposedly depleted rations for the festivities surrounding the expected child's appearance.

Elspeth went immediately to her erstwhile house whilst Tobias went to a more respectable tavern than the one Jess worked at to bribe a couple of better-dressed ruffians; under Tobias' instructions, they went to the house as watchmen and made a supposed arrest of the hapless Benjamin, accusing him of not paying a gambling debt.

With Benjamin dragged off, Tobias stood guard, wrapped in scarves and a thick, rough and high-collared coat to hide his appearance. The baby – thankfully for the plan, a boy - arrived immediately after: Jess had a difficult birth, her screams of pain only being muffled by swathes of material over her mouth and a few tots of rum to make her discomfort more bearable. The child was suckled by Jess for an hour and then the mess of the birth was cleared up, the baby wrapped in copious blankets, then removed forever from Jess's sources of nourishment for the journey back to Mulberry Hall. Alice, now being seven months pregnant, was by now bearing a small amount of milk and so the need to find, bribe and keep a wet-nurse onside at the Hall was fortuitously avoided.

The baby had been given a finger-lick of gin to make it sleep but by the time they all arrived it was waking up and so was taken to the Lodge where Alice tried to silence the infant before its next perilous journey across the stretch of land between the two buildings and into Lucinda's bed.

As dusk fell, Tobias and Elspeth could be seen taking a large hamper from Alice Lodge to Mulberry Hall, whereupon the baby was deposited into Lucinda's waiting arms and bed; the padding was hidden away to be surreptitiously burned the next day as Lucinda's bogus screams of childbirth pain rent the Hall from top to bottom; Sir Walton had been disbarred from the room due to the 'difficulties' of the baby's birth and grumpily strode up and down until Elspeth reckoned he was tired enough to go in and see his wife and heir.

It would be an awkward few weeks…

*

As for Jess, she soon returned to the tavern, where her clients were glad to see her return; but the experience of childbirth had forced her to see the world as an adult. She had subsequently resolved to use the money wisely and to make what was now essentially her own little house more homely: she would save as much as she could while she was still young and pretty but – being the object of men several times a day – had pledged to never have a regular man living with her in her home, much to the despair of Benjamin, who had hoped to replace Giles: one could have too much of a good thing, she deemed. Also, he would get in the way of her burgeoning plans, for with her new-found relative wealth, she had also gained a sense of revenge: she had worked out who her baby had almost certainly been destined for soon after the pain of looking into her infant's eyes: then it had been whisked away and left her wondering what she had done. This realisation had compelled her – one day - to exact revenge on the people who had taken her baby from her. Like her child, her blackmail plan was in its infancy… but she was in no hurry to enact it.

Not yet, anyway…

CHAPTER 29

The Act's Early Legacy

When the Act for the Abolition of Slavery had passed its final hurdle and become law in 1807, it had presented Sir Walton Grimley with a number of dilemmas: whilst he knew he had done the right thing by supporting the Act, the responsibility of being forced to either free or pay his slaves – perhaps both – had dropped like a ton weight onto his shoulders at the time. He had always known it might ruin his business but after it had happened the full force of its probable outcome had appeared devastating. Of course, its effects would not happen overnight but the extra stresses, obligations and deliberations suddenly made him feel sick with worry. Fortunately, he had already come up with a plan, although now its necessary execution was staring him in the face. Perhaps thinking that it had taken so long to get to this point already – the Act had been going in and out of the Commons since before 1797 – he had perhaps believed it would never happen in his lifetime. But it had - and rocked him to the core.

Yet sometimes the predictions of future calamity are unfounded and although the Act was passed, those who had slaves were allowed to keep them. His, at least, were well looked after but he had wondered how his other slave-owner acquaintances would fare. With a surge of pride and altruism, therefore, he had recently decided to make further improvements for his workers and started to pay them, which - whilst putting a greater financial burden on his shoulders - he wagered he could just afford, such was the high price of sugar at the time. So, for the moment at least, he had satisfied his conscience, his finances... and also retained his workforce. Yet he had not told anyone of his munificence – not even his own family. So he just bathed in the warm glow of his good actions and sat tight...

BOOK TWO

1822

CHAPTER 30

The Children Become Adults...

Fifteen years had subsequently passed without further conflict, intrigue or complication within the Mulberry Hall estate. With the end of the Napoleonic Wars in 1815, a new mood of optimism had swept the country and by 1822 a feeling of enlightenment, liberation and tolerance had become palpable. As a result, Sir Walton had felt ever keener to make a stand and release his daughters, Sophie and Jemima - now both stunningly beautiful young women of nearly eighteen and fifteen respectively - from the restrictions of incarceration at Alice Lodge and into the wider population; however, despite his good status as a politician, he did not wish to rock the boat too much for - should his dalliance with Alice and their resultant children become too well-known - his opponents in the Commons would almost certainly twist this fact into a damning indictment of his lust and double standards should they wish to do so.

Fortunately for Lady Lucinda and Elspeth, Sir Walton had swallowed the ruse of his son's birth without question; indeed, he was generally delighted with his now fifteen-year-old son, Sebastian, whom he and Lucinda loved deeply despite his tendency to be sneering and curt on occasion – although this was more apparent to Elspeth than anyone else. However, he also had a lustful propensity towards women which, even at his young age, seemed to be uncontrollable. Two parlour-maids had recently been paid off due to his successful advances into their nether regions, which Lucinda had kept from her husband as she knew all too well where his genes had almost certainly come from – as, again, did Elspeth. This also put a damper on Sophie and Jemima, only being allowed out of the lodge's confines when Lucinda and - particularly - Sebastian were away. Yet they wanted to be young adults and the confines of Alice Lodge were stifling. So as Sophie's eighteenth birthday approached it had been decided that some latitude should be granted: she must have the chance 'to make her way in the world', whatever the 'slings and arrows of noble misfortune' - much to the annoyance of Lucinda, who wanted Sebastian to be the principal child. Inevitably, this slight freedom would also be applied to Jemima when it was propitious to do so and Lucinda was forced to consent. Yet her annoyance was becoming less relevant as attitudes were changing and most new servants just accepted the occasional sighting of two young women of colour without questioning their provenance, however unusual it was at the time: and Sebastian was the heir to the estate, so was afforded greater respect anyway... and they had quite enough work to do at Mulberry Hall to keep them busy and away from speculative tittle-tattle – as well as Sebastian's roving eye...

Tobias and Elspeth's son, Edward – now also fifteen years old - was a quiet lad, unlike the more expressively outward girls borne by Alice or the rowdier Sebastian; he did not need telling to be discreet because he was of that countenance by nature and although a strikingly good-looking youth he paid little attention to his pretty neighbours, accepting that he was a servant. So he stuck with the social attitudes of the time and, the two girls being potential aristocracy, he treated them as such. He was also more likely to be found in the library studying than outside whenever he had the time to do so and the words 'industrious' and 'studious' were the epithets most used to describe him, much to the distress of a young parlour-maid whose carnal lust for him could not compete with his desire for knowledge. He had become a footman at fourteen, melding into the daily routines of the Hall without comment, and although he was generally assumed to be the son of Tobias and Elspeth, it was a taboo subject and was neither mentioned nor discussed.

In Parliament, additions to the Abolition of Slavery Act 1807 were afoot; these further changes would abolish slavery not only in Britain but all its colonies. Whilst Sir Walton felt he had done more than any slave-owner to better the lives of his charges in Jamaica, he was again pushing for this final act, called The Slavery Abolition Act - which would obliterate the practice for good. As ever, its passage through Parliament was a tortuous affair and would ultimately not eventually enter the statute books for several more years so Sir Walton found himself spending more time away from Mulberry Hall than ever as he tried to get the bill enacted. However, this had given him the opportunity to parade his son both in London and over a wider local area, his national fame enhancing his local popularity. Lady Lucinda, too, had been a help in his politicking, which had the dual effect of allowing her to show off her sparkling personality to the London elites and also leave Alice and her two children behind - those two constant reminders of her second-class state. Her only sadness was that her father, Lancelot, had expired a year before: the good news for her, on the other hand, was that as all the Mulberry Hall building work had been completed some years previously, she had persuaded Sir Walton to release Josiah Prentice from his job as the Mulberry Hall estate manager to run what was now her thriving business, only occasionally needing to return to Wirksworth herself to guide the company's progress under him, which she hardly needed to do as he took to managing it so well. Being so extensively occupied in Wirksworth, therefore, Josiah's lack of being needed at Mulberry Hall meant he did not see anyone or anything there for long periods. Yet Lucinda had a secret ulterior motive: since her wedlock with Sir Walton and its many shortcomings, she had wanted to keep this fine young man within her grasp as a kind of stop-gap if her marriage declined further or terminally; hence the appointment. Yet any chance of this had been put on hold since the 'birth' of Sebastian...

Jess, too – who had learned much and surmised even more over the years - was keeping an eye on the best time to pounce, restricted only by her thriving business as a madam in what had been Giles and Elspeth's house...

In short, it seemed that the past would, at some time, catch up with the present with possibly explosive results.

CHAPTER 31

An Unexpected Meeting

One fine summer's day, Josiah Prentice had returned from Wirksworth to Mulberry Hall in order to discuss with Lady Lucinda some changes he wished to make to the running of Noncey & Daughter, as her business had now been renamed. On arrival, however, he was informed that both Sir Walton and Lady Lucinda were in London. By now, it was not unsurprising that most of the servants had at least had a glimpse or more of both Sophie and Jemima, but any speculation as to parentage or reason for being there was forbidden to be talked about; yet with the master and lady away and the servants either oblivious or uncaring about the occasional sighting, the girls became less cautious about their movements.

Thwarted in his quest to meet Lady Lucinda, Josiah decided to take a stroll around the beautiful lake and follies he had created all those years ago. The sun shone, the bees buzzed and the birds tweeted as he descended the incline and noted that the mulberry tree had grown significantly, its blooming leaves green and healthy. On reaching the lake, he gazed across it and – at the far side – noticed movement. Enjoying the break from work on such a beautiful day, and his curiosity piqued, he walked slowly round the watery expanse; by halfway round, he could see that the movement was from two parasols being twirled and moved, behind which were two figures dressed in white. As he neared the scene, he saw that these were two young girls reading, sitting on filigree iron chairs with a like table between them. They suddenly noticed him and a little squeal of embarrassment wafted over the lake as they turned the parasols across their faces. Not wishing to frighten them, he held up his hands and shouted just loud enough for them to hear, "Please! Don't be afraid! I am Josiah Prentice, master builder and constructor of these works. I am come to see Lady Lucinda but I find she is not here; may I join you for a moment as I take the air for a few minutes?"

A small voice replied: "As long as you are not surprised or demeaned by our appearances, sir, then of course you are very welcome." Unsure what the sweet voice had meant by this, he moved closer. As he arrived, the two parasols parted and two laughing faces were revealed; he instantly understood the meaning of the voice's condition to him but what struck him most was the indescribable beauty of both the young women before him. One in particular, whom he presumed to be the elder, was so striking that his knees momentarily failed him and he nearly collapsed into the lake. At this, they laughed even more; he bowed and smiled back... and knew immediately that he was in love.

*

After Josiah had heard the news that Lady Lucinda was away for the season, Tobias and Elspeth had wondered how they could further help him, this pleasant man who had spent so much time building the magnificent Hall, Alice Lodge, the lake, follies and other beauties, so when he stated he would like to inspect his work by wandering down to the lake, they had been quite happy to let him, not knowing that Sophie and Jemima were there too. It was over an hour later that they wondered why he had not returned but presumed he had left to go back to Wirksworth – or at least an inn nearby before his long trek home.

In London, Sir Walton Grimley was tied up in the Commons, leaving Lady Lucinda alone to enjoy an At Home event with the Marquess of Devizes, a voluminous woman in body and personality with a voice to match; she had heard that Lucinda's husband was vocal in stopping slavery and raised the impertinent question as to what he would do for a workforce in Jamaica – and the resulting diminution of funds - if he had to pay people, which could so easily affect his considerable fortune and, therefore, his social standing. She then made a deprecating remark about people 'in trade' taking over the country: as someone so immersed in the iron business, Lucinda found this a slur too far, promptly made her excuses and left. Yet what she realised in that short encounter was that there were tiers of snobbery that even she was guilty of: the aristocracy, the trading classes, artists, service, peasants... and now even race; her husband was at least accepting of people's colour even if, through current necessity, he had generally kept it quiet. Yet the implied insult that she was a trader who had been lucky to marry into the aristocracy was something which piqued and angered her and she resolved there and then to support her husband more vocally in his quest to finally abolish slavery, even if it did mean a deeper acceptance of Alice: in fact, she would do all she could to increase her own prowess as an industrialist to support him even if her husband lost all his wealth.

Future events would, however, challenge this pledge –

but for very unexpected reasons.

*

Josiah recovered his poise, stated his name and position again and fell into easy conversation with the two young women, who seemed extremely pleased to be talking with someone else – and an apparently successful young man, no less - a novelty! - which their intense incarceration over the years had mostly precluded. Correspondingly, they were slightly gauche but their genuine warmth of emotion and feeling was as enlightening to Josiah as that which he felt he was exuding towards them. He realised he may have caught sight of one of them when much younger as he was building not just the Hall and the lake but Alice Lodge, too, and suddenly the penny dropped that this elder one was rumoured to be the child of Sir Walton and his once slave-girl Alice. The other child must have followed after he had left the Hall to run Lady Lucinda's business; he inwardly cursed the ability of the aristocracy to bend life to their will but also concluded that, without them and their attendant secrecies, he would not be either so well-to-do now nor meeting such delightfully unusual young women.

They had introduced themselves as Sophie and Jemima and also volunteered their ages - eighteen and fifteen respectively. He could see that the books they were reading were of a light but semi-literary bent – probably each a love story. As the afternoon progressed, he felt that he should leave them alone but found himself unable to do so, as if a magnet was attracting him to Sophie and she to him. At one point, a footman arrived asking whether they would like some refreshment, and a pot of tea and some excellent cakes duly arrived which complemented the proceedings further and happily lengthened Josiah's stay.

A little later, Jemima tactfully excused herself, leaving Sophie and Josiah alone. A palpable aura of trust and attraction was so evident that soon they were broaching the subject of hopefully seeing each other again. Josiah knew that there was a nineteen years age difference between them but this seemed irrelevant as they were getting on so well; nevertheless, he felt duty bound to tell Sophie this, to which she just said, "Dear sir, that just means you can teach me nineteen years' worth of knowledge without my having to bother!" her glistening perfect white teeth a counterpoint to her dark complexion framed by her white dress and parasol. The conversation continued in this vein for a while longer, Sophie eventually concluding to herself that this man was certainly one to be considered for wedlock (an emotion which Josiah had also concluded but could not yet dare proclaim for fear of compromising this unexpected situation). Eventually, as the shadows lengthened, she asked where he was staying that night as the evening would soon draw in and he had not yet eaten. In his reverie with the delightful Sophie, neither necessity had crossed his mind so when they walked back to the Hall, he was delighted when she invited him for supper in Alice Lodge.

Yet propriety being what it was at that time in the early nineteenth century, Josiah knew he could not spend any longer with Sophie than a light supper and he eventually - reluctantly – made his excuses to leave. They both vowed to see each other again when he returned for more business dealings at Mulberry Hall or to discuss events regarding the Wirksworth factory and its products with Lady Lucinda. In addition, he asked Sophie if she would discreetly send word to him on Lucinda's return after the London Season: having discovered this dusky butterfly whose every tone, movement and uttering enhanced any sweet emotion he had ever sensed was thus someone whom he could not bear to let go. Sophie happily agreed to the request, discreetly harbouring similar sentiments - this amusing, competent and successful good-looking beau who had unexpectedly dropped into her lap.

They eventually parted, each privately wishing that the courteous bows they gave each other could be replaced by kisses but which neither dared admit lest the spell be broken. Josiah returned to his cart and drove off down the drive, the last rays of a golden-tinged cloud burnishing his thoughts as the beauty of the day crowded in on him. It was only when he reached the track where the palatial arch denoting the entrance to the Mulberry Hall estate ended that he suddenly realised he had no idea where he was going to stay.

CHAPTER 32

Anticipation...

& A Surprise Revelation

Lucinda's child, Sebastian, was completely unaware of his provenance. He wondered why he seemed so different to his parents and many were the days when Lucinda wished she had not entered into the arrangement. However, the social advantages appeared to outweigh the pitfalls and so her life had improved immeasurably; she and Walton had gained a mutual point of focus together and the ease of enjoying high society as a lady and mother was most useful to her. Yet Sebastian's behaviour and lack of ambition were a constant concern and he was also running up gambling debts in both Derby and London, disappearing for days on end; yet, to her and Walton – although not mutually discussed – for the moment, at least, his existence was of benefit to both.

At around the same time, Jess was deciding that it was an ever more propitious time to pounce but was finding it difficult to formulate a plan which would not also incriminate her. Yet fate has a way of progressing events that are not always apparent at the time and a week or so later – not long after accepting that her looks were flagging

- she had decided to manage rather than experience her licentious tendencies by engaging two further young girls as harlots to work in her house and so expand her clientele. As fate would have it, she also found herself in the town on market day when she spied an obviously well-to-do young man and, as was her wont, sidled up to him to 'accidentally' gain his attention.

The man was instantly attracted to this still appealing young woman and decided to oblige her come-ons, whereupon she guided him back to her house. He was a good lover and although he was unexpectedly gruff for his class she found herself uncharacteristically enjoying the closeness of his person, unlike the many others whom had become routine; he seemed to have a presence and an aroma which attracted her too so, after the event, she made it obvious that she would like to pleasure him again. This he acceded to and he then disappeared back into the town.

*

A month or so later, Sophie received word of Sir Walton and Lady Lucinda's return and took no time in passing on their expected arrival day to Josiah, who subsequently planned to attend the estate the day after under the pretence of demonstrating and selling new wares and – of course – ensuring that his buildings did not need any maintenance: he also connived that this could become a handy excuse to return more frequently to see his dusky lover.

Sophie had not told her mother, Alice, of her sudden infatuation with Josiah, lest she tried to dissuade her; being a confined young woman who was now itching to get out into the world, this charming and talented builder was not only a prospective key to that escape but also the type she had always imagined in her dreams, such as they were.

She mused that, if she married him, then she could live far away from Mulberry Hall and arrive in Wirksworth as a total stranger rather than being this ghost-like figure hiding away in the rooms of Alice Lodge. She would miss her mother, of course, but like a caged bird now wanted to be free of all restrictions - even if living in Wirksworth would bring her into more frequent and awkward contact with Lady Lucinda: from a very early age she had realised that there was a frost between her mother and Lady Lucinda so had avoided the latter as much as possible. Yet she was too naïve to understand the reason; as far as she knew, her father had disappeared long ago and had never realised she spoke to him nearly every day, despite the languorous looks between her mother and Sir Walton and subsequent frequent disappearances at the same time. Jemima was even less aware…

The day came when the Grimleys arrived back and Sophie was becoming ever more excited about the prospect of seeing Josiah again the day after. She had anticipated greeting them all by taking tea in the Great Parlour to exchange gossip but found neither her mother nor Sir Walton there when she did so; the only inhabitant was a very annoyed, discomfited and unconversational Lucinda whose apparent disdain for her was even cooler than usual.

Sophie took tea and made pleasantries but realised that there was no point in trying to defrost Lucinda and eventually left. As she passed into the main hall, Sir Walton jauntily entered the hallway, his cheeks ruddy and sporting a countenance diametrically opposed to the person she had just left. His jolly mood was infectious and after a few moments catching up with their London season's events she decided to tell him of the visit of Josiah the next day. Not wishing to go back into the Great Parlour, she asked him to come into the library with her; unsure of what she would tell him, he acquiesced and they sat down together.

"So, what is it you wish to tell me, my pretty Sophie?" Sir Walton enquired. She recounted the meeting with a fine young man she met quite unexpectedly by the lake and that they had subsequently spent several hours together. His face grew more and more inquisitive and as the tenor of her tale advanced, a slight smile pervaded his lips.

"And who is this young man, pray? And why was he down by the lake? If he was trespassing…"

"No! No, he came to see you but you weren't here. You know him well, Sir!"

"So who is he, then?"

"Your master builder and the man running Lady Lucinda's business! Josiah Prentice."

Sir Walton's face fell. "Oh," he said.

Sophie was confused; "Sir, why do you look so glum? You should be happy for me."

He took her hand. "Dear Sophie. I want you to be happy but do remember that he has not asked you for your hand yet and you must get to know him better over a period of time. One meeting is not enough."

"There will be another," she said cautiously, then: "He's coming here tomorrow - to see you and Lady Lucinda."

"Ah… well, that's fine… yes. Good… very good." Yet she could tell there was still a reluctance to endorse her happiness.

He looked at the floor and then back at her. "But… if you *were* to marry him… Er, it might cause some complications if… *if* you married him."

"Why, Sir?"

"Because when you fly the nest I would still wish to see you from time to time with your mother."

"But Josiah is the manager of Lucinda's company."

"Indeed." Another pause, then his voice dropped: "But one day I will probably divorce Lady Lucinda and never see her again."

It was Sophie's turn to look confused. "But why, Sir?" she muttered.

"She married me under false pretences as I, I suppose… did her. At least I got an heir out of her, but…"

"Well, why is that of import to me, Sir?"

"Because it would be difficult… what with Josiah being in her employ … and seeing her and you together over the years when you meet her and have children of your own."

"Children of my own? What's the issue with that?"

"Because I would be the grandfather to them." By now, Sophie was completely confused. "Grandfather? How?"

"Because I am your father."

CHAPTER 33

An Admission, A Plan

& A Dark Deed Uncovered

The next day, Josiah arrived at Mulberry Hall. A footman announced his presence and Sir Walton went out to meet him. Sophie – impatiently awaiting her intended suitor – had seen him appear as his covered cart passed Alice Lodge and, seeing this handsome man again thrilled her senses. Yet as she traversed the greensward between the two buildings, the voice of Sir Walton resounded again around her head: "I am your father!" The news had both relieved and daunted her, especially with the other intention he had betrayed: Sophie did not mind that he wished to leave Lady Lucinda – in fact, it pleased her - but, as the only one who currently knew, she felt burdened by the news. She was, though, thoroughly elated: she had a father! Strangely, the admission had neither shocked nor surprised her – it was as if there had always been someone there who was a father figure but it had never crossed her mind that it was actually Sir Walton. Yet now she did know, she was ecstatic. As for the fact that she and he were of different hues, this neither bothered her nor seemed relevant.

THE SLAVE-OWNER'S DILEMMA

She had gone to Alice after her emotions had calmed and quietly but excitedly told her that she now knew what had hitherto been a family secret – of which Jemima was obviously the subsequent part; Alice just said, "Walton – well, your papa, now! – always said he would tell you both after your respective eighteenth birthdays and I am so pleased he has now done so to you: it has made us an even closer family than I knew we were already. But it is not wise to tell Jemima yet, please – I don't think she is quite old enough yet to understand the social implications." Sophie accepted this, but admitting her infatuation with Josiah to her mother was something she doubted her father had had the time to impart since their meeting in the library the night before; she was therefore unsure how Alice would react when she did so. Instinctively, she felt that perhaps this was not the moment and the news would better come from Sir Walton; but to her growing panoply of emotions would now be added guilt, for although Jemima had teased Sophie regarding her feelings towards Josiah but quite rightly withheld that knowledge from anyone, she – Sophie - was now hiding the most important family secret from Jemima!

All these admissions, secrets and hopes had suddenly crowded in on her: if her hopeful romance with Josiah did lead to marriage - and therefore the leaving of Mulberry Hall - she would now miss her father even more. His concern regarding the Noncey business and her potential awkward position within it added to that: she would also be mostly stuck within the environs of the same home in Wirksworth with the man she loved - but also the owner of the foundry who would be a constant brooding cloud.

As she reached the door to enter the Hall, she also had

the sudden realisation that Lady Lucinda might well proscribe her mother, Alice, from seeing her; so as she entered the building, her eyes were moist with tears. As she was about to open the Great Parlour door, it opened and Josiah and Sir Walton stepped out. Instantly observing her tearful eyes, Josiah mistook them for pent-up emotion at seeing him and, momentarily forgetting etiquette, bent and kissed her hand.

"I see you must have already met my d- , er, Sophie," Sir Walton almost carelessly stated as Josiah, slightly sheepishly, withdrew a couple of paces, inwardly cursing himself for his forwardness, in that same moment believing that Sir Walton did not yet know of their tryst. So, slightly awkwardly, he stated, "Indeed, Sir; we met some weeks ago when I came here to see you but you were away for the Season and this kind, sweet young lady was good enough to take care of me."

"I'm sure she did," smiled Sir Walton with a hidden wink to Sophie; "A splendid young lady if I say so myself."

"I am in full agreement with you, Sir – a splendid young lady indeed!"

Sophie curtseyed and looked pleadingly at Josiah as Sir Walton walked away to the entrance. He then turned back and said, "Sophie, get Tobias or Miss Shaw to arrange a fine lunch for us three in the dining-room in an hour or so..." then added quietly, "... but don't tell anyone else." This was with reference to Lady Lucinda, Sophie assumed. "Oh, and ask Tobias to inform Lady Lucinda that her manager is here and would like to speak with her – but later this afternoon. I believe she's out riding now, anyway," and he secretly winked at Sophie again as Josiah was now discreetly looking away from them.

THE SLAVE-OWNER'S DILEMMA

Sophie did as she was told and an hour later found herself in the company of Josiah and her father – augmented halfway through by the unexpectedly early appearance of Lady Lucinda who was not best pleased that no-one had informed her of her manager's presence on the premises.

Lady Lucinda's foul mood ensured she soon tired of her familial obligations and curtly asked if she could speak to Josiah privately for a while to discuss business, to which the others – by now keen to leave - acceded. Sir Walton was bored with her company anyway and keen to get back to Alice; being in such a good mood, as he and Sophie left the Great Parlour, leaving Lucinda and Josiah there for discussions, Sophie caught up with her father in the main hall and asked if they could have a quiet word again in the library.

Once there, she admitted in hushed tones that she just knew she and Josiah had fallen in love and if things proceeded well over the next few days, would he agree to its manifestation in marriage as soon as possible? His answer was an ebullient and happy one: "My dear daughter Sophie; last night it was a bit of a shock but now I've seen you together… even under oppressive circumstances…" he added with a nod in Lucinda's direction, "Well, I could tell immediately – you can't take yer eyes off each other! And he's a splendid fellow – always has been… he built all this, of course! You'll make a lovely couple!" Then he dropped his voice: "But I haven't told yer mother – you should do that - but tell her I'm all for it. Let's keep it quiet from everyone else for now, though – especially Lady Lucinda: she'll be furious you're marrying her manager - particularly with all its attendant complications… and when I eventually tell her I'm divorcing her – or at least kicking her out - it'll get even worse. As far as I care, she can live either in Wirksworth or anywhere else as long as it's not here! Your dear mother and I can then live together in the Hall. Josiah I will take on again as my estate manager so he can be here with you. Or Lucinda can stay in Alice Lodge while you live with Josiah in Wirksworth! She'll probably go for that – she'll still be Lady Walton and ... no! A better idea: she can hob-nob with her sort up there, far away from us. In fact, that's what I'll suggest when the time comes. I'll support her, financially of course – until she finds another duke or whatever to sponge off. Then you and Josiah can live *alone* in Alice Lodge and we'll all be here together without her!" And he walked off, humming... Absorbed by his exuberance, Sophie realised she had not told him that Alice already knew of her love for Josiah and was positive about it; she also surmised that, in his happiness, he had forgotten about Jemima's future – or Sebastian's; but she presumed those resolutions could wait. In fact, they would soon become very apparent...

*

Jess, meanwhile, was doing well as the local 'madam' and her increasingly fine clothes due to her endeavours had caused people to regard her as a woman of supposed taste and substance. Whilst her profession was well-known in the town to those that were privy, it also gave her standing as her clientele now consisted of people with influence of whom she could ask favours - and blackmail if necessary – including lawyers, a bank manager, a judge and a local squire or two. One of these was, unexpectedly, the local pastor whose capacious wife had so upset Alice all those years ago when enquiring of her paternity. Jess' girls had been instructed to winkle out – if that was the right word – any scandal, secrets or compromising tittle-tattle regarding anyone ... but especially the gentry or those whose positions might be compromised for money.

And so it was that Sebastian let slip one drunken, lewd night, that he was the son of Sir Walton and Lady Grimley.

Jess had not been the one to whom he had let slip this fact; that belonged to a very pretty girl she had taken on called Polly who could, it had become apparent, talk secrets out of any one of her clients. On being told this news, Jess was in a panic: was this not the young man she had once inveigled into her bed for money? She shuddered at what she might have done but dismissed the fear of this possible truth as a mistake - an anonymous act between two consenting adults and apparently total strangers. Yet it still niggled: but if it was him, it would remain her secret: for now, being the vindictive self that she was, it hardened her resolve for revenge against the Grimley family who had sacked and compromised her, then taken her son. And also, somehow, rid her of Giles, his father, her useful idiot, who had been her best conduit back into Mulberry Hall.

Yet when revenge occludes rationality, details can be overlooked; consequently, it seemed unlikely her plans would turn out as she expected.

CHAPTER 34

A Devious Postulation, A Singer & A Decision

In London and other large English cities, changes of opinion regarding enslavement since the Abolition of Slavery Act of 1807 were at last slowly gaining traction after years of febrile debate. Consequently, the previous arguments for and against were becoming better documented in the newspapers and coffee-houses and whether it was a good or bad thing still caused division; yet provincial towns like Bakewell were slower to catch up with all the issues and where a cavity of misunderstanding exists, jealousy breeds, resentment follows and Alice's stunning looks caused further division. Whilst the lads whistled, the women loured but, being the charismatic person she was, the various opinions directed at her were generally ignored.

For Jess, though, if that really had been her son whom she had unwittingly bedded that unfortunate night, her twisted logic was to blame the easiest target – and that was Alice. For she argued that if Sir Walton had married his slave-girl as he should have done – with all his agitating for slavery's abolition, that should have been his course of action - then there would have been no reason to marry

Lady Lucinda for propriety's sake. Then she, Jess, would not have had to sell her son to that barren aristocrat – nor ever called him that pretentious name! Her only solace was that he was now better off in every way than she had ever been.

Whilst Alice did not go into Bakewell often, by now she was quite well known in the town and although there were various rumours and counter-rumours regarding her provenance and situation, it was generally assumed that she was something to do with Mulberry Hall – although in what capacity, very few knew or even bothered with, which is what Sir Walton Grimley had always planned; to add to the speculation, Tobias – who had aged with his duties and worries - was now more frequently assumed to be Alice's father with no more than rumours as to whom her mother was. Yet Jess had acquired the truth… and if she could avenge herself by getting at Sir Walton and Lady Lucinda through this more vulnerable woman or her children, she would do it. The one thing everyone agreed upon – or resented - was that Alice was beautiful: yet her expensive clothes and attractive looks were occasionally begrudged by the poorer womenfolk, especially as she was not quite 'one of them' – although that was more due to the combination of her class and race than race itself, which was still mostly a curiosity in those parts.

*

Tobias and Elspeth's son, Edward, meanwhile, had grown into a fine-looking, placid young man who had inherited his father's physique and his mother's sensibilities. His skin was also a blend of theirs, being of a more Mediterranean hue than either of his parents' and, as often happens, where there is a lack of ambition in an individual, someone else recognises a talent that is hidden to them: this revelation was about to be exposed in Edward. He often found that singing to himself rendered him relaxed and happy as he did his duties around Mulberry Hall, a fact that was picked up by his father. Wishing to encourage him, Tobias one day asked Sir Walton what he thought he should do to help him, the master being so much more worldly than he. Sir Walton thought for a moment and then said, "Yes, I have heard him singing too and he has a good voice. Perhaps he should take lessons? He's a good-looking lad and I wager he would do well if he was in London. There are two competing opera companies there..." He thought a moment longer then looked Tobias in the eye and continued, "Well, Tobias, you have been a superb butler to us all and I would like to help you and Elspeth. So why don't I engage a singing teacher to assess his merits when I next go down to London? The air's not so good for his lungs as here, but... if he does well... then the world's his oyster. Italy, the Americas, Germany... who knows?"

Tobias thanked his master and went to tell both Elspeth and his son who, being somewhat shy, was rather overwhelmed by the possibility but instantly started singing more loudly and more often, much to the amusement – and occasional irritation – of the other servants.

Yet this possibility had also given Sir Walton an idea, which would help his planned estrangement from Lady Lucinda no end...

Lady Lucinda had begrudgingly accepted that there was a strong romance going on between her manager, Josiah, and Sophie, which she jealously resented. This offspring of her husband's mistress marrying her manager was definitely neither something she had expected nor wished for and the complications surrounding the expected transfer of Josiah to Mulberry Hall – or, worse, the couples' removal to her factory and access to her wealth and influence in Wirksworth – was a source of extreme annoyance. She disliked it further because her sneaking passion for Josiah had grown into an obsession, borne out of resentment and fertilised by envy; and as Sir Walton now had an heir, consequently her previously rare reproductive attempts with Sir Walton had dried up completely. So she resented Sophie further for stealing her only lingering hope of an occasional coupling and her moodiness and sullen demeanour thus became more oppressive to Sir Walton, who decided to strike, feeling that the timing was right. He found Lucinda brooding contemptuously in the Great Parlour under the guise of reading a book, closed the door positively, then confronted her.

"Lucinda," he began: "I wish to take Edward to London to see if he has the voice we all here believe he has."

"I was not aware of that fact," she said coldly.

"Well, he has. So I am going to pay for him to have singing lessons there."

"I see."

"And I am going to take Alice with me." Her eyes narrowed disdainfully. "This is because they will think she's his mother, which might help her, too."

"What further help does *she* need?" Lucinda replied curtly. "You give her everything she needs – and certainly more than me." There was a pause, then: "And that's not your reason at all, as you well know. You just want to be with her, not me."

Sir Walton took a deep breath. "Well, I was coming to that, Lucinda…" Anticipating admonishment, she looked up from her book: she had been expecting this for a long time.

"I think you should leave Mulberry Hall and look after your business in Wirksworth."

A tundran chill enveloped the room, any heat from her rising blood pressure no match for its severity. "I see. And where does that leave me? Homeless?"

"Not at all Lucinda. I would not do that to you."

"You've done just about everything else, Walton. Married me under false pretences for an acceptable heir, spent more time with Alice than me, sired two children by her - "

"And you," he interjected. "You have a son."

"Well – that's not all it seems either."

"What is that supposed to mean?"

She stood to look more threatening and then stared at him with a glacial frost that surprised him. "The child is not yours."

"What d'you mean, not mine?"

"Sebastian was a foundling," she lied.

Sir Walton found his knees weak and sat down on one of the settees. "But the pregnancy – you were pregnant. I saw it."

"It was padding. Which I enlarged as the months went by. I knew you would never want to touch me while I was in that condition... and it gave you another excuse to stay away from me and go with your beloved Alice."

There was a pause as he came to terms with this revelation; yet he felt not surprised by the deceit, as if he had always suspected something was wrong without ever quite being aware of what it was. Or caring: that was the truth of it. The betrayal by his wife for her own betterment jarred at his senses but he had to admit that the addition of an heir – however unusual or immoral – had helped him, too. So at length he just said weakly, "No wonder Sebastian is such a disappointment – a wastrel… a gambler and a whoreson." Lucinda kept quiet: he was right. "'Pon my soul…" he kept saying, then: "But you betrayed my trust, Lucinda. I never kept anything from you."

"Never kept anything from me? What about Alice?"

"You knew all about Alice from the beginning."

"Not when you first asked me to marry you!"

"You understood the arrangement! You got a life of wealth and plenty. Money for your business… helped your good father… I think you have done well by me."

There was a pause which seemed to plumb the depths as deep as any ocean.

"So what do you propose?" Lucinda eventually enquired.

"I propose that we stay married for propriety's sake but you leave to go back to Wirksworth and run your business. You – we – can say it's for the necessary good running of the business – financial reasons… whatever. I will have Josiah build you a good house there and sustain you if your business falters. Then you will return Josiah to me here so that he can marry Sophie. They will live in Alice Lodge while Alice moves here with me. As for Sebastian… well, you'd better take him with you."

"So you are banishing us?"

"Not really; you are not happy here and your roots are further North. Added to which, your spendthrift son can help you in place of Josiah, whom I need here."

"You are very cruel," she said icily. "I have given you respectability – people like us as a couple."

"Which is why I am suggesting we do not divorce.

Nothing has changed much except that you will cease to live here bar welcoming guests from time to time - and certain 'collusions' during the London Season together will be maintained. The illusion must be upheld."

"The only illusion is your son," she spat tartly.

"And that illusion was visited *upon* me – not *by* me," he retorted. "I am fertile, you are not. Tomorrow, I will leave for London with Edward and Alice. By the time I return, I will hope that you have returned to Wirksworth. I will speak to Josiah about building you your house there as soon as possible."

He then walked resolutely to the door and then stopped, turning back to Lucinda. "Does Sebastian know of his situation?"

"Not as far as I am aware, no."

"Good – let's keep it like that. Good afternoon... wife." And he walked boldly out, firmly closing the door.

Lucinda just sat there and looked around her, the opulent surroundings causing a tear to collect in her eye. Then, under her breath, she said, "Well, if I am to be driven out of here then my new house must be as palatial as this one. I deserve it." Then she burst into tears, revelling in her concocted feeling of misfortune, despair and pique.

Actually, she was quite relieved: she would still be Lady Grimley and back in control of her business again in the region she knew best - away from the servants' sniggers that accompanied her life here at Mulberry Hall thanks to the presence of Alice; so, in fact, she mused, it could all actually work out rather well...

CHAPTER 35

An Engagement, A Singing Teacher & A Removal

Two weeks later, Josiah returned to Wirksworth with the knowledge that he and Sophie would wed; he had been surprised by the request to load his cart with a couple of large trunks containing some of Lady Lucinda's effects although no reason had been given; she, too, was heading to Wirksworth 'for business purposes' although Sir Walton's instructions had left him somewhat perplexed: he wanted him to build Lady Lucinda a good, big palatial house in Wirksworth - but why? Was she not happy at Mulberry Hall? Or were there business problems he had not been made aware of, requiring her presence there instead? Was he, Josiah, not doing his job well enough, he wondered? Well, as his slow horse tugged the load up and down hills and dales, he knew that at least his proposal to Sophie had been gladly accepted and eventually, after the house was built, he would not be stuck in the rains of Wirksworth but the snows of Mulberry Hall – with the girl he loved. Most pressingly, he would have to build the new house in Wirksworth as fast as possible in order to return to his Sophie as soon as he could. If Lady Lucinda wanted him to stay as his manager after that though, this would cause some rancour - and might ultimately mean giving up his job with her, despite Lady Lucinda's wrath not being something he wished to experience. Yet he could not rely on Sir Walton to support him.... So, he decided that he would stay with Lucinda for as long as it took to finish the construction and then flee to the comforts of a newly-married life with Sophie thereafter... whatever the consequences.

Around evening, he pulled into an inn where he had stopped before and took a large meal after leaving his horse, Rosie, in stables for the night. Rosie was less willing and slower than Bessie, his previous steed, which had died many years before but still missed: he had loved that loyal horse, which seemed to represent his early struggles getting established after his father, too, had died. Then the guardian angel in the guise of Sir Walton had taken him on full time and here he was about to build him another house which he could only imagine was a means to keep Lucinda away from him. That Sir Walton was in love with Alice – and always had been – was now obvious to him, whatever he had believed all those years ago. And now he was marrying his angelic daughter by her, his beautiful, beloved, black Sophie...

*

Sir Walton had left for London with Edward and Alice the night after his ultimatum to Lucinda. He felt bad about the decision in one way but knew it was for the best: even London rumour was now catching up with him regarding his coloured paramour but social attitudes were changing so he was less concerned about presenting Alice to his closer friends in London society than he might have been some years before. Every man he knew in his social circle had a mistress or two – he was just the only one with a lady of colour, which rather marked him out as a free thinker and renegade: he liked that. It might also help his efforts to convince his fellow Lords and MPs that as Alice was such an intelligent, courteous and responsible lady he could make them see that these qualities were less to do with any colour of skin than whom they were as a person. He accepted that there would be snide remarks but as long as they kept them to him and not Alice, he would consider having her there as an advantage to his cause. In the event - and notwithstanding some waspish comments from the wives and mistresses of Sir Walton's circle of acquaintances due to having Alice on his arm rather than Lady Lucinda - the drinking and social friends whom he met in his club made it quite clear that they were insanely envious. More importantly for him and Alice, any questions which arose regarding Edward's parentage was a secret they kept to themselves, which not only gave them great pleasure but also ensured that Edward had all the support they could give to their talented young ward. So, some days later, after a good meeting with a singing teacher who concurred that Edward did indeed have a very fine tenor voice, he added that, with his striking looks and the right training, Edward could well become a star at the Theatre Royal in Haymarket. Buoyed by this opinion, Sir Walton booked him lessons there and then and installed Edward in rooms in Brook Street which were only a few doors away from what had been the residence of George Frideric Handel, which he optimistically hoped would have some relevance.

*

Happy with the journey's positive outcome, Sir Walton and Alice returned to Mulberry Hall, only to find the supposedly banished Sebastian draped across one of the

Great Parlour settees and in some degree of intoxication by various substances. Sir Walton decided to leave him there until the morning, despite Tobias imploring him to allow the son's removal by carrying him up to his room.

"Let him rot here for the night," he said to Tobias - and they both angrily retired.

In the morning, however, when Sir Walton found his son still in the same place and state, he was far more forthright and, poking him with his stick, woke him and shouted: "Sebastian! I am not going to pay your gambling, drinking and whoring debts any more – not one of them! Go and join your mother and find yourself a proper position. You are no son of mine!"

The young man wanted to think of a sharply witty riposte but could not, his head still thick with the aftereffects of drink, snuff and opium: any reply would only have accentuated his father's wrath, he knew, so he slunk out of the parlour and went to sit outside to get some fresh air. Since his mother had left – been banished – he had no-one to support him and now he had no idea what to do. His father would not actually throw him out completely, he believed... but he had to do something: revenge came into his mind, but that would not repay his debts and if he allowed his temper to flare as often as it did then he would probably hang for patricide. Blackmail seeped into his consciousness as another spur... but what did he have on his father? Nothing. The profligate heir of a successful, prestigious and well-respected member of the aristocracy and a Member of Parliament to boot: that made any indiscretion easier to fell him, of course... but he had to find something that would do this first. Yet even the fact that he was known to be with his concubine Alice did not seem to cut any ice now; despite the fact that she had been his slave, she had dazzled and delighted London society on the rare occasions she had been there and her wit had been the talk of the town; this meant any memory of his mother Lady Lucinda had been hidden until they had met her again, their guarded welcomes hardly hiding the fact that they all knew what was going on, the hushed, lewd comments angering him because that was what they thought of her.

He did not wish to stay there that night and instructed the ostler to prepare a horse to take him into the town. He would spend the little he had made on recent gambling on a final night of licentiousness with Polly if she was available and the next day would travel to Wirksworth to see if he could help his mother in her business.

It would be a groundbreaking decision.

CHAPTER 36

An Unexpected Truth

& A Plan For Revenge

Jess opened the door to reveal Sebastian – her son - and contritely guided him to Polly who had just finished with a Justice of the Peace and was washing herself out. Polly was happy to welcome him, however, as he was a good lover and she had heard a rumour with which she felt she could blackmail him and so get a better fee.

After the pleasure of his intercourse with Polly, they lay back: during the final convulsions she had been planning on how to broach what would be a tricky subject which had to be carefully handled.

"Sebastian," she said after some more reflection. A grunt revealed the realisation she had spoken. She continued: "Do you know who your mother is?"

"Lady Lucinda Grimley," he said carelessly.

"Not what I heard," she said casually.

"What do you mean by that?" he grunted again, his eyes still closed.

"I mean what I mean."

"I was brought up at Mulberry Hall by Lady Lucinda so she's my mother," he stated slightly testily.

"Lots of money, there, then," she remarked after a moment.

"She doesn't give me any. It's my father's."

"So do you know who your father is?"

He sat up and looked at her, enquiring gruffly, "Why are you asking these questions?"

"Because I don't think you know who either of your real parents are."

"What are you talking about? I know who both my parents are, you silly whore. And my father's just cut me off... for doing too much of this sort of thing. But doesn't matter: I'll be going soon – up to Wirksworth – to help my mother with her business."

"Getting too warm for her here, is it?" she asked cheekily.

"What d'you mean by that?" he asked again, somewhat vindictively.

"If I tell you who your real parents are... will you give me some more money for the knowledge?" Now he was wide awake. "Especially as you've just said you're leaving here," she added.

"No! You *won't* get any more! Especially as I think you're trying to get money out of me that I now don't have." This was said with an air of despair.

"You mean, you're not going to pay me?" she darted, with a threatening chill.

"I'll pay you your usual rate – not a penny more!"

"Oh. I see. That's a pity, then."

"Why's that?" He was even wider awake, now.

"Well, I daresay that some people might like to know the truth of your birth."

"What sort of people?"

"Oh, the justices of the peace I know… people in the tavern… you know, they might think the knowledge was worth something. For blackmail."

"Isn't that what *you're* doing?"

"Call it what you like… but my fee will be far less than what others will get from you if they know what I know."

"So what is it you know that's so damning?" He was more contrite now.

She held out her hand, as if asking for payment. "And then," she added, with her lascivious smile, "I'll keep my mouth shut forever."

Sebastian hesitatingly reached for his purse. "How much?"

"Oh… five pounds should do it."

"Five pounds?" he exploded. "That's a year's worth of bawdiness with you!"

"Suit yourself." She rose and went to clean herself out from a washstand in the corner. He was stuck.

"All right, then; but it'd better be good."

"Oh, it's good all right. You won't like it, but it is good." He was speechless as she finished washing and held out her hand again. He handed her five pounds, adding, "And that includes our coupling just now."

"I think I can agree to that, good sir."

She then told him who his father was rumoured to be – Giles Burrows, the previous butler to Sir Walton Grimley of Mulberry Hall. She wanted to tease him who his mother was for the moment – she was enjoying this moment of power.

"Who told you that?" was all he could say when she finished. "It can't be true…" Polly shrugged her shoulders. Then she continued: "I speak to a lot of people in my job… they all have tales to tell."

"So who was it, then, who told you?" he demanded.

"Now let me think…" she pretended, a wry smile on her face. "Oh, yes – that's it: a Reverend…"

"Reverend?" he thundered, "You mean, a man of God? Coupling with you?"

"Men of God have earthly needs too, you know."

"But which reverend? There are several around here!"

She smiled coquettishly. "You'll have to give me more money if I tell you that. He swore me to secrecy… and his wife doesn't know he comes here, of course…"

"I bet she doesn't!" There was a pause, then he got out his last shilling and gave it to her. "That's not much for such a big secret," she said patronisingly.

"It's all I've got. So you *have* to tell me." He could see she was resisting. "Look, you've taken my last money but if I can get a fortune out of blackmail with what you've just told me, I can come and see you more often."

"Deal. You're lucky I like shagging you – you're rough and ready… just like your mother said your father was. I like that. And so did she."

"Tell me who told you, damn you!"

"It was Reverend Louwerse."

"This *town's* reverend?"

She nodded. "The one who witnessed your father's divorce from Elspeth Yarley."

"But as a man of God in his own town he must have

been mad going with you!"

"*He* didn't think so – and nor did you!" She giggled. "Quite a 'celestial event' he told me." She paused, then mused unemotionally, "Amazing what you can pick up during…" and she giggled again.

He liked her giggle – but its usual infectiousness was lost on him at that moment. So he darted: "Sorry, Polly – I don't believe you."

She looked annoyed. Then she went to a small table in the corner on which the washbowl and jug stood and which contained a single drawer, out of which she took a small silk handkerchief with two letters embroidered upon it: HL. "There," she said triumphantly. "Proof. Henry Louwerse. He left it here by mistake."

Sebastian suddenly saw an opportunity. "May I borrow it for a few days?"

"Why?"

"Blackmail."

She smiled. "Ah, I see; you're learning fast." She gave him the handkerchief, then: "But I want it back. I might need it again sometime…"

"Of course. But… what has Elspeth Yarley got to do with my *real* mother?"

"Elspeth Yarley – Burrows - was your father's wife before he met… your mother."

She could see he was flummoxed, so added, "But that was after your father left her to stay here in Bakewell while she took a position at the Hall… and your mother and he had associations, so to say."

"And I was the result?" She nodded. "So where is my father now then?"

She shrugged. "Don't know. Hasn't been seen for ages. Disappeared off the face of the Earth." There was a pause as Sebastian took this all in. Then she added dramatically, "Murdered, probably... At least, that's what your mother thinks."

"So who is my real mother, then?" he asked warily; "You still haven't told me that."

She smiled a conquering grin at him, then replied, "You know her as Jess."

There was a moment's incomprehension, then the penny dropped: "You mean the Jess who runs this place?" Polly nodded. "So when I first started coming here, I had sex with my own mother?"

She nodded again. "But I wouldn't discuss it with her. She knows it was a terrible mistake but she hadn't seen you since you were taken at birth. And she doesn't know I've told you." Then with an acidic tone, added, "And *I* didn't tell you all that, so keep it quiet – or the deal's off."

Sebastian realised he had been compromised, used and kept in the dark; but he also had a wealthy, titled mother who was not his own but did not know that he knew - and whom he could threaten or blackmail accordingly...

None the less, it was a very shocked young man who soon left the premises, studiously ignoring his true mother Jess on the stairs as he did so. Someone would pay for this secret, he vowed... and that was Sir Walton Grimley. It was surely all his fault for demanding the divorce between his real father and the housekeeper of Mulberry Hall – and all in cahoots with the Reverend Louwerse, whom he could now destroy – unless he gave him hush money. Which he now needed even more urgently; so – being the closest - the unsuspecting churchman would be his first visit...

*

The Reverend Louwerse was at his rectory near the centre of the town when his housekeeper announced the arrival of Sebastian Grimley. Totally unaware of the reason for his visit, the Reverend welcomed the young man in.

After the housekeeper had closed the door, Sebastian came straight to the point.

"Reverend Louwerse: I believe it was you who arranged the divorce between Giles and Elspeth Burrows of Mulberry Hall."

Slightly shocked by his aggressive tone, the churchman declined to offer Sebastian a sherry and said, "But that was nigh on twenty years ago: why do you ask now?"

"Because I have reason to believe it was all a plot to get rid of my father."

"Your father? But your father is Sir Walton Grimley."

"I do not now believe that to be the case."

"But I married him to Lady Lucinda myself: he *must* be your father."

"Not necessarily. And I also believe that he is not only not my father but also that Lady Lucinda is not my true mother."

The reverend looked shocked but not surprised: so much so, that he suspected where Sebastian was heading – without at that moment realising the young man's knowledge which he would soon impart.

"So why are you telling me this? I divorced Mr. and Mrs. Burrows and witnessed the financial settlement. But after that… well, that was that."

"Except it wasn't. I have it on good authority that I am the issue of a certain Jess Rigby."

THE SLAVE-OWNER'S DILEMMA

Louwerse went pale as the blood drained from his face. "Ah, the fallen woman," he mused sadly. Then he reddened again as the connection became apparent. "You mean… Lady Lucinda did not give birth to you?"

"Indeed, sir. But my *real* mother sold her baby – me – to Sir Walton and Lady Grimley so that he would have an heir."

"That is preposterous! I attended the birth soon after the child was born."

"Perhaps. But apparently my father was actually Giles Burrows and - for some reason I know not - his wife at the time, the Mulberry Hall housekeeper now known as Miss Yarley, had issue by someone else some time before. I don't know what happened to that child but I am now beginning to have my suspicions."

"I see. And by whom did you learn of this insinuating accusation?"

"Polly Lister." The reverend went red again and looked away; then he said – more to the wall than the man in front of him, "Ah, *another* fallen woman." There was a pause, then he turned back to Sebastian and continued patronisingly: "But you should never believe the machinations of a low-life woman such as her, my dear sir. She probably wants to entrap you for the benefit of - "

"Low-life she may be, sir, but you have benefitted from her too, I understand."

Louwerse went redder still and Sebastian could see he was sweating. Then he said, "That is a preposterous allegation, sir. I have never been near the girl. This is a calumny. In my work I have come to know what the girl does – and that she works with – for – Jess Rigby. But I have never touched her, nor been to that bawdy-house."

"I think you lost a silk handkerchief embroidered with your initials a week or two ago, sir." Louwerse gave him a sharp but frightened glance, then, trying to re-establish his composure, said, "Yes, that is true. But how did you know that?"

"Polly told me." And with that, he pulled it out of his pocket and dangled it in front of the reverend's eyes.

"And where did you find that, then?"

"I didn't find it – Polly did. In her bed, after you left her."

Louwerse by now was trembling and perspiring even more profusely. Then: "Well, sometimes the narrow avenue to righteousness takes men like me *into* such salacious places... I only went there to try and get her back onto the path of God..."

"Huh! And that path to God lay through Polly's bed, did it?" he chuckled. "You must have lost your way because you said you'd never been inside that house."

Louwerse stood up shakily, his whole body trembling with guilt and anger. "I think it is time you left both me and your accusations in the hallway when you leave," he tried to state boldly but which came out as a whimper. "And keep your rumours to yourself."

"Oh, I shall, sir. As long as you pay me five pounds for my silence."

Louwerse hesitated: "That is blackmail," he riposted weakly.

"Then you should have been the man of God you profess to be and resisted the 7th of the Ten Commandments, I believe."

Louwerse knew he was beaten, his uncertain journey to a strongbox in the corner slow and unsure, as if hoping the hand of God would smite this reprobate who was threatening his wealth and reputation. When this did not happen, he slowly took out a key hanging from around his neck, unlocked the strongbox and took out five pounds; then he locked the strongbox again and gave the money to Sebastian, adding, "But my donation to your colourful story also means that I refute everything you have charged of me and I will visit the girl in question to reprimand her for lying and the debasing of my character."

"If you lie, you will be committing yet another breach of the ten commandments, *'Thou shalt not bear false witness against your neighbour'*," Sebastian riposted with a sneer. Louwerse looked lost again.

"Go on your way, sir, immediately - and never return."

"I hope I will not have to, dear Reverend Louwerse. Because if I do it will be to extract more money from you for betraying my secret. And remember... I still have your handkerchief."

And with that, he swept out.

CHAPTER 37

A Hidden Threat, A Realisation

& An Advancement

Sebastian delayed his journey to Wirksworth for a day before returning to Mulberry Hall; he found Sir Walton in the library and strode purposefully up to him.

"Dear Father... or so they say," he added sneeringly.

"What do you mean by that?" Sir Walton said offhandedly but with a hint of caution. Sebastian knew he could not divulge what he knew or his father would disconnect him completely: but for now, any hint of his knowing the truth would do. He could now blackmail his father – but only when the time was right. And that time was not now.

"I shall return to Wirksworth tomorrow to accompany my... 'mother'... in her business. So please give me some money for my journey and I will endeavour to pay back my debts when I help her make her business even more successful than it is now."

The slight reticence to say 'mother' without inference troubled Sir Walton: had Lucinda told him of his progeniture? Surely that would be bad for both herself and her supposed son? Her best claim to propriety was for all to believe that Sebastian was of her own blood. It would also ensure that Sebastian was accepted as aristocratic stock... So had Lucinda told anyone else of her subterfuge? Was she really that stupid or vindictive to take her own son down - real or not - by telling him the truth of his birth? A foundling of low descent? What was the point of that? Lucinda was many things but she was definitely not that careless... Then a suspicion darkened his thoughts: someone else knew and had told Sebastian... and if that person knew, then whoever it was would doubtless have told others.

He agreed to give Sebastian some money – more than he might have donated before this realisation – and charitably, if not with much relish, wished him well. As Sebastian disappeared, he felt a sense of relief: he would not miss his 'son'. Since he had become Edward's ward, he regarded that fine upstanding young man as more of the son he had wanted and was following his progress in detail, which was more than he had ever done with Sebastian; indeed, there was no career to follow other than a trail of bills and licentiousness. Edward was so much better a man and he decried the secrecy of the social mores of his times: if only the Act for the Abolition of Slavery had happened many years before... But then he would not have met his slave-girl at all: or be so rich. Such conflicting times... He sighed.

As for Sebastian, he would also not miss his official father either – until he needed him again. That seed had been sown...

*

Elspeth and Tobias had been careful to ensure that their sexual relations had been at menstrually-correct times but still they wondered why they had not created another child, such was the continuing passion of their liaisons. It then occurred to Elspeth that perhaps the episode with the knitting-needles all those years ago had actually neutered her despite mercifully not affecting their son, Edward. Thank God! He was now singing minor parts in operas by Bellini and Donizetti at vogueish London theatres and had started to make a name for himself in that arena, his darkish skin an advantage, looking more like an Italian in the fashionable preponderance of that operatic style. To that end, he had also adopted the stage name of Eduardo Grimaldi, which certainly helped his ascent and also deflected any aspersions as to his lineage. Tobias and Elspeth had been informed of his rise through many letters arriving at Mulberry Hall and when Edward secured a minor lead as Belcore in "L'Elisir d'Amore", Sir Walton – as his benefactor – arranged for them all to travel to London to see him perform.

Sebastian had left for Wirksworth the day after his meeting with Sir Walton and was by now immersing himself in Lucinda's business, which had already started gaining in profitability, much to her appreciation and, it has to be said, surprise; but he did not tell her what he knew and increasingly called her 'mother' to continue the illusion. Yet its more frequent use unnerved Lucinda – the word had never before been so often applied and seemed imbued with a slight sarcasm – or was that just her imagination? Yet it made her wonder if someone had revealed her secret... Elspeth? Surely not... but she was too far away from that woman to ask and was suddenly glad that it would not now be long before Josiah finished her house and would be well away from her for good: indeed, the structure was progressing well but that, she regretted, was only because Josiah was hurrying to return to Mulberry Hall to wed Sophie. That was not something she was looking forward to – and still harboured plans to entice him to stay with her instead.

Yet, as so often, circumstance would get in the way of intent.

CHAPTER 38

A Proposal, An Escape, A Performance & An Emigration

Three further months had passed and Josiah looked on with some satisfaction at the building he had constructed for Lady Lucinda: the finishing touches were being applied which could not be completed fast enough – he so wanted to leave the mills, noise, smoke and incipient squalor of the burgeoning town as it industrially wrested itself into the 19th century and get back to Sophie and the open parklands of Mulberry Hall...

The house was situated in the highest part of the town so looked down upon it, standing in the middle of a plot filled with small trees and shrubs and the whole surrounded by high black railings. It was tiny compared with Mulberry Hall and although also smaller than Alice Lodge had many of the same architectural quirks and embellishments: balustrades, long slender windows and a palatial staircase leading up from the iron gates to a grand Palladian portico lined with ionic columns where the front doors opened into a spacious, if diminished, hall. Sir Walton had stipulated that: he did not want his unwanted, cast-off wife to have somewhere as grand as his own! Despite wishing it to be bigger, Lady Lucinda was generally pleased with the result and finally glad that she had used her wiles to snare Sir Walton in the first place, despite the inevitable speculative gossip surrounding her solo return to the area.

Sebastian appeared to be a changed man: he had taken to being the supposed squire of the manor with gusto and after a few short weeks had gradually relieved Josiah of many business issues and turned them to increasingly profitable use, paying off his debts and helping his 'mother' into the bargain; his presence had also given Josiah more time to concentrate on completing the house.

Despite outward appearances, however, Sebastian had not changed his inner persona and his traces of resentment and revenge still haunted him. Yet he was making his own money now and he had consequently become well-known in the town for his licentious and bawdy desires, which diminished him in the face of polite society but was gratefully accepted within the taverns and whore-houses which had sprung up as the town grew to satisfy the desires of its expanding population.

As Lucinda became increasingly aware of this, so her attentions turned more objectively to the honest, business-like charm of Josiah; if only her son, rather than putting her into awkward positions, could be more like him… Nothing was too much trouble, he was efficient, still good-looking despite his receding hairline and advancing stomach, and had a quiet but sharp sense of humour. In fact, she found herself being attracted to him more every day and subsequently kept adding requests for the house in a ploy to keep him there longer. Josiah became aware of this incipient development and was disturbed by it: he just wanted to leave and get back to Mulberry Hall …

One day, he requested a personal audience with Lady Lucinda in the office above the clanking foundry which spat fire, brimstone and the sounds of hammers and seared metals, its confirmation of industry for which the locals were grateful and meant full bellies for their families. He entered the dingy room and approached Lady Lucinda as she sat near the window, the light illuminating papers, pencils, quills and inks which surrounded large plans for future and existing ironwares and products. He was glad Sebastian was not there: he wished to say what was on his mind, which he would find difficult enough anyway without the presence of her gruff son.

"Do enter, dear Josiah," Lucinda said to her architect and business manager. "A tot of sherry or gin for you?"

"No, thank you milady… I come on important business and need a clear head to express it."

"That sounds ominous," she retorted with the twist of a smile: "What can that be all about?"

"Well, milady… as you know, your house is now complete – bar a few odds and ends – and so I humbly request that you allow me to leave your business as planned as soon as I may." Anticipating her reluctance, he added, "And Sebastian is a very good manager now and very competent. And creative," he added as another sop before she could reply.

There was a pause as she looked down at the plans in front of her, a strange smile playing on her lips. "Do you still want to leave me here, Josiah? With all this?" as she waved at the papers in front of her.

"It's not that I want to leave you, exactly, milady; but I do wish to return to Mulberry Hall so I can wed my Sophie."

There was a pause. "Do you really want to?" she eventually said flatly. "I mean, she's a pleasant girl and very pretty but... do you truly wish to marry someone like that? Her mother was a slave-girl, you know..." The endemic bitterness of that comment chilled Josiah but he was adamant he had to leave so ignored it and continued in a more urgent tone, "I am fully aware of that, milady; but Sophie possesses every trait that a man like me could wish for: yes, she is pretty but also has great charm, wit and a thirst for knowledge which I find appealing."

"Are you saying that I do not possess those same qualities?" she said in a sweet tone enwrapping a shard of iron.

Josiah knew what she meant and had been expecting it. "Milady, whether I think you do or do not have the same qualities is not the point. I just wish to wed my Sophie."

"After all I have done for you?"

"You have indeed, milady – and I am most grateful. You have taught me the other side of business – the planning, the manufacturing – which I knew not before I came into your life. But my heart beats in Mulberry Hall, not here."

"What a pity," she said after a moment's reflection. "I was going to make you a wonderful offer."

Josiah started to feel his neck prickle as the not unexpected proposition which he feared was coming made him sweat somewhat. Yet he had to remain calm. "And what offer is that, milady?" he asked out of politeness rather than interest. He dreaded the answer which nonetheless came sharply towards him in an instant.

"I wish to take you as my husband, so I can be rid of Sir Walton forever."

"I see," he said, feigning surprise. Then, resolutely, he added, "But I do not wish that. I admire your fortitude, business acumen and creativity to design and manufacture all these superb implements... but I am a builder, architect and sometime estate manager and wish to do those things rather than manage a business which is not to my desires."

"And *my* desires have no influence in this matter?" she asked coyly.

"Your desires are your concern, milady."

"I see. So what if I offered you five hundred pounds a year to be with me?"

"Emotions have no price, milady – only influences."

"Then you are resisting my offer?"

"Indeed I am, milady."

"I see. How sad. I have taken quite a liking to you and would prefer you in my bed to anyone else I know – especially Sir Walton." A silence draped the room, engulfing the noises from below. Then she added, "And it would mean being permanently rid of that little grasping woman, Alice..."

"The mother of the girl I wish to marry," he parried tartly.

"Indeed. Oh, well... have it your own way. But don't forget me up here all alone when things go wrong. Which they will, I wager."

"So I will leave at the end of the week, if it suits you."

"No, it doesn't suit me at all. But... just remember my offer, which still stands."

"That is very good of you. And I will still need your magnificent implements and tools, so we will always be in contact."

"And when the house needs repairing," she said ominously.

"Indeed, milady."

Suddenly, the door opened and Sebastian swept in, which fortuitously ended the conversation. Josiah had never been so pleased to see Sebastian in his life and left for Mulberry Hall two days later. Yet on his long journey back to Mulberry Hall, Lady Lucinda's offer continued to make an unwanted impression on his mind, which unnerved him.

*

At around this same time, the journey to London undertaken by Sir Walton, Alice, Tobias and Elspeth had resulted in a feeling of huge pride for the latter two and immense pleasure for the former as they attended The King's Theatre in The Haymarket. Eduardo Grimaldi, as Edward now asked them to address him, had received very good reviews for his performances there and his rising popularity amongst the opera-going London public was boding well for his future. For Tobias and Elspeth, who had never set foot in a theatre before, it was a magical occasion as their almost-aborted son was ecstatically acclaimed for his renditions. To hear the applause from such a fashionable high society audience was something neither could ever have imagined and engaging with such beautiful music played by true musicians rather than travelling troubadours was a revelation.

After the performance, they went round to the stage door where Sir Walton used his political influence to gain entrance. They wound up the stairs almost to the top of the building where their son was awaiting them, accompanied by a most beautiful young woman, dressed in exquisite finery, who was introduced as the Duchess of Salisbury – and who obviously adored Edward with a passion, reminding Elspeth of how she had felt when she first encountered Tobias.

The pleasantries accorded, they were all taken to a sumptuous banqueting hall where Eduardo was similarly mobbed by much of the gentry and their fawning daughters.

Yet on seeing the parents of such a handsome young man such as Eduardo had also attracted mixed feelings regarding his progeniture, most of them previously believing he was Italian, which had been Eduardo's intention: yet now the cat was out of the bag, gossip ensued and while abolitionists were keen to applaud him, many others suddenly found his ancestry troubling. The day after, notices in the newspapers were definitely muted even amongst those who supported him for his talents but did not wish to go too far for fear of upsetting a slightly more sceptical general public.

A dark cloud thus appeared over the proceedings. Yet in the auditorium that night had also been an Italian impresario who had travelled to London with the intense desire of returning as many Italian singers to his home country as possible, their popularity in England having decimated numbers due to the nobility's passion for Italian opera in London.

And so it was that the next afternoon, in Eduardo's lodgings, a maid announced the presence of a Signore Alessandro Cavalli; not knowing the man but always pleased to meet someone new, Eduardo invited him in. He was surprised to welcome this bucolic but flamboyantly-dressed man who flattered Eduardo's talent and immediately offered him a contract in Italy, singing in all the finest opera-houses there. Wary due to the prevailing situation, Eduardo awkwardly explained the man's mistaken expectations, being not Italian but of mixed-race ethnicity – despite realising that this knowledge might further destroy his future in London and also Italy. But Cavalli was unmoved: to him, Eduardo looked, sounded and sang like an Italian and that was good enough - and if there was a little mystique in his birthright, so what? In fact, it would add a hint of romance to his past – good for business!

Thus, there and then, a draft contract was discussed: inevitably, Eduardo was hesitant, and after later meeting with Walton, Elspeth and Tobias, he was unsure whether to accept; understandably, they all wished him to remain in England.

After a few days, however, it was obvious that Eduardo's star had been eclipsed by discomforting sentiments and, his contract with the King's Theatre soon finishing, they all agreed that his departure to Italy would be in his best interests.

And so it was that three weeks later Eduardo departed for Italy where no-one would know of his parental background and, some monstrous fees agreed, left to sing in Milan, Rome and Turin. He was also accompanied by his young duchess, who promised to provide him with love and support should he need it… and which conveniently hid the secret that she was pregnant by him: her declared 'Grand Tour', therefore, would cover up any scandal that might have found itself attached to the couple had they stayed in London.

Whereas Tobias and Elspeth were only saddened at losing their son to another country just when he had started to succeed in London, Sir Walton was furious; he wrote to the papers decrying this incipient prejudice but only got criticism for his relationship with a slave-girl -

whom the press had erroneously decided was the mother of Eduardo – with an unknown father.

Sir Walton and his party subsequently returned to Mulberry Hall in various states of anger, annoyance and depression.

CHAPTER 39

A Trip To Bakewell, A Meeting & An Admonishment...

Josiah had now escaped the clutches of Lady Lucinda and was back at Mulberry Hall with Sophie: wedding plans were in preparation. Yet Lady Lucinda's offer to Josiah continued to haunt him: if things went wrong with Sophie then at least he had somewhere to escape to, he mused... and he had enjoyed the job: would he now just sit back and get fat and lazy with much less to do at Mulberry Hall? He still had his building business, of course, and he was now geographically closer to it than he had been before. And Sophie was wonderful. Yes, how lucky he had been to meet her. And yet...

Sophie's younger sister, Jemima, was also now blossoming into a stunning young woman but was not as vivacious, thirsty for knowledge or engaging as her elder sibling. Nor did she share Sophie's intellect. One day, on a trip into Bakewell chaperoning Josiah and Sophie and wanting them to have some time on their own, she wandered off into the town's hinterland and eventually found herself by a canal, suddenly realising she was lost. Staring down a dingy back street and unsure how to get back into the centre of the town, she saw the door of a house open and a young, pretty woman came out. Seeing her, Jemima asked for the best way back to the centre of town. Polly, realising instantly that this young black woman must be related in some way to either Sophie or Tobias - and always out for a chance of blackmail or financial appropriation – offered to accompany Jemima back to the centre of the town. But wanting to know more about the girl and how she could perhaps entrap her, Polly took Jemima by a circuitous route to better ascertain her chances. Being friendly but naïve, Jemima answered all Polly's questions, particularly regarding where she lived and, worse, who her parents were. Polly's suspicions confirmed, she wondered whether this not particularly bright but very attractive young woman could be enticed into Jess's employ – less for the expectation that she would agree but enough, perhaps, to incriminate her and blackmail Sir Walton – a double triumph should she succeed.

After a lengthier time than necessary, they arrived back near the centre of town and Polly nonchalantly asked if Jemima – being such an intelligent, attractive woman – might be interested in employment one or two days a week... obviously, living at Mulberry Hall might be a problem *every* day, but... Jemima looked interested and asked what the work might entail: Polly casually answered that it was just meeting with people and chatting to them... mainly. Her interest whetted, Jemima asked for the address of where she could apply as she had no idea where she had become lost. As Polly started to tell her, a shout from behind calling Jemima's name made her turn to see Josiah and Sophie and she called back to say she was coming; but when she looked back to thank Polly for her help and proposal... she found that the girl had disappeared.

Surprised, she rejoined Sophie and her fiancé.

*

At that same moment in her factory in Wirksworth, Lady Lucinda was again missing her previous manager, Josiah. Not just his calm, worldly presence but his business acumen, wit and creativity, which was now in short supply with Sebastian, with whom she had had some feisty rows since Josiah's departure. Whilst he often had some radical ideas, they would have fallen on stony ground had not the methodical but ingenious Josiah not been there to take them forward. That they were opposites and disliked one another was obvious but the conflicting chemistries worked, she had noted; it was just that the meticulous and mild-mannered Josiah was better with customers – less abrasive, pushy and… so much more. She sighed. The workers toiling below had liked him, too for he understood their concerns, having come from a lowlier background, whereas Sebastian… well, he had, too, she knew, but had been offered all the advantages in life… which he was now so good at squandering.

Perhaps it was time to double her offer to get Josiah back… with Sophie, too, if really need be. A solution to her could be sorted later.

*

As their coach set off from Bakewell to return to Mulberry Hall, Josiah asked who it was that Jemima had been talking to. She explained how she had got lost in the town and that this nice girl living down some side street had befriended and guided her back to the market square, adding that she had not realised how much larger Bakewell was than she thought, it taking so much longer to return to the centre than it did to get lost.

Josiah, becoming anxious at this, asked, "What was her name?"

"Polly."

His blood ran cold. One night in Wirksworth - when he had reluctantly accompanied Sebastian on a bibulous tour of the town's taverns - the latter had divulged one of the better whore-houses in Bakewell – and a particularly pretty girl called Polly...

On return, Josiah quickly availed Alice of his concerns regarding Jemima's meeting with this girl; not really having seen her clearly nor ever having met her, he was unsure if it was the Polly alluded to by Sebastian but, Bakewell being a small town, he felt it was not unlikely. For her part, Alice wondered whether Jemima had inherited some of her own instinctively opportunistic nature – she had ensnared Sir Walton, after all! – but was anxious that her naïve daughter should cast her net in more appropriately aristocratic directions than those Josiah had implied. She summoned her daughter and sat her down.

"Jemima; you were in the town earlier..."

"Yes, mama... with Sophie and Josiah."

"Indeed. And you got lost, I hear."

Jemima could feel an admonishment coming, so hesitantly replied, "Yes, for a little while... but is there anything wrong with that?"

"No. But was the young girl who took you back to the market-place called Polly?"

"Yes."

"And what did she say to you?"

Jemima started to feel annoyed; she was almost eighteen now and could see whom she wished, so why the sudden questions? "She talked to me of my being such an unusual but pretty girl that I could use this to my advantage."

"Advantage in what way?"

"Meeting people and getting paid for it one or two days a week. She said she'd been - "

"Doing that for some time?"

"Yes."

"And did she look like us?"

"You mean... black?"

"No! Of our *social* kind – aristocratic... well-heeled."

"Well, she was nicely dressed... she *looked* aristocratic... although her clothes were a bit soiled..."

"I should imagine so – she probably takes them off and puts them back on again twenty times a day!"

Jemima looked confused: "Why would she do that, pray?"

Alice ignored her and continued. "Was she also very pretty?"

"Yes – very. I wager most men would think so, anyway..."

"Yes, *I* wager they do, too!", Alice retorted viciously - so much so that Jemima recoiled. "Jemima- you must not go anywhere near that woman again. She is of ill-repute – a harlot."

"What's a harlot?"

Alice's poor sheltered daughter! All she had ever known were the comforts and platitudes of her fortunately very comfortable existence, miles away from any licentiousness except when the odd bumbling squire, duke or mercantilist appeared at Mulberry Hall; they all adored her and told her she was very beautiful. It then occurred that she had noticed Jemima seemingly enjoying these overtures but had previously thought little of it; perhaps she should be more wary... Her tone softened.

"Jemima... a harlot is someone who hires herself out to men for sex and then, of course, money. It is dangerous, dirty and would destroy you – as well as your life. Stay away from that woman."

"Yes, mama," she intoned sweetly. Yet she had to admit that it all sounded more worldly talking to people in the town and enjoying their company – she had not fully understood the seedier implications – rather than just existing in a stately home in the middle of the countryside, making small-talk and doing embroidery all day. Actually, remembering also that she had experienced some pleasant pubescent urges when enjoying the attentions of men, she rather naively put two and two together and concluded that it all seemed rather exciting...

CHAPTER 40

Approaching Nuptials,

A Further Offer & An Escapade

Jess and Polly were in hushed conversation, Polly having just told Jess the news gleaned from Jemima that Josiah was now living at Mulberry Hall with Alice's daughter Sophie and that their marriage was imminent. A good time to highlight the racial side of the family and cause some disturbance which might result in a successful blackmail... But they had to ensnare Jemima into their web first... and were fortunate in that events had delivered the girl into their laps with little contrivance at all.

A week later, the wedding guests started to arrive and the usual tensions, undercurrents and embarrassments of large family gatherings were already palpable. Lady Lucinda had arrived, which gave her the chance for another tilt at Josiah before he tied the knot with Sophie, while Sebastian – who had accompanied his supposed mother from Wirksworth – was as much bent upon having a session with Polly if he could get to Bakewell long enough to fit her in. He missed Polly: she was fun, pretty and did all sorts of things to him that no other girl had ever done either emotionally or physically. Yet the proximity to his true mother always floundered him and that feeling was particularly acute at this moment.

As for Sir Walton, he was delighted that his beautiful daughter, Sophie, was finally getting married and that there would be a family line at Mulberry Hall after the heirs started to appear. He still thought of Sebastian as an embarrassment and treated him thus, which, as always, riled his official son and made the latter's urge to get away and see Polly all the more acute.

Despite Jemima having lived a relatively sheltered life, her interest in men had only grown as puberty had further enveloped her; indeed, her mother's warnings only encouraged her to rebel against these restrictions, her youth enjoying the urges without realising their consequences. That Sebastian wanted to see Polly had come about by an offhand comment made to someone else but – having heard it –Jemima realised she could at least take the opportunity to learn more about what that girl's offer entailed and Sebastian would be the perfect chaperone to do so. She had not bothered to look up the word 'harlot' but as it sounded mystical and naughty, she wanted to find out. So she asked Sebastian when he was going into the town again and, when he did, could she please accompany him there for a few hours? Sebastian was intrigued at the sparkle in her eye and put it down to some beau she must have struck up an acquaintance with so thought little of her request: what he did not know was that they both wished to go to the same destination.

Josiah had tried to avoid Lucinda for as long as possible but inevitably the moment arrived when they found themselves facing each other with no means of escape for the young man. Meeting as they had - going in different directions on the grand hallway staircase - etiquette meant that he was obliged to accompany her to the bottom, where she engaged him in conversation.

"Dear Josiah," she began: Josiah was sure he knew what she would ask next – a request to return to the managership of Noncey and Daughter – but was not prepared for what she actually offered. "I have missed your abilities – and your presence," she added flirtatiously, "and therefore renew my offer to give you an even larger stipend… doubled, indeed… to one thousand pounds a year and a share in the business." Josiah was speechless.

"But, Milady," he eventually stuttered as her piercing steel blue eyes bored into him, "That is most generous… but as you know I am betrothed to be married to Sophie just next week and my life will be here from then on."

"Bring her up to live with you in Wirksworth." Josiah was again stumped for a moment: he had anticipated this conversation, knowing that she obviously found him attractive as well as useful; but it was the intensity and speed with which she had confronted him which was surprising. She was trying to make him call off the wedding, he could tell – which would have the added effect of angering Sir Walton – not to mention upsetting Sophie.

"I will not renege on my promise to my dear Sophie," he said through partially clenched teeth, his ambition and the offered pecuniary benefits grating against his love for his intended – but still worrying about what he would do with himself without work and reliant upon the whim of Sir Walton. In fact, this had increasingly concerned him since his return as the probability of his incumbent father-in-law soon losing his right to use slaves could leave him with nothing. And, thus, he himself…

He excused himself and walked away, his mind a

ferment of contradiction. His love for Sophie was strong, but the promise of his own wealth rather than inherited was a powerful attraction – with the added piquance of a woman who was after him for much more besides.

*

"So what are you travelling in to the town for, my dear?" asked Sebastian of Jemima as the carriage bumped and bounced over the uneven track.

"I have come to see someone," she said evasively, yet with a sparkle in her eye that Sebastian easily detected.

"Me, too," he countered, then added, "A beau?"

"Not exactly."

"*Two* beaus, then?"

"Perhaps," she parried, subconsciously adding, 'and possibly more.'

Silence mostly ensued until the outskirts of the town were reached and the horse and carriage were left at livery stables. "Three hours, then?" he proposed. Jemima nodded. "Three hours," she concurred. Then waited as he jauntily walked off - in the direction she would soon follow…

*

Tobias and Elspeth were so busy organising the impending wedding that they had little time to cast the occasional eye over what Alice had asked them to do, which was to discreetly observe Jemima's movements; Josiah's observation in the town had disturbed her and whilst she did not want to monitor her young daughter too much, she wondered whether she should have been more forceful in her warnings. Jemima was almost as pretty as Sophie but did not possess her sister's common sense and she had witnessed a teasing nature towards one or two of the younger male servants and also any man of note who visited the estate. She suddenly realised she had not seen Jemima that morning and wondered where her younger daughter was to be found. She tried the usual places – the library, her room, the dining-hall and the lake - but no-one seemed to have seen her. Her concerns rising, she went to the servants' hall to seek Tobias and Elspeth but the former had not seen her and Elspeth was at the top of the house so Alice progressed to the stables and asked if anyone had seen her daughter: one of the stable-lads came forward to inform her that Miss Jemima had gone to town in the carriage with Master Sebastian. Her spirits plummeted further; that man was no good and all his philandering, drinking and gambling were not the influence on her daughter she desired: she had been so pleased when he had left for Wirksworth and ever since his return Mulberry Hall had felt as if a menacing omen was about to break. She reflected on how Sebastian seemed to malignly influence anyone he came into contact with and would almost certainly warp Jemima in a harmful way if there was prolonged close contact. And she wanted no scandal… At any time – but especially with the wedding next week; so she asked the lad to saddle a horse and went to change into her riding habit. It was at least a pleasant day and there seemed little chance of rain so the exercise would do her good. With Sir Walton elsewhere on the estate and her having assumed a sense of danger, she decided to leave quickly without telling anyone where she was going.

*

Jemima had waited a good fifteen minutes before setting off in Sebastian's footsteps: although she did not fully understand what Polly did or in what capacity Sebastian would engage with her, she suspected he would have to spend some time waiting for her and wanted to arrive when he was most likely out of the way: then she could talk to someone else to get a better idea of the enticing opportunity she believed she had stumbled across.

Sebastian was in flagrante delicto with Polly when the bell was rung but neither heard it; Jess, though, sensing some unexpected business, quickly opened the door and instantly recognised the young girl from a few years back when a child. Jemima, though, did not recognise Jess, who had never been allowed to enter Alice Lodge and any distant view of the former seamstress from the windows of Alice Lodge would have made any recognition unlikely – more so now that Jess looked slightly haggard, with an excess of whitish make-up and a prominent beauty spot. Her mental acuity still unimpaired, however, the conversation with Polly suddenly flooded back to her and the portents that this unexpected meeting could unleash prompted a huge smile as she welcomed the young girl in and the door was closed resolutely behind them.

*

Alice rode as fast as she dared; she was not a natural rider and the movements chafed various parts of her anatomy; she wished she had sought out Walton to come with her but also surmised that he was not the right person to accompany her in this quest; he hated Sebastian even more since Lucinda had informed him he was not her real son. So, if he had seen Sebastian in the company of his younger daughter - in what would almost certainly with Sebastian be licentious circumstances - he might have caused a scene and either skewered him with his sword or blown his head off with a pistol. He was not the heir Sir Walton had wished for and would relish any excuse to be rid of him forever. If only she, Alice, had managed to provide a male heir then this predicament might never have arisen.

She arrived in the town square and went to the stables; sure enough, there was the carriage, the nag and the sleeping coachman… but neither Jemima nor Sebastian were to be seen. She did not wake the coachman for information, which might prove awkward, so went outside and started asking people if they had seen the heir of Mulberry Hall or, perhaps, her own daughter? Being of a different colour would jog a few memories, inevitably; and after a few enquiries a young lad said he had seen a pretty young lady of colour, like herself, going down a back street less than an hour before. She thanked the boy and gave him a sixpence for his information, which she saw him swiftly escort into a nearby public house.

The street was dirty and unswept, with rotting dung, human faeces and animal parts in various stages of decomposition strewn about: a knacker's yard or butcher must be somewhere close she surmised - and took out a perfumed handkerchief to cover her nose; the pungent smell slightly alleviated, she looked about but there was no sign of either quarry.

Alice then noticed a well-dressed man approaching, his silver shoe-buckles and cane gleaming conspicuously against the rotting desuetude and grime; not wishing to be recognised, she turned her head away and stepped into a doorway. The man walked on and went to a door about thirty yards distant, stopped, looked around furtively, then knocked lightly on the door. It soon opened and in the brief glimpse of the face knew it was almost certainly Jess.

Then she considered the face of the young man… and it was not one she would have expected to see in company with *that* woman: it struck her in that moment that this was almost certainly where Sebastian would also be… and with a chill hoped Jemima was not there too.

CHAPTER 41

A Confirmation, A New Experience & A Realisation

"So you're interested in finding out about what we do here, are you?" Jess enquired of Jemima after the man had been whisked away upstairs with a girl called Tess. Slightly bemused by Tess's dishevelled clothing, Jemima nodded.

"We sell happiness and release here…" Jess was saying to her. "Release from the woes of the world for gentlemen otherwise trapped in boring marriages or, perhaps no marriage at all."

"Are they always 'gentlemen'?" Jemima asked pointedly.

"Of course! Did you see that man just now? He's a Justice of the Peace!"

Jemima's hopes rose. "I'd like to find a gentleman," she added. "I'm bored with no-one to talk to… and now my sister, Sophie, is about to be wed, there'll be even less chance to talk to anyone."

Jess assessed her coldly. "Have you ever had sex?" she asked starkly.

Jemima blushed. "No! Of course not! I'm only just eighteen!"

Jess shrugged. Jemima was obviously a virgin – she could get a premium price for that. "I first had sex when I was thirteen," she said dispassionately. "You should try it... a pretty girl like you... and with one particular difference to most, of course; with your colour you'd be in high demand. Unusual, mystical... I know several gentlemen who come here looking for a wife... I'm sure you'd be very popular here. You could take your pick."

There was a pause. Then Jemima said, "I think I like men... I get a pleasant feeling when I'm with them. They look at me in a nice way."

"I'll bet they do!" Jess retorted. "You're very attractive..." There was a pause, then she said calmly, "Tell you what; I'll give you a try. There's a nice man due any moment who I think would like you – and you him, of course. You don't need to do anything – just talk. And I'll pay you, too." Another pause, then: "And if you let him kiss you... then I'll pay you some more."

"Is that all I have to do?"

There was a pause. "Ye-es... For now, anyway. And if you like his company, then you can see him again. And then I'll pay you even more."

"All right. As long as I like him, too."

"Of course! If you don't, just let me know and I'll introduce you to someone else."

*

Outside, Alice was becoming cold. The promise of a bright day with the prospect of no rain now looked dubious and it had become an uncharacteristically grey, dank day for early summer. She was also unsure what to do: knock on the door and ask if Jemima was there – and then perhaps bump into Sebastian? Or if Jemima wasn't there, where would she find her? Her colour and quality clothes would be a giveaway, too: no, she had to stay unrecognised. Yet she was sure that Sebastian was there and Jemima would obviously be going back to Mulberry Hall with him. So what was the point of waiting here? She decided to go back to the square and return home. Turning to go, she then saw a very well-dressed young man coming down the street: early twenties, *a la mode* fashion, a jaunty feathered hat and silk breeches adorning good legs… nice face, well-to-do… She sighed. She loved what Sir Walton had done for her and the life she now had thanks to him. But it had always been an arrangement - much as she had enjoyed it. Yet now he often spent so many days in Parliament she seldom saw him… She was still relatively young… and the sight of this attractive man had provoked the unexpected thrill of a 'little adventure' which surprised and excited her soul. After all, she was sure Sir Walton was not as pure as she was, with all that temptation in London and he a knight of the realm to boot… She had seen women throw themselves at him and was sure he must have succumbed to flirtation at least a few times. So why should she not have these thoughts, too? Then she felt ashamed of herself and her little reverie evaporated.

The man did not pass the door but looked round assuredly then knocked on it; again, Alice saw the face of Jess as the man was invited in. She had just started to move in order to return to the town when the door opened again and Sebastian came out, lightly giving a different pretty girl a peck; he then sauntered towards Alice as the door closed behind him. She recessed herself into the doorway and turned her face into its damp frame as Sebastian contentedly lit a pipe, drew a few puffs, then happily meandered away from her, heading for the square.

So where was her daughter, Jemima?

*

This second young man who had entered the building was newly-trained as a lawyer and Jess had introduced him to Jemima. He had never seen a person of colour before and was intrigued not only by her looks but by the fact it was obvious this was her first time. He had heard that there was a rumoured black slave-girl ensconced with the master of Mulberry Hall but did not think this beautiful young girl would be anything to do with that man: what would she need of prostitution? So they made small talk and then he asked if he could kiss her. Liking him as much as he did her, Jemima consented... and eventually the deed was done in its entirety. Satisfied, he thanked the young girl and asked if he could see her again, then promptly left, depositing a large sum of money into Jess's outstretched hand as he left the building. Yet Jemima was upset: she had enjoyed what the man had done with her and was disappointed he had suddenly left; and she did not even know his name: what was going on?

Jess was immediately in the room, informing Jemima there would be another man coming soon who would like her as much, so would she like to stay a little longer? Suddenly aware of the time she had been away from the square, Jemima declined the offer but asked if she could come back to see the same man again. Jess concurred: his name was Jonquil and he had been visiting at this time every Tuesday for only the past month, being new to the town. So she could come back again next week if she wanted to... Desperate to have this girl in the palm of her hand while she and Polly worked out their plan to compromise Sir Walton, she was only concerned that she might overplay her hand; yet a smile had now crossed Jemima's face and she consented, much to Jess's relief. For now, her plan was working and fortune had smiled on her in the shape of this charming if not very bright young girl. Give her enough rope…

Outside, Alice had followed Sebastian from a safe distance as he returned to the centre of the town and when he went into the market tavern she slipped past and retrieved her horse, mounted it and rode a mile out of town; then she waited, hidden by a clump of trees a few yards back from the road.

Jemima had left the whore-house a good half-hour after Jonquil; she felt excited and had a feeling of righteous defiance in her young body despite not really understanding what she had allowed herself to do. But she knew she had enjoyed it and that was enough for now… As she entered the square, she saw Sebastian leaving the tavern for the livery stables and her step quickened.

Then she remembered that Jess had not paid her; she would have to return for it - but not today. She would come back again. She was looking forward to that already.

She arrived at the livery stable and found Sebastian about to leave in the carriage, the horse already harnessed and the coachman seated. "You were going to wait for me, weren't you?" she asked angrily.

"Erm, yes, I suppose so…" he murmured. Actually, his exertions with Polly, some complimentary drinks as he did so and then a few more afterwards in the tavern had dulled his memory – and the snuff hadn't helped either. Jemima was annoyed: she wanted to impart that she had had a good time in town and wanted to ask him some questions. But Sebastian was soon asleep despite the carriage bumping back to Mulberry Hall and so her torrent of interrogations would have to wait.

From the clump of trees she had secreted herself in, Alice saw the carriage approaching and, seeing both Jemima and Sebastian contained within it as they passed, decided to ride back to the Hall via a shorter route along a ridge that was impassable for the carriage; she wanted to be home before them so she could confront the pair more assuredly...

CHAPTER 42

Things Come Dramatically

To A Head

Alice was waiting calmly for Jemima in the Great Parlour: she had told the stable-lad to direct her to this room instantly on her arrival, which was three-quarters of an hour later; this had enabled a change of clothing and a hardened composure for the inquisition she had prepared for her daughter.

Eventually, an outwardly contrite but internally jubilant Jemima entered the room and sweetly asked her mother what she wanted.

Starkly, Alice asked: "Jemima – where have you been?"

Feeling the frost, she evasively answered, "Out."

"I know that. But where – and who with?"

There was a pause as Jemima quickly wondered what to admit to. "In the town. With Sebastian."

"You know I have forbidden you to consort with that young man whenever possible."

"It wasn't possible."

"What d'you mean?"

"I wanted to go to the town... he was going too, so I asked if I could go with him."

"You did not get permission from me."

"I couldn't find you."

"Did you try?" Jemima petulantly shrugged her shoulders. "So what was so special about the town?" Alice persisted.

"I went to see a friend," Jemima responded guardedly.

"I didn't know you had any friends in the town. I do not know of any 'friends' you have there," she said with a slight snarl.

"Well, I do." There was a pause.

"What's his name?"

"Why do you think it's a man?" Jemima exclaimed.

"I can see it in your eyes. They're alight. With a passion... I can tell these things."

The fires in Jemima's eyes were doused by this correct interpretation: seeing her suddenly subdued, Alice added: "And I am fairly certain I know where you went."

"How?"

"Because I followed you." This was the dangerous part: she was fairly sure that the house which she had stood outside was where Jemima had gone because she had seen Sebastian leave it; but the connection with him and Jemima being with him there was a guess. Yet it was obvious that the place was a whore-house – not least because she had heard rumour that it once belonged to Elspeth and had been bequeathed to some prostitute as a deal to ensure the cover-up of Edward's birth... Then suddenly it all made sense: the girl she had seen was *definitely* Jess, the dismissed servant and probable mother of Sebastian! It was she who had been bequeathed what had been Elspeth's house and was now using it as a brothel! Like glistening blocks of quartz interlocking into a perfect heptahedron shape, she could see the plan of everything: Jess had realised her son was the heir to Mulberry Hall and was now trying to wrest the house and its estate from her and Sir Walton as revenge for her dismissal; in addition, Jess was hiding Sebastian's provenance so that she could eventually cause a scandal to deny her daughters any claim to it - *but* using her innocent Jemima as a pawn to help do so! That was definitely a dig at her own lowly birth in Jamaica and Jess's feeling of racial superiority regarding both of them... what a vicious, scheming, bitter wench! She walked around the room for a few moments to calm down, then became angry once more as she concluded with a chill that Jess must have been trying to inveigle her high-born but supposedly second-class Jemima into her web of intrigue as the final part of some dastardly plan. The proof would be if Jemima had actually done the deed.

She turned to Jemima, the fury on her face causing the young girl to cower.

"Did you just visit a house down a side street in the town? Back Lane?"

"Why do you want to know?" Jemima asked with a tremor in her voice: she had never seen her fragile, obsequious mother like this before and the countenance which stared furiously before her was terrifying.

"Because I am your mother and I demand it."

Flatly, Jemima answered, "I did."

"And was there a girl called Jess in that building?"

"I don't know," she lied.

"Polly?" Jemima's startled silence answered her in the affirmative. "And did you meet a good-looking young man there with silver-buckled shoes and a silver-topped walking cane?" With that, Jemima nodded, tears beginning to well in her eyes.

Alice looked away. "I warned you about this, didn't I?" she said as if a shard of ice had chilled her. Jemima started crying more unrestrainedly. Alice walked to the other end of the long room, then shouted back to Jemima: "And I suppose he kissed you, did he?" Jemima nodded, the tears in free flow now. Then she marched back to Jemima and, placing her face directly in front of it so their noses were almost touching, viciously stated: "And then he took your clothes off?" Jemima nodded again, wailing, her eyes now like a river in flood, coughing as the phlegm mingled with her tears. Alice stood up and went to one of the huge windows overlooking the mulberry tree, its magnificent bloom and promise of fecundity and strength a counterpoint to the blubbing child behind her. She had no reason to wonder what happened next – it was obvious. The man who had deflowered her daughter was the one she had found quite attractive herself – how ironic! Her young daughter had been appropriated as part of a grasping plan to embarrass the whole household and ensure the shame scandalised Sir Walton Grimley and evicted him from his estate. And her. Sophie and Josiah, too; everyone. The supposed indignity of Sir Walton and her was an open secret but one which, with a little fanning of the embers would create an inferno. Hypocrisy! Exploitation! Scandal! Well, she would not let it happen. Jess and Polly would be found guilty – Sir Walton could see to that - and transported to Australia. Or worse, if she could influence it.

That made her feel better: they would get their just desserts before they had even had a chance for their plan to be implemented. Yet her sudden clarity made her turn back to her daughter: how weak is the human spirit, she reflected... Then she remembered how she had been only *six*teen when Tobias, the catalyst for all that had happened since – had deflowered *her*... and she felt suddenly sorry for her young daughter; she was human, too, after all...

Penitently, she crossed back to Jemima who was now much more quietly moaning; she put her arm around her. "You have done a silly thing, Jemima," she whispered "but I forgive you. Just don't do it again." Jemima shook her head: "Sorry, mother," she cried as the tears came again, "But he was a very nice gentleman at least..."

"Yes... he *was* quite good-looking, wasn't he? Early twenties, *a la mode* fashion, a jaunty feathered hat and silk breeches adorning good legs... nice face, well-to-do...!"

Jemima started and looked at her mother. "You noticed all that?" she snorted through her blocked nose.

"Yes, I did! As I said... I followed you. But now, we're going upstairs and you are going to have the longest and most thorough bath of your life – we need to clean you out. We want no more ghosts to keep secret..."

"Ghosts?"

Alice nodded. "Mm. You and I, Sophie, Tobias and Edward are all ghosts, like dark secrets to be kept away from the wider world lest we embarrass the status quo... We are the ghosts of Mulberry Hall."

*

After this, events moved rapidly. Alice told Sophie of what had happened and articulated her perceived summation of the two harlots' plot; when Sophie told Josiah, he went into a deep, morose mood, despite the wedding being now just two days away. To complicate the situation, Lucinda had accosted him again with her plan, emphasising the larger sum of money she would pay him and also being somewhat less subtle about what 'perks' his placement in her midst would be available. Josiah went out into the park and sat under the mulberry tree, its branches soothing him as the breeze blew through the leaves. He looked at the two mansions he had built and realised not only how happy he always felt here – they were like his children, his progeny – but that he had to stay. Then, with a jolt, he wondered if Lucinda was in league with the two harlots, Jess and Polly... If Jess had come to realise that Sebastian was her son, then Lucinda – as Sir Walton's legal wife - might also have an even stronger claim to the house if these two avaricious harridans were together clever enough to realise it. Mulberry Hall would then be appropriated by... Sebastian, Lucinda and the two harlots! Sir Walton, Alice, he and Sophie would be turfed out, as would Jemima and – probably – Elspeth as the seductress of Tobias: jealousy had deep roots... So he there and then vowed to ensure that no extra bribes or enticements would ever allow him to accept Lucinda's advances – pecuniary or sexual. He had gained much experience as her manager and he would forthwith use that to enlarge his building business with his dear Sophie, using the house as his base. Then the children would come and he would be a father in his magnificent building, too.

He then saw Sebastian wandering towards him with Lucinda and his mood soured again. Yet the day after tomorrow, he was going to marry Sophie, which cheered him once more - and that would be terminally that. He just hoped that these two scheming people approaching him would not have the time to thwart his marriage to her, despite having the ability, if they but knew it. And he was sure they did.

*

Jess and Polly, now knowing that the wedding at Mulberry Hall – so essential to their plans - was on Saturday, had realised that Jemima would not therefore return to them before the event. So, the day after, they sent one of their new girls to the mansion on the pretence of seeking casual employment for the wedding. The girl, Tess, was not from the area and so they gambled she would unlikely be known to anyone at Mulberry Hall: but Jemima, having noticed Tess when she first entered the bawdy-house, recognised her from a window in Alice Lodge as she walked up the drive. Initially tempted to run and get Tess to pass on the message that she was not now interested in Jess's proposal – but chastened by the only beating she had ever had from Sir Walton in her short life for her 'shameful behaviour' - she was also doubly sure that Tess's appearance was to do with the further undermining of Sir Walton and her family, as Alice had deeply impressed upon her. As she weighed up whether to intercede, her thoughts returned momentarily to that revealing forty minutes – in every sense – with Jonquil and she sighed: yet she knew her rebellious instincts had to be subsumed, at least for now... she could wait until after the wedding if her yearnings persisted but knew she would be ejected from the family if she was known to be consorting with him again. So she took a deep breath and ran to tell her mother where Tess was from: the girl was summarily dismissed a few minutes later by a very stern Tobias.

Alice's concerns regarding their predicament - and the wedding possibly being disrupted as a result of Jemima's deed - hung over her like a looming storm which might break at any moment, especially if her perceived belief that Sebastian was involved might cause a thunderously catalytic reaction. Yet time was on their side, now: the banns had been read some weeks before and Sir Walton had been immediately availed of all these latest happenings and possible defamatory plots, all so perilously fanned by his younger daughter's actions: he was in a vengeful mood and even refused to talk to either Lucinda or Sebastian, to which they did not take kindly, particularly as they did not know the reason why…

Yet an unanticipated event would throw the next day's wedding into confusion for two of the guests which neither could possibly have foreseen.

CHAPTER 43

The Marriage

& An Unexpected Guest

The huge marquee's canopy heaved and fluttered in the chill breeze under the boughs of the Mulberry tree; despite a hesitant late spring sunshine, the promise of full summer had not yet arrived. This wind, however, was of benefit to the servants, cooling them as they busied themselves rushing hither and thither, preparing for the wedding feast. A mile away in the village, the church buzzed with happy chatter and laughter as the proximity of the betrothal drew ever nearer. There were the usual conspiratorial voices mumbling as to the 'suitability' of a mixed-race marriage but these were respectfully and instantly subdued when either Alice or Jemima – or especially Sir Walton - were adjacent. Yet as always with large gatherings, further rumours were also abroad, one being that the vicar had been reluctant to conduct the marriage due to its 'ungodly' overtones and what his parishioners might think about his Christian morality in confirming such a liaison - which had never been done before in the north of England as far as he was aware. His doubts, however, had apparently been extinguished by a large donation from Sir Walton for the church's upkeep and distribution to the needy of his locality – interpreted by most as a charitable act for a good cause by Sir Walton but as a sop by him; for, while he himself had been happy to donate the money, he disliked being forced - and to him the fact that even the church could be bought off smacked of blackmail and hypocrisy.

The marriage was soon completed and the church's distant bells wafting across the fields alerted the servants at Mulberry Hall to the imminent arrival of about a hundred guests, whereupon a flurried intensity took over as drinks were poured into fine glasses on several sleek silver salvers in anticipation. It was a large celebration for the times but gave Sir Walton a chance to make a point and display his largesse.

The gilded open wedding carriage arrived at the front of Mulberry Hall and Sophie and Josiah descended from it, looking lovingly at each other as it was driven away, their sparkling eyes and happiness ready for inspection by the guests as they appeared in their wake. Sophie's bouquet was discreet but splendidly colourful and her ivory dress, satin shoes and flowered white chintz head adornment contrasted beautifully with her luminous black skin, so burnished by excitement, love for Josiah and innate bloom of youth.

Sir Walton and Alice stood proudly next to the couple as an array of servants stood with champagne, canapés and softer drinks for those wishing a less intoxicating beverage. Jemima was next in line, then a fidgety, morose Sebastian and awkward Lucinda, followed by Edward and his young duchess – the latter bursting less with happiness than an advanced pregnancy – who had both travelled from Italy. Edward would regale the guests that evening with operatic arias fresh from the Teatro alla Scala in Milan, accompanied by a quartet of musicians.

An hour later, the guests were drinking and eating under the huge marquee, the mulberry tree's leaves never tiring of caressing its canvas roof in the slight breeze and making gentle scraping sounds as a complement to the merriment of the throng. Sebastian looked sourly on and Lucinda glowered in concert, her gaze fixed upon the groom whom she had so wished to steal away from Sophie for her own business purposes - not to mention her dashed hope of personal carnal pleasure: indeed, jealousy coursed through her veins. Jemima found herself talking to a young duke who was enjoying her spirited beauty and hoping for a chance to get to know her better – much better; yet there was another person who, sitting at a distant table, had just noticed Jemima through the throng. He had not met the welcoming party, having arrived late due to his carriage suffering a broken wheel on the way from Bakewell to Mulberry Hall. His name was Barnabas and few knew of his invitation…

*

Back at the Hall, the kitchen was a ferment of industry as broths and vegetables were boiled, various birds and animals baked, braised or roasted, pans clashed and shouted orders were being disseminated by all. To a casual observer it was chaos but above it all the calm presence of Tobias, Elspeth and Miss Shaw held the event together with abilities honed over many years; Tobias's hair was now more flecked with grey and Elspeth's once trim figure had by now taken on a more matronly demeanour whilst the cook, Miss Shaw, looked as she had done for many years and was still a spinster, never having found any time or inclination for the fripperies of marriage – as, indeed, that prospect had never inclined itself towards her.

A maid dropped a skillet of scalding water, tripping over one of the kitchen cats as she rushed from the hearth to the scullery, causing confusion and consternation for a moment; fortunately, no-one was hurt and neither was the cat, which fled with its life intact, if not its usual tranquillity. Within moments, the industry was back at full pace and the minor disturbance resigned to oblivion.

In the marquee, the servants were in a similar state of inward panic and outward calm. One of them, though, had a different intent to the wellbeing of the guests; her clothes did not quite match those of the other servants, having made them from memory; unusually for her, a pair of glasses surmounted her small nose and she wore no powder or other application. She did her best to make herself look busy without ever serving any guests or going back to the kitchen, only helping others less strong than her or clearing up dishes and piling them on a huge table behind the marquee for supposed restitution to the scullery when the frenzy had later passed its zenith. It was also particularly essential for her to keep away from the gaze of Jemima, Tobias, Lady Lucinda or Sebastian...

It was Jess, and she was waiting for an opportunity.

*

At the top table, during a pause in conversation with Alice on one side or Sebastian on the other, Jemima cast her eyes around the sea of merriment and dreamed of meeting Jonquil again; she would love to see him once more, she thought – no, more than just the once! - and then perhaps she could have a wedding like this. So many happy faces, all here to witness two people getting married who had fallen in love: a frisson ran up her body as she contemplated the idea.

Some distance away, at the far end of the marquee, sideways on to Jemima, sat a young man, talking earnestly to what looked like a cavalry officer and his wife. She looked away again, only to find herself quizzically looking back: something in the young man's movements had reminded her of someone she knew. Jonquil. Well, he wouldn't be here, sadly, she concluded. And yet, the more she saw of his animated personality, the more she was reminded of him. Somewhat distressed, she tried to think of any possible reason he could have been invited – but there was none. Disappointed, she looked away. Yet the next time she looked back, she could see the man was looking straight at her – and smiled.

It *was* Jonquil! As discreetly as possible, she smiled back and with her eyes and a discreet head gesture only, intimated that they should meet outside the tent, behind it. He discreetly nodded back. After a moment's composure – her legs wobbly with a thrilled anticipation now – she made her excuses as if to go to the powder room and left the tent, turning out of it and behind rather than going up to the Hall. There was no-one there. Her heartbeat gaining in speed, she got to the furthest point by the back of the tent and turned the corner to find a beaming Jonquil there. They instantly embraced and kissed wildly, aware that there were over a hundred people just a few inches to the other side of the restless canvas, which heaved and sighed in the breeze in concert with their young hearts.

"What are you doing here?" she enquired, whispering breathlessly after the first long, lush kiss had been satisfied.

"I was invited," he said simply.

"By whom?"

"Sir Walton."

She was confused. "But why did he invite *you*?" she said somewhat patronisingly.

"Steady on!" he parried, unused to being treated as if a lesser mortal.

"But *why*?" she repeated.

"Because I became his lawyer two weeks ago."

"I didn't know that!"

"Well, you do now!"

Her head was spinning. "But – why did you not tell me?"

"How could I have done? I did not know you were the daughter of Sir Walton. However much I should have realised the possibility of that fact!"

She threw her arms around him and kissed him again. "I have missed you – hoping that I could come back to see you in that, that... -"

"Don't mention that place. I'm glad you didn't go back there. Now I know who you are... You should never have been there anyway."

That observation cut her so she darted back quickly, "And neither, Jonquil, should you!"

He looked guilty and dropped his eyes then, needing an escape, furtively stated: "Actually... that's another thing. My name's not actually Jonquil."

"What d'you mean?"

"When you met me I was *introduced* as Jonquil... but actually my name's Barnabas."

Jemima looked at him intensely, holding his shoulders

THE SLAVE-OWNER'S DILEMMA

at arms' length for emphasis. "Why a different name?"

He looked awkward, sheepish. "Because a man in my position should not have been in such a place," he declared, as if berating himself. Then he looked at Jemima with a slightly admonishing smile and said, "But there again, neither should you have been!"

Jemima blushed and suddenly wondered if – rather than the banished Tess being sent to betray her it was he, her Jonquil - whom she had fantasised about ever since their meeting - who was the stooge to destroy her and her family; but rather than blurt out an accusation, an inner indignation parried his information with, "Well, if you're a man in such a lofty position, why *were* you there?"

"Indeed." He looked around awkwardly, as if concerned that someone else there might have known of his visits. "For reasons of pleasure, of course. As, I suppose, were you," and his gaze bore down on her like a judgement from heaven. Jemima looked around, half expecting Sebastian to appear as part of some dastardly plot; perhaps Jonquil and he had passed each other, had a drink together, compared their experiences? "How many times have you been there?" she suddenly demanded.

Slightly taken aback, he replied, "When I met you it was only my second time. And I came back for you, too, just the day before yesterday – but you weren't there."

"Did you have your way with someone else, then?" she asked tartly, taking a step back. He hesitated, then nodded.

"Who?"

"Jess." Jemima's spirits crashed to the floor, fragmenting into a thousand splinters of emotion. A tear of despair and panic welled in her eye: she was being set up, she was now sure. Seeing this, he moved closer and whispered, "But, honestly, Jemima, I wanted to see *you* again, not her."

"That's not the point," she hissed. "They want to destroy me – and my family. I was curious, attracted to… oh, I don't know… something new, an adventure, an escape. It's so boring reading books and poetry here all day…"

"I can sympathise with that," he agreed, "despite it being such a magical place." A sudden gust of wind made her grab her hat as the branches scoured the canvas roof again, rustling their self-esteem in tune with their mutual concerns.

"So what do you actually do, then?" she hazarded, "apart from…"

Barnabas ignored her barb and answered, "As I said, I am a lawyer. I trained in London but could not bear my employer. So I passed my articles and decided to come here. My father left me some money when he died recently and Bakewell seemed a pleasant, respectable town in need of legal services, I found… so I bought a house here and… well, here I am."

Suddenly wary again, she asked, "Who *really* invited you?"

"Well, indirectly, Sir Walton, as I said. But more specifically it was Josiah – the groom. I did some business for him – he was my first client in this district. He mentioned he was to marry the delightful Sophie and asked if I'd like to attend. I did not know she had a sister – you – or, at that time, that her father was who he was. Or, indeed, that Sophie was of colour. So, for better or worse… that is why I am here today."

Jemima did not know what to say next. Her mind was like a battlefield in which conflicting armies were lacerating each other with swords, pikes and halberds, each opposing soldier a metaphor for each of her thoughts: was his name really Barnabas, not Jonquil; was he really there as the guest of Josiah; was Jess involved: was he honourable or a scoundrel?

All these emotions – captained by one like a knight in shining armour coming to save her – raged through her beating breast. Then, as if a truce had suddenly been declared, Barnabas' calm, warm and authoritative voice quelled the mental torment. "Dear Jemima: I have no ulterior motive. I am here at the invitation of Josiah, as I said. I apologise for meeting you in that demonic place but we should look upon it as an unlikely but beautiful piece of good fortune brought on by angelic forces. We were neither of us where we should have been – and I will never go there again as, I suspect, neither will you. So let's look upon this as a divine intervention and reap the reward it has offered us. If I had not made the most beautiful love with you I would still not know what to expect. Now I do, I wish to do it again – probably for the rest of my life. I hope you will believe me in that."

Seeing her wrestling with what he had said, he told her he would return to the feast and that she should, too, after a few minutes' delay. She nodded and he walked briskly off.

"Wait a moment!" she said in a hoarse whisper. "I want to ask you something." She pulled him to the edge of the tent and peered round into its cavernous space. She instantly spotted Sebastian talking to a lively middle-aged lady with a loud laugh and even louder apparel, her hat sporting a stuffed turquoise cockatoo. "Do you know that tall man there, standing up?" she enquired cautiously, retreating out of sight. He peered around the edge and looked: "Speaking to that ghastly woman with the bird nesting on her head?" Jemima suddenly felt the urge to laugh but restrained it until she knew the answer, so just nodded.

"No, I do not," he concluded, as he retreated back. Relieved, Jemima let out a little laugh.

"Well, who is he, then?"

"No matter. I'll tell you in due course."

"So that *does* mean we might see each other again?"

The fiend! She was going to ask *him* that! "Look, we have both admitted that we both met in unusual circumstances but being the outward person I really am under all this encumbrance" – as she implied her dress – "I think we should start again. If we can secure a formal introduction... then we can ignore how we met and put it behind us." There was a pause.

"I like that idea," he said, a smile crossing his face.

"But you really must *never* go back to that dreadful place – never! And certainly if we are seeing each other."

"If you would like that, then so would I."

"I believe I most certainly would."

They parted, leaving severally for their respective allocated places within the throng. Some time later, as the evening fell and the guests became louder and less sober, Jemima and Barnabas kissed behind the folly once more and then took a circuitous, hidden route back to Alice Lodge. With all the servants involved in their many duties, the building was empty and soon they were in the same position they had been just days before...

For Jemima, she had dismissed all her concerns about Barnabas; they each had a secret which would compel them to stay together – how they really met was an easy lie to concoct; for now, she knew she really liked him and would happily spend her life with him if he asked.

For Barnabas, he felt the same... with the added benefit of hopefully soon being part of a very wealthy, influential family and would thus be made for life. How fate had intervened for both of them...

Yet it was a secret that had to be kept away from Jess – at least for now. If she got to hear of their liaison, she would have the perfect means to destroy not just these two but the entire edifice that was Mulberry Hall.

Sadly for them, she had witnessed the latter part of their furtive meeting behind the marquee.

CHAPTER 44

A Decision, An Explanation

& Defiance

Jess dissolved away behind the marquee as the guests started to make their way up to the Hall where further entertainments were anticipated, including the concert by Edward, whom many knew had made a name for himself in Italy and was now being wooed to return to England by various impresarios. She had left Bakewell at first light that morning and walked the nine miles motivated by a seething bitterness and urge to foment a scandal; she had therefore been hungry all day, yet servants were expressly not allowed to eat on duty. Any pilfering would have not gone unnoticed and much resented by any servant who might have seen or recognised her. On top of her hunger, she was even angrier at having missed any opportunity to make a scene - despite realising that it would have done her no good to cause a disturbance in front of so many people for which she would inevitably be imprisoned. This result would also have drawn attention to her business and it would have been subsequently closed down – most likely by the very people who frequented it! Yes, blackmail using what she had witnessed happening between Jemima and the man she knew as Jonquil was now her best course – and much more credible as others may have seen that convivial moment behind the marquee, too. And the fact that she knew where they had met – at her own brothel – was her ace card, she reasoned. She could blackmail Sir Walton Grimley to keep quiet about that, too, especially as it was frequented by his supposed son!

Therefore, as the day had progressed, she had resolved instead to ask someone to write an anonymous letter to Sir Walton – her own reading skills were still only rudimentary - and spill the facts of his daughter's liaison with the man she now knew must have had dealings with the family: he would not have been invited to the wedding otherwise. This way, she could also blackmail Sir Walton Grimley to keep quiet about her business and then have enough money to open another bawdy-house somewhere else if things became too hot. On top of that, it would give her an opportunity to embellish them with the truth that Sebastian was her son, cruelly taken from her by Lucinda and Sir Walton Grimley: unless hush money was paid, the papers would hear of it and he and the family would be ruined. How she would laugh at that! Serve him right for dismissing her… *and* she would also avenge that stupid stable-lad, Jack, who had caused her dismissal in the first place! She would get Elspeth fired, too, for her part in the arrangement, a fitting epitaph for that woman's previous husband, Giles, the man she owed her house and profession to – and who had mysteriously disappeared without trace. She had an opinion on that, too.

She was daunted by the walk back to Bakewell, however, and needed something to eat first: the hunger pangs had been demanding satiation all day and the small bun she had brought had been eaten hours ago: seeing so much food left over, though, and her plan now firm in her mind, she decided to pick up a chicken leg, a potato and a piece of cake to eat as she made her way home. No-one was looking, so she darted to a table and grabbed them... only, as she turned to go, to find herself looking into the stern gaze of Tobias.

"What are you doing here, Miss Jess?" he asked forcefully. "I have told you before to be gone and never return."

She made a sarcastic expression and did a mock curtsey – then turned and ran. Yet Tobias had already put down the silver salver he was carrying so was ready to chase after her. His strong legs – unencumbered by long dresses as Jess was – rendered her escape futile and he soon caught up with her; she fought back viciously but Tobias quickly overpowered her then marched her back to the kitchens where she was tied to a chair – and barracked by the patronising and waspish comments of the footmen and kitchen-maids as Tobias sought out Sir Walton.

*

Jemima and Barnabas had realised that they would both be missed and gossip would follow if they did not return to the throng, so severally returned to the main house where people were assembling for the pending entertainments. Yet they were finding it difficult to stay apart and a little later were spotted together by Alice who, recognising Barnabas, angrily accosted them and, in some consternation, took the couple aside.

"Jemima! I forbade you to see this man again... and how did you come by being here anyway?" she asked Barnabas abruptly.

"No, mama, you forbade me to see him *in that place*,"

she emphasised, "and now Barnabas will never return there, as neither will I."

"I should hope not," Alice replied curtly. Then, after a moment, she looked at him sternly and said, "So your name's Barnabas: well, perhaps you had better explain yourself and why I should allow you to see my young daughter."

Between them, they explained what had happened and that the episode in the Bakewell house had been a terrible mistake for both of them but that its occurrence had started what looked like a very promising relationship. At first, Alice was unmoved but their earnest apologies and requests that they would appreciate being permitted to see each other again eventually softened her resistance and she instructed them to behave decorously whilst she went to discuss the situation with Sir Walton. They both looked relieved as she left and eventually found Sir Walton in deep humorous conversation with Josiah. Prising them apart, she discreetly took him into a corner and availed him of what had happened.

Being initially angry at what she told him, he admitted that it was he who had invited Barnabas on Josiah's part and, being in a somewhat inebriated mood and wishing to appear conciliatory, asked Alice to fetch the couple. Soon they found themselves in the smoking-room which was at that moment the only place not filled with people. Jemima and Barnabas had looked rather sheepish as Sir Walton entered and he sternly interrogated them.

After a few minutes, it was obvious to him that their affection was genuine and, liking Barnabas and having heard good reports of his character and abilities from Josiah, he accepted their explanations and the manner in which they had met – albeit with some regret. However, in order for them to be allowed to see each other further, he demanded an agreement: that Barnabas marry Jemima as soon as possible – not just to permit him to continue his nascent position as a lawyer in Bakewell but in case there was the chance of any issue from the initial or any subsequent clandestine couplings: he wanted no scandals. As this happily suited them both, the entire case was agreed – after which he left them and returned to the Great Parlour.

Only to be immediately approached by a slightly breathless Tobias with another predicament: that Jess Rigby had been accosted at the wedding where she had hoped to cause 'some sort of disturbance', as he put it.

"Jess Rigby? Again?" he asked disbelievingly. Tobias nodded. This immediately returned Sir Walton into his sour mood again: all he wanted was to enjoy the festivities but had to admit that it was important for him to address and chastise this woman who kept re-appearing like a bad penny.

Some minutes later, he was in the library, this having been quickly requisitioned due to the number of guests in the Great Parlour: he stood with his legs akimbo to denote a firmness of strength and authority in the manner of Holbein's portrait of King Henry the VIIIth while, further away, Alice sat quietly. The door opened and Jess was shown in by Tobias, her hands bound behind her back. Sir Walton gave her a cold look but said nothing, while the girl writhed and started shouting abuse at him, which did her cause little good.

"Calm down, Miss Jess," Tobias advised; "This will not help your predicament." It went quiet for a moment, the tense air only punctuated by the heavy breathing of Jess and the thickly bookish silence that pervaded everything.

Then Sir Walton spoke.

"I understand you have something to say to me," he stated. Tobias shoved Jess to respond. After a pause, she replied: "No. I've nothing to say."

"*Sir*," Tobias prompted, shoving her again.

"Sir," she reluctantly added.

"Then why are you here when you have been banished?"

Jess stayed silent, so Sir Walton continued: "Tobias tells me that, apparently, you were going to write me a letter and send it to me anonymously."

"That was my original intention, sir. But I had thought better of it."

"Why?"

"Because I realised I had missed the moment when I got here – things had moved on."

"Things?"

"When I was relieved of my position here I told Mrs. Burrows - "

"Miss Yarley."

"Miss *Yarley*… how badly I had been treated here and that I had found out things about your family which perhaps people didn't know but should…"

"What sort of things?"

"Things I was supposed to ignore, not see…"

"Like what?"

"Your children by Miss Alice and how you ignored Lady Lucinda… that sort of thing…"

"For what purpose?"

"Only so you knew that I knew, Sir – and you might then re-instate me to my position here."

"Is that all?" he asked. "Was there not some intent to extract money from me by blackmail so my position and reputation were impugned?"

"Me, Sir? No, Sir!"

"I don't believe you." Jess writhed.

"I'm just a poor girl, sir, trying to make an honest living."

"Poor? Honest? I hear your bawdy-house is doing very well – the one I gave you to live in as part of the divorce agreement – but never to turn it into a house of ill-repute." This silenced Jess, so he continued: "Miss Rigby, I think I know more about you than you do about me. I know my son – supposed son – visits your establishment and somehow my daughter, Jemima, was lured there by you."

"That's not true, sir! It was my friend Polly bumped into your daughter when she was lost in the town, sir! We just showed her the way, sir!"

"Indeed you did, Miss Rigby; indeed you did."

Alice could not help smile at this, despite her still raw anger at how her daughter had been taken in and then defiled.

"And there you introduced her to Barnabas."

"I know no Barnabas, sir."

"Well, he knows you." Jess looked confused.

"No, sir. I know no Barnabas, sir."

"For reasons of propriety, he called himself Jonquil to you." Jess looked surprised.

"You see, Miss Jess... we all have to respect our positions. Even you."

"How d'you mean, sir?"

"Well, most people – well, men, anyway – know your

trade but keep it secret - "

"That's for their own positions, not mine!" she blurted. "I was forced into my business by you after you dismissed me for loving a man whom I found attractive."

"But Jack the stable-lad did not want *you*, Jess. You harassed him."

There was a pause, then she responded waspishly, "Well, they want me now, sir, don't they?"

"Yes, they do. And you were lucky enough to know me, who got you that house in the town because of your relationship with my erstwhile butler, Giles Burrows. You enticed him into your web and got his house. No-one has tried to take that away from you since. Until now." Jess went white as he continued: "Elspeth Yarley, as she has reverted to calling herself – kept quiet for my sake and yours. She wanted no lingering problems with that dreadful man so gave in – and you were the beneficiary."

"What d'you mean, 'until now', sir?"

Sir Walton Grimley looked at his shoes, then back at her. "Well, as I said a moment ago... I believe you were going to try and blackmail me to destroy my reputation ... and bring my house and family into ruin. You also thought that I didn't know Sebastian was probably your son - "

"*Probably* my son? He *is* my son!"

"In your business? How can you be sure of that? Could have been many a man's son."

"No! I had only gone with Giles by then!"

"I think not. The way you went after our stable-lad, Jack, made us all aware of your propensity for lustful conquest... so it would appear you went into the right profession." He smirked at his little jibe then continued:

"There were many of them... Giles was just the excuse as he was drunken, gullible and you could use him. All I did was offer an escape route for him and Elspeth from which you ultimately benefitted."

Jess stayed quiet: she was not enjoying this situation. How could people like Sir Walton Grimley know all this and sleep soundly, she wondered to herself. But Sir Walton had continued his discourse: "Another benefit, of course, is that out of all this I can now blackmail *you* into getting Elspeth's house back." Jess took a sharp intake of breath but he held up his hand. "Stay quiet, Jess, until I have finished. I am not as harsh or unkindly a person as you would have us all believe... As you gave me a son to a wife I had little love for, and he was virtually banished by me for his frequenting places such as yours – and gambling, carousing, getting into debt - nonetheless he has a title which I can either acknowledge or deny – especially under the circumstances of his coming by it. So, you see, I can blackmail *you*." The intensity in the room was only interrupted by the sounds of distant grouse as Jess awaited his decision - and that she was about to lose everything she had acquired due to her malicious scheming. Now she was paying the price: never take on the gentry, they always win, she found herself relenting.

Sir Walton then continued. "So I will make a proposal, Miss Jess. And it is this. In due course, Miss Yarley and Tobias will have to retire and will need a house. That house will be yours, returned to its rightful owner."

Jess went to protest but thought better of it.

"But today is supposed to be a happy occasion so I am going to give you a second chance. You will move far away from Bakewell and I will provide you a small amount of money for a house - as long as all the conditions I will lay out today are adhered to. These will include not having any claim on your supposed son's birthright – he may not be my own wife's but he also might not be yours, as I have implied – and I will give you a small amount to live on for a year whilst you establish a business, preferably more reputable than the one you are in now. I am doing this because I believe you are only guilty of a licentious nature and cannot control it – but that will pass. We are all licentious in some degree or another – it is God's will. Without it, there would be no children. Even I have been licentious in my youth and – yes - visited one or two places resembling yours. I was licentious again by bringing Alice's daughters into being. But, most importantly to this situation regarding you... For devious outcomes, you introduced my younger daughter to my lawyer who – as a result - I believe may find themselves very happy together. So, you see, all your anger, bile and resentment has actually been of benefit to them – and so that has given me pleasure, too."

Jess just stood there, disbelieving. Sir Walton Grimley was not the ogre she wished him to be; he had graciously dealt her a good hand and a chance at respectability. She looked down and just said sheepishly, "Thank you, Sir; thank you very much indeed, Sir."

Sir Walton nodded with a slight smile of both satisfaction and triumph and then went to a reading-desk on which was a quill and an inkstand, at the same time sending Tobias to fetch Barnabas. Tobias left the room and Jess asked if she could be untied, which Sir Walton agreed to and the footman did so.

With that, the door opened and Tobias showed in

Barnabas, who looked slightly embarrassed by the situation but, as agreed only a few minutes before with Sir Walton, had swiftly made out a legal document, stipulating that she, Jess Rigby, would be beholden to what she signed to or else would be out on the street with no home or living and probably destitute. She nodded with a sense of conflicting regret and relief as Barnabas laid it out on the reading-desk and motioned her to come and sign it. As she went over to it, Sir Walton stated, "This, Jess Rigby, is a binding legal document, drawn up by your good friend, Jonquil – or Barnabas, as his real name is. See? We *all* have secrets…!" Barnabas reddened as the document was signed and Sir Walton watched her do so. "It seems you have learned to read since you were here, Miss Rigby," he observed approvingly.

"I been learning to read, Sir…"

"Good – at least some of your ill-gotten gains have been put to good use…"

Jess wanted to make a face at that comment but declined - she was still under observation and now at the whim of the law. Yet the one thing she knew without any doubt was that Sebastian was her son: mothers know these things. And now she had to move away from Bakewell and start all over again somewhere else. That annoyed her. So despite Sir Walton's apparent kindness, she would make herself believe it was underpinned by a blatant self-interest which would benefit him more than her in the long run … and a burning revenge would still burn in her maternal breast. And this only became more intense as she walked back to Bakewell in the gathering gloom…

*

Some months passed: Jemima and Barnabas married

quietly without pomp or ceremony and to avoid any embarrassing questions, whilst Sir Walton Grimley's plans regarding Jess had been enacted in full by Barnabas, now his new lawyer and son-in-law. Unknown to them, however, Lady Lucinda had been contacted by Jess, who had seen a loophole in her agreement with Sir Walton: so despite signing a written agreement, her vitriolic wishes against Sir Walton Grimley, his family and the entire staff pertaining to Mulberry Hall were fanned by their being of more benefit to him than her. However, she needed to wait a while and, by releasing her house as acceptance of Sir Walton's edict, had cleverly then decided to live in Wirksworth. There, she could be close to any news of the Grimley household through Lucinda and Sebastian, the latter who would, of course, quietly help set up her existing trade there – and also be her founding client once other girls had been engaged. With the money donated by Sir Walton Grimley – and by now not a small amount of her own - she bought a slightly larger building than she had received in Bakewell to expand her business and profits. It would soon, therefore, be an auspicious moment for Jess to approach Lady Lucinda at her Wirksworth factory with a proposal…

BOOK THREE

1832

CHAPTER 45

Finances, Rankling Revenge, A Plot & Acts Of Parliament

Sir Walton had always wanted Tobias, Alice, Sophie and Jemima to live without prejudice now the convulsions of slavery's abolition were calming down; yet his personal concern was that although the Act had indeed caused a negligible reduction in Britain's wealth, with him being at the sharp end he had suffered disproportionately more than the country as a whole. Subsequently, he was finding it increasingly difficult to pay his outgoings and worried that soon this would mean paying his workpeople in both countries less, which he was loath to do: with that, he could suffer more disdain, rather than less, and might backfire on his initial morality, kindness and largesse over the coming years. His tenure of even the workers he employed in Jamaica could technically be cast into jeopardy, such had been the febrile outcome of the Act's passing and its lingering after-effects. He sighed: epoch-making events like this took so much time to settle in as, he suspected, similar major national ones would do in future years and centuries... So he wondered whether, perhaps, it was the moment to sell Mulberry Hall and retire to Jamaica: after all, he had to admit, the cold northern weather was now beginning to affect him more acutely...

He knew Edward would be immune to whatever happened as he was successful in Milan and across other parts of Italy, too; in addition, his Duchess was such a favourite due to her beauty that she was able to deflect any rancour with her additional effervescent wit. Their only criticism came from the Catholic church for not being married. Sadly, she had lost her child on the rough crossing back to Europe after Sophie and Josiah's wedding but their affection would soon provoke a replacement, Sir Walton was sure. Both Sophie and Jemima had recently given birth, too; so perhaps he would – if things all went wrong – not retire to Jamaica yet but take himself, his family and dependants to Italy for a few years. He was still just young enough to do that, he felt...

*

It was a cold, grey morning in Wirksworth and although the rain had stopped, its threatened continuation cast a damp pall over the town. A few blurs of polluted yellowy cloud challenged the gloom but it was a feeble attempt. Jess was making her way through the cobbled streets, most of them flanked by tall, drab factories which created canyons of murk as she progressed towards Lucinda's manufactory. She had recently begun to realise how much the openness of

Bakewell had previously lifted her mood: whilst Wirksworth was similarly surrounded by steep hills, their presence was mostly obliterated by these buildings, worsened by their plumes of belching smoke which loured the sky. Still, she had made a good start in the town and had already sought out some prospective clients, easier now she had found two pretty girls whom she had taken in. She had been unexpectedly glad for the opportunity to start again because, without prostitution, she would have missed the physical contact and easy money – much to the satisfaction of Sebastian.

"Good morning, Miss Jess."

"Good morning, Lady Lucinda."

"And what is it I can help you with? I hear you have settled in well in Wirksworth."

"Indeed, Lady Lucinda – and with much help from your good son."

"Or, *your* good son."

There was a brief pause as Jess looked round to check he had not entered. "So he is not here at this moment?"

"No. Out hunting."

"For what, may I ask?"

"Probably some pretty women to fill your new house and venture."

An awkward embarrassment filled the air, only the clanking of the steam-hammers in the factory below interrupting the moment.

"So how can I help you?" Lucinda asked again.

"It would not surprise you to know that I still have a strong feeling of resentment towards Sir Walton Grimley."

Lucinda shifted uneasily; "I am surprised. You have

come very well out of this, have you not?"

"That is not quite the point, milady."

"I see." There was another pause as Lucinda gazed out of the window towards the tips of the trees just visible on the other side of the valley through which the river Medlock ran, powering her business, their bright green a distant contrast to the drabness beneath and beyond her lofty office. Then she looked at Jess as her countenance hardened and she stated quietly but bluntly, "It may not surprise you to know that I, too, have a feeling of resentment towards Sir Walton Grimley."

"As I suspected."

"Is that why you've moved here, to be far away from Bakewell but close to your son?"

"That is part of it; also, that I will hear news of Mulberry Hall more readily from you and Sebastian than I would anywhere else."

"Hmm… clever… you *do* have a resentment, don't you? Waiting for a chance to pounce and discredit him?"

"If possible."

"And so ruin him?"

"That would be a satisfactory outcome."

"But if you did that, it would also affect me. He gives me an annual amount."

"If you think more deeply, however, Lady Lucinda," flattery was now of benefit, she surmised, "if he was forced to leave Mulberry Hall – in whatever manner - " she added darkly, "then as your legal wife it would fall to you; whereupon you could either sell or lease the estate and make a handsome profit – and make much more than he could ever begrudgingly give you."

"Continue."

"Although the Act for the Abolition of the Slave Trade was passed through Parliament years ago in 1807, there is now a new Act - "

"You are very up with political affairs for a woman of your lowly disposition."

Jess brushed the slur aside: she knew that Lady Lucinda had come from a similar background, so she countered: "I have needed to be in the know of things in order to create my business with what little I had - a grasp of facts, a pretty face and a good body. After that, I started to take an interest in national events. It helps me with my clients – they like to talk. So I learn things which are useful."

Lucinda gave her a disparaging glance. "I find the whole Parliament thing of little interest. What will be will be - and my business is of greater importance. And of what significance is, *was*, this Act for the Abolition of the Slave Trade, pray?"

"The Act only concerned *future* slaves; those who were already in slavery still have few rights, if any. So with the possibility of a new Act coming up in Parliament very soon - "

"And I suppose you know what this Act is called?" Lucinda interrupted, with a slight sneer.

"Yes – the Slavery Abolition Act. It will mean not only that new slaves cannot be carried from the colonies but that Sir Walton will either have to take on new slaves by paying them as freemen or not take on any at all. Either way, his sugar will soon be far more expensive. Other nations are resisting the abolition of slavery – Holland, France, Portugal, Belgium, to name but a few - so Sir Walton's sugar will become too costly and he will subsequently be ruined."

"So it means that Sir Walton will legally have to free all his slaves. Or pay them."

"Yes."

"Well, I believe he has actually already done that – and has been doing so for some time – ever since the, the, the other Act you mentioned."

"What – the Abolition of the Slave Trade Act of 1807?"

"Yes, I believe that was the one; they all sound the same to me."

Jess was annoyed: had he? That was something that had escaped her. Not that it would make any difference to her plan.

In the silence, Lucinda continued: "Mind you, I thought all that had been sorted out years ago. I seem to remember some silly Act or other being passed…"

"Well, it was; it was called the Slave Trade Bill and was passed in 1792. But it took ages to get through the Lords and was only enacted in 1807… as you probably know," she added mischievously.

Lucinda flinched, then replied, "Well, these things always take time… I think it *has* impacted on his wealth… but not enough for *me* to worry about."

'*But I do*,' thought Jess, as the swift execution of what she hoped would be their joint plan suddenly seemed more urgent.

While Jess momentarily wrestled with this new immediacy, Lucinda was beginning to realise how much more this upstart whore knew about national events than she did and resented it, feeling Jess should not know these things when she herself did not. Miffed, she tried to think of something that would make her sound more knowledgeable

– and suddenly remembered something. "I seem to be aware of the formation of a Royal Naval Squadron after that Act, which Sir Walton earnestly championed."

She hoped Jess would be flummoxed by that, but she instantly answered, "That's true – and it's already reduced the number of slaves being transported by other countries. It hasn't completely succeeded yet, but it's beginning to… so the sooner that happens, the quicker Sir Walton will be losing money."

Again annoyed at her lack of current affairs, Lucinda looked at the plans on her desk as a distraction: yet the penny had dropped. She was suddenly worried and looked up. Without her annual stipend from Sir Walton she would have to put her prices up, too – and that would mean losing many embryonic and lucrative contracts. Jess was right: as Sir Walton's wife she might be able to wrest Mulberry Hall from him which would satisfy her financial needs for life. Since her business prospered she had rather lost touch with the financial side, preferring instead to design and create useful tools and implements, which is what she was good at. But that was where Josiah had been such a blessing: his mastery of detail and finance had been instrumental in growing her business. Yet Jess's acute perception of Sir Walton's approaching vulnerability was now stoking a glow of revenge in her solar plexus, too, which might even cause the return of Josiah to her business. Then with a dash of disappointment she remembered that he was already installed in Mulberry Hall since his marriage to that little trollop, Sophie. Well, she could banish Sophie if she became mistress of the Hall – and then ingratiate Josiah into her bed instead! With that thought, she felt quite flushed and, picking up a plan for a pressure valve she was designing, fanned herself with it – an action which was well understood by Jess and confirmed that her plan was working. As for Lucinda, she was suddenly and lucidly aware that Jess's assessment of the situation might bear fruit for all of them bar Sir Walton Grimley. With this Slavery Abolition Act soon apparently expected to cause widespread financial disturbance, she might be able to both hasten the ruin of Sir Walton *and* avenge him for preferring his little black whore Alice to her as well. She turned to Jess. "I will get some victuals prepared at my house shortly. We need to talk further."

They found themselves in deep conversation for the rest of the evening.

CHAPTER 46

Stark Realisations

& A Momentous Decision

Sir Walton Grimley was arriving back at Bakewell in deep thought and not a little depressed. He was unsure how his family – both close and rejected – would take to his proposition but felt that he had seen the writing on the wall and must go through with his plan to retire to Jamaica. They spoke English there, too, unlike Italy, and had decided that, as he did not speak Italian, he would be too dependent upon Edward and Philomena... His ruminations were not helped by a foul journey with torrential rain, a few late arrivals at staging-posts and an unpleasant altercation with a highwayman near Stamford, who was eventually shot by the watchman travelling on the rear of the coach. Initially only wounded, it was requested of Sir Walton as the most senior and important person to dispatch him; this momentarily relieved Sir Walton of his pressing thoughts but subsequently gave him nightmares for years to come. The coachman and the watchman were allowed the proceeds of what the man had stolen from a previous endeavour for their valour and they threw the assailant over the edge of a high, adjacent cliff, with everyone sworn to secrecy.

It was dusk when they arrived in Bakewell and Sir Walton decided to stay at the Rutland Arms for the night; he could not face the further nine miles to Mulberry Hall being already tired, dirty, stressed and very irritable. Again it hit him – he was getting old: and this damp weather was making his joints ache. He must put his plan into action.

*

Since their last meeting, Lady Lucinda and Jess had become far more friendly with one another, a situation not lost on Sebastian, who felt that the only reason for this new dalliance must be subterfuge. His position between the two women – his true mother and his adopted one – was awkward and, whatever this alliance meant, he did not like it. He was glad having Jess around, though, despite strange pulls of emotion where he felt he was beholden to one rather than the other, then the opposite; although many men would feel that one mother was enough, the unusual juxtaposition of conflicting yet symbiotic feelings kept him in a state of affectionate awareness as to their very contrasting places in his life. Whilst he felt constricted in one sense he was free in another: neither could scold or berate him for fear he could use the other for emotional advantage. Neither told him to get a wife, for example, and although Jess was in no position to promote the idea, he wondered whether Lucinda would do so if pushed. So his existence continued in a mutual ambivalence, which did nothing to help what happened next.

*

By resisting his return to Mulberry Hall for another day, Sir Walton Grimley had found that being in the hotel without distractions had allowed him to think more clearly. He had thus decided to consult Josiah for a discreet private talk while his thoughts settled into a coherent train before returning home to confront the family with the plan which was pervading his every thought. He sent a message to Josiah at Mulberry Hall via a stable-lad, requesting a meeting in the town with him as soon as possible and to come with his horse - he had had enough of stage-coaches: he would wait for either him or a response. As the lad rode away into the hills, he began to realise that he felt Josiah was like a younger brother he had never had and once again found he was chastising himself for his decision to marry Lucinda when he had already been so happy with Alice: a brother would have warned against such a move, he was sure. Things were so different in those days, he mused; in London there were now a good many people of different races and backgrounds blown in by desire, shipwrecks, insurrections, reputation and, occasionally, affluence. There were mixed-race children now, too, and few took any notice; in fact, the English were more likely to make open fun of the French, Dutch or Germans than anyone with a different coloured skin; it was as if the continentals were an open enemy due to constant wars, alliances and consequent betrayals than the few who had arrived almost by chance: perhaps it was because they had a mystique which was unknown, unfathomable. And that is what took him back to thinking about his own plan; would his true family think of him as he thought of them – benignly, without prejudice, and kindly? Or would they harbour rancour and resentment? Only time would tell; but he somehow felt that, for him, this was running out.

Eventually, he heard horses clattering through the archway of the coaching-inn and, through the window, he saw the stable-lad and then Josiah leading Sir Walton's own steed go past. A few moments later, a hot and flustered Josiah appeared.

"Sir Walton," he said as he entered, as if concerned about some terrible news his father-in-law was about to impart. "What's happened?"

"Nothing to worry about," Sir Walton replied somewhat unassuredly; "Just something I need to discuss with you before I return to the family."

"Ah… so how can I help you?"

"It's some legal advice I need."

Josiah stopped: "Ah – wouldn't it have been better to summon Barnabas for that?"

"Not yet; I want to run this past someone I have known longer… and who feels more of a brother to me."

"Ah – I am flattered. That is a huge honour."

"And I mean it as such. I have reserved a room where we can talk – let's go there. There are drinks and victuals ordered…"

He rose and they went into a back room; the drinks were already waiting and after they had both sat down and filled their glasses, Sir Walton started to reveal his proposal.

"I am getting old," he prefaced, then, "and now that this protracted act of Parliament will soon be most likely passed – thanks to God - I have to make some changes in anticipation to help both me and my dependants, which includes you, of course." A silence descended on the room, as if portending something dreadful, which seriously concerned Josiah. He noticed Sir Walton staring into the fireplace and, as the flames danced in denial of the prevailing mood, he noticed a tear in the old man's eye.

"What is it, Sir Walton?" he ventured after a few

moments' silence,

"I wish to sell Mulberry Hall," he murmured.

Josiah was dumbstruck. "But... but what are the family going to do? And where will *we* all go?" He suddenly realised how selfish that sounded and wished he had kept quiet.

Sir Walton sighed deeply and then began to offload his thoughts. "I inherited a lot of money when my father died and made the estate in Jamaica a much better place for my people to work. When moves were started to abolish the trade I knew that it was the right thing to do – future generations would never forgive us for what many owners did, even though other nations have still yet done nothing to share our lead. But neither did I think this would ever come in my lifetime. Yet if it did, I knew then that one day I would have to face a reckoning; that day is this one." Josiah sat back in his chair and waited for him to continue, fortifying the stillness with a sip of his brandy. "I always loved my people – well, except one or two troublemakers... but because they knew I was a good master – and word travels fast in places like that – they never took advantage of me, which is why I liked them all the more. So I decided to make as much money as I could, while I could, as long as it didn't disadvantage the wellbeing of my people." Josiah was touched at how he never called them 'slaves' in the possessive, but always 'my people' or 'workers' – he had heard him use these terms before. "As you know, the Act for the Abolition of Slavery is almost certain to be passed very soon – and I'm heartily glad of it. However, it poses some changes, which grow out of the associated problems. As I also said, I am getting old but have had a wonderful life – how could I not without the good Tobias at my side at first, and then my beautiful, wonderful and dear Alice?"

The tears were becoming bigger as he said this, and one dripped over his eyelid and into his sherry. He brushed the remains away and continued. "Without her, I would have been nothing – and I am so pleased you have married our daughter, Sophie, which brings us closer together as in-laws. When I first met you as a young apprentice builder I knew that you could go far and I have done all I can to progress that – and so I thank you for building the splendid Mulberry Hall and Alice Lodge – as well as whatever it is you have built for Lucinda which, of course, I have never seen. Nor do I wish to, for fear of seeing her again, whose subterfuge with my supposed bastard son and that whore called Jess has blighted my life at what should have been a happy time."

Josiah was becoming ever more concerned, as each sentence seemed to procrastinate his solution due to this torrent of both joy and conflicting remorse. "So why do you want to sell Mulberry Hall?" he enquired warily.

"I'm coming to that. I am aware that Lucinda has been very quiet for a while, which usually means she's plotting something – despite being so far away."

"I fail to see where this is going…" remarked Josiah.

"Let me explain. … You know some of this, but perhaps not all… Some years ago, I dismissed that servant girl, Jess Rigby, for harassing a stable-lad. Later, though, I bequeathed this Jess woman Elspeth's home in Bakewell as part of forcing her wastrel husband Giles to divorce her because he had taken this girl over and she was living in their house. I did that – and gave her some money - because I wanted Elspeth to be happy with Tobias. Yet she keeps cropping up like a bad penny – as you saw at your wedding. Jemima was compromised by the same girl, too; that, in the event, worked out well for her and Barnabas but it was also this girl who provided the child that Lucinda took as her own so I would not banish her - and also have an heir. This Miss Rigby then moved up to Wirksworth."

"The same town as Lucinda…"

"Yes. But despite my largesse I think she may be in league with Lucinda to try and destroy me once more, as they have a connection via my son and heir, Sebastian."

"She sounds like a scheming young lady," remarked Josiah.

"Not a lady, Josiah, a scheming harridan." A hint of a smile crossed his face. "And whilst I was very diplomatic in giving Jess Rigby the house in Bakewell and sorted her out financially in Wirksworth, I know she still hates me and all I stand for; I was sure she would be back in some vengeful fashion one day, I was sure of it; one can feel it in people, y'know… And again, that day is now."

"*Now*?", interjected Josiah.

"Yes.

"Why do you suddenly think this *now*?"

"Because I have received a vindictive, grasping letter from Lucinda's counsel and it's obvious to me that its contents could only have been concocted with intelligence from Jess: they're in cahoots, I would wager, as they have a connection – my 'son' Sebastian. That means that, when I die, they will fight over the estate, which will be bad for you, Alice, Sophie, Jemima and now, also, Barnabas."

"I see. But - " Sir Walton raised his hand to stop him. "Please… just wait for me to finish, then you can ask all the questions you want."

Josiah nodded and sat back in his chair again, pouring

another brandy as he did so.

Sir Walton continued. "There was a time not long ago when I thought I would stay here until I died but having spent much of my youth and subsequent life on and off in the West Indies, I find myself attracted back there, if for no other reason than my aching joints. If I returned there, I could also better ensure that my people were well looked after and also do good for the other estates whose owners are not as enlightened as I am. In fact, it has become a calling for me. Now, whether Tobias and his dear Elspeth Yarley wish to return there – or go there, in her case - I know not; I suspect Alice will come with me – well, if she doesn't then I will stay here with her and we will await our armageddon together. But I suspect she will want to come – she too is concerned that Lucinda has not finished her hatred of her and so would do well to be out of her way. As for you with Sophie, and Barnabas with Jemima, that is for you all to decide. But in order to do all of these things, that is why I will have to sell Mulberry Hall."

Josiah was in a quandary; he loved Mulberry Hall, his greatest achievement. "And what of Alice Lodge?"

"Ah… that I intend to leave to you and Sophie if you want it, as well as Barnabas and Jemima. There's room for you all there as well as a few servants… and you can always build an extension if you need to on the amount of land I will leave around it. And a suitable stipend, of course, to keep you in the manner to which you are now accustomed."

Josiah noticed his mouth was hanging open and quickly shut it. "I see," was all he could say.

"So… what do you think of my plan?"

Josiah had so many responses in his mind that he did not know where to start. Eventually, his feelings regarding the Hall seemed the most pertinent to him so he started there.

"Sir Walton; you know it is no secret that I love Mulberry Hall - it is my first and greatest achievement and without your confidence in my finishing it after my dear father died, I would be nothing. I have built a few other mansions – when I was not pre-occupied with Lucinda's business – but none are as great or beautiful as Mulberry Hall. But... who do you think would buy such a great pile? Things are becoming tighter financially for the aristocracy and servants are so expensive now... and I doubt Lucinda would allow its sale without a fight – unless you can get in first."

"That's a good point; you see, that's why I had to run it past you." There was a pause, then he added, "Talking of Lady Lucinda, did she ever betray any affection for you?"

After a moment, Josiah almost angrily blurted out, "Indeed she did, Sir. It was incessant – more so after you went back to Alice."

"I never actually 'left' Alice – but that is a detail. Hmmm, I thought as much..."

"And when I was building her house in Wirksworth she never stopped - although I think it was as much because she was aware that I wanted to leave to marry Sophie and that would diminish any money she might get from you; overall, somehow I think she wanted to entrap me - "

"For both pecuniary *and* emotional reasons, then?"

"Yes – and, of course, revenge."

"Ah... revenge – another thing I hadn't thought of. Seems obvious now I think of it."

"She last tried the day before Sophie's wedding to me, would you believe?"

"Damn the woman! How I ever found her so attractive I shall never know…"

"Well, she has a pretty face and an engaging personality, Sir… At least, when she *wants* something, she does."

"Hah! Well… now she's *definitely* not getting any part of Mulberry Hall, I assure you! She's done quite well enough out of me… so we must keep her trapped in Wirksworth!"

They each emitted a hollow laugh, a release against the stark problems they could soon be facing. It went quiet for a moment, only interrupted by two barmaids bringing in a hearty lunch. After they had disappeared, the two men went to the table and started eating, each harbouring some similar, and other disparate, concerns.

Josiah eventually broke the silence: "Sir Walton, why don't you just sell Alice Lodge instead? It will not bring in so much income but it means less to you than the Hall itself."

Sir Walton contemplated the idea for a moment, then replied, "I see why you say that; you wish to keep the Hall in the family – and it's your achievement. I understand that. Yet it all comes down to money. Which I will need to pay off the inevitable legal fees that Lucinda and possibly even Jess will fight me over – whether or not I sell Mulberry Hall. Either way, it seems, I am damned: I lose the Hall by selling it but get money for a good life in Jamaica or I win the case but am ruined in the process."

Another momentary silence descended on the room. Then Sir Walton continued: "You see, as well as the increased costs I have in Jamaica because I treat my workers properly… I know a claim is coming – in the letter I had from Lucinda's counsel it is clear that I will need the money to fight her … but… if I sell it first, and as soon as I can, she has far less chance of getting it."

"Hmmm... Pity... If you had divorced her and married Alice this dilemma would be less of a concern..."

"True... but then she'd just have tried it on earlier which would have caused a scandal... and, anyway, it's too late for that now."

There was another pause. Then, with a heavy sigh, Josiah said, "I think you should, then, talk to Barnabas – and quickly. I remember Sophie saying to me once that she and Jemima felt like ghosts as they were virtually banished from the Hall due to any scurrilous backlash against you, Sir Walton... Perhaps we should leave it like that and you're right - sell the Hall and leave the memories with it. I would be more than happy with just Alice Lodge as long as I have my Sophie with me. And every morning I could look out of the window and view my beautiful masterpiece..."

"You wouldn't want to if Lady Lucinda was living there," Sir Walton added pointedly.

This took the wind out of Josiah's sails for a moment; then, with the conviction of a fresh, untried approach, he said, "Then we would definitely join you in Jamaica!"

"And leave the ghosts of Mulberry Hall intact but alone."

"Indeed..."

There was another silence; then Sir Walton sighed again and said quietly, "One last thing, then, dear Josiah; not a word of this to anyone, please. I will address the family soon when my way forward is clearer."

Josiah nodded. The debate over, Sir Walton Grimley stood with a wince – and a little difficulty and pain, Josiah noted; yes, the better climate and distance from the jealousies and bitterness of past events would do him good, he realised. And Tobias and Alice could return to their spiritual home, perhaps... Sophie and Jemima would obviously prefer to stay in England. At least, he hoped so... Then a wicked perception crossed Josiah's mind: if Sophie did wish to leave for Jamaica, he would not - and he could live in his masterpiece with Lucinda. Then he felt ashamed of his thought and soon they had finished their lunch and were riding back towards Mulberry Hall.

CHAPTER 47

A Plan Is Proposed

& A Brawl Avoided

It was a week or so later when Sir Walton Grimley received a further letter from Lady Lucinda's lawyer and it suddenly became the catalyst for him to finally break his plan to the rest of the family. The letter stated baldly that as she had been evicted from Mulberry Hall for well over a year – and that her business was facing turbulent headwinds – she had no other choice but to demand that she was due to half the current value of the estate, either as continuous remuneration from its proceeds or occasioned by 'other solutions', as she had evasively termed it. This spooked Sir Walton, who realised he now really had to act in haste lest Lucinda got wind somehow of his desire to sell up: this was all the more urgent now he suspected that her secret plan was to wrest the Hall from him completely – no half measures for her. Fortunately, a conversation with Barnabas on his return from the meeting with Josiah had resulted in a letter of intent being swiftly written, witnessed and sent to Lucinda's lawyers explaining his decision to sell the Hall – if not the entire estate – some days before the date of

THE SLAVE-OWNER'S DILEMMA

Lucinda's letter; thereby, the arrival of Lucinda's ultimatum could be proved that it was received by Sir Walton *after* that date. All that had to happen, therefore, was for someone to have bought the house before any negotiations could begin. In this, Barnabas had already been in touch with agents and a putative sale had been agreed – dated even further back – in case that any expected reply arrived. Some monies had changed hands but the proviso would be that the whole family had to accept its terms when the time arrived.

Suddenly, the whole family were summoned to the Great Parlour – as were Tobias and Elspeth, Miss Shaw and other loyal and long-standing servants of authority. Fevered speculation caused a bubbling ferment of conflicting expectations but the over-riding sense was one of worry that their employment was about to be terminated.

Sir Walton Grimley strode as purposefully into the room as he was now able and it went quiet. No other members of the family – except Alice - had been privy to the putative plans so were all there in a state of bafflement, if not particularly concerned: they lived gilded lives so had no expectation of the upheaval about to be foisted upon them.

"Dear family and loyal servants," he began. "I shall be brief. For reasons that I wish to keep private – except the fact that I am getting old..." as a muted sound of denial went around the room – "I have decided to sell Mulberry Hall and its estate." A gasp of fear and surprise pervaded the room, but he held up his hand. "None of you need to worry, however; you will all have the option to stay here under the new owner if you wish... or come with me to my final home and eventual resting-place." Another babble of suppressed surprise went around. "I cannot tell you yet who the new owner of Mulberry Hall will be as it is secret for reasons I need to keep so. For my part, Lady Alice" – he had called her that ever since the banishment of Lady Lucinda – "and I will be permanently departing soon to Jamaica." Another gasp went around the room. "However, anyone here will be free to come with me. I have a beautiful mansion on that wonderful island which also has smaller houses dotted around the estate for servants – and with the sale of this I can build more if necessary. I wish for Alice's children – who are also mine, of course" and a ripple of suppressed laughter went around the room "– to have the opportunity to live in the country of their mother's birth if they wish to. However, if they don't, they can stay here in Alice Lodge – which I will not include in the sale - with their new English husbands. Elspeth: you and Tobias must decide where you wish to rest and I accept that this will be a difficult decision for you both but one which must be addressed." He instantly noticed a look of panic on Elspeth's face and realised what a conundrum he was putting them in: if Tobias wanted to return to his homeland, would she go with him? And if she did, she would probably never see Edward again – Jamaica was too distant and difficult to get to from Italy. He felt suddenly responsible, so added, "I will discuss things with you both in private if you wish, should that help you." Then he turned to Barnabas, sitting just behind him, and continued. "Barnabas here will give you all some time to make your decisions but they must, please, be made today – for pressing legal reasons. Finally, as a thank you to all of you here, my dear servants, I will leave you all a year's wages whether you decide to stay or not as a thank-you for your loyal service which has been so appreciated over the years." Someone started clapping as a murmur of grateful thanks swept the room. Sir Walton continued: "Obviously, those who wish to come with me will have the same terms and conditions – and chores – as here; but I can say that Jamaica is a most wonderful place; yet it is mostly hot but sometimes cold; it does have hurricanes and violent rainstorms, too; also insects, some dangerous snakes, fish and animals and various other unpleasantries. Yet, on balance, it is a beautiful island which I wish to return to for my last days. I shall now allow you all to discuss your thoughts but, again, please tell Barnabas what decision you have made today. Discuss freely… and I will see you all later in person or at dinner as usual."

Tobias, though, needed to know the answer to one question first and asked, "Sir, can you tell us all, please, who the new owner will be?"

He stopped and looked down for a moment, then carefully answered, "Probably someone less to your liking, Tobias – nor who wishes to understand you as I do."

With that, he swept out as Barnabas sharpened his quill in expectation of a torrent of questions and difficult decisions… The most frequent he expected was why they had to make their decisions so quickly; the answer was that it had to be signed and sealed before word got out into the wider world that the estate was for sale.

*

A few hours after these discussions had been taking place, Sebastian – having no idea that his adopted mother was trying to wrest Mulberry Hall from Sir Walton Grimley - was, as so often, drinking heavily in a Wirksworth tavern. It was a very large tavern but not a good one and full of loud, ribald and dangerous men; some were sailors who had been at Trafalgar and others soldiers at Waterloo. Many were missing limbs or otherwise emaciated - and one or two were known to have become violent thieves, pickpockets and malcontents – by personality or desperation. Sebastian, being better dressed than any of the others, stood out and it was not long before a couple of these rogues started provoking him. Being much in his cups by that time, he could not think clearly and told them in no uncertain terms to leave him alone or there would be trouble.

"Trouble?" the two men said together. "It's the likes of you who cause trouble," added the more aggressive of the two; "You're the ones causing trouble; we fight for our country but now we're crippled we're on the scrapheap with no money. But look at *you*… exploiting us workmen so you can lord it over us and keep us down… all silver buckles, silk breeches and, no doubt, a clasp full of snuff!"

"And a cellar-full of claret!" another shouted from the back.

A ripple of disdain echoed around the parlour as Sebastian unsteadily stood up and faced the man. "You, sir, are a varlet, a rogue and a malcontent. You can afford to drink here, so what are you worried about?"

"We drink to forget!" another shouted; "Give us some money so we can eat - to forget how hungry we are!" Another roar of approval rent the air.

"Bloody toff!" another cried, to a similar response. The barman, a rotund, balding man with a dirty white apron, tried to calm them down. "I'll 'ave no trouble in my 'ouse," he shouted in his thick Derbyshire accent: "Be ye gone or there'll be no grog for any o' you!"

"Oh, sticking up for the masters, are you?" the first villain said, turning his attention to the barman. "And why should we not kill him and take his money?" The pub went quiet at this. "Because," the barman said, "it is the likes of people like 'im who keep this tavern open. I wonder 'ow many of you should actually be grateful to this man?" There was a silence as the topers worked out the reason: it soon came. "Because 'e pays 'is way, 'e does, which keeps me in business to the benefit of you lot – but how many of *you* thieving rascals owe me money?" as his raised arm swept the room with an accusatory finger. Then, "This place doesn't run itself. Leave 'im alone."

The bar went quiet. Sebastian sat down again. At that moment, a female voice broke the silence. "Yes – leave him alone! I know all of you here, pretty much – and especially you two," as she pointed at the two ringleaders. "You touch my son and there'll be no pretty young girls to pleasure you in any nugging-houses around this town!"

"How can you arrange that?" sneered the first.

"Because I own the best ones!"

A ripple of surprise went around the tavern.

"Well, I'll say one thing then; there's money in sex!" said the man, assessing her well-dressed attire. Then, turning to Sebastian, he said loudly: "I never knew I'd had it off with your mother!" Raucous laughter filled the pub but some hid their mirth: they did not want to jeopardise their carnal pleasures. Jess stood there, defiant, then looked coldly at the man and said, "Silas, I know a few things about you which could incriminate you so be careful."

"You know nowt about me!" he bellowed.

"Oh, I think I do – it's amazing the secrets that slip from men's lips when they're stoking the fire."

Silas looked stunned as the nervous laughter erupted then receded: he did not like being made fun of. Then, unable to articulate his feelings, he roared like a lion and, pulling his friend with him, went to the door, turned and delivered his parting shot: "No-one makes a fool of Silas Wood! C'mon, Jasper – we're going to drink somewhere else!"

The two left, the only subsequent sound being the slamming of the door and the shouted response of the barman. "See? They've left again without paying! 'Ow can I keep this place open if you lot don't pay? Come on – pay up now or this tavern will be shutting down."

Instantly, the sound of coins being counted was heard and the owner suddenly looked far happier than he had some moments before.

CHAPTER 48

Decisions Made, A Thwarted Plan,

A Flight & A Murder

Elspeth and Tobias had spent as many hours as their time restriction and chores would permit to contemplate a decision. Of the two, Tobias was more uncertain; he had become, in his view at least, the quintessential English butler and a sudden return to his roots was something he had never contemplated after coming to England with Sir Walton. He now had authority, a fine reputation and – now that the Abolition of Slavery Act was on the cusp of being passed – felt more at home in England than he had ever done in Jamaica. Elspeth, not knowing what she was comparing things with, could only rely on Tobias' interpretations. She was attracted by the sound of the warmer weather – the Peak District could be harsh on even the mildest of days – but terrified of the insects and animals Sir Walton Grimley had described. So, just by the deadline, they decided to stay and trust that the new owner would be as kind and generous as the current one.

Alice was pleased to be returning, if more for Sir Walton's sake than hers; they were still so very happy together that it made perfect sense to go back – their location was less important than their deep mutual affection. Her children and new spouses were a trickier proposition but - as they were each doing well in their respective businesses - a move to Alice Lodge was not an onerous choice. Sophie and Jemima were as English as they could possibly be and so wanted to stay, despite not wishing to see their mother and father go. And if the new owner was unpleasant, then they could sell Alice Lodge and Josiah could build a substantial home for them all somewhere else.

Three servants decided to accompany Sir Walton Grimley to Jamaica – the cook, Miss Shaw, a footman and his sweetheart Daisy, who also worked at the Hall.

For his part, Sir Walton Grimley was disappointed to be losing Tobias, who had become a loyal confidante, friend and good counsel throughout his time at Mulberry Hall. Yet he understood his butler's reasons for staying: to leave and then try to return to England after his death would be difficult, so appreciated his decision.

What he had not anticipated – nor anyone else – was who would actually end up buying Mulberry Hall...

*

Jess had left the tavern with her son and told him she was going back home – and he should go back to his rooms in Lucinda's house to sleep off his excesses: she would see him on the morrow and would not accompany him - she was too annoyed with his state of inebriation. Yet the confrontation had stirred a number of concerns; a sense of prescient foreboding had enveloped her and, being anxious for his safety as any mother would, she approached two more honest-looking men leaving the tavern and offered them money for witnessing any attack on her son, which she was sure might happen due to the vindictive unpleasantness of the two rogues, Silas and Jasper. She knew, too, that she would be unable to help him in his drunken state and – despite thinking this somewhat selfishly – also knew she might end up being attacked, too. So perhaps the presence of these two men would deter them… Sebastian had walked away, still in a daze, not helped by the remnants of his snuff. She went on ahead and when she last saw him was glad that the two drinkers she had paid were studiously following him…

*

Lady Lucinda, quite used to Sebastian returning home at all hours - if at all - decided to go to bed; she would leave the candle burning in the window in case he arrived back before it burned out; it was a dark night so any light to help him find his way home would help. Then she retired upstairs; there was no-one else in the house and the daily housekeeper, maid and butler had been sent home; she did not like having people around her during the night – they would arrive back in the morning. Something to do with her lowly upbringing, she surmised: as a child, servants could never be afforded and she usually preferred to do things herself, anyway - just like her mother, God rest her soul…

*

Jess had arrived home but forty minutes later there was a hammering on her door: on opening it, she was horrified to see the two guardians she had paid, both badly cut and bleeding profusely. On seeing their terrified faces she instinctively knew what had happened: they told her that – at great risk to themselves – they had witnessed an attack on Sebastian. Her son had been stabbed several times with daggers and whilst they had tried to defend him, they were certain that the two assailants had succeeded in their deed and then run off so, not wishing to be implicated, they had hobbled off themselves, leaving Sebastian to die as they went to tell her the news. Having recounted the event and fearing being seen in such a condition with her, they started to limp off but Jess, although somewhat numb with shock, nevertheless swore them to secrecy regarding her payment to them and – more pertinently – that they had not seen her since – even to tell her the news. Surprised, they agreed with the help of a shilling apiece and she closed the door on the two witnesses. She slumped heavily to the floor and thought for a moment, ashamed to admit little sense of regret that her son was dead as, for the most part, he had caused her so many emotions which conflicted with her maternal instincts. Yet, dead or alive, he was still essential to her ongoing acquisitive plans. So she forced herself to think straight: her ability to foresee reactions to possible events had been instilled in her through necessity since childhood for whatever circumstance and as she had always fended for herself, so she was permanently prepared for a swift change of tack – or escape. This was one such occasion, and she was ready. Yet it was essential that the fact of Sebastian's death did not leave Wirksworth – or reach Lady Lucinda for as long as possible: well, she wouldn't tell her. Then she remembered that Lucinda had said she was going to be away from Wirksworth for a day or two but could not remember when; she racked her brains... yes, it was around now, she was certain. So Lucinda would not know of Sebastian's death for a while, which gave her a chance. And Lucinda was a distraction, she coldly surmised: *she* wanted Mulberry Hall, *without* Lucinda. Yet, annoyingly, Lucinda was still useful... The thought had often crossed her mind that - being a titled lady - Lucinda would probably be able to claim a superior challenge for the ownership of Mulberry Hall whether Sebastian was living or not but her increasing jealousy always swept that fact aside: something would happen, she was sure, to help her – for a working-class girl she had led a charmed life so far and would eventually prevail. For now, her instincts told her that she had to keep the fiction that Sebastian was alive going for as long as possible: her plan would only work if he were still perceived to be living by those who currently resided at the Hall – no true son, no chance of entitlement ... Yet she knew that was the biggest potential flaw in her plan; how soon would it be before Lucinda found out about Sebastian's death and told Sir Walton Grimley? Although a two-pronged attack on Sir Walton's estate would have been better, now she wagered that this was out of the question: in her increasingly fevered brain she felt that to get to Mulberry Hall with her claim to the estate as Sebastian's true mother was her best chance at this precise moment... so speed was paramount: she had to leave immediately. She could say that she had already left Wirksworth before the assault on her son and so was oblivious to his demise; this would also give her time to get to Mulberry Hall before Lucinda had even realised and she could steal a very significant march on her. She was aware that by leaving this fine small house bequeathed her by Sir Walton Grimley she might not see it again, yet comforted herself with the hope that if she could gain Mulberry Hall instead, it would be worth it – and preferably without Lady Lucinda's knowledge.

She ran upstairs and picked up a bag of clothing already prepared for such an occasion and all the not insignificant amount of money she dared from the strong-box in her bedroom for her escape south. The lock on this was big and robust: being very heavy, the casket had also been perfect for dissuading any thief because it was so difficult to tell if it was empty or full. After she had taken out her cash, mostly paper bills for lightness – again, she had thought of everything for such an occasion, whatever the situation - it was almost empty. She was forever aware that even if this attack on her son had not happened, the law might approach her; it was common knowledge he was her son – she had even stupidly announced it in the tavern: lawyers would therefore ask too many questions of her so-called 'immoral earnings' which her bawdy-houses in Wirksworth had procured.

However, retribution often fosters muddled conclusions and, spurred by her increasingly ruthless but irrational sense of revenge, her usual ability to weigh things up and arrive at logical deduction had deserted her: hubris had clouded her reason, persuading her to do things that normally would have stayed her hand... This was her chance at last! In this fevered mental state, she concluded it was time to go and confront the people of Mulberry Hall *now*; it was her life's motivating objective and would brook no refusal ...

*

Sebastian had walked uncertainly up the cobbled hill towards his and Lady Lucinda's home; still over a hundred or so yards away, its uncertain candlelight danced in the bottom window to the left of the porticoed front door and gave out a dim radius of flickering light in the otherwise dark street. The walk in the fresh, damp breeze had woken him up a little and the fog of insouciance which had clouded his soul in the tavern had evaporated like a plume of steam. Suddenly, behind him, he was aware of movement and turned just in time to draw his sword and resist two assailants – those who had chastised him in the tavern. Then two more were behind the first two, and it seemed as if he was being attacked by them from behind as well: he found himself parrying he knew not which one as they all seemed to be attacking him at once – or were two of them trying to defend him? In the mêlée and darkness, it was difficult to tell. But Dutch courage and a new perception of his existence had given him strength and the will to survive, stinging him into action… and after a few moments, two of them lay injured; they were not dead but bleeding, their blood running in tiny square rivulets between the cobblestones. The other two – Silas and Jasper – ran off into the darkness, bloodied and cursing. In a starkly cold realisation, Sebastian understood that there were people in this town who obviously resented him, his arrogant display of money and his class: he sat on the ground, exhausted by his sudden actions and thought deeply in the gloom. After a couple of minutes, his senses restored, he resolved to disappear into his adjacent home for a few days while he nursed his wounds. He did not even recognise those lying bleeding in front of him: they were slowly getting up and supporting each other as they slowly and painfully disappeared into the darkness: the feeling of envy must be general and deep-seated, he surmised... He sat there for a while longer, then told himself to summon his strength and get up: he must return as quickly as his injuries would allow to Lucinda's home to tend them… Then someone bludgeoned the back of his head and his world went black and lifeless.

*

In anticipation of any furtive escape, for whatever reason, Jess had some months before ensured she knew the way to a village nearby called Upper Haddon. By studying a detailed map and learning the route, she reckoned she could follow it even in the dark; this was a high, small hamlet just within a short riding distance of Bakewell. She would not go directly to that town – too many people might still recognise her and any time spent there had to be short, precise and constructive: perhaps, even, a modicum of disguise might be helpful... She had therefore dressed herself in black - not so much to reflect her dark thoughts or her son's departure from this life as to blend into the night. Quietly, she locked the door of her house and, keeping to the darkest shadows, went to some stables to procure a horse: she had business to do before her arrival at Mulberry Hall.

She had been taught the rudiments of riding by Jack the stable-lad whom she had unsuccessfully wooed at Mulberry Hall all those years ago, which – seeing as it was him who had caused her banishment - was the only good thing to come out of the relationship. Fortunately, away from the town, the dark factories did not occlude what was a moonlit night and the beast, with her uncomfortably on top, were soon out into the open countryside. As it plodded along, her thoughts swirled around her head: she had not known the boy from whom she procured the horse, which had been a blessing. She had worn a veil over her face, too, which would come in handy again, she speculated: any cognisance would inevitably invite questions or, worse, confirm who or where she was – which would ruin her plan: for now, the authorities had to believe she was away, dead or missing and subsequently unaware of her Sebastian's fate. Herself, she had seldom felt so alive in her life, her resolve strengthening in the brisk air, which was fresh with a dash of rain; a chill wind blew intermittently, seemingly from all directions at once, yet she had the firm feeling – fuelled by her unquenchable desire for revenge – that finally she was going to achieve something in her life.

A few hours later, only stopping twice – once when the moon went behind a cloud and the tracks were indistinct, and then to hide in a wood for half an hour when she saw a flare ahead and suspected it was a highwayman – she eventually found herself approaching Upper Haddon. The sun was rising behind the peaks but drifts of cloud draped them in an assortment of colours, some above her in the brightening sky, others thin and fragile wisps floating in the valleys below. It would be an hour later before she reached the cluster of dwellings which constituted Upper Haddon; remote and high up in the Derbyshire hills, it was a good vantage point should any representatives of the law be spotted, whereupon she could make a swift getaway in almost any direction, using the valleys for cover. Her salient, nagging thought, was that having fled Wirksworth, she was now even more sure she would be cited as a possible witness to – or perpetrator of – Sebastian's murder, whether they thought her dead or not. Still, that was a bridge she could cross later. It would all work out well, she was sure…

Ten minutes after she had left, a constable and a watchman had indeed arrived at her home but found her absent… which inevitably started discussion: why was she not there? Had she fled? With rumour the handmaiden of truth, they inevitably asked: was it her who had murdered her son?

*

By the early morning, around the time she arrived at Upper Haddon, Jess's disappearance was provoking widespread discourse in Wirksworth; as she had neither been seen nor her corpse found within the precincts of the town, many were of the opinion it must have been she who had killed her own son – hence her sudden disappearance. But events had actually moved quickly to her unknown advantage: the two men paid to witness her son's possible assault had actually testified to the magistrate what had happened – without mentioning Jess's payment or knowledge, as agreed; consequently, Silas and Jasper had been quickly identified, arrested and swiftly taken to court. Unfortunately for them, the travelling county judge just happened to be in the town at the time; notorious for his quick sentencing and brutal justice - and disappointed that no felon at this session had been found guilty enough to be hanged that morning - he was eager to get on his way to a more promising sessions in the afternoon. He subsequently skipped through the trial and delightedly charged Silas and Jasper with the death of Sebastian and - despite their protestations of innocence - denied any clemency. They were then quickly and summarily sentenced to be hanged in public at first light the morning after.

Meanwhile, Lucinda had not been away as Jess had hoped and, like many others, was surprised that Jess had not been at the trial. She had been present, however, overtly crying the tears of a bereaved mother at the appropriate moments. Yet this display of emotion was not all that it seemed and, behind the black veil, her eyes sparkled with a pleasured expectation: now free of her son and his spendthrift habits - and the intelligence and acumen gleaned from Jess so helpful, (particularly the various scurrilous accusations to further undermine the reputation of Sir Walton Grimley) – her mind had been a ferment of creativity during the proceedings: and with the news that Jess had disappeared she knew not where, it seemed propitious to assume that she had fled, thinking that she would be arrested for the death of Sebastian. This meant that there was no-one else to stand between her obtaining either a knockdown purchase price when wresting Mulberry Hall from her husband or, indeed, the legal right to the whole estate without paying a penny. In short, she was now free to expose all the skeletons in Sir Walton Grimley's cupboard without demur, humiliate him for banishing her, nationally expose his godless relationship with Alice and subsequently illegitimate children, generally play the part of the wronged wife and then become the true Lady of the manor again. Like Jess, a chill, poisonous river of revenge was flowing from her and would motivate every action as retribution came closer to her grasp.

To further that ambition - but without Jess's knowledge and prior to these unexpected events - she had fortuitously made an appointment in Bakewell for 4 o'clock that very afternoon. So upon leaving the courthouse she climbed into her coach for the journey, a very happy woman indeed.

Yet there was another twist to the tale which was completely unanticipated – and would surprise both conspirators in very different ways.

CHAPTER 49

An Arrival, A Confrontation

& A Protraction

At the same time as Lucinda was leaving in her coach, Jess, having slept a few hours at the tiny inn, decided she had recovered enough from her night-time ride to mount her horse again. She restored the black widow's veil across her face to complement her black clothing and, dressed thus, appeared to be in mourning and less likely be recognised as she rode into Bakewell. It was market day and the town was busy, which would further help her to stay unrecognised as she searched for intelligence regarding the sale of Mulberry Hall.

She entered a few shops and made polite tittle-tattle as she browsed goods with their owners, feigning an offhand interest in any matters pertaining to local news generally and the Mulberry Hall estate as an aside. In one, a shopper said she had heard rumours the Hall was for sale but was unsure. In another, she heard from a bright young man that it was said the Hall was to be split in two, with the main estate being separated from Alice Lodge. This alarmed Jess: why would that be so? Further proddings revealed that Sir Walton Grimley and Alice, his 'woman', as

THE SLAVE-OWNER'S DILEMMA

the fellow called her, were apparently moving to Jamaica but their children, along with their new husbands, would stay on at an enlarged Alice Lodge. Jess was unsure what to ask next, but the young man did divulge another piece of information – that Lady Lucinda was rumoured to be returning to Mulberry Hall but without her son, who had apparently been murdered under strange circumstances. This surprised Jess – in her mind, she had not actually expected this news to have arrived in Bakewell quite so soon, especially when so pertinent to the Grimley family, whom she was sure would have suppressed it. Mulberry Hall gossip, yes, which would have slipped out and festered for months… but not a murder quite so speedily: how strange it was that the gruesome always finds a ready ear, she reflected... then wondered whether these rumours of a murder had accompanied news of a hanging, which always generated an intensely morbid interest far beyond the confines of the event. "So is there to be a hanging?" she enquired nervously.

"I believe so," came the reply; "Two felons, I heard, to be hung at first light tomorrow…"

Two felons! Well, that made sense, at least: and her son… *her* true son! – had been avenged. Better still, she was now in the clear and any hanging had rendered her swift flight from Wirksworth unnecessary: perhaps she had been too hasty, she pondered, only drawing attention to herself by her absence. She remembered that there had been a case some years ago where the wrong felons were hung and the true perpetrators got clean away, so it was worth another question: "And did Lady Lucinda identify the body, do you know?" she enquired of the shopkeeper, aware she was showing too much interest and could so cause suspicion: but she had to ask.

"All I heard was that he was cut by daggers. The traveller who told me the news said he believed Lady Lucinda was too distraught to look at the mess they made of him."

Jess suddenly felt sick, made her excuses and left the shop as decorously as she could; no tears coursed down her cheeks and she still did not feel saddened at his demise. She quickly left the market-place and went down to the river to sit and collect her thoughts. Yet she still had to know conclusively that Sebastian really was dead; it had seemed to be based more on speculation than fact. What obsessed her more was news of Mulberry Hall.

Being away from the market-place at that moment, however, Jess missed seeing a smart new carriage entering Bakewell with both Lucinda and her lawyer inside. They had arrived to attend an appointment with Sir Walton Grimley for a legal meeting in Barnabas' chambers.

*

Sir Walton Grimley and Barnabas were already waiting for the arrival of Lady Lucinda, who sat preening herself in her brand new Grimley-crested carriage as it entered the main square, delighting in the attention of the townsfolk who had not seen her for some years. The coach stopped outside Barnabas' offices and when Lucinda alighted, she took as much time as possible entering them so all could see that she was dressed in a striking black silk dress with a veil, as testament to her son and heir's death. She was helped by her also new footman, dressed in a less sober finery; this was all part of her plan - she was anticipating making a big splash and was so sure of her ability to seize the Hall at a low price or inherit it completely that she had decided to invest in some ostentation to substantiate her claim – and also to make her appear the equal of Sir Walton Grimley. In her mind, having come from a lowlier background, pretension was everything.

A slight frost accompanied Lucinda as she entered the room for her first meeting with her husband for some years; Sir Walton held out a hand of welcome but she ignored it and sat at a chair more distant than the one expected. Then her own lawyer entered, which occasioned a similar frost descending upon Sir Walton. He was not aware that there would be anyone else present and instantly resented this unknown and very unwelcome addition to the meeting - which also made it obvious that Lucinda was out for more than 'a pound of flesh'.

The proceedings started tersely and without humour; Sir Walton explained that he wished to retire to Jamaica with Alice, provided he could get the good anticipated price for Mulberry Hall - but was willing to split the estate and hive off Alice Lodge if the purchaser could not afford both; this was all laid out in the reply sent to her lawyer before Sir Walton received her ultimatum. This immediately pricked Lucinda's revenge further – she wanted the whole estate, not bits; then she could dictate what would happen to the rest of the family. And she did not want Alice's children around - which would be a permanent reminder of her displacement.

"I do not wish the estate to be split," she stated baldly, and let silence fill the ensuing chill, despite the hearty fire doing its best to dislodge it. "I wish to have the whole of it – and you will bequeath it to me as your legal wife."

There was a silence; then Sir Walton Grimley went to speak but Barnabas held up his hand and intervened. "Good morning, Lady Lucinda; we have not met formally, although we were both at the recent wedding together. I am Sir Walton Grimley's lawyer, Barnabas Ludd. I also have chambers in London." If this was supposed to impress Lady Lucinda, it did not and she just cursorily responded with, "I am sure that is very pleasant for you, good sir." Again, a silence pervaded the room.

Barnabas breathed deeply and continued. "As you know, Sir Walton Grimley has laid out what he wishes to do and if you would like again to see his proposal - "

"*My* lawyer has his own proposal, sir, drawn up by *me*," Lucinda interrupted, as she motioned to her own advocate, a quisling, bald and bespectacled man of about forty who looked far in excess of that age and spoke as if the wind was escaping from a church organ pipe, creating a sporadic whine. "Good morning, sire – I am Uriah Hawtrey – very good to make your acquaintance, Sir -"

"Please skip the pleasantries, Mr. Hawtrey, and deliver our terms," Lucinda interrupted again.

Somewhat disconcerted, Hawtrey winced and then continued. "Of course, your ladyship, Erm... well, the situation is this. Lady Lucinda, who is still legally your wife, of course... erm, well, wishes you to bequeath her the whole estate – every building, lake, house, stables, the mansion..."

"And Alice Lodge, too," Lucinda finished for him.

There was another silence, bar the crackling of the fire, whose flames had still not made any impression on the proceedings. So the lawyer continued, "Our terms on the original date were - "

"I cannot do that," Sir Walton interrupted. "I cannot just let it go; I am about to lose much of my income for reasons you must have recognised, what with the passing of the Act - "

"I care nothing for the Act, whatever its contents," Lucinda retorted dismissively. "I am your wife and I am entitled to the estate in its entirety. I have also had to undergo the humiliation of being ousted for, for... that slave-girl with whom you have had two children!"

Hawtrey leaned over to Lucinda to try and progress the impasse by saying, "You had a son by Sir Walton as well, milady, who also has a claim ... "

"No – he was *not* her son," Sir Walton explained firmly. "Lady Lucinda tried to deceive me into *believing* I had a son – but he was a foundling child who possessed many unpleasant characteristics due to his lowly birth – and a mother who was... Well, anyway - I do not even know where he is now."

This astonished Lucinda: did he not know that his son had been murdered? Others in the town knew of Sebastian's death; surely Sir Walton knew? It was not unusual for news to take days, even weeks, to find a new audience but... She looked furtively around, suspecting a trap, then, spotting an opportunity, decided to see if she could prolong that fiction. If he really had not heard yet, then she might be able to get an agreement today if she acted quickly...

Sir Walton was continuing his rambling as she thought this, saying, "Mind you, even if he had died, I doubt I'd care any more... no blood of mine, the thieving little..." He trailed off.

"He *is* still my son," Lucinda posited purposefully, if warily. "And he is heir to this estate."

"That is the truth," Uriah Hawtrey confirmed.

"His mother was a whore," Sir Walton riposted darkly.

Lucinda's eyes took fire at this, embarrassing the true

flames in the hearth with their passion. "So what was *your* little fancy, then, Walton? She was just as much a whore as Sebastian's mother."

"Alice was my *lover*. And not only was I already with her when I met you – which you obviously knew: I took you under my wing for the sake of propriety and because I admired your father and wanted to help him but - "

"Propriety? Yours or mine?" Lucinda spat.

"Yours, mine, Alice's. I was the only one to impregnate Alice. Sophie and Jemima are our children – there is no denying that." Sir Walton stared at her and then added coldly: "Which brings us nicely to the fact that I wish to divorce you."

With that, Lucinda's jaw dropped. For a moment, she had suspected there was still a chance to inherit the estate without her paying anything – especially, she realised, when Sir Walton did not even seem to know that his son and heir was dead. Yet if Sir Walton now wanted to divorce her, then Sebastian's death would soon come up and she would be heirless, disconnected, and Sir Walton could do what he liked. He had set a trap; so she must resist divorce with all her might and pretend that not even she knew Sebastian was no more or all would be lost. She was not going to give up easily.

*

Jess decided to return to the centre of the town, her head a jumble of possibilities, contradictions and fears. She felt uneasy being back in Bakewell with all her memories, successes and failures and - despite her disguise - was anxious should anyone recognise her, especially one of her previous clients, of whom there were many. She walked past her old house as if searching for inspiration but soon found

THE SLAVE-OWNER'S DILEMMA

herself in a street leading back to the market square where a splendid new, shiny coach stood outside a building proclaiming the legend, 'Barnabas Ludd – Lawyer & Attorney'. The name Barnabas arrested her; was that not the real name of Jonquil, the lawyer whom she had introduced to Jemima and then seen with her again at the wedding that day and then forced her to sign that nasty agreement? Her heartbeat increased: and whose coach was that, then? She peered inside, attracting the attention of the coach driver who told her this was private property and he was guarding it, the implication being that she should instantly leave. She apologised and took a step or two back, then looked up at him again and enquired, "Whose coach is this, sir? I have lived here many years but have not seen it before."

"If it's of any interest to you, madam, it belongs to Lady Lucinda Grimley."

"But she does not live here."

Sarcastically, he smirked, "That's what coaches are for, madam – travelling. They take people from one place to another."

She ignored the mockery, contemplated for a moment, then said, "I see. So she is come from Wirksworth, then?"

"Ah, so you know of her, do you? Well, the answer is 'yes' and a horrible journey it was, too."

Jess nearly said, "I know," but stopped herself. So Lucinda was here! Why had she not told her? They were supposed to be in this together - had Lucinda betrayed their agreement? Then she admonished herself for doing exactly the same thing – even if she had only come to get an idea of the lay of the land; but in her soul, she just knew that Lucinda must have deceived her and was in those very chambers – now – using her knowledge and intelligence to steal a march on her.

"Do you happen to know who he is seeing?" she enquired.

"Not that it's any of your business, madam... but it's Sir Walton Grimley of Mulberry Hall."

Lucinda *was* betraying her! The devious witch! She was suddenly aware of the coachman studying her reaction to his news, a quizzical look on his face, so she thanked him for his information and he returned a more kindly air by saying, "That's fine, madam – and I hope you recover from your sorrow soon," as he started descending from the carriage to wipe away some of the mud from its chassis. Jess turned away, an emotion like a red-hot poker having taken hold of her chest. She saw a young boy return with some pies for himself and the coachman and hid herself in an alleyway to think...

She could not enter the chambers and cause a scene: this would betray both their plots. She was not permitted in Bakewell anyway as part of the settlement agreement with Sir Walton – that was why she was in disguise, she reminded herself. Yet that woman, Lady Lucinda Grimley, was, she was sure, now trying to forestall her and get the whole estate for herself. Well, she was not having that, she resolved: she returned to the coachman who was now with the boy, eating his pie with one hand as he removed the mud with the other.

"Good sir," she said to attract his attention; "where will you be tarrying the night, pray?"

He looked at her cautiously: "And why would you wish to know that?" he replied with the flicker of a smile on his face.

"Your knowledge has been of great use to me and if you'd like a little company tonight I could be there for you."

He looked at her, as did the boy. "Got over your sorrow quick enough, then," he said, smiling.

"A woman has to eat," she replied cheekily. The boy looked disgusted, stood up and went to start cleaning the other side of the carriage.

After a moment, he replied cagily to her question: "She's here at the Rutland Arms... But *we're* over there at that little inn," and he pointed across the square to a squalid building opposite. "Be there at ten o'clock tonight after her ladyship has gone to bed and should have no more need of me. My name's George: what's yours?" She almost gave her real name but mercifully remembered not to: "Matilda."

"Good to meet you, Matilda - I'll see you later, then."

"I shall look forward to it, George," she replied, and slipped away to think further.

*

Tempers were becoming exercised in Barnabas's chambers. He and Hawtrey were arguing together and Sir Walton was in deep contest with Lady Lucinda.

"I even had a house – a good house – built for you in Wirksworth – what more do you want of me? I cannot afford to let you have the whole estate," he was angrily saying again. Then he was adding, "You should be grateful that I am allowing you to have half at a very reduced price – but I must retain Alice Lodge at the very least for my children and their husbands. That is sacrosanct. And if you don't like it then I shall sell to someone else at a greater price who is very interested, damn you. Do not exercise my generosity further!"

Lucinda stood defiant but inside conceded that he was not to be moved. Unless he died – now – there was no way out and the loss of Sebastian had not made things easier as she had hoped because they had not heard of it; in fact, it had muddied the waters as she now realised the chilling possibility that Jess Rigby might have had some input into the proposal: she doubted it, but it was possible – that girl had a clever brain and was even more devious and grasping than she was – and more desperate. By selling her home in Wirksworth – and using the Noncey & Daughter business as collateral – she could just afford the price of Mulberry Hall alone at Sir Walton Grimley's reduced price for her; secretly, she had conceded that it was a good offer but still wanted everything – and to be rid of those illegitimate children and their grasping husbands on her doorstep in Alice Lodge.

Suddenly realising how pressing time was to get a conclusion, she tried again to start the discussions but they eventually broke off for the day in a state of mutual distrust and mounting anger. She was further angered when she found that Sir Walton had also taken a room in the Rutland Arms Hotel which meant that now she would have to avoid him. Having retired there, however, the splendid brand new edifice on the square where her coach was now in its coachyard and the horses stabled, calmed her. Barnabas would sleep the night in his chambers as he often did when the ride back to Mulberry Hall was considered too onerous and Hawtrey lived in the town anyway. They were all due to meet at 11 o'clock the next day after tempers had cooled... and, perhaps, some of the demands had been softened.

Jess had not gone back to Upper Haddon – she had some business to do, of course. Not only that, but she had made a plan. And her liaison with George the coachman would be her alibi if necessary.

CHAPTER 50

A Despicable Deed

Jess had spent a lucrative hour pleasuring George the coachman but did not wish to spend the night with him any longer. She had brought with her a small coloured bag she had purchased in the town along with a few other items to complement the rest of her plan. She was still wearing widows' weeds and the veil went back on as soon as she had finished with George. Then she slipped out of the inn through the back, having ensured no-one had seen her enter. It was a dark night, and despite the plethora of flares and candles in windows around the square, she merged easily into the puddles of darkness. She took a circuitous route, wishing to enter the Rutland Arms from the rear. Most of the staff had gone to bed, the night giving them a brief respite of sleep before their chores started at daylight. She located the reception desk and opened the ledger where the names of the guests were logged: 'Lady Lucinda Grimley – Room 12', it was written. Further down, 'Sir Walton Grimley – Room 18'. Good. That meant they were not close to each other and probably on different floors.

She quietly climbed the stairs; the building, being quite new, had few squeaky steps and soon she was on the first floor; lightly passing down the corridor, she arrived at the end, only to find that the room must be on the next floor. She retraced her steps and ascended the stairs again, then went along the same corridor one floor up. There it was – room 12. She gently tried the door; it made a noise but opened – Lucinda had trustingly forgotten to bolt it. The bed was near the window and just enough light came through a chink in the lustrous curtains for her to see; the soft sound of gentle breathing could be heard. After she had closed the door – and locked it – she traversed the room towards the bed and took off the widow's veil. This episode took over a minute, such was her care to be noiseless. She put her hand in the bag and took out a large knife; then she reached for a pillow beside Lucinda's head and quickly pushed it hard onto her face. Lucinda woke immediately and started to scream and kick her legs but the stifling feathers allowed very little sound to escape; when Jess felt that Lucinda was almost dead she raised the pillow and whispered loudly into her ear, "Quiet, Lucinda – quiet! It's me, Jess. But if you do not stay quiet I will stab you through the heart with this knife." She peeled the pillow back further so Lucinda could see the glint of the blade and then replaced it across her mouth, leaving her nose free to breathe. Lucinda's terrified eyes stared with a ghostly pallor into Jess's and she nodded her head as if to accede to the instruction. Jess leaned in and whispered into her ear, "You have betrayed me, Lucinda; we were going to wrest the Hall from Sir Walton together. And do you know what happens to traitors?" Lucinda shook her head. "There is retribution. Unless they are contrite and stay quiet while I discuss those issues with them." Lucinda nodded again. "I hear you've been discussing things with Sir Walton… so what's the outcome?" She lifted the pillow a little so Lucinda could speak but put her finger across her mouth to denote quietness.

"I was not going to betray you," Lucinda whispered breathlessly; "You disappeared – how did I know where you were if you didn't tell me where you had gone?" That was a fair point, Jess conceded. "And if you disappeared then why should I not feel you were about to betray *me*? I had to act quickly, before… before - "

"Before I found out about my son's death?"

Lucinda looked shocked. "You know about that?"

Jess nodded. "Someone in the town told me. Who killed him?"

Lucinda's eyes opened wider in increased terror, confusing Jess for a moment. "It was two people in a tavern," she said unconvincingly. "He was drunk and, and, dressed in his best clothes so these two ruffians were envious… and he said some silly things to them which made them angrier and, and so they followed him home and…" Jess looked more closely at her; something did not feel right. "How do you know all that?" she asked gruffly.

"It all came out at the trial this morning."

Something was still not right… Lucinda saw the doubt and even more histrionically continued: "They cut him down with daggers, Jess… and, and then they must have clubbed him over the head for it was a terrible mess."

"So you saw the body, did you?"

"Yes… yes, I did."

"A young man I spoke to in the town implied you were too distraught to look at it." Lucinda seemed momentarily to be lost for words as if she was trying to recollect – or, perhaps, check her story for errors before speaking, then blurted: "Yes – well, initially – but I had to identify him, didn't I?"

Again, something did not sound true.

Jess put her face closer to Lucinda and said: "It was you who had Sebastian murdered, wasn't it? – so I didn't have an heir."

Lucinda's eyes opened wider and her mouth went to speak but no words came out. Then the floodgates opened and tears began to run down her cheeks as her perspiring face exclaimed, "It was for both of us, Jess; he would have squandered all our money! Yes, I paid two ruffians to do it but two others tried to stop him! I don't know where they came from... I saw the whole thing through my window! He managed to fight off the other two but... Well, Sebastian was half dead anyway – I just finished him off! It was going to save us so much time! And he was a wastrel – you know that!"

"He was still my son: MY son!" Jess croaked in a hoarse whisper.

"But you hated him, too – you said so... he was never going to change. He would have ruined us both in the end!"

"He was still *my son* – never yours! You might have got the Hall as his wife but now you have made it even more difficult for *me* to get the Hall from that dreadful Sir Walton because Sebastian was my *only* path to the estate. You have betrayed me! And when Sir Walton finds out there's no heir now, he'll have no need to knock down the price anyway. So we are *both* ruined."

"Yes, I know that now but I didn't until this afternoon at the lawyer's when it became obvious that they didn't know Sebastian was dead yet..."

"So I still have a chance?" Jess almost shrieked.

"Yes! But I didn't know that until this afternoon! I would have told you – honestly!"

"How? You thought I was still in Wirksworth so with you here how could you have told me? It would have been too late! You'd have done the deal without me!"

"No! No – I'd have found a way…"

There was a momentary pause, then Jess sneeringly looked at Lucinda and whispered: "You're a liar." She sat up a little, then leant back into Lucinda's face and said threateningly, "So how did you 'finish him off', then, as you say?"

"I beat him over the head with a cudgel."

Jess took a last patronising look at Lucinda as the anger raced up her body to her head and in a blind rage threw the pillow back over Lucinda's mouth with a strength she never knew she had, then raised the knife and plunged it into the woman's chest, whispering hoarsely again and again: "You killed my son, you killed my son!"

She did it again and again in a frenzy, the sheets and covers becoming shredded and soaked in blood. When Lucinda's body stopped twitching, she calmly stood, went over to the washstand and cleaned her hands, her knife and a few gouts of blood from her face; then she returned the knife to her bag. She put her veil of mourning back on and quietly made for the door. She listened for any noise, then quietly opened the door a little and, seeing or hearing nothing, crept out, quietly closing the door again. Then she went down the stairs and, checking that the veil still covered her face, nonchalantly walked out of the door and into the square. She had nowhere to go and could not retrieve her horse at this hour so went back down by the river where an arch over the towpath would shield her from any rain.

Then she waited until morning.

CHAPTER 51

A Discovery, A Resolution

& A Departure

Just after daylight, there was a hubbub at The Rutland Arms; a maid entered Lady Lucinda's room to open the curtains and enquire of any further services needed when the scream from room 12 was enough to wake and alert the entire building. Soon, various officials, hotel employees, constables and justices of the peace were observing the scene, maids and the housekeeper running hither and thither to clean up the mess, remove the body and ask for any suspects – and all the while trying to dissuade not a few guests from wishing to glimpse the carnage.

One young hotel orderly said he had observed a woman in black mourning dress and a widow's veil ascending the stairs but had assumed that it was Lady Lucinda going to her room; this was generally accepted as fact as it appeared that her death occurred sometime after that event. He did, however, note that she was carrying a bag which seemed out of place with the rest of her appearance, being somewhat more colourful. Immediately, a search was made for the bag but even after an exhaustive exploration, none was found.

*

Jess spent a damp, uncomfortable night under the arch but had been woken at daylight by a horse pulling a barge; the bargeman did not see her but she was aware she should move as others would soon be following. She picked up her bag and made her way into the town. It was already becoming busy and she found a newly-opened pie-shop which she felt she could patronise with some certainty of not being recognised.

Her stomach contented, she decided to reclaim her horse and go back to Upper Haddon before anyone recognised her. She arrived at the stables but, just outside, found there was a small crowd of men with muskets and pistols being addressed by a justice of the peace who was exhorting them to scour the town and look for a woman in widows' weeds and veil. She melted back into an alleyway and waited for them to disperse before entering the stables; with the men and their steeds soon distributed across the town, they were now empty. She recognised her horse – indeed, it was about the only one left, the others all being out and ridden by those men trying to find her, she shuddered. Quickly saddling it up, she quietly led it out into the yard, ascended a mounting-block and started riding out as quickly as she dared, clutching the bag close to her stomach. It was at that moment that the young man who had seen her ascend the stairs the night before, running an errand in the square, noticed the very coloured bag he had previously observed and sounded the alarm. But by the time that the alert had summoned enough people to either witness or arrest her flight, Jess was riding out of the town towards Upper Haddon – but completely unaware that she had been recognised ...

*

Suspicion had meanwhile fallen on Sir Walton Grimley: it was perceived that he was the only one with a motive to kill his wife as it had become known they were haggling over the price for the Mulberry Hall estate: and being in the same hotel would surely mean he had had a good opportunity to kill Lady Lucinda. By the same yardstick, however, it seemed an odd thing to accuse him of when his estranged wife was also the only person who currently seemed distinctly interested in acquiring the estate. In addition, it would be too obvious. The accusation was subsequently met with a firm denial and, admitting that he had had a tot or two to help him sleep, his rebuttal was generally accepted – until or unless any other evidence became available. This 'slur on my spotless reputation', as he termed it, put him in a foul mood but with the event rendering any further legal meeting unnecessary it was summarily cancelled, with the outcome that he was now virtually forced to accept any other price for his estate that was proffered. The problem was that the one person interested had gone off the idea: furthermore, the estate in its entirety, or even split in half, would still entail a huge sum – one that few could afford… Especially if they were slave owners who would soon start to feel the financial effects of the Act of the Abolition of Slavery.

*

As Jess neared Upper Haddon, she rode into a copse, dismounted and removed her veil and widow's clothes. When in Bakewell, she had purchased some simple clothing and a warm jacket, which she had secreted in the bag and now donned. The knife she threw into a stream, the remaining blood on its blade dissolving into the water in

THE SLAVE-OWNER'S DILEMMA

tiny wisps of red as it flowed down the scar towards, she suspected, Bakewell – how apposite, she mused. Remounting her horse, the increased height allowed her to see further down the valley from whence she had just come – and saw a number of mounted men ascending it and heading straight for Upper Haddon. Even from this distance, she could see they were armed and a chill of fear surged through her: the observation had put her into a dilemma; she could either avoid Upper Haddon completely and head back into the direction of Wirksworth or – and a surge of excitement surged through her – why not the environs of Mulberry Hall? That was the last place anyone would expect her! She could arrive there long before Sir Walton Grimley or his retinue and – now she knew precisely what had happened in Wirksworth – realised it was unwise to return to her home there until things calmed down. Also, they still did not know that Sebastian was dead: it was now or never. So she spurred her horse to go as fast as either dared or were able to and started her descent, motivated by her deranged belief that she would soon be able to claim Mulberry Hall as Lady Lucinda was dead.

Yet whereas a desirous revenge can often make wayward facts seem advantageous, the hard truth can also prove the opposite…

So as she rode on, the daunting task of trying to argue any claim at all to the Hall weighed down on her; she had enough money on her person to buy a small house but not an estate the size of Mulberry Hall – or even Alice Lodge on its own… Perhaps she should return to Wirksworth after all and say she had been seeing a relative; it was dawning on her, too, that – despite Lady Lucinda's betrayal of her – she had been Jess's best chance of eventually getting the estate, even if they had to share it: with Lucinda's money, and, in the eyes of the upper classes and propriety, that Sebastian was actually hers, there was a tie, a bond – and an avoidance of scandal... In a sudden, blinding moment of realisation it struck Jess that she had let her temper kill the very person she could have betrayed in turn later on ... and got the Hall for nothing. She stopped her horse, dismounted and almost fell as she did so, her legs were so weak. She steadied herself and, scanning the horizon for any assailants, let the fresh wind drive some sanity into her being: perhaps a return to Wirksworth would be more advisable rather than a sortie to Mulberry Hall. There she at least had a house and a business - if her whores had not already left; but she doubted that – they were probably doing well enough without her and she had only been away two nights... But, she reminded herself, that house was legally hers, bought with money given to her by Sir Walton Grimley. That still gave her a connection... and so why would she wish to compromise Sir Walton Grimley, she could argue? Then her possessive side kicked in again - whether she managed to compromise Sir Walton or not, with Lucinda now dead she wanted that woman's money as well: after all, she had been helping Lucinda expand her business, hadn't she? It was all the same family, too, wasn't it? ... and the root of her vengeance was the head of it – Sir Walton Grimley! Perhaps she could get some papers forged to the effect that should anything happen to Lady Lucinda, then the Noncey & Daughter business would pass to her...? There was now no Sebastian... but he had been her *true* son... perhaps that would give her access to the Noncey business too? And there was no-one else now... Then she wondered whether she would be apprehended for Sebastian's murder... No! Before she killed her, Lucinda had said that the two men had been hanged for that... So if she could return with no supposed knowledge of either her son's murder or Lady Lucinda's death... then she was in the clear. That was it. She would return to Wirksworth, continue her business as before and forge some papers which would claim entitlement to the Noncey & Daughter business in the event of anything terrible happening to Lady Lucinda. Which it already had – but it was doubtful anyone in Wirksworth knew about that yet. Once again, speed was now of the essence – but in a different direction.

Despite being troubled by what she had done, like a sunlit dawn rising over a troubled sea she suddenly concluded in her febrile mind that murdering Lucinda might have actually *increased* her likelihood of wresting Mulberry Hall from Sir Walton Grimley after all: with no son or wife to succeed him, nobody now had any legal claim to it as he had never married Alice.

With a renewed sense of purpose, she made sure that no-one was following, re-mounted her horse and rode at a less frantic pace than before towards her home. She had unwittingly, through an act of passion, cleverly worked out the surest way of eventually acquiring Mulberry Hall after all.

Or so she thought.

*

Sir Walton Grimley arrived with Barnabas at Mulberry Hall later that same night; they had left Bakewell at the earliest opportunity after his name had been cleared but the journey seemed much longer than when they had travelled there. Barnabas went straight up to see Jemima but, alone in this Great Parlour, surrounded by his wealth and beautiful things, Sir Walton suddenly felt alone, fragile, small and vulnerable - just like one of his ornaments; they were worth a great deal but could easily be shattered. Like him... he was now a broken man. This was less for the loss of Lucinda herself so much as now he wondered who would buy his estate. Perhaps he should have done the munificent thing and let her have it for little, as she had demanded. Yet that had been the point: she had *demanded* it and that had made him more stubbornly minded to refuse her – she had no sense of consideration... He soon fell asleep in his armchair, still vexed about Lucinda's death and the consequences, so when his reveries were interrupted by the re-arrival of Barnabas he felt refreshed enough to spend some hours discussing his concerns regarding what to do next.

By midnight, however, they were still no further advanced.

CHAPTER 52

A Tricky Confrontation, A Revelation & Conjecture

Jess arrived home at Wirksworth in darkness a few hours later; she had stopped at an inn on the way for refreshments and had then returned the horse on arrival; she had bought the horse at a high price in case she never came back so managed to regain some money for it - yet this was less important than working out what to do next. She quietly walked home from the stables and finding nothing untoward, entered her bedroom, closing and locking the door; she then took the strongbox key from a hidden pocket in her bodice and, undoing the hefty lock, replaced her fortune. That done, she decided to go to her two 'business' houses with the aim of ensuring all was well… and to hear of any rumours or gossip floating round the town which might be relevant to her.

All seemed much as she had left them; in the first, a girl was hanging around but only claimed they had wondered where she had disappeared to; beyond that, all seemed as normal. In the other, the girls were *in flagrante delicto* with clients but as these emerged from their predilections the girls seemed relieved to acknowledge her return. She heard the church bell strike two o'clock and decided, after some financial settlement for their endeavours, to return home. Only to find a serjeant-at-arms and a nightwatchman awaiting her.

"Miss Jess Rigby?" the serjeant demanded.

"I am, sir. What is your business?"

"Is this your home?"

"It is, sir."

"Nice home for a working-class woman," the nightwatchman sneered. "How d'you come by this, then?"

"I was bequeathed it by Sir Walton Grimley, the famous member of Parliament, in settlement of a debt."

"Money?"

"Honour."

"I see," the serjeant said with a resentful tone. "May we come in?"

"May I ask why?"

"We'll tell you when we're inside." Jess unlocked the front door and stood aside to let them. As the door closed behind them, she had the feeling of being suddenly imprisoned in her own property.

They regarded Jess with further disdain; they obviously resented the fact that, unlike most other houses in the district, it was not dirty, squalid or poverty-stricken but clean, tidy and well-ordered.

"I have heard you are a keeper of a bawdy-house," the serjeant said at length.

"Can you see any bawds here?" replied Jess innocently.

"We should look," said the nightwatchman indignantly, nastily. The serjeant nodded. Without asking, they went around the house, opening doors, drawers, cupboards and boxes. Jess suddenly wished she had not put all her money back in the strong-box because she was sure they would ask her to open it.

"What's in the strong-box?" the serjeant asked as they returned downstairs.

"My valuables."

"Big box," observed the nightwatchman.

Jess said nothing; best to stay quiet and let their imaginations trump their suspicions.

They looked lost for a moment; then the serjeant asked another question – one which Jess had hoped they would not.

"You were away for nearly three nights. Where were you?"

"Away."

"Obviously. But where?"

"I went to see a relative." That wasn't quite true, of course – but she had at least been in *league* with Lucinda.

"And where was that?"

"Upper Haddon." They looked blank. "Never heard of it," said one.

"It's small."

"Near Bakewell, at all?" enquired the serjeant.

"As a matter of fact, yes – about three miles. But Bakewell was not the purpose of my visit."

"And so what *was* the purpose of your visit?"

"As I said – to see a relative." There was a pause: she was on dangerous ground now. "Sadly, she died," she added.

"I see. Her name wasn't Lady Lucinda Grimley, was it?"

With this, a shaft of fear shot up through her body but she somehow emitted a convincing retort: "No – she is the owner of Noncey & Daughter, here in Wirksworth. I often do consultative work with her. She's a busy, successful woman, as I'm sure you know. Why on earth would she be in Upper Haddon?"

"Close to Bakewell," said the serjeant vindictively. Jess could feel her throat going tight, dry... *'Stay calm'*, she told herself.

"And we're looking for a coloured bag," he added. "And a woman in a widow's dress, wearing a veil."

Jess's heart sank. The widow's weeds, veil and coloured bag were in her strong-box.

*

Barnabas had been about to go to bed and leave Sir Walton to wallow in his regrets when a lone horseman arrived at the Hall just after midnight; with Tobias and the staff having been released from their duties for the day, it was Barnabas who went to the main entrance to receive him.

"What news do you bring at this time of night?" he enquired.

"Pardon me, Sir, but are you Sir Walton Grimley?" the young lad asked.

"No – but he's still up. We've been in discussions. Why do you wish to see him?"

"I have urgent news for his ears only, sir."

"You'd better come in, then."

The lad nodded and dismounted, carrying a scroll encircled with red ribbon and fastened with a crested seal. He followed Barnabas into the Great Parlour, who introduced him to Sir Walton, who looked slightly dazed at this interruption but asked him his business. "Sir, I have a document for you from the mayor of Wirksworth," he stated.

"The mayor of Wirksworth? Whatever for?"

"News of your son, Sir Walton."

"My son? What's that squandering damber done now?"

He took the document, opened the seal and read its contents. His face went whiter as his eyes scanned the page. "'Pon my soul," he said after a few moments. "Sebastian has been murdered in Wirksworth." Barnabas was shocked, too. "Good heavens," was all he could say.

"Barnabas get me a brandy – and take one for yourself." Then he looked to the lad and asked if he was hungry after his ride. The boy nodded. "Barnabas, would you also go and look in the kitchens for something this lad can eat?" Barnabas handed him his drink, put his own down and left the room.

"I'm sorry to bring bad news, Sir," the lad said as the room went quiet. Sir Walton nodded. "Although it's not as bad as what I have already just suffered," he added.

"Sorry again to have brought it to you, Sir."

"The message says that he was murdered – what...? – nearly four nights ago now? Why did the news take so long to reach me?"

"I understand that his mother, Lady Lucinda, asked them not to tell you, Sir. She wanted to tell you herself."

"Then why didn't she?" he enquired flatly, as if the boy would know. "I was with her only two days ago – less." Then in a flash it dawned on him - it was because she could have used Sebastian, technically the legal heir after his death: without him, her claim to the estate would be less promising. Perhaps, even, that was why she had requested their meeting: did she already know of Sebastian's demise, when he had not? The scheming little harridan! With that, any previous mild sadness at her death was now very much less felt.

*

The serjeant-at-arms and nightwatchman were looking very closely at Jess and if she was showing any guilt there was little she could do about it. She volunteered a side-step: "I would imagine that the woman you're looking for is Lady Lucinda Grimley herself," she ventured. "I hear she lost her son, Sebastian, not a few days ago, so may be wearing a widow's dress and veil. I can go and ask her if you wish – her factory and offices are not far away, as you must know."

They looked at her suspiciously. Then, with a sigh, the serjeant said, "No need."

Stupidly, Jess asked, "And why is that?"

"Because she's dead."

Jess tried to look shocked. "Oh, no! That's awful! How?"

"Stabbed to death in Bakewell."

"Oh, my goodness! What a tragedy... and so soon after her son was murdered, too. Oh! It is all too distressing! Have you told the foreman at her factory what has happened? He'll wonder where she is."

They found themselves wrong-footed and shook their heads, as if annoyed that a relevant part of their duties had been omitted.

"Then I must go and tell him! As I said, I have - had - been doing business with Lady Lucinda – helping her with day-to-day things on occasion. So why would it be in my interests to murder her, as you seem to be suggesting?"

As a final retort, it seemed to Jess, the serjeant then asked: "Where did you stay in, where was it?"

"Upper Haddon."

"Upper Haddon…"

"There's a small inn there. The landlord can vouch for me."

It went quiet for a moment. "We will do," he said ominously, then flicked his head towards the door as if implying they should leave, which they did. Outside, the serjeant turned back to her and said, "You're still under suspicion, Jess Rigby. We'll be watching you."

She closed the door and emitted a sigh of relief, sinking to her knees as she did so; the journey and then this interrogation had made her feel very weak. After a few moments, she knew she had to tell the foreman at Noncey & Daughter of the news, which would further validate her story; with no other relative alive to run the business, she might now be able to take it over herself – the foreman knew her, after all. Perhaps she might soon be rich enough to buy Mulberry Hall after all … along with some threats to keep the price down. It now seemed possible that things had turned in her favour again… Then she remembered the allusion to the coloured bag and widow's weeds, swiftly went upstairs, opened the strong-box and retrieved them; then summarily burned the damning evidence in the fireplace.

*

Sir Walton was still talking to the messenger lad when Barnabas arrived with some bread and cheese and a tankard of ale for their bearer of news. "You can eat that in here," said Sir Walton: "There may be other things I wish to ask you…"

"Thank you, Sir," and he went into the corner and tried to eat his meal as surreptitiously as possible.

There was a knock on the door and Tobias came in, dressed less formally than usual. "Excuse me, Sir, but I heard the horseman arrive and thought I should come down to assist with whatever may be needed."

"Ah, thank you Tobias but the mortar has already exploded, so to speak."

"Sebastian has been murdered, Tobias, in Wirksworth," Barnabas explained quietly. Tobias let out a sigh of disbelief.

"The felons who did it have been hanged already, according to this," Walton added as he gestured to the document. "Pleaded not guilty, though…"

"Well, they would have done, wouldn't they?" Barnabas responded.

"Hmmm… Perhaps they were set up..?" There was a pause, then: "Tobias, you can go back to bed – get some sleep."

"I'll just tidy up, Sir…"

Walton was already in deep thought. How things had dramatically changed over the past few days – his estranged wife and now his bastard son had been murdered and, as Tobias refilled his brandy glass, was wondering further if the two events were linked. He knew that Sebastian had always expected to inherit the Hall after his mother Lucinda died – surrogate mother, he corrected himself – and probably before he, Sir Walton, died too, if possible; he needed money for his wenching and gambling. Yet Walton could not fathom why they had both been killed so close together; perhaps it was just coincidence but his instincts told him otherwise. Was he next in line to be bumped off? Perhaps… He furtively looked over at the messenger but he was finishing his cheese – and he hardly looked like an assassin…

THE SLAVE-OWNER'S DILEMMA

The lad finished his meal, so Sir Walton thanked and dismissed him, donating a few shillings as he did so. Then he turned to Tobias: "After you have seen our young friend out, that will be all for now, thank you, Tobias."

"Thank you, Sir."

Tobias tidied up the plate and tankard and ushered the messenger out. A silence descended on the room as they heard the main doors being bolted and the sound of receding horse hooves. Sir Walton turned to Barnabas and, still feeling that Jess Rigby might have a part in all this, explained her history at Mulberry Hall to Barnabas, who started taking notes; then they discussed what to do next, which they were still doing when daylight broke and the sounds of servants rising to do their chores were heard. Sir Walton told Barnabas to go to bed - Jemima would be missing him, so he departed.

After he had left, Sir Walton looked into his brandy glass and then out through the long, tall windows to the mulberry tree. It was a magnificent specimen, now; the early sunlight frolicked on its heart-shaped leaves and it was the perfect foil, he mused, giving foreground to the view of the sparkling lake a little lower down the estate's parklands, then The Peak crowning the scene in the far distance. It was as beautiful as one of those rustic theatrical sets that his ward Edward sang in front of at the opera – confected perfection. He sighed. Yet despite its beauty and the splendour of the Hall, recent events suddenly made him decisively wish to leave it all behind and get back to the warmth of Jamaica. And away from all the intrigue.

CHAPTER 53

A Journey, A Meeting, A Plan

& A Warning

Jess spent a troubled night, half expecting another rap on the door; she finally drifted to sleep around four o'clock and was woken by the town clock chiming 7. She rose, washed and dressed, being out of the house a half hour later. A heavy mist had descended from the moors which she was glad of as visibility was down to twenty feet, fortuitously rendering her less conspicuous. On arrival at Noncey & Daughter, she sought the foreman, Arnold, who, with a slightly worried tone, informed her that Lady Lucinda had not been seen for a few days.

"I know," she said, "I have some news for you so I think it best that we go up to the office." Not saying any more, they went to the top of the building, Arnold somewhat alarmed at her peremptory attitude. On arrival – and both slightly breathless at the speed of their ascent - he stood hesitantly as he waited for her to speak. Not bothering to sit, she turned to face the man and spoke frankly and positively.

"Arnold; I'm afraid I have to tell you that Lady Lucinda was murdered in her hotel room in Bakewell the night before last." The man's face went white but as he grasped a nearby chair for support, grappling for words to say, she continued: "You may have noticed that I have been here on several occasions over the past few months, advising and helping Lady Lucinda with her business, of which we were going to do much more. So much so, that we drew up an agreement which stated that should anything happen to her I would, in the event that there was no heir – which there isn't now, as you know, her son Sebastian being dead too – be the legal heir to this business." This was not true, of course, but speed and surprise was necessary for her plan – and the hope this relatively simple man would accept her story. Arnold's mouth had fallen open during this; then, after a moment, he croaked, "But it's Lady Lucinda's business, Miss Rigby."

She continued: "I'm coming to that. Fortunately for you and the others' employment, as I am now legally entitled to this business – and her house here in Wirksworth - there is no need for any of you to worry. The business will continue as before." Then, with a firmer emphasis, she added, "As long as you do as I say." He went to speak but she held up her hand to ensure she could finish her diatribe. "In that strong-box over there is a document which describes this agreement in full... but until I can find the key I have no way of showing it to you." This was a gamble: did Arnold know where the key was kept? Unlikely... so she was relieved when he said, "I think she kept the key on her person, Miss Rigby."

"Well, I shall find it somehow," she said dismissively. "It's a very sad event and I hope they catch the perpetrator soon." Having run of things to say or lies to tell, she waited for Arnold to respond.

After a moment, he did so, uttering the words in a weak, deflated voice: "Why would anyone wish to kill Lady Lucinda Grimley?"

"That is for the law to find out," Jess answered evasively. "Until then, please take me around the factory so that I know everything there is to know to permit me to carry on this successful business."

Actually, this was not her real intent: she wanted to get an idea of how much she could sell it for. That knowledge would frame the context and conditions of the legal document she would soon have to forge.

For his part, Arnold had suspected that something was not right: he had always assumed that Josiah would be the one to inherit the business, having been a partner in it with Lady Lucinda - but the suddenness of the news and the outright chutzpah of Jess Rigby had alerted him to say nothing: he was not as simple or stupid as Jess had presumed. Or hoped.

*

That same morning, Josiah was told by Sir Walton Grimley of Lucinda's death – and that of Sebastian, too; he also told Josiah the background to what he felt to be the motives and those involved – with particular emphasis on Jess Rigby and Sebastian. The revelations shocked Josiah – but none more than his realisation that Noncey & Daughter now had no manager. Very concerned, he knew he had to return to the Wirksworth factory for a few days to sort things out for the future. He had a significant stake in the business and had also invested more money into it whilst working there as it grew and strengthened. He could not, however, shake off a feeling of being relieved that Lucinda was no more: her constant harassment of him for both

THE SLAVE-OWNER'S DILEMMA

licentious and pecuniary gain had at times been awkward, if not extremely embarrassing. He had eventually told Sophie of her attraction for him and how it had severely discomfited him but she had just giggled. In fact, his wife had stated that, in her opinion, the 'attraction' was more to do with slighting her and her mother than any for him – which rather put him in his place as he reluctantly realised her perspicacity was most likely to be true.

With a heavy heart, he therefore decided to return to Wirksworth to see how he could help with the takeover and what to do with the house he had built for Lucinda those few years before. At least Sophie would accompany him this time – which would turn out to be of great relevance to their future.

At first light the next morning they departed in the main carriage; their two strongest horses had been harnessed and they hoped to make the journey in around six hours – delays, stops and the changeable Pennine weather permitting. Their coachman had been armed, as had a young, nervous footman to play watchman at the rear; it was a relatively new vehicle and had superior springs fitted which would make the journey less onerous. It was market day in Bakewell which slowed them down as they passed through and then rain and a sudden wind slowed the horses so they rested them and took some refreshment later than expected at Darley. They eventually pulled into Wirksworth at four in the afternoon, just as the winter sun was beginning to set.

Josiah had sets of keys to both the factory and Lucinda's house – the latter fact raising Sophie's eyebrows for an instant – so after stabling the horses and the carriage he let Sophie into the house, where the servants – the housekeeper, butler and maid – were in a state of disquiet, being unsure what was to happen to them following Lucinda's sudden death.

Josiah put their minds at rest for the time being and left for the factory but as Sophie relaxed after the journey and took some tea, she suddenly realised that something was nagging her. Focussing her thoughts, she eventually grasped that it was due to having seen a face she recognised as they passed through the town – and although for the moment not quite able to place it, knew it was one she rather disdained.

*

Jess was leaving the printing shop as the coach had passed her and, rather pre-occupied with the deed she was hoping to get away with, did not take any notice of it. Earlier that day she had gone to see one of her girl's clients who was training to be a lawyer and, with an unusually large amount of silver placed in his hand, had happily worded what was necessary in the unfortunate event that Lady Lucinda either had no heir or became deceased. Knowing another client at a printer's, a forged new document had swiftly been created, dated some months previously; this man had done business with Lucinda on occasion and therefore possessed a good example of her signature, which he carefully but gladly added after a similarly requisite amount of silver had changed hands. The bogus law firm heading was one supposedly existing in London and the whole was festooned with a splendid red seal and ribbon: how grateful she was that so many people would do her favours due to the unspoken threat of blackmail! It was when she was leaving this second establishment that the coach had passed without her realising who was inside it.

So when she arrived back at the factory, she was

surprised to find Josiah there.

*

Back at Mulberry Hall, Sir Walton Grimley was still trying to persuade Tobias and Elspeth to go with him to Jamaica, despite initially stipulating a swift decision. Whilst Tobias was open to persuasion, however, Elspeth was adamant. She did not wish to 'perform my duties' in such heat and was still terrified of the allusion to insects – which she vehemently hated, constantly waging a war of attrition against much less dangerous species here in Mulberry Hall: heaven knows what she might have to fight off in such much warmer climes! And the wild animals - she even dreaded meeting cows on a country walk! She had also not dared to find out what meats she would be confronted by... and the sweat of the clothes disturbed her too, which would be so much more apparent than here in cold England... She also suspected that there would be all sorts of water-borne diseases to contend with – or even airborne ones secreted within the many hurricanes they had which would surely lift her off the ground and whisk her out to sea! There had been cholera in England and there was talk of people dying of it even in London... So, over there in Jamaica? No! She could not countenance it. She would also be even further away from their son, Edward, becoming ever more famous and making so much money in Italy; if only Sir Walton had had a plantation there, then that is where she would have happily gone...

Then she felt guilty, for without Sir Walton's help and finance, Edward would never have become whom he now was... so perhaps she should go with him to Jamaica after all... These swings of decision had unbalanced her senses several times over the past few weeks and Tobias had got used to them; being a mild, contemplative type he would do whatever she wished as long as he had books to read – which only made her decision ever more difficult.

*

Josiah had been just as surprised to find this flamboyantly well-dressed woman arrive and be introduced by Arnold as Miss Rigby, a resident of the town and 'recent friend and occasional business associate' to the late Lady Lucinda. This alerted Josiah: so this was 'the harridan' whom Sir Walton had described, yet he now realised he was involved too as it was he who was the business associate and no-one else. Arnold's eyes darted between the two: having known Josiah for over two or three years, he was keenly observing their features as pleasantries were exchanged: but he had to be careful. If he blurted something out, it might cost him his job or even put Josiah in an awkward position, perhaps not being privy to any arrangements which might have been made between him and Lady Lucinda in the light of – or prior to - recent events. Yet he had his doubts and increasingly knew he had to speak to Josiah in private. He suggested that they all went upstairs, away from the clanking factory and shouts from the workmen as they shaped and honed their artefacts and, this advice being well received, they did so.

As the noises receded in intensity, Jess was wondering how to extricate herself from this unexpected situation; she was still holding the document in its very new-looking long box and wished she had covered it somehow; her hurry had made her careless, she admonished herself. Her plan had been to 'find' the document in the office and present it to Arnold as proof of her claim but the unexpected presence of Josiah had surprised her and now this was impossible. Josiah, meanwhile, was interested to know in what capacity Jess was 'a business associate' of Lady Lucinda's but presumed it was all part of Sir Walton's perceived plot against him... Perhaps he was right... His own genial nature pushed him to wonder whether she had become such only after his departure to marry Sophie – and yet it did not seem right: it appeared to have deeper roots. He also had a suspicion that he might have met her briefly before around the time he had been building the Mulberry Hall lake... Perhaps... but he could not be sure, that being so many years ago...

They reached the relative quiet of the office. For her part, Jess was just as aware of Arnold's searching eyes and suspected that he did not trust or believe her claim to the business, so had to get Arnold and Josiah apart at all costs. The next few minutes were spent in diplomatic evasion until Arnold realised nothing would be discussed in front of him: he was just the foreman. So he made his excuses and left, being careful to close the door firmly behind him. He made much of descending the stairs, then very quietly crept back up to listen at the door.

"So what brings you to Wirksworth?" he heard Josiah asking of Jess.

"Business," she replied evasively.

"I see. In the town?"

"You could say that."

"I see."

"And you?"

"I was the manager here for some years." Jess's heart sank.

"But not still?" she asked more in hope than certainty.

"No." Her heart bounded again.

"But I still have a claim to the business, having invested a lot of money into it."

Jess felt perturbed once more. "I have shares," he added with emphasis. He was beginning to dislike this woman on his own account, not just Sir Walton's: she either avoided questions or asked awkward ones. Jess was nursing similar sentiments. If this man was going to thwart her clever plan…

"And where do you reside normally?" she asked.

"Mulberry Hall, just before Bakewell."

"Ah…" So he must be the man Sophie wedded that day she slipped into the reception: he looked vaguely familiar but was more portly than then and she had of necessity kept quite distant from him. But he was now one of the Grimley family so something had to be done. In for a penny… Yet for now he obviously did not recognise her, so she had to act fast while she still had that advantage.

There was suddenly the sound of hissing steam and a hoarse whistle emanated from below them; it was six o'clock and time for the men to stop work for the day. They could hear some of the machines winding down and, after a few moments, there was a knock on the door and Arnold entered.

"Begging your pardon, sir, Miss Rigby, but it's time for the men to leave, so shall I see either of you in the morning?"

"You'll certainly be seeing me," Josiah answered.

'*Not if I have anything to do with it*', Jess thought, then said, "I have some business in the morning but may drop by later on. I have to locate a document."

"Not *that* one, then," Arnold interjected, pointing to the one she held tenaciously in her hand..

THE SLAVE-OWNER'S DILEMMA

"No – another one," Jess responded almost viciously. Then, waspishly, "I do have several in my possession."

Josiah noted her defensiveness and wondered why. So he announced his departure and made for the stairs but Arnold was there before him; they passed through the doorway and Arnold quickly turned to Josiah and urgently mouthed, 'I have to talk to you' just before Jess's swift presence appeared behind them. Josiah was bemused but nodded and followed Arnold down.

Once there in the now empty factory, it became obvious to Josiah that Jess would not leave until he had, so after a few minutes' small-talk he departed and – Arnold having disappeared into the factory, made his excuses to Miss Rigby and went some hundred yards down the road, stopping to hide behind a statue of the local hero and industrialist Richard Arkwright, where he could observe the main door of the factory and wait for Jess to leave, whereupon he would return to meet Arnold. But Jess did not come. After some ten minutes waiting, and suspecting the imminence of rain, he decided to go back to Lucinda's house; Arnold would realise where he was staying so he could wait for him there in comfort.

He arrived there a few minutes later and was surprised to be met by a distressed Sophie after the maid had let him in. "My sweetheart, what's the matter?" he asked as the maid helped him off with his coat.

"There's a Mr. Arnold Strapley waiting for you in the parlour," said Sophie breathlessly. She waited for the maid to disappear then conspiratorially added in a whisper, "And he has suspicions I think you should hear."

"Strange – I was waiting for him for ages outside the factory because he implied there was something of importance to tell me."

"And it is, my dearest. And I, too, have some news, which I think is relevant and will impart when you see him. Come, come – quick! It is indeed of extreme importance," and she ushered him into the room where an apologetic-looking Arnold stood, his cap in hand and still in his leather apron from the factory – he must have left in a great hurry.

"Mr. Strapley – I was waiting for you for some time but- "

"Sorry, sir," Arnold interrupted, "but that woman would not go so I left through a back door. I think she's an impostor and is after your factory…"

"And also, he believes, Mulberry Hall," added Sophie. "That was what I was going to add: as we entered the town I recognised her face and have only just remembered who it must be. It was the servant that Sir Walton dismissed some years ago – and who also tried to compromise Jemima. She's evil."

"Yes," Josiah replied, "Jess Rigby; she's the one Sir Walton fears is plotting against him."

With a quaver in his voice, Arnold stated in a voice full of foreboding: "I have to say, sir, that I fear you and your family may be in great danger."

CHAPTER 54

A Plan Thwarted, Suspicions Arise

& Evidence Is Found

It had not taken Jess long to realise that Arnold had given her the slip but – rather than draw attention to herself by finding him and possibly Josiah in the town and risking a rowdy altercation - decided to take advantage of the empty upstairs office where she hoped she could pick the lock of the strong-box and place the forged document – without its box - within it; re-locking the casket would be the bigger challenge but she had to try. Then she would consider her next move. She raced back up the stairs and after several minutes with her hairpin, the lock eventually sprang open; she lifted the heavy lid… only to find that the casket was completely empty. Nothing. Surprised, she angrily knew she could not now add the document. She looked around the room and started searching for any hint of a hidey-hole or loose floorboard – but the building's frame was of iron and the cracks in the boards laid across it revealed the floor below. She started to panic… if there was nowhere to find a document, then she would not be able to claim its retrieval. She pondered her reckless intimation to Arnold that the document was inside the strong-box: no wonder Arnold was suspicious of her for he must have known there was nothing in it. Worse, any important papers must be somewhere else... Or, Lucinda had entrusted him with a key and he had cleared them out for safety.

Either way, her plan was thwarted and an irrepressible anger rose within her.

*

Josiah was by now angry, too. Arnold had regaled him of his suspicions regarding Miss Rigby and stated that after she told him Lady Lucinda had been murdered, he instinctively suspected she was covering something up - also opining that he would not be surprised if she had done that deed herself. And when she had said that there was a document in the strong-box, he knew she was lying. He had never taken to Miss Rigby, he said, as she had arrived like a tornado in the town some years ago and then made a not inconsiderable amount of money with her bawdy-houses, always one step ahead of the law due to 'knowing' people she could blackmail. Yet there were rumours, too, of some connection between her and Lady Lucinda which no-one had dared talk of because they were always meeting in private. Indeed, as Jess became by wealth more of a 'lady', Arnold felt that she had openly been ingratiating herself with Lady Lucinda – and more so after Josiah had left the town for Mulberry Hall and his love, Sophie. Lucinda, being then somewhat lonely with Sebastian often away whoring and drinking or in London, had been glad of a friend and had all too readily taken this woman into her confidence, he stated.

It went quiet for a moment as this sank in. Eventually, Arnold continued: "And now Lady Lucinda is murdered... this technically leaves Miss Rigby in a good position to make a claim on this business – if she really has managed to forge what appears to be a legal document, that is…"

"What are you saying?" interjected Josiah.

"Well, sir… just a few hours ago, when Miss Rigby came to tell me that Lady Lucinda had been murdered in Bakewell - and as she was what she termed 'a business associate' of Lady Lucinda's - she said she had a claim on it if anything befell her. Well, instantly I thought, '*That's not right.*' Then she mentioned that, in Lady Lucinda's strong-box, there was a document drawn up by some legal firm that bequeathed her the Noncey & Daughter business in such circumstances - and when she found the key she would show it to me as proof. Well, I knew what was inside it – Lady Lucinda often left it open." He laughed.

"And had she left it open?"

"Not this time, sir, no."

"So, presumably, you had a key?"

"Yes, sir. Lady Lucinda gave me one in case she lost hers. So while you were talking to Miss Rigby – she waiting for you to go and me hoping you could keep her chatting as long as possible - I managed to disappear and immediately crept back upstairs and quickly took the papers out: Lady Lucinda was very tidy and the papers were all in one large bag – presumably for a quick retrieval if necessary. Then, as you were leaving, I just managed to get back down the stairs to hide myself and the bag in the cellar. She called for me and must have thought I'd gone because she went straight back upstairs. I could hear her cursing as she picked the lock but as soon as I heard the heavy lid open I knew I should escape with the documents."

"So where *are* Lady Lucinda's documents now, then?" Josiah eventually asked.

"I have them in my cottage," Arnold replied.

"Are they safe, there?" Josiah enquired nervously.

"Safer there than where that woman can find them," he replied firmly, then added, "But I'd like to get them to you as soon as I can, sir..."

"Indeed." There was a pause, then Josiah asked, "So I see now why you suspect that she's after this business... but I fail to see how you are of the opinion that Miss Rigby could ever acquire Mulberry Hall."

"Well, begging your pardon, sir, for the insolence but... well, I knew that Lady Lucinda was after the Hall as well, sir... she talked to Miss Rigby of little else. They might have talked in private but if you listen carefully you can hear through the cracks in the floorboards... So together – one real wife and one real mother - I understood from several bits of conversations over the months that initially they wanted to use Sebastian – the supposed heir – as the reason for grasping the estate from Sir Walton Grimley *together* - before he could give it to anyone else."

"Or Sir Walton Grimley died," Josiah mused.

"Or Sebastian," Arnold added ominously. Then, more darkly: "Mind you, I don't think Sebastian knew of their plan – I'm pretty sure that they kept it from him: he was the one who could be dispensed with..."

"The reason rather than the solution..." Sophie commented.

"Indeed, madam. But then, I think, petty jealousies started getting in the way; they didn't want to *share* the spoils – they each wanted the Hall for themselves."

After a moment, Josiah looked at Arnold and said, "So you, Arnold, took the papers out to protect us – and to ensure she could not add her document to whatever was in it?"

"Yes, sir."

"Well – thank you. That will be remembered."

"Thank you, sir. Much obliged, sir."

A pause descended upon the room; then Sophie enquired: "But I still don't understand how on earth you think Miss Rigby could inherit Mulberry Hall. I just don't see that."

"Because she had so much on Sebastian, madam," Arnold interjected. "And he was in her pocket... and she was probably sure that he would be just as keen to live back at the Hall with all its opulence and all. After all, he was Miss Rigby's true son, it's rumoured. Makes sense, sir..."

"What?!" Sophie exclaimed; "How do you arrive at that?"

"Well, madam... begging your pardon again... and, well, this must have been quite a few years back... I heard that Lady Lucinda couldn't conceive but knew Sir Walton Grimley would divorce her if she didn't bear him a son. So she made an arrangement with Jess - her being in that business, if you know what I mean, madam," and he reddened slightly, "she soon became with child ... and that was Sebastian, who officially became the designated heir to the Mulberry Hall estate."

"Without my father knowing of the subterfuge at the time?"

"That's right, madam."

"*I* only heard about all this for the first time yesterday, dearest," said Josiah. "And I'm not surprised they didn't tell you, it's all so... so machiavellian..."

"Mmm... no wonder my father didn't tell me, then – he

didn't know," said Sophie, somewhat disconsolately.

"He certainly does now," affirmed Josiah.

"But now Lucinda and Sebastian are *both* dead," Arnold added.

Sophie lowered her voice and said touchingly, "My father loved my mother more than he ever loved Lady Lucinda – she was just for show. And would provide an 'acceptable' heir, rather than me or Jemima. But we were never privy to *that* secret." Then she asked Josiah, "So you knew about this possible plot and the history behind it, did you?"

"Yes – but only since yesterday! ... but I kept it quiet for obvious reasons – and not least because I didn't know whether you knew." Sophie looked despondent, as if someone had taken away her favourite toy. Seeing this, Josiah continued: "I mean, I obviously knew about Sir Walton and your mother – almost everyone did on the estate – despite everyone being forbidden to say it. But not anything else... Sebastian's parentage, Lucinda, Jess Rigby... None of it! And to think I was even living in rooms here with Lucinda but never knew!"

A silence descended as they all contemplated the situation. Then Josiah turned to Sophie and asked, "Did Alice know of the subterfuge, do you think?"

She contemplated the question, then said slowly, "I think she must have done – in fact, now I think of it, she must have acted as a wet-nurse to the child after it was taken from Miss Rigby. I saw her feeding the baby once, so that would explain why - because Lucinda couldn't."

"How did she manage that?" asked Josiah, confused.

"Because I think that must have been the time she was pregnant with Jemima."

"Oh, no… How awful for Alice … to be used by someone who would then be her superior."

"And who would despise her because my father always truly loved Alice. Lucinda never came to terms with that," Sophie added bitterly.

"And I built her this house…" Josiah murmured. "I thought it strange… although it wasn't *that* odd because this was where Lucinda's father's business was. How naïve I was… And Miss Rigby was evicted from employment at Mulberry Hall because she harassed a young stable-lad there to such an extent that he asked to be relieved of his duties – but Sir Walton liked him and dismissed Miss Rigby instead."

"So you think it's revenge?" Arnold asked.

Sophie concurred: "That would certainly make sense to me now," she said. A silence descended once again upon the room.

It was eventually broken by Josiah: "I don't think that Jess Rigby murdered Sebastian, being her real son… Being so desperate, it would be easier to appropriate the Hall using Sebastian *with* Lucinda, as you said, Mr. Strapley… wouldn't it? I mean, they'd have a better common claim on Sebastian and the money, after all, *together*..."

There was a silence as the logic began dawning on him: "Aah… But if Jess had the money from the sale of *this* business… *and* had a true heir to Mulberry Hall… then she would have enough money to buy Mulberry Hall and a supposed heir into the bargain."

Arnold then drew a deep breath and said, "Begging your pardon again, sir… but may I make another supposition?"

"Of course," Josiah agreed. "Speak out."

"Two felons were hanged for Sebastian's murder but I thought at the time – before they were apprehended - it *might* have been Jess Rigby but, if I'm honest, I don't think it was her, either. I think it was Lady Lucinda."

The room went cold.

"How so?" Josiah enquired timorously.

"Well, sir... no real mother would murder her own true son, would she, as you just said? Particularly with him being so important to her only real claim on Mulberry Hall? I mean, what with propriety being what it is... well, sir Walton being an aristocrat now with wealth and a seat in Parliament... it would have been easier for Lucinda to supposedly prove Sebastian was her son than Jess because that knowledge would have caused a scandal. And he was a liability, what with all his spending and all. No, I think Lady Lucinda killed Sebastian – she had a better and easier claim to Mulberry Hall solely as Sir Walton's wife."

Josiah looked unmoved, then asked. "So who do you think killed Lady Lucinda, then?"

There was a silence as each quietly came to the same conclusion. Then Josiah confirmed it: "Jess Rigby. Because Lucinda killed her son - the only real claim she had to Mulberry Hall."

*

By early the next morning, Jess had realised that it was perhaps more important to show her bogus document to one of her clients in the legal business to assure it would pass verification, rather than try to foist it on Arnold. She could see that things were becoming awkward and that it was imperative to get this legal screed in front of someone who could act quickly: Judge Sir Ainsley Hoult was her best prospect. Better, he lived a little way out of Wirksworth in a small manor and she hoped this more direct but less conspicuous route would yield results faster than influencing Arnold first and then going to a lawyer in the town. It was only a mile or two away and so, as light dawned, she left Wirksworth for his home, the indicting document under her arm, wrapped in a cloth to keep off the damp. Arriving at the front door, she pulled the bell and waited for a response. But none came. Now even angrier, she left the premises and started her return to the town. To make things worse, it was drizzling, so she took refuge in a clump of trees and waited for the rain to pass. What she had not known was that Judge Hoult had seen her arriving and instructed his footman not to answer. Rumours were swirling about this girl and he did not want anything to do with her; he had also contracted the pox from one of her girls and was therefore not best minded to entertain her – in any sense of the word.

When Jess eventually returned to her home some two hours later, she turned the corner to see again the serjeant-at-arms and his assistant awaiting her arrival. And with them was Josiah Prentice. Things did not look good – so she turned and fled as decorously as possible. After some time waiting, the men barged at her front door until it burst open and the three went inside. This time, they searched her house more thoroughly than before, having been instructed to find a document which might have a bearing upon the ownership of Noncey & Daughter; but even after forcing her strong-box open and mostly only finding money, no document was found.

But they did find a charred vestige of coloured material in the fireplace…

CHAPTER 55

The Net Closes In

꧁༺❀❀❀❀❀❀❀❀❀❀❀❀❀❀❀❀❀❀❀❀❀❀❀༻꧂

Sir Walton Grimley was unwell and had taken to his bed. It was now late afternoon and a cloudy day which did little to raise his spirits, despite Alice spending her time beside him, mopping his fevered brow and reading him stories from his now impressively vast collection of books in the Mulberry Hall library: Tobias and Elspeth had hitherto been helping him pack his favoured belongings into trunks for the intended journey to Jamaica but his illness had precluded any further progress.

It was then that they heard a carriage pull up outside. Alice went to the window and said, "Ah, Josiah and Sophie have arrived back from Wirksworth! I must go and see them!" She gave Sir Walton a kiss on the forehead and skipped down the stairs; where she got her energy from was a mystery to Sir Walton but it had always been thus – Alice was still energetic and winsome even after all these years. She bounded into the hallway as the doors were opened by two footmen and Josiah and Sophie entered. Yet their expressions portended some sort of foreboding and whilst they were friendly, a pall hung over their greetings.

"Is there something wrong?" Alice asked.

"It's quite possible," Sophie replied. "We need to see Sir

Walton immediately."

"He is in bed, unwell," replied Alice.

"We must still see him," said Josiah, as he deposited his cloak, hat and gloves with a footman and made his way up the stairs. Alice looked bemused. "It will all be made clear," Sophie said; "Come upstairs and listen while we recount the story."

The revelations they exposed to Sir Walton perversely gave him some strength and he sat up to listen to the details, occasionally asking for clarifications and embellishments. When the facts had been exhausted, he sat back against his pillow and reflected for a moment, then said, "So before Lucinda was murdered in the town… you think that she had already killed Sebastian so that she would inherit this estate without any complications…?"

They all nodded. He continued: "…Such as, in case it was found out that Sebastian was not our true heir…" They nodded again. "And in the meantime, that scurrilous wench Miss Rigby whom I fired for harassing the stable-lad has been plotting my downfall – and in cahoots with Lucinda."

"Indeed, that seems to be correct," Josiah agreed.

"I just knew in my old bones something was up; I told you, Josiah, remember?"

Josiah nodded: "Indeed you did… But perhaps because they *both* wanted the estate, that's where they fell foul of each other… and where it all went wrong for them."

There was a short silence as the facts sunk in. "Well, blow me down," said Sir Walton eventually, "who'd have thought it? Am I that unpleasant that my ex-wife hated me so much? And a lowly, vengeful servant girl whom I did my best for still does?"

"It's not you, father," said Sophie sweetly; "It's what you represent in Jess's case - and pure greed in both of them."

"Excellently put," Josiah concurred. Then he added, "Yet we must be on our guard, for that scoundrel of a girl will try anything to wrest the Hall and estate from you. And we don't know what she has in that document – legal or not."

"And we also don't know if there are any nasty surprises from Lucinda's side, either," Sir Walton emitted faintly. "We have no idea what she might have concluded with that girl... perhaps there *are* some potentially damning facts or agreements between them ... *I* don't know... What I would wager, though, is that she's quite close. And, armed with that document, we don't know what to expect regarding the Noncey & Daughter business – even if we do all suspect it's a forgery." He looked out of the window into the distance. "So we'd better find the girl; if she's on the run then it's likely her last chance rests here at Mulberry Hall."

At that moment, two horses were heard cantering up the drive. Josiah went to the window and saw two swarthy men dismounting and Tobias walking towards them to enquire of their business. They were both armed.

Josiah said that he would deal with it, descended the stairs and went out into the evening air, which was refreshing after the stuffy ambiance of the sickroom.

"Sir Walton Grimley?" one of them asked, seeing him. Josiah corrected them. "Oh... pardon us, sir, but we need to speak to Sir Walton Grimley – King's business. And we also have a warrant for the arrest of a Miss Jess Rigby."

Josiah explained that she did not work at the Hall but they, too, wanted to see her – probably for the same reasons.

"I see," the more senior of the two men countered.

"So why *are* you looking for her?" Josiah enquired.

"She is wanted for the suspected murder of Lady Lucinda Grimley."

*

Jess was furious with herself: she had played all this very badly. When she went to find Judge Ainsley Hoult with her document she should have taken some of her wealth with her to have the chance of having enough money to hire a horse, stay in a hostel and eat if she suddenly had to escape for any reason… but in her desire for revenge she had not kept a clear head and gone there with very little financial support. Now she was on the run, cold, wet and penniless – all she had was the document. And that, now, was more of an indictment than a help. Yet it was all she had. She would have to beg for food and shelter on what would now be a very long walk from Wirksworth to Mulberry Hall.

And then she had an idea.

*

Josiah took the two men up to Sir Walton Grimley's sickroom and introduced them. They went straight to the point.

"Sir, Walton, good evening. We are sorry to disturb you but we are hunting for a previous employee of yours, we believe – a Miss Jess Rigby."

"Indeed," replied Sir Walton: "So are we. But I have to tell you I terminated her employment back in around 1808, I think it was – a couple of years or so after Trafalgar, anyway - for harassment of a stable-lad and an unsuitable disposition. She did not take it well. So, from your unexpected arrival, I suspect that she has done something wrong – as do we."

"Yes, Sir. We believe she may have committed a murder – of your wife, Lady Lucinda Grimley."

Sir Walton did not look shocked, but commented, "As far as I am concerned, sir, Lucinda is as much my wife now as that bedhead." The men looked confused, so he continued: "We separated some years ago and she went back to her late father's business in Wirksworth. Josiah here was the manager of that enterprise until recently."

"So can you give us any more details, Sir?" the man asked, turning to Josiah.

Josiah, not expecting to be part of this interrogation, was caught slightly unawares: "Er, well, er... upon hearing that Lady Lucinda had been murdered, I went up there with my wife, Sophie, because there was no-one to run the business – despite not being the manager now I do have an investment in it, you see... It was then that I unexpectedly met this Jess woman – trying to force a document onto the factory foreman, Mr. Arnold Strapley, supposedly proving that she had a claim to that business should anything befall Lady Lucinda. But Strapley told us that he also thought it was she who had murdered Lady Lucinda and that we might be in danger here as she may try to wrest this estate – Mulberry Hall – from us as revenge now that there was no heir since Sebastian Grimley's death."

"Sebastian Grimley being your son, Sir Walton?" the first officer enquired.

"Sort of..." Sir Walton answered, somewhat unhelpfully.

"And that her document is proof – if it is legal – to the appropriation of this estate?" the officer probed further.

"Not *this* estate directly, so much," Josiah explained. "But it probably pertains to a false claim on Noncey & Daughter, with which funds - if Miss Rigby sold it with the help of a probably bogus document of entitlement - she could possibly buy this estate. And with the help of the fact that Sebastian was *her* true son, not Lady Lucinda's." He looked at Sir Walton, expecting a glaring look for the betrayal of this confidence but, much to his relief, found his expression unchanged.

"She'll never manage it," said Sir Walton, stiffly resisting the idea, if not its possibility.

"You wouldn't believe, Sir, how some of these uneducated people can manipulate events to their choosing; I would advise you to be on your guard, Sir."

Sir Walton looked annoyed – why should this serjeant or whatever he was advise him? Cheeky fellow!

The man continued. "If she has, indeed, killed Lady Lucinda, do you think she may have killed Sebastian as well?"

A silence ensued as Sir Walton and Josiah reflected, then Sir Walton answered, "I suppose it's possible, although we think it more likely it was Lady Lucinda herself, actually."

"Why so?" the man asked.

"Because I had banished the boy for not being my son after all. I only found that out around the time he came of age. That's one of the reasons I finally gave Lucinda a house in her home town of Wirksworth – built by my now son-in-law Josiah here – to keep her quiet and get rid of her. Yet whether Jess Rigby killed Sebastian is unlikely because he was technically the heir as 'our' son – though, in practice, nothing to do with either me or my ex-wife."

"Two felons were hanged for that murder," the man said smugly. "I apprehended them myself, in fact."

"Yes, I daresay: but you're missing the point. For Jess Rigby to kill him would have destroyed her claim to the estate."

"How so, Sir?"

"Because – as Mr. Josiah Prentice here has tried to explain - he was *her* real son, provided secretly to my wife when she could not conceive and so supposedly give us an heir which would tie her to the estate. I never knew of the plot at the time."

"And did you banish Jess Rigby at the same time?"

"No – that was much earlier, as I have said. But I was charitable to the girl and gave her money to buy the house in Bakewell that my housekeeper had once lived in but which her husband, Giles Burrows, appropriated when she moved permanently here and, and... well, became involved with someone else in this house..."

"'In this house'," the man reiterated. "I see. Can you give us more information about that event?"

Sir Walton was becoming annoyed again. Testily, he said, "My housekeeper, Elspeth Burrows, eventually married my new butler, Tobias. Giles Burrows *had* been her husband and my butler before this house was built but I made him divorce Elspeth for a pretty sum so he could stop upsetting her, which enabled him to carry on with this Jess, who had become his whore by then; I did it also so Jess would not be on the streets. All good intentions – I am not a cruel man and wanted the best for the girl as well as my housekeeper and butler... I believe Jess Rigby did well out of her 'profession' but then she moved away when I told her - once again – never to come here again when she turned up at my daughter's wedding. I even made her sign a document to that effect... Anyway, she left – to go to

THE SLAVE-OWNER'S DILEMMA

Wirksworth, I understand, to be close to her son and also, as it turns out, Lady Lucinda Grimley."

"So she moved to Wirksworth, Sir, to be near your son, on whom she must have realised she could both use and depend on – and he her, of course?"

"Yes, that's as I understand it now, but I didn't then."

"Charity does not always get repaid," the second man suddenly interjected sagely. "It is often resented." Then, he changed tack and asked, "So what happened to this Giles Burrows?"

"I have no idea. Disappeared. Why?"

"Well... I'm told he was never seen again in Bakewell by people who knew him... Is it possible that Jess might have killed him as well – after she got what she wanted?" They all looked shocked. "You see, Sir, that's why we're concerned for you. He suddenly disappeared and it was rumoured that he ran out of money... so we wondered whether Jess got tired of his abusive and drunken behaviour. But by then, of course, he may have already sown the seed of revenge in her, despite your charitable intentions."

Sir Walton nodded. "Indeed. It's possible, I suppose; but it was several years ago now." There was a reflective pause, then he became more thoughtful and asked, "So, going back to where we were... and bearing in mind this Jess woman seems to have become increasingly inured in murder... are you concluding that she was by then aware that Lady Lucinda was a threat to *her* gaining the estate after all since her real son was now dead?"

The second man answered again: "In a convoluted way, yes - it's more than possible. His death removed any entitlement for said Jess Rigby to this estate. But this also meant that, with Lady Lucinda being still your legal wife,

Sir Walton, she would be the sole inheritor."

"Damn her!" Sir Walton said under his breath. "I told her I would divorce her but after she'd gone I kept forgetting to do so. How stupid of me..."

The room went quiet again as the summation of probable events and reasons sank in to those who had suspected them but also to those who had not.

"Which is also why we think Jess Rigby will try to kill you if she can. Because you are not married to the mother of your children, are you Sir?"

Sir Walton Grimley looked thunder at him. "No, I am not, damn you. What of it?"

"Well, there is no legal heir by marriage. And as we have no idea what's in Miss Rigby's document... if it *is* legal, then... she may have a greater claim to this estate than you think."

A chill went through the air as a silence ensued. Sir Walton then decided the meeting was over and gruffly addressed the men. "Well, thank you for your visit... most considerate but rather frightening, under the circumstances. Now I will marry Alice with all speed."

"Being a widower will permit that prospect now, of course," the second man remarked wryly. Sir Walton suddenly realised that it was this man who was superior, just standing back, assessing, watching, as the other laid out the facts.

"Are you the serjeant?" he enquired. The man nodded. "It's very late – or early, depending on your point of view... so you're welcome to put your horses into the stables and sleep in the room over them if you have nowhere else..."

"Thank you, Sir Walton – that's very much appreciated,

Sir; it has been a long day and a long ride at the end of it..."

Sir Walton nodded and addressed Josiah. "Josiah, will you alert Tobias and get him to do the necessary? And give these men something to eat, too."

"Of course," and he left.

"And have a brandy to warm you up before you get over there – it's probably a bit damp; but comfortable."

"That will do fine, Sir, thank you," the serjeant replied. Then he took out a small piece of charred, coloured cloth from his pouch and held it up for Sir Walton to see, and asked, "By the way, Sir Walton... do you recognise this material at all?"

Sir Walton took out a glass and looked at it carefully, then shook his head.

"Pity," the man said; "We found it in Jess Rigby's fireplace and tomorrow we hope to ascertain from a young lad working at The Rutland Arms in Bakewell that it was in the hands of Jess Rigby at the time we believe she murdered Lady Lucinda Grimley."

*

It had been just after nine o'clock when Jess knocked on the door of the man's lodging-house; a light burned in the window, casting flickering shadows onto the unkempt turf. She was searching for a kindly young man training to be a notary. Like so many men of his age who wanted some experience of life before marriage, his lustful instincts had led him to one of Jess's girls. Because he had been so young – and Jess being at that time of a more generous nature than she had latterly become - she had given him a reduced rate: it was now time to cash in her generosity. She had expected the door to be opened by the landlady but her brazenness paid off as this time it was opened by the very man she sought. He was horrified at seeing her again and tried to seal the door as much as possible behind him without actually closing it. By then, Jess was manufacturing copious tears to embellish her tale of woe and wondered if – under her poor and straitened circumstances – he could give her the remainder of the fee he had earlier paid. Somewhat perturbed at what this visit might do for his reputation and religious prospects, he rushed inside, brought out a larger fee than had been expected – Jess could hear from the back of the house the landlady enquiring who was there – and did not request any change, firmly closing the door afterwards. Jess dried her tears and, financially recharged, decided to walk to the next village in the hope that she could find a place for the night and a horse to take her to Mulberry Hall the next morning...

CHAPTER 56

A Change Of Heart, A Confrontation & A Conclusion

Sir Walton Grimley was angry; not just that he now had to go through the rigmarole of marrying Alice but more because he could not understand why his personal lawyer, Barnabas, had not foreseen this inheritance loophole. He had demanded an audience with him for early the next morning and was determined to rise in order to deliver his broadside fully dressed in formal attire rather than as an ageing man in his nightgown. The two officials had left for their room over the stables around midnight with a trail of supposition in their wake; Alice had retired to bed some hours before and would be informed of the proceedings in the morning, hopefully happy that at last her saviour had been persuaded to marry her. After the demise of Lady Lucinda it seemed the right thing to do – even without the pressing necessity of wills, inheritance and potential claims of Sir Walton possibly dying intestate.

Barnabas stood in front of him, trembling. He had never experienced Sir Walton Grimley's wrath before which, although muted, was clearly evident. The tirade finished with Sir Walton saying, "... so how did you not know that, with my wretched supposed son Sebastian dead, and also Lady Lucinda, that I would have no lineage unless I married Alice!"

"Well, Sir, it all happened rather quickly... and until these terrible events happened, you never actually had the ability to divorce Lady Lucinda anyway because she would never have consented to it. I thought her banishment to Wirksworth was the closest you could get to being rid of her. Sir!"

"But what of this ruddy girl who might pop out of the woodwork any moment? I will have to marry Alice immediately! Or... all this could suddenly disappear!"

"That would be the best option, Sir Walton. Shall I have a word with Miss Alice to confirm it? Then I can get the vicar to the village for a ceremony... well, what with banns and so on... within about three weeks?"

"Three weeks? To hell with the banns! Fix it with the parson – a donation to his spire fund – anything! The girl might be here any moment! Marriage tomorrow at the latest! Here, in the church, in your chambers... anywhere! Even Van Diemen's Land! Just arrange it and fast!"

Barnabas left with his tail between his legs. Sir Walton then rang for Tobias. When his butler arrived, he asked him to inform Alice that they were getting married tomorrow and to alert Elspeth that there would be a marriage dinner afterwards; then he asked Tobias to arrange for various invitations to be sent to some local notables so there was a sense of celebration. It was all very hasty and indecorous but it had to be done this way or it might be too late.

With that, Alice entered; she had not seen Tobias and was unaware of Sir Walton's plan, so was surprised to see him so animated.

"Dearest, what are you so disturbed about, pacing the room like a caged tiger?"

"My darling Alice," he exclaimed, approaching and embracing her. "You are about to become Lady Alice Grimley!"

"Oh, Walton… er, well, that's wonderful! But… but why now?"

"Because I should have done it in the first place, before I got involved with that damned woman, Lucinda. But I had to do it for, for… "

"Appearances?"

"Well, yes, I suppose so… No! For legal reasons."

"And appearances, dearest! But, no matter, I am delighted."

"Oh, you were always so wonderfully understanding… but now that scheming witch is dead I am going to do the right thing. So… will you marry me?"

"Of course, dearest! But when?"

"As soon as possible! Today – or, latest – tomorrow."

"But why the rush?"

"To ensure that another scheming witch does not get the estate from us now that Lucinda and Sebastian are no more."

"And who is that, pray?"

"Jess Rigby – our ex-servant girl."

"But she left years ago and you gave her a house, if I remember rightly - *and* made her sign a document to stay away after what happened more recently with Jemima."

"Yes. But she is evil, *evil*! And despite all that she may

appear at any moment, so we must be on our guard."

"I see."

"No, you probably don't my little sweetheart... but if you see or hear of her tell me immediately." She nodded. So he finished with, "And at last you will have the rightful title of Lady Alice Grimley."

"But what will your peers say to this? I am but a humble slave-girl!"

"Not after we're married! And anyway, I don't care what they say – sod 'em! I love *you*." With that, they spontaneously waltzed happily around the parlour as if dancing to an imaginary quartet but with the music supplied by the joy in their hearts.

What they did not know was that Jess Rigby was nearing the palatial front gates to Mulberry Hall at that very moment, with the similarly desperate intent of acquiring the same title for herself.

*

Jess had not been able to find lodgings and the open landscape provided little shelter; consequently, she was cold and wet, as was her horse. They were both hungry. A damp, grey pallor coloured the sky in the distance, a feeble excuse for dawn, but even this and her saturated condition could not suppress the thrill which coursed through her body as the gates came into view: she was here... Mulberry Hall was just over the rise and the document in her saddle-bag was going to prove that she had rights to the Noncey & Daughter business... from then on, she would argue that the Hall was hers, too, through Lucinda's demise *and* the fact that Sebastian was *her* son and – according to Lucinda's final confession before she killed her – they believed he was still alive! In her increasingly lurid and covetous state she had made herself believe this – her last chance. How clever she was! She smirked as she thought of Sir Walton Grimley less than a mile away now, who had no idea what was about to hit him... he would soon regret ever dismissing her for chasing Jack the stable-lad. Yet without that catalyst she would still be a poor, overworked servant girl and probably married with several children, worn out and unfulfilled. It was all working out well and a surge of pride welled within her: she was not going to be one of life's have-nots and would soon have dukes and barons fawning over her for the favours she could tantalise them with – and those they could bestow upon her! She would rise from being a humble whore to wealthy courtesan!

She left the muddy track and, passing under the palatial entrance arch, dismounted and set foot on the firm, well-made drive. Leading her tired steed towards her objective, however, she suddenly heard horses' hooves ahead of her; yet she was out in the open and the expansive parkland stretched either side of her with no place to hide. She panicked for a moment, then her steely nerve returned and she strode on. After a few moments, two bouncing heads appeared on the drive's horizon, each capped by a feathered leather hat. The two horsemen were talking to each other so did not immediately notice her but as soon as she saw them, she knew exactly who they were: the serjeant-at-arms and his accomplice she had almost walked into outside her house in Wirksworth. They had got here before her! She quickly tried to mount her horse to make a getaway but kept sliding off its damp flank; then they had seen her, just a hundred yards away... Not for an instant realising who it was, they rode on until suddenly the serjeant cried, "It's Jess Rigby! Get her!" and they were upon her, dismounting and tying her hands as she screamed that they had no right to be apprehending her. They took the document and the serjeant unscrolled it, his eyes lighting up on reading its contents: "A-ha!" he cried, "A forgery if ever I saw one!"

"It's a legal document!" Jess screamed back, "Made out in London with a lawyer!"

"Made *up*, more like!" he riposted.

They tied a rope to her hands and remounted their steeds, half pulling and half dragging her and her horse along the drive and back to her goal – which, even as they approached it, now suddenly seemed further away than ever before.

As they came to a halt outside the entrance, the doors flew open and Sir Walton Grimley and Josiah ran out and down the steps, each putting on their coats against the dank day. Behind them were Tobias, Alice and two footmen who surged up to and around them. The serjeant looked at Sir Walton and stated, "Sir Walton Grimley, we have reason to believe that this is Jess Rigby, resident of Wirksworth."

"My goodness, yes, it is," Sir Walton confirmed.

"I also believe that this document – with which I suspect she was eventually hoping to defraud you of your estate – is a counterfeit piece of nonsense."

Jess started screaming abuse at them all until she grew hoarse and eventually quietened as they all laughed at her.

"Let's all go inside," Sir Walton suggested, "and interrogate the wench there. The sport will be more pleasurable in the warm."

They entered the building and assembled in the Great Parlour. Tobias and the two footmen stood close to Jess as the others formed a circle around her, forcing her to face Sir Walton and the two officers of the law.

Sir Walton looked pitilessly at her and looked her up and down, as if trying to amass the facts of the situation when he fired her all those years ago – and more recently besides. Then he drew a deep breath which seemed to emanate from the depths of his soul and quietly but firmly asked, "Did you murder Lady Lucinda Grimley at the Rutland Arms last week?"

"No!" Jess shouted.

Sir Walton took a pace back to avoid any spittle landing on his person and asked a second question: "Did you kill my son, Sebastian, before that?"

"No! And he was *my* son... MY son – not yours *or* Lady Grimley's! But because he was taken from me and lived both here with Lady Grimley so he is my heir and I lay claim to this estate!"

"But he is dead, dear girl... so whether he was your son or not is of no importance."

That information momentarily stunned her: they knew he was dead after all: Lucinda had misled her again! So she took a deep breath and launched another tirade: "That document gives me claim to the Noncey & Daughter business so now Lady Grimley is dead I am the only surviving claimant to her son's estate."

"I thought you just said he was *your* son." They all sniggered.

"He was *my* son – and I have a claim to the Noncey & Daughter business so by rights I have a claim to this estate as well!"

Sir Walton smiled patronisingly: "But *I* am the rightful owner of this estate, my girl – and you signed *two* documents, not one – agreeing never to come back here.

Which you have now done. So you're trespassing as well."

"My claim overrides that!" she shouted loudly at him.

"And even after I tried twice to help you and give you a chance in life, you still despise me... You were well looked after by me; I even gave you a house so you could be with Giles Burrows... you poor thing."

"That's chicken-feed to you!" she spat.

"Not the point. I was trying to help you but you insulted my charity. Now you will pay the price."

The serjeant stepped forward: it was time to make some accusations. "I put it to you, Miss Rigby, that *you* killed your son because you believed that Lady Lucinda's claim – being of the nobility – would trump yours. Although how you expected to gain this estate by doing so I still cannot fathom."

"Exactly! I don't *know* who killed my son – but I don't believe it was the people who hanged for it."

"Hmm. Tidy..." the serjeant responded. "So was it Lady Lucinda Grimley?"

Jess turned to him, trying to look confused. "Don't be stupid: why would she wish to kill her adopted son? And he was good to me, confided in me and helped set me up – so it's obvious *again* that *I* wouldn't have killed him."

"Perhaps, then, as I implied... Lady Lucinda did. Especially as he was running up gambling and whoring debts..."

"To which you were a helping hand," added Sir Walton.

Jess looked daggers at him.

The serjeant continued: "And then perhaps – if he had lived - you and he *could* have taken over Noncey & Daughter, as this forged piece of parchment attests... But never, of course, this place."

Jess could feel the earth slipping away from under her so, trying to change the course of the conversation, shouted "This is not a court!"

"Just trying to establish the facts... before you attend one."

Elspeth had entered the room during the latter part of this inquisition and was horrified to recognise Jess; but needing to ascertain whether she would have to prepare food and drink for the assembled throng, was biding her time for an appropriate moment.

Sir Walton, now wanting to get Jess out of his house at the earliest opportunity, then asked, "So you say you did not murder Lady Lucinda Grimley?"

"No!"

"Nor Sebastian Grimley?"

"No."

"I see. So, did you, then, as a matter of interest, murder Giles Burrows? His misdemeanours had landed you with a house after all – and he was of no use to you after that..."

She hesitated for an instant, surprised at this question out of the blue. "No! I did not! Anyway, I'd left him long before I heard he'd disappeared." She darted a look at Elspeth, who suddenly flushed red and quickly left the room.

The serjeant then put his hand into his pouch and brought out a charred piece of coloured cloth. "This is yours, isn't it?"

Jess reddened and, somewhat flustered by the unexpected relic from her hearth, could not immediately find an answer, her normal sang-froid deserting her. "N-No... No, it isn't!"

"Then what was it doing in your hearth, then?"

"I don't know!... Perhaps you put it there! To incriminate me!"

"So you admit it's from your house?"

"No – I just said you put it there." Her confidence was returning. But it did not last long.

The serjeant paused a moment and moved closer to Jess, staring her in the eye. Then, slowly, he dangled the remnant of cloth in front of her and said purposefully: "When we first accosted you at your house in Wirksworth we stated that a young lad at The Rutland Arms had seen a woman of your description there carrying a coloured bag on the same night Lady Lucinda Grimley was murdered. You told us you didn't have a coloured bag. Yet when we returned a second time – and you'd fled – we found this in your hearth. So I suggest that you were trying to burn the evidence. I will swear that on the holy bible. So, Miss Jess Rigby, I accuse you of the murder of Lady Lucinda Grimley on that very night."

Everyone stared at her. She did not know what to say. And, with that, she knew the game was up.

CHAPTER 57

A Change Of Plan & A Resolution

As if the case against her was not enough, the further charge – added to her murder trial – was that she had disobeyed her agreement made at the time of Sophie and Josiah's wedding. So it was hardly a surprise when Jess Rigby was sentenced to be publicly hanged in the centre of Bakewell two weeks later.

There were some who would benefit from her demise, however: the small fortune from her strong-box was distributed to the poor of Wirksworth on the orders of Sir Walton, who had been gifted her three houses there by the judiciary as no-one knew who owned the other two; in fact Jess had subtly managed to make everyone believe they were hers but appropriated them as they had fallen derelict and unoccupied. Over a relatively short time, she had restored them sumptuously enough for her sordid – but very lucrative – business. Jess's girls all disappeared, most likely not wanting to be arrested for their trade; it was generally supposed that they dispersed to other towns in the area along with the experience and business acumen which Jess had instilled in them – but none were ever seen again in Wirksworth. As for the house in Bakewell, this had already been bestowed on Tobias and Elspeth as part of the original agreement with Jess. Yet fate would produce a very much better outcome for them.

Just prior to Jess's trial, Arnold Strapley had found an unexpected document amongst those he had retrieved from Lady Lucinda's strong-box. This he gratefully gave to those administering the legal process; it revealed that Josiah's financial investment in Noncey & Daughter – and Lucinda's romantic interest in him, along with his managerial capabilities - had secretly occasioned her to draw up a legal entitlement bequeathing Josiah the business if any tragedy might befall her – rather than her errant and not true son, Sebastian: perhaps she had wondered whether, at some stage, he might have wished to administer the same brutal fate to her. Consequently, Josiah had the advantage of acquiring a small fortune should he wish to sell the business. Sophie, however, was minded to move with him to Wirksworth and make it even more successful: she was more resourceful and ambitious than Jemima and by living in the Wirksworth house Josiah had built for Lucinda – but which, of course, still belonged to Sir Walton Grimley – she had seen in that flash of fortune that she would be less fettered by the past should she and Josiah live there. So it was not long before she had persuaded Josiah to run the Noncey & Daughter business again, which would also pay the dues on Mulberry Hall if it could not be sold and so help her father.

Jemima and Barnabas were also grateful to be living in Alice Lodge as the sole occupants.

CHAPTER 58

A Marriage & A Change Of Heart...

Whilst the events at Mulberry Hall that night had eliminated the need for Sir Walton Grimley to marry Alice after all, he now fervently wanted a sense of family continuity to linger down the ages: Alice had been his rock, he had forced himself to admit – the very reason for his being, which was why he had belatedly felt duty bound to make her 'an honest woman': it would be she and their children who would inherit the estate without any possible challenges on his death - recent events had clearly illustrated that necessity. Yet nothing provokes action regarding this as much as the wish to forestall it, and this seemed all the more likely if he stayed any longer at Mulberry Hall: he needed warmth in his old age - and with Alice being so much younger, she could go with him to Jamaica and return to the family home, or Alice Lodge, after he died, should she wish to, without fear of having her inheritance usurped.

The funeral of Lady Lucinda happened a few days later in the village church. Few came, mostly as none were formally invited: but just a few hours later, Sir Walton - wishing the past to be firmly buried before any marriage to Alice – wedded his paramour in the same church in the presence of a much increased and happy, colourful throng. As for Sebastian's body, this had already been deposited and forgotten in a Wirksworth churchyard.

The sudden brush with guilt which Elspeth had experienced by that look from Jess, regarding the killing of her husband Giles all those years ago, however, had made her reassess leaving England for Jamaica; without exposing why, she discussed her changed wish with Tobias but he now firmly wanted to stay in England: whereas Jamaica reminded him of relative hardship, Elspeth moving there suddenly offered a chance to escape the vicinity of her crime and possible arrest. She had watched Jess hang and was terrified that the same fate would await her if Giles' body was ever found. Tobias, not ever having known of this episode, could not understand her sudden change of heart but it was so passionately – and frequently - put that he eventually relented. This was much to the delight of Sir Walton and Alice – and soon, accompanied by the other three servants, they all began their long and hazardous journey to Jamaica...

On arrival there, Sir Walton Grimley and Alice were fêted by his workers and the local population: having freed his slaves or re-employed them with decent wages a few years earlier, his actions had eventually been copied by other slave owners – if seldom to their liking. Yet because the Hall had not been sold - and with his sugar now more expensive to produce - his income had fallen dramatically and some of the less enlightened slave owners laughed at him; yet the enactment of legislation soon made it incumbent on them to adapt to a more benevolent society, too, and with a happier, better-fed and more productive workforce, dissent diminished and their profits subsequently began to increase. As the new legislation took hold, Sir Walton was soon regarded as a hero thanks to his altruism and he increasingly became known locally as 'Saint Sir Walton'.

Yet with no-one living in Mulberry Hall – only Alice Lodge – the future of this wonderful house looked bleak… but there would be a twist to the tale…

CHAPTER 59

A Letter From Italy

& A Welcome Setback

Throughout all the goings-on in England and Jamaica, Edward had steadily become a huge operatic star across Italy and Europe, singing to packed houses wherever he went. Sadly, much of his success went unknown in the vast expanses of rural Derbyshire due to his being too busy and a poor letter-writer; in addition, what scant letters did get through to England sometimes did not get as far as Mulberry Hall. One day, however, a letter did arrive from Edward, addressed to Jemima, asking where his mother Elspeth and father Tobias were as they never replied to his letters… Edward was now based in Rome, he wrote, where he was now living with his duchess; they were very happy and now had three children. However, he had strained his voice by singing too much and consequently had to rest it for a few months… so they wished to travel to England to see his parents but could not contact them. Could they stay at Mulberry Hall? Jemima immediately sent a reply to Rome explaining the situation and that his parents were now living in Jamaica with Sir Walton Grimley and Alice. She forwarded Edward's letter to Jamaica and replied to him thus:

Dear Edward and Lady Philomena,

I was greatly excited by your news and your wonderful success in Italy. Of course you can come and stay with us at Mulberry Hall but things have changed here significantly. Sir Walton is now very frail and is living back in Jamaica with Alice, whom he married but a month or so ago after the death of Lady Lucinda. (More on that when we see you!) With them are your parents, Tobias and Elspeth, who decided for reasons none of us could fathom to live there with them. Sophie now lives with her husband, Josiah – whom you know as he built both the Hall and then Alice Lodge and now runs what was Lady Lucinda Grimley's factory in Wirksworth. I have wedded my husband, Barnabas, who is a lawyer living and working in Bakewell – he was at Sophie's wedding but you probably did not meet him for reasons I will have to discreetly explain! I cannot remember how much you know – you have been away from us for so long! But I will only say that much intrigue, plotting and circumstance has occasioned since you left us all – and only a long sojourn here will give us all the time to catch up with one another! Should you wish to come and stay with us in the empty Hall, that would be more than convenient but wonderful too – unless it is sold by then. If it is, then you can stay with us in Alice Lodge. If you can come in the summer months then perhaps Sir Walton may return too – but not the winter months: the cold here in Northern England is all too much for him now. Also, I cannot help feeling that his health would improve if someone would only buy Mulberry Hall. So try to come sometime between June and September and I will organise as many of the family to be here as possible. Please let us know as soon as you can what suits you and I will make any arrangements. Reply soon, dear Edward! Your good childhood friend, Jemima. February, 1835.

Only three weeks later, Jemima received a letter from Edward, which said:

Dear Jemima and Barnabas,

My goodness! So much has happened since I left – and seemingly so full of intrigue! I cannot wait to see you all again and will arrive at the Hall the first week in June. The party will consist of me, my darling Philomena, our three children, Ersinda, Segeste and Alessandro, my manservant Howard and Philomena's maid, Simona, who is Italian and a delight. Please inform Sir Walton Grimley and Lady Alice and we hope that they will feel it worthwhile to return to England to see us – sadly, Jamaica is a sea too far for us! But he has done so much for me that I truly wish to be able to see and thank him for his help in making me famous: perhaps my presence might even help him to get better as anything I can do for that man would be such a pleasure - I am eternally indebted to his favour and largesse! Yours sincerely, hopefully and eternally, Edward – or Eduardo, as I am known in these climes! Alla prossima!

Jemima duly wrote to Sir Walton, Tobias and Elspeth, availing them of the news that Edward, his family and retinue would be arriving in June... and waited.

Five weeks later, in early May, she received a letter saying that Sir Walton desperately wanted to see his ward once again, and Elspeth and Tobias would accompany them as they too, obviously, wished to see their famous son once more. Sir Walton had recovered well in the Jamaican climate, was fighting fit and raring to see them all again. They were preparing for the long journey now...

CHAPTER 60

A Reunion, A Relief & A Debt Repaid

Sir Walton, Lady Alice, Elspeth and Tobias duly arrived at the end of May in order to prepare for the arrival of Edward and his family in early June. Tobias was happy to return to England and – if she would admit to it – so was Elspeth; in the warm climes of Jamaica, her clothing was often too hot and although Sir Walton had provided her with lighter, cooler clothes, her strict upbringing had made her a stickler for impractical sartorial convention.

The Hall had its furniture covers removed, the depleted staff were bolstered by extra hands to do the dusting, cleaning, scullery and garden work and so by the time Edward and Philomena arrived in the second week of June, all was ready for them.

The Great Parlour rang again to excited conversation, laughter, whoops of surprise, clinking glasses and even some music, for although Edward would only sing very carefully, Philomena was an accomplished pianist and it seemed that even the portraits on the walls depicting past ancestors and acquired scenes of nymphs, sylphs and cherubins were in concert with the festivities. The strict mores of previous years were relaxed so that Tobias and Elspeth could enjoy their son's return without doing any chores; these were apportioned to other staff, who nonetheless found themselves being caught up in this very enjoyable reunion.

Sir Walton had not mentioned the fact that he was still trying to sell the Hall but the point had been picked up in Jemima's reply to Edward and, one evening after a lavish dinner, Sir Walton and Edward found themselves talking alone in the smoking-room.

After some minutes of small talk, Edward took on a resolute air, stood to pour himself and Sir Walton another brandy and - as he offered the glass to Sir Walton - said quietly, "Sir Walton; there is something I wish to discuss with you."

"And what is that, dear boy?" Sir Walton enquired.

Edward took a gulp of brandy and settled himself down again into the lush leather seat, exuding a deep sigh of contentment. "Sir Walton, I cannot tell you how grateful I am – and Philomena, of course – for all you have done for me over the years. Without your encouragement, extraordinary prescience, belief and – yes, money, too – I would never have been able to become the person I am now."

"Eduardo!" laughed Sir Walton, histrionically, in an Italian accent.

"Indeed, Sir. Without your lessons, connections and – as I say, belief – I would still be nothing."

"You were never 'nothing', Edward."

"Relatively speaking, I was, Sir. But now…" There was a pause.

"Continue," said Sir Walton, his interest piqued. He could see there was something Edward wanted to say but was unsure how to say it. Edward looked at his fine Italian leather shoes, silk breeches and the rings on his fingers but still the words seem to elude him.

"Go on, man, spit it out! We have no secrets here!"

"I wonder if you realise how much money I make now for every performance I sing…"

"I have no idea. Why should I?"

"Well… it's a great deal – a *great* deal… and whilst Philomena relieves me of much of it, there is still plenty left over."

"That's very heartening; but what is your point?"

"My point… is… I hear you wish to sell this wonderful Hall."

"Ah… that. Well, no I do not *wish* to but… it's a necessity. What with political considerations and all…"

"But you don't *really* want to sell it – that's the truth."

"Yes – it is, but - "

"Then I have a proposition. I was gifted a palazzo in Venice by a beautiful widow whom I got to know rather too well…"

Sir Walton's eyes lit up and he leaned forward in anticipation, saying, "Ah! Scandal? Tell me more!"

"Well, when Philomena was pregnant with Ersinda, she was confined to Rome but I had a long contract singing at La Fenice in Venice and… well, we had a short relationship. Yet she was – unknown to me – dying of some disease and she suddenly passed away. I had been living in her palazzo and suddenly found that she had bequeathed it to me as she had no children and her husband was already dead."

"Good heavens," said Sir Walton in the ensuing silence. Then: "Must be worth a fortune."

"It is. But I had previously bought a large mansion in Rome, which is where Philomena was staying during her confinement. Now, as you know, I have to rest my voice for a few months or I will not be able to sing at all. But our plan is to move into the Venetian palazzo when I am recovered."

"Marvellous!" said Sir Walton, believing that was all he had to say, but Edward put up his hand to continue.

"But singing is a relatively short career and even after I have recovered, I will not be able to sing forever. So I will sell the Rome mansion and set up a singing school in the Venice palazzo as well as living there. But that is not all. If you are agreeable, I have decided to buy Mulberry Hall from you for when we wish to be in England, which will be most summers as the heat in Italy is too much for either me or Philomena. It is also a way of saying 'thank you' to you for all you have done for me." He looked up to see tears welling in Sir Walton's eyes.

"But Edward, do you know what I am asking for this pile?"

"I do. And I can afford it. I might even set up a singing school here, too – who knows? Residential courses pay very well, you know!"

Sir Walton was speechless. Eventually he managed to croak, "Well, 'pon my soul... does anyone else know of your plan?"

"Only Philomena. And she loves it here." There was a silence as Sir Walton took the offer in, so Edward continued: "I would like to keep this place in your family – *our* family," he emphasised. "But there is one favour I would ask of you in return."

"Of course! Anything! What do you wish?"

"That my father and mother can retire and live here in the Hall as … as…, well, not servants… but as a sort of lowly aristocracy, if you like. I think Tobias much prefers here, as does mother… but it's more to do with dignity and, as you know, they are very loyal to you – and you have already helped them immensely."

"And they, me," Walton attested. "Yes – that is absolutely agreed… but with one minor caveat…"

"Which is?"

He went quiet for a moment, then spoke softly, leaning forward, secretly, confidentially. "Edward… Alice does not know this but I will be dead soon. I have an incurable disease which does not show but is fatal – rather like your beautiful widow." Edward went to interject but it was Sir Walton's hand which went up this time. "When I go back to Jamaica, it will be for the last time. I wish to die there, not here, because it's hot and I can bathe in the warm sea. I love the light there, as well – it's softer than here, much as I also truly love England and this place, too. So when I heard you were coming I knew I had to make a final return… and I am so pleased I did."

"Then you are agreeable to my purchase of the Mulberry Hall estate – including Alice Lodge, of course?"

"Absolutely. And it is for me to thank you for taking away my financial millstone." He clasped Edward's hand, then looked into the middle distance and said reflectively, "And to think, this is all because although I brought Alice over for your father, he had already fallen for your mother by the time I returned from Jamaica … and I had similarly fallen in love with Alice on the crossing - despite bringing her back for him… And then, you were the result."

"Well… it has all worked out rather well, then, hasn't

it?" Edward said. They poured another drink and started talking of what it would mean to all of them, keeping Mulberry Hall in the family and its entourage. They stood, shook hands and then embraced, signifying a deep, close bond between the two of them.

"One thing," said Edward: "No mention of the wealthy widow to Philomena. She thinks I *bought* the palazzo – was not gifted it by a beautiful widow!"

"Don't know what you're talking about!" replied Walton with a sly look in his eye. They shook hands again, their hands staying clasped, as a pause ensued and Sir Walton's demeanour became more serious. "Actually, I have something you should know too but which must also never be mentioned," Sir Walton added darkly.

"And what is that, pray?"

"She doesn't know I know this… but I know your mother, Elspeth, murdered her first husband."

"What?" retorted, Edward, astonished, sitting down again.

Sir Walton sat again, too. "Yes… Giles. He had been my butler before this was all built but he had it coming to him. Ghastly man… embezzled my money, beat your mother, compromised her, was unfaithful to her… and, after I forced him to divorce your mother and forbade him to return to the Hall, and even after I arranged a house for him with his harlot, he nonetheless tried to. But that's another tale, entirely…" He looked askance, as if recalling many such stories.

"But that's terrible. I mean, my mother's such a quiet, submissive woman…"

"She was forced into it. And she could be very persuasive and resolute if need be – what made her such an excellent housekeeper. Firm but fair…"

"But are you sure my mother still doesn't know you know? Even now?"

Sir Walton nodded his head. "Absolutely certain: there was no need to tell her – it would have worried her too much. For if she thought I knew, then she would have been terrified that others might, too. But I just suspected something…"

"And why *was* that?" Edward asked, intrigued.

"Well, Elspeth seemed unusually furtive, fearful, pre-occupied when I got back once after being away and she wasn't wearing her wedding-ring, which she always did – as much for Tobias' sake as for apparent propriety. Then I noticed that a dagger and a sword had been switched around on the wall – normally the sword was below the dagger but their positions had been reversed… and as I put them back into their rightful positions, I noticed a smear of blood on the hilt of the sword so after dark that night, I went over to Alice Lodge with a flare and found Giles' body in a hole under some scant earth and twigs in the garden, with a pile of laundry over it. It was obvious that it was there to hurriedly cover something – I mean, why would a pile of laundry be out in the garden at night? - and when I removed it and brushed away the twigs, there was Giles, mutilated as if in a frenzy. And lying on top of his body was something that glistened in the flarelight which I recognised as Elspeth's wedding ring – thrown in with disgust, I suspect. I knew what had happened immediately and did not blame her, so I re-covered the body as I had found it and returned to my bed. I came back a few nights later and saw Giles had been properly buried under the tree that's there now. Fecund chap, obviously – because the tree is very large now…!" and he laughed. "Probably why Elspeth decided to come to Jamaica with me to get away in case the murder was ever found out about," he added lightly. "And that suited me as well!"

"But… why d'you think she buried him in the Alice Lodge garden?"

"Well, first because Alice Lodge was where I think she must have done him in and, secondly, because so few people went there – especially me… and Lady Lucinda was forbidden to go there… for obvious reasons," he added as a wry smile crossed his lips. "And I don't think Alice knows I know, either, but I'm sure *she's* privy to what happened because she hardly ever left the place in those days, bringing up the children…"

Edward did not know what to say next and just stared at him. Then he asked, with a tremor, "How many other stories like that do you have for me?"

"Ah…there are many stories more I could tell you… but not as dastardly as that one… and not tonight. All this has made me rather tired."

And with that, they each retired severally to bed.

EPILOGUE

With the sale of Mulberry Hall to Edward, Sir Walton Grimley acquired the money to do what he had always dreamed of doing – even further improve the lives of his workforce in Jamaica: he built them ever better accommodation and paid increased wages – much to the further anger of many other plantation owners who were now beginning to suffer seriously from a reduced flow of slaves thanks to the Royal Naval Squadron's effectiveness clearing the seas of slave-ships since 1807; this had been something he had vociferously supported in Parliament. Also, in a final bid to stamp out slavery by offering compensation to slave owners following the Abolition of Slavery across the British Empire in 1833, the slow passage of bills in Parliament was eventually supplanted by The Slave Compensation Act of 1837 and was the final – if contentious – nail in the coffin of British slavery. Although Sir Walton Grimley saw this as an imperfect Act because it compensated the owners rather than the slaves, due to having already improved conditions, banned beatings, chains, incarceration, manacling, 'pickling', branding and other horrors on his plantations voluntarily, he did not apply for compensation himself, believing it was the slave owners who should pay the compensation, not the British state. Championed by some but resisted by those owners with many slaves who were therefore avaricious of the final sum, he again felt vindicated, despite the imperfection.

By now feeling increasingly part of Jamaica, he formally decreed his body be buried there after his death, where he felt his soul should reside, lying among those whose lives he had spent a lifetime trying to improve...

Yet this desire, stated to Alice, fired her imagination – and also a streak of rebelliousness. With Edward's blessing, she asked Josiah to design and build what would be his last architectural project at the Hall - a mausoleum overlooking the lake and house into which she, her contemporaries and descendants would eventually lie to admire the view in perpetuity. She had told Walton that she would return to live at Mulberry Hall as Lady Alice Grimley after his death, back in England and closer to her daughters, broader family and the life she had become accustomed to: what she did not divulge was that he would – whatever his wishes – be the first to occupy it ... for she wanted to be with him forever, in England, not Jamaica. After all, he would never know...

Edward, meanwhile, having paid for the Mulberry Hall estate, decreed that his mother and father could live there in splendour; yet after Sir Walton Grimley's death in 1848, at the age of 74, they decided to return to his more humble home on the plantation in Jamaica, where it was run by them until they died - with the same consideration for its workpeople as Sir Walton had stipulated.

Before Edward retired from the international opera circuit as a performer, he and his wife, Philomena, and their three children lived either there or in Italy as was expedient;

Mulberry Hall also became the permanent home for Barnabas and Jemima, whose fortunes were not as great as Edward's. Eventually, Edward built a small theatre between the two Mulberry Hall houses to stage productions and foster a love of music in the north of England, which did not at that time have the same depth of artistic venues as London…to this, he also initiated a singing school to complement the one by then thriving in Venice; these eventually expanded during his lifetime into major international venues, famous for performances of new operas… His philanthropy therefore contributed much to the globalisation of Italian music in the area during the 19th century and, as his singing diminished, so his impresarial abilities grew; he knew so many singers from his life in Italy that he could engage them for international festivals as far away as the United States and South America. In London, too, after 1843, the restriction on opera performances being allowed only in the two 'patent' theatres of Drury Lane and Covent Garden had been lifted; after this, so many other theatres could stage these glittering, sumptuous productions that this also later allowed Edward to become ever more influential and wealthy.

Josiah and Sophie's business in Wirksworth had, over the same period, expanded and made ever larger amounts of money supplying implements mostly for the cotton and weaving trades that were still springing up in the area; knowing that they could afford to effectively retire to Alice Lodge when the time came and as social mores changed and travel became easier and less dangerous, many were the occasions when this unusual family and past servants found themselves enjoying each others' company together. This subtle mix of race, aristocracy and supposed 'inferior classes' was seen as a harbinger of the changing attitudes which would eventually become normal over the next hundred years and more.

The ownership of the Jamaican plantation eventually passed to Edward, his family and children. Yet by the mid-1900s, global corporations were the only ones rich enough to own and manage such large tracts of land and as more enlightened and beneficial laws were passed in a newly-independent Jamaica from 1962 onwards, so the cruelty and disdain for human life there became an affliction of the past. The plantation was sold by Edward and Philomena's descendants at that time and a trust was set up for the advancement of musical education in Jamaica as their father had done in Italy and England.

Alice had returned to Mulberry Hall soon after Sir Walton's death and was the last to join them in the mausoleum when she died in 1874, aged 89, complementing the cold, reluctant bones of Sir Walton: her youth had outlived them all, this beautiful, finely-boned woman taking up the least space as they all rested, overlooking this perfect representation of an innovative, just and pioneering England... especially considering that it would only be many years later that slavery was finally abolished in the rest of the Western world.

Alice Lodge, being so much smaller than the main Hall, was turned into a military hospital during the First World War, and again in the Second; it then became an office for a wealthy hedge fund company in the 1970s and after that an international business school, where people from all climes and cultures came to learn the secrets of trade and business.

Yet no such good fate befell Mulberry Hall itself: by the time that the eponymous tree was blown down during a fierce gale one autumn night in the 1960s, the great edifice had fallen into ruin, the victim of swingeing death duties and political jealousies. The fallen tree was disrespectfully cut up for firewood but on subsequent windy nights it is said that the ghosts of Mulberry Hall warm themselves by its eery, spectral flames, congregating happily in the draughty, cavernous and empty Great Parlour to recount the tales of years gone by… and as far as anyone knows, the body of Giles Burrows is still trapped, sneering and snarling, as the roots of the now huge tree in the Alice Lodge garden continue to grow around him…

But whether the ghost of Jess Rigby ever joins him is something we shall never know…

Idea and text © SIMON HOLDER, 2024

ABOUT THE AUTHOR

Simon Holder worked for most of his life in broadcast television for the BBC, Channel 4, ITV, Sky and more before turning to writing novels. His topics are wide and varied - love stories, short stories, the environment and a humorous thriller set in a TV background are his most recent before this work. His interests include the environment, film and theatre, politics, music (especially Baroque opera), English literature (especially Thomas Hardy) and freedom of expression.

Printed in Dunstable, United Kingdom